NORA NAISH

Nora Naish was born in India, one of seven children of an Irish father in the Indian Civil Service, and did not come to England until she was eight years old. She was educated at a convent in Wimbledon and London University before qualifying as a doctor at King's College Hospital during the war. She married and brought up four children in Gloucestershire. In middle life she went back to medicine as a GP in Avon. Her elder brother was the late P. R. Reid, the author of *The Colditz Story*. Nora Naish has written three previous novels, *Sunday Lunch*, *The Butterfly Box* and *The Magistrate's Tale*.

By the same author

SUNDAY LUNCH
THE BUTTERFLY BOX
THE MAGISTRATE'S TALE

A TIME TO LEARN

NORA NAISH

ARROW

Published in the United Kingdom in 1999 by
Arrow Books

1 3 5 7 9 10 8 6 4 2

Copyright © Nora Naish 1998

The right of Nora Naish to be identified as the author of this work has been asserted by her in accordance with the Copyright, Designs and Patents Act, 1988

This novel is a work of fiction. Names and characters are the product of the author's imagination and any resemblance to actual persons, living or dead, is entirely coincidental

First published in the United Kingdom in 1998 by William Heinemann

Arrow Books Limited
Random House UK Limited
20 Vauxhall Bridge Road, London, SW1V 2SA

Random House Australia (Pty) Limited
20 Alfred Street, Milsons Point, Sydney, New South Wales 2061, Australia

Random House New Zealand Limited
18 Poland Road, Glenfield
Auckland 10, New Zealand

Random House South Africa (Pty) Limited
Endulini, 5a Jubilee Road, Parktown 2193, South Africa

Random House UK Limited Reg. No. 954009

A CIP catalogue record for this book is available from the British Library

Papers used by Random House UK Limited are natural, recyclable products made from wood grown in sustainable forests. The manufacturing processes conform to the environmental regulations of the country of origin

Printed and bound in Norway by
AIT Trondheim AS, 1999

ISBN 0 7493 2585 2

To women doctors wherever they live and work

A Time to Learn

PART ONE

A Yorkshire Childhood

PART ONE

ONE

Baby Alice drummed with her spoon on the wooden tray in front of her high chair. There were two women looking after her that dinner time, but they weren't paying her the attention she demanded.

'Mud! Mud!' she shouted. It was what she called her mother.

Matilda leaned towards the child and wiped her mouth with the cleanest part of her bib. 'You can take her out to the castle this afternoon,' she said, 'or down to the beach in her pram. I shall be back in time for tea.'

Clara looked across the table at her sister, so pale in her black mourning clothes, her eyes ringed with shadows from sleepless nights. Forlorn, thought Clara; that was the word to describe her – forlorn. She couldn't help comparing her appearance today, with that of the radiant bride who'd mounted the step of Henry Thorburn's trap as he sat smiling, reins held lightly, waiting to carry her off to Trafalgar House. And it was a house which, to Clara's mind, resembled her brother-in-law: big, square and sturdy, made of warm red brick, but built to stand up to the winds whistling round it on that tongue of land which divides Scarborough's two bays. It was a house where Matilda had been happy, and a marriage that she declared had been made for her in heaven.

'My appointment with the bankers is at half-past two,' said Matilda. She dreaded the visit, but it was necessary, so it must be made, though she would much rather have stayed at home and played with baby Alice till the older children came home from school.

In the hall she put on her black straw bonnet and pulled the black veil down over her face, noticing in the hat-stand mirror how pale she looked. Suddenly, with a surge of sorrow and a rush of tears to her eyes, which was the last thing she needed at this moment, she thought of Henry, so full of health, so brimming over with fun and jokes and with bright new ideas and schemes for his business, till only a fortnight ago.

He had been at the shop when he'd died. Somebody had delivered a sack of flour and left it at the door. It must have annoyed him as being out of place and, perhaps, in the way of customers. It was an exceptionally heavy sack, but it needed shifting. He was a powerful man, and also, by nature, impatient; he would not wait for a helper and so he seized it by the neck and swung it up on his back. As he moved he felt a violent, tearing pain in his chest and staggered into the little sitting-room at the back of the store, where he died immediately. The cause of death on his death certificate was 'Ruptured valve of heart'. Matilda was thus left at the age of thirty with everything he possessed, including considerable debts, and five children. It was during the month of May.

The next day Henry's mother and brother, Wallace, had arrived at the shop to take charge of things. Matilda was grateful for their help, but in her desire to be alone, was irritated by their talk, so she went into the little sitting-room where Henry had died. Here there were several chairs around a table where he used to do business with travelling salesman, there was a desk against one wall, and against another stood – or, more accurately, reclined – a battered *chaise longue*. Matilda sat down on this and put her feet up on a patch of upholstery so worn that the horsehair stuffing was beginning to protrude. She was, as yet, too stunned by what had happened to be grief-stricken; but she felt very tired after a long, bewildered, sleepless night, which had been unusually hot and airless for May, and her head ached. Resting her head against the end of the *chaise longue*, she closed her eyes.

As she lay there, her mother-in-law and Wallace entered the room and, thinking her asleep, they sat down at the table and began to talk in subdued tones, discussing freely what they intended doing with Henry's property. Wallace offered to take over the farm, and his mother suggested putting a manager in the shop. As they elaborated their plans, Matilda realised with growing horror, first that she was unwittingly an eavesdropper, and second, that in all their schemes she and her five children were not being considered at all.

'She can go back to the Millses,' said Wallace. 'There's a bit of brass tied up there in Robin Hood's Bay.'

'She brought little enough of it with her,' commented Henry's mother.

It was not until after the funeral that Matilda had learned that she was Henry's sole legatee, and realised that she must visit his bankers, Messrs Gooding and Grigson, without delay. She needed their support and goodwill in the great decision she was about to make.

She was ushered, with due solemnity, into their private office. The two men stood stiffly in their long black coats, and stared at her in complete silence. She was not a woman of fashion, but in the matter of the new mourning gown she'd just bought she had succumbed to the prevailing whim for bustles. She had chosen the dress carefully because she'd known she'd have to wear it for a long time. It was made of a silky material light enough for the coming summer, the cut of it flattered her tall, slim figure, and, from below a pleated frill attached to the hem of its skirt, her shapely foot and ankle emerged. The bankers were impressed. Mr Gooding, the senior partner, who had had no classical schooling, but knew his *Hamlet*, thought of her as Niobe all in tears; Mr Grigson was simply charmed. He pushed forward a chair for her, and she sat down, lifting the black veils over her bonnet to reveal her face. They both saw, with some surprise, what a young woman she still was, and how beautiful; and Grigson, who had an avid curiosity about all things feminine, noticed with pleasure her full bodice with its high collar to which was pinned an oval brooch of Whitby jet, carved intricately into a full-blown, black rose.

She was a stranger to them, never having stepped inside the bank before. Of course, they'd known Henry well, and were, as the whole town had been, shocked by his tragic death – in his prime too! – and were very sorry about it because Henry had been universally liked and, what was more, banked large sums of money with them. And here was his pretty widow, thrown helpless into a rapacious world and onto a bank account for the moment rather heavily encumbered with debt. They didn't know quite how to begin the interview.

'I've received this cheque,' she said, pulling an envelope out of her large black handbag. 'Five hundred pounds from my husband's life insurance policy. Will it be enough to pay off what he owes?'

There was a pause.

'Perhaps you would be able to go on living at Trafalgar House,' suggested Mr Gooding. 'Mr Wallace Thorburn will have to pay you rent for his use of the shop premises, and I daresay, with great economy, you could manage to live on that.'

'Oh, no!' said Matilda. 'I won't be taking any rent

from Mr Wallace Thorburn! I intend carrying on the shop myself. I may allow him to supervise the farms. And I shall have to sell Trafalgar House. Yes, I know it's a pity to lose a family home, and such a happy one too, but I will have to do it. I can see that. I shall bring the children to live with me over the shop.' She was not, after all, such a poor, helpless widow, though undoubtedly beautiful and young. And Mr Grigson, wishing he was still a bachelor, suddenly had visions of her marrying again. After a decent interval of course . . . A potentially highly lucrative grocery business, too . . . But five children! That, sadly, would be a handicap in the marriage stakes.

Mr Gooding spoke again, telling her to keep the five hundred pounds to cover immediate expenses, until such time as she had sold Trafalgar House, or made sufficient profits from the shop to pay off her husband's overdraft.

'There may be other debts of which I, as yet, have little cognisance,' he said. The winged collar of his white shirt was too tight and too stiffly starched, and rubbed his neck whenever he turned it, and his old-fashioned speech was stiff, too; but the kindness of his meaning shone through the eyes he rested on her, and she appreciated it. 'And there will be sums outstanding owing to him too, you know.'

Grigson took her hand when she rose to go. 'We shall always be ready to help you, Mrs Thorburn, in any way we can, should you ever need it,' he said and, bowing low over her hand, he pressed it sympathetically. Looking down on his well-oiled hair, she thought him servile, although she knew it was unfair to compare him, or indeed any man, with Henry, which was what she was doing. No man, no man on earth could ever match up to her Henry. She dropped her veils around her face before stepping into the public office; and as she walked proudly out, pretended not to notice the surreptitiously

7

lifted heads and furtive glances of the clerks behind the counter.

When the door closed behind her, Grigson remarked: 'What a disaster for the poor lady! Henry Thorburn – at the peak of his powers! – But what a lovely wife he had! I had no idea . . .'

They fell silent for a moment, both wondering about her future.

'Do you think she'll make a go of the business?' asked Grigson. 'A woman on her own?'

'We shall see,' said Gooding. He was not going to commit himself.

A faraway look came into Grigson's eyes. 'This new bustle the ladies have taken to . . . rather fetching, isn't it? Does something for them, doesn't it? Enhances a woman's bum, don't you think?'

Gooding frowned. He didn't like his partner's turn of phrase, nor did he approve of his enthusiasm for women's fashions, still less his appreciation of their forms beneath the fashions, which was risky in a married man, and in a married banker, downright dangerous. He himself, even when young, had never experienced uncontrolled appreciation. He sometimes feared Grigson might.

'We shall see,' he repeated, putting a finger between his collar and his neck in an attempt to loosen the collar's hold. 'What business acumen Mrs Thorburn possesses will soon come to light. Bustles are neither here nor there.'

Grigson, slightly chastened, bowed his oiled head and went quickly to his desk; but as he sat down he couldn't suppress a snigger. Neither here nor there indeed! The bustle certainly was there – and in the right place too!

Matilda didn't feel half as confident in her own capabilities by the time she got home, nor did the name of Nelson's famous victory, cut into the stone arch above her front door, bolster her courage much. Baby Alice was sitting in her pram in the porch. 'Liss! Liss!' she shouted as soon as she saw her mother. It was a happy noise of greeting, this name she gave herself, and had led to her being known as Lizzie. Matilda picked her out of the pram and carried her through the door. As soon as she was inside the narrow hallway her two young servants, Bessie and Flo, rushed out from the back premises to meet her, to take her hat and to murmur little sympathies. They were honest, rough, but warm-hearted girls who were being particularly attentive to her during this time of crisis. Not only did they feel the sadness and the drama of it all, but they were anxious about what would happen to themselves.

'Miss Clara has the tea ready for you, Ma'am,' said Bessie.

'You look that tired, Ma'am dear,' said Flo.

They hovered round her as she walked towards the sitting-room. She turned at the door and spoke, wearily. 'You may as well come too, and hear about what's been planned.' They followed her in and then stood there trying, with difficulty, to put on faces solemn enough for the occasion. They are like unbroken colts, thought Matilda. She couldn't help smiling at the thought. They were so young – fourteen and fifteen – and eagerly affectionate too.

'It's all been decided,' she said. 'We shall have to sell this house and move into the shop. But I shall need both you girls – Bessie to be cook and Flo to do the cleaning. There's a bedroom there for the two of you. I myself shall be busy behind the counter, and doing all the buying, and the accounts.'

'Oh, Ma'am! So you'll be a great grocer woman now!' exclaimed Bessie.

'Thank you, Ma'am! I'm glad we can all be together still!' cried Flo.

'You may go now,' said Clara, rather sharply. She was

always afraid her sister's easy manner with servants would make them rebellious and more demanding.

They made their exit, bumping each other in their haste to leave the room. Matilda could hear their suppressed giggles as they scurried away down the corridor to the kitchen.

'This is all going to be very hard on you, Matilda,' said her sister, pouring out tea into pretty porcelain cups embellished with red and blue flowers.

'The hardest thing will be parting from Alice,' said Matilda. 'My poor, fatherless baby girl!' she murmured, kissing the child as her tears began to flow easily and fast.

'Baby Lizzie's too young to suffer much,' said Clara.

'No. She'll never know what she's lost.'

The baby pushed her fist into her mother's cheek and then into her own mouth and, tasting the salty tears she seemed surprised and repeated the experiment.

'She likes the salt,' said Clara, and laughed; and Matilda, too, laughed through her tears.

'I know she'll be in good hands, and perfectly happy with you,' she said. It was obvious to them that although it would be possible for Matilda to care for the older four children in their new home, since they already spent most of the daytime in school, it would be impossible for her to be a lady grocer and wine merchant and care for Alice as well. To hire a trained nanny would be too costly, and to accommodate one on the premises, awkward. So Clara had offered to look after the baby in Robin Hood's Bay. It was where the sisters had spent their carefree childhood, so they both loved the place. 'But I shall miss her, of course,' said Matilda.

'She'll have plenty of company,' said Clara. 'Mother will help keep an eye on her. And you know how I love the little dear.'

'I shall miss her,' repeated Matilda.

'But you'll be busy. And that will keep your mind off things. Mother wants it, and Uncle Mills is willing. As a matter of fact,' Clara pursued, in her comforting, persuasive tone, 'he wants the older ones all to come to us, too, for the summer holidays.'

Matilda nodded. Uncle Mills was the owner of Esplanade House, the old family home, which stood on the cliff top above the bay. 'It's very good of him,' she said. And looking at Clara she sighed: 'But what would I do without you?' Precious little, was what Clara thought, although she didn't speak it aloud. It was merely a private self-satisfaction.

The coastal strip of the North Riding is separated from the rest of Yorkshire by moors. Here, an enormous turbulent sky hangs over a wilderness of heather, wave upon wave as far as the eye can see. From the dazzling but inhospitable beauty of this place the road descends into a green folding of fields through which the river Esk seeks the steel grey water of the North Sea, by way of Whitby. It was in that old sea port that Alice's ancestors first made a living, then a bit of brass, by fishing and exporting herrings packed into brine-filled barrels lashed into the holds of sailing boats. Later, they built ships: round-bottomed collier brigs to carry coal from Newcastle around the coast of England, faster sailing ships for the merchant fleet which sped across the North Sea to Scandinavian and Russian ports, and great whalers with hulls strong enough to resist the crushing ice of arctic waters.

John Mills (Great-uncle Mills to baby Alice) had sailed in many ships, but in old age he allowed himself to be stranded in a village built on cliffs crumbling slowly into the sea around a small indentation of the coastline a few miles south of Whitby. In the 1880s, when Lizzie spent her childhood here in Robin Hood's Bay, it was a fishing village, a tightly-knit community surviving only by an

11

unremitting struggle against the implacable enemies of wind and sea. It was a small, separate world, enclosed by the North Sea below and the great moors above. The high road between Whitby and Scarborough was several miles away, and could only be reached on foot, or by the carter, who travelled every Thursday to Scarborough and back. From time to time traders' packhorses brought treasured things from distant industrial towns: cloth and thread and other draper's goods, or pots and pans and cutlery, and even fragile crockery packed into big baskets on their backs, as they picked their way gingerly down the cobbled street.

The very first thing Lizzie could remember was holding Great-uncle Mills's big conch shell in her little hands. The inside was smooth, satiny pink, the colour of salmon flesh, the outside rough and the colour of the sandy beach.

'Put it to thee ear, lass,' said Great-uncle Mills, 'an' listen to t' sea.' So she did; and her large, blue eyes grew solemn as she heard the mighty ocean heaving. It was magic: all that fierce water tamed to a murmur inside the shell.

From her attic window under the roof she had a good view of the sea, and from an early age she learned to watch its moods. Even when it was smiling, calm, green and glistening under sunlight, the white waves on its surface shone like bared teeth, and a windy day soon whipped it up into a grey snarl. On wild winter nights when it hurled itself against the cliff, making her tremble in her bed as the house reverberated with its thunder, she would murmur to herself the words of that hymn they sometimes sang in church for those in peril on the sea. So Lizzie regarded the sea with mixed feelings of awe and pleasure. It could be, like a tyrant, laughing and generous on warm summer days, but wicked in winter, unpredictable like those bad Roman emperors in Great-uncle Mills's book about the fall of Rome, who possessed power and could distribute wealth or stupid cruelty as they chose.

Great-uncle Mills had been a whaler in his youth, and a master mariner in his heyday. He was lucky because he had survived into his seventies; but his sister's husband, Captain Harrison, was drowned at sea on a return voyage from Archangel, leaving Grandma Harrison widowed with two little girls to look after, and only her skill with the needle and her sharp eye for measuring and cutting cloth with minimal waste to earn her a living as a travelling dressmaker. While she was away plying her trade, sometimes staying for a week at a time in neighbouring farmhouses, the girls lived with their Uncle John in Esplanade House. They never went to school, but as soon as they could read well enough they were let loose in his library where they read, without check or discrimination, any book they fancied, including Gibbon's *Decline and Fall of the Roman Empire*, in which so many murders were committed that in the end the horror of it all became boring; but they did relish reading about the mad emperor who fell in love with his horse; and they called their kitten after him: Caligula.

Clara, who was the elder of the two sisters, was the first to fall in love. Her heart was captured by Benjamin Tuck, Captain of the *Whitby Ariel*, a speedy ship that crossed back and forth across the North Sea through Skaggerak and into the Baltic with salted herrings for Hamburg, and home again to Whitby with a cargo of Scandinavian timber. He was a robust man who liked playing harmless practical jokes, and he sang a lusty bass in the church choir on Sunday whenever he came home from sea to his mother's cottage. Clara seemed to come to life when he looked at her from under his great, black, bushy eyebrows; and she trembled when he smiled his friendly smile at her from the depths of his massive beard.

'He has a roving eye,' remarked Grandma Harrison, who was rather given to uttering doom-laden prophecies. It alighted and lingered awhile on Clara. He didn't look much at Matilda, who was only fourteen at the time, but he tickled her knees under the tablecloth when invited to Sunday lunch at Esplanade House. Matilda never breathed a word of the tickling to her sister, though it did worry her a bit. She even wondered if it was the prerogative of a future brother-in-law, when he proposed to Clara and was accepted.

Grandma Harrison's warning was never put to the test, however, because the *Whitby Ariel* was wrecked in a terrible storm only six months after the engagement was announced. Captain Tuck went down with her, and most of his crew as well, though a few survivors, clinging to planks loosened by the crack-up of the hull, and half-dead from the cold, were picked up by the Whitby lifeboat. When, years later, Clara told Lizzie the story, time had censored Grandma Harrison's judgement of Benjamin, and the knee-tickling episode was omitted since Clara knew nothing of it; but the tale brought tears to Lizzie's eyes. It was sad for poor Captain Benjamin and all the drowned sailors, and sad for Aunt Clara as well, who was left a disappointed spinster.

She was not, however, as sour as spinsters were supposed to be, and was often quite jolly. She had accepted the loss of her lover, whom she regarded as having died an honourable death. In common with many women of that region of England she had made in her heart a pact with the sea. The sea was like God: it gave, and it took away. Once, on hearing of a certain fisherman who was so unfortunate as to die in bed, she expressed contempt.

'Why shouldn't he die in bed?' asked Lizzie innocently.

'He should go down with his ship!' replied Aunt Clara. It was the right and proper thing to do.

The women, left alone at home by their menfolk, who

remained at sea for long periods and were so often snatched away by violent death, had to be independent, hardy, courageous and realistic. Lizzie's home was inevitably matriarchal. Her grandmother and aunt Clara, as well as her own mother, had all lost their men suddenly, while still young, and all had to fight for survival in a harsh world.

Clara made bread twice a week. While she stood at the kitchen table kneading dough, Grandma Harrison sat by the stove mending socks, and Lizzie sat near her on a three-legged stool listening to their talk. Sometimes she stood with Clara and kneaded her own little loaf, patting it smooth with a smear of milk. When the loaves were risen Clara took them to the village bakehouse where Fletcher, armed with a long-handled, flat-ended shovel manoeuvred the many loaves, and many whole dinners too, in and out of an enormous oven built into the wall of his house.

One day, while helping to make bread, Lizzie asked: 'Where do I come from, Aunt Clara?'

'Scarborough,' replied Grandma Harrison promptly.

'No. I mean . . . before I was born . . .'

'From an egg, child!' Clara was busy kneading dough in her big, pottery basin, but Lizzie's flour-flaked hands were suspended above her own little bowl as she listened. 'You remember that broody bantam we saw sitting on her eggs? That's how they were hatched.'

'But Aunt Clara . . .' persisted logical and doubting Lizzie. It seemed to her impossible that her mother, who was always rushing from one task to the next, too busy to sit down even on Thursdays when they went over the moor in the carter's van to visit her, could ever find time to sit close like the little bantam hen. 'Where . . . and how did Mother do it?'

'You were hatched in her bustle,' said Clara. 'That way she could keep moving about while she were doing it.'

Lizzie was aware that grown-ups told you only the half of it, especially in certain matters, which, for their own reasons, they wanted to keep secret; but she found this explanation, though not entirely satisfactory, rather attractive. Her mother's bustle as 'baby-bag' accorded reasonably with her alphabet book in which *k* stood for kangaroo, out of whose forward-facing pouch long-eared babies peeped. So, rather pensively, she resumed mixing her dough.

'Bakin' meks ye speculative,' said Grandma Harrison.

'What's speculative?'

'Askin' questions.' The child was always asking questions. She was not easily fobbed off with quick answers either.

During the summer months a collier brig from Newcastle used to sail in and tie up in the bay; and at low tide all the able-bodied villagers went out to it to buy coal. There was no quay, but the Wayfoot, a slipway of great boulders worn smooth by many feet and the pounding of heavy seas, stretched from the bottom of the street out across the beach and into the sea. Carts were driven over it towards the ship; mules and donkeys had to stand patiently in the water while coal was loaded from the deck above; and women waded out with sacks and buckets to be filled. Lizzie carried her own small bucket, Aunt Clara two large ones as, tucking up their petticoats, they paddled out to the brig. When their buckets were full they carried them home uphill and tipped the contents on to the floor of an outhouse. So they continued their coal hauling, till the shed was full and Lizzie's face was black. 'You look like a chimney sweep's lad,' said Grandma Harrison. 'Tha mun sit in tub by fire now an' get thee washed.'

On coaling days two uniformed coastguards paraded above the Wayfoot. They were the only visible representatives of the law, as the nearest policeman lived in Whitby. It was said, usually in undertones so Lizzie had to hold her breath and strain her ears to hear, that they sometimes turned a blind eye to the smuggling that went on.

'What's smuggling?' asked Lizzie.

'It's high time t' lass went to school,' said Great-uncle Mills. 'Schoolmistress'll 'ave to answer all her questions then.'

'Aye. It'll cost us sixpence a week,' said Grandma Harrison, 'but t' lass'll learn her letters, an' 'appen a few sums.'

Lizzie did her sums with a piece of chalk on a slate. She had a damp bit of sponge for wiping out her errors, which were not many because she was careful. Poor Billy Boothby wasn't careful. He didn't care at all what he scribbled on his slate, so he was often in terrible trouble and had to stand in a corner of the room with his back to the rest of the class and wear a cone of paper on his head, marked with a big *D* for Dunce to shame him. But Billy Boothby wasn't shamed, not even when the teacher hit him across the seat of his trousers with a cane. He came swaggering back to his desk after it was done, and sat down with a cheeky grin. It was Lizzie who felt the shame of it for him. She learned a bit about smuggling, then, when she passed him a jelly baby out of her apron pocket under the lid of the desk to comfort him, and thus became his friend.

She was even allowed to join his gang, the only girl among his men, when they played games of being smugglers, pirates or Viking invaders on the beach and among rocks around the bay. She was proud of belonging to him.

'Where've you been?' Clara would demand when she arrived home late for tea, flushed and important after following Billy to victory over the Saxons (Billy was always on the winning side).

'On the beach,' Lizzie would reply.

17

'You're growing into a tomboy,' was Clara's judgement. 'No harm in that, just so long as you don't go too far.'

Thursday was the best day of the week. It was when Lizzie travelled with Aunt Clara across the moor in the carter's van to visit her mother in Scarborough, and have tea with her sister on her return from school. Lizzie adored her mother with a passionate devotion, partly owing to their natural bond, but particularly because of their separation. For Matilda it was half day in the shop, so she could give her little daughter two or three hours of uninterrupted attention, showering on her a love heightened by her feelings of guilt in being forced by circumstances to deny the child her presence for the rest of the week. There was usually a new book for Lizzie to read, and a special plate of Yorkshire parkin for tea and, what Lizzie loved best of all, the string of sugar crystals to dangle in her tea before breaking off some of the lumps and popping them in her mouth. To Lizzie, her mother was not only the source of Thursday pleasures but an icon of what a woman could achieve, for Clara filled their travelling time with stories about Matilda's past, beginning with her wedding day when she was dressed in an ivory silk suit made by Grandma Harrison, and of how the bells of St Stephen's church rang out as Lizzie's father, Henry, drove his bride away.

'He were six foot tall, and fair,' said Clara. 'And he made us all laugh with his jokes and his schemes. Your mother called him her Viking Chief.'

He was champion weight lifter of the North Riding; he owned a grocer's shop and flourishing wine business established in 1813 ('When Napoleon was still prancin' about', said Grandma Harrison), as well as a couple of small holdings that supplied butter, eggs and vegetables for sale over the counter. 'And as if that weren't enough to keep him out of mischief, he were a town councillor as well,' was Clara's verdict. A tragic mask then fell over her face as she described his death: 'Hit by a bolt from the blue he were.'

So Lizzie learned the story of his sudden death, and how her mother bravely shouldered the responsibilities of running the shop single-handed, as well as making a home for her older brothers and sisters. Lizzie knew she had a special mother, stronger, better and wiser than other girls' mothers; but she had no proper father. There was God, of course, who was Our Father in Heaven. She liked to think of God as like that person in the poem they sometimes recited at school: 'God leans out to hear the noise/Made by His happy girls and boys.'

The person nearest to this kindly figure on earth was Great-uncle Mills. Lizzie often sat with him in the evenings by the fire in his sitting-room, he in his big wide armchair, she on the floor between his knees. It was then that he told her his stories. He used to pick up one of his treasures from the mantelpiece and weave a tale around it. There was his nest of wooden Russian dolls with pink painted cheeks and bright red skirts, six of them fitting one inside the other, getting smaller and smaller as you took them apart till at last you came to the smallest one of all which was no bigger than a thimble.

'I got 'em in Archangel,' he said. Lizzie saw, in her imagination, the White Sea harbour with shores of ice instead of sand. In the sky above the water hovered a white angel, huge, with golden wings and a sword of fire. He was the one who pushed Satan off the clouds and sent him hurtling down into the pit of hell, so Grandma Harrison said. When Great-uncle Mills was a young master mariner he sailed into the harbour one very cold night. After he'd anchored his ship safely he went ashore to find food and a bed; but it was late, and no one was moving in the deserted streets, not a soul awake in the quiet houses. At last, he saw a light in a window. He banged on the door, and after a long time an old woman appeared. He couldn't speak Russian, and she couldn't speak English, but he mimed his needs. The old woman seemed very unwilling to give him shelter, but finally, after he'd pulled some money out of a pocket and given it to her, she let him into the house where, by the light of a single candle, she fed him a bowl of soup. Then he went up a creaking ladder to a room above. He had no light, so he had to feel his way to the bed, and fell, fully-clothed, into it. It was a feather bed, and warm, and he slept well. He woke in the cold, colourless dawn, sat up, and rubbed his eyes. There on the floor beside him, with eyes closed and hands crossed on his breast, lay the corpse of an old man in a coffin. The way Great-uncle Mills said the word 'coffin' made Lizzie shiver.

A different story grew out of a Staffordshire pottery group, modelled only at the front and known as a flatback, of a boy in lilac pants and a girl in a bouncy green skirt with a white apron over it. They were leaning together across a rock from which spouted a waterfall.

'They wanted to play together,' Great-uncle Mills said, 'but neither one nor t'other could cross t'watter, and so they stood forever on t'banks, only gawpin.' His voice was sad.

'Where's the river?' she asked.

'It wor t'Esk what runs down off t'moors into Whitby between East Cliff where ruined abbey stands and West Cliff where People's Park is.'

'Was the boy called John?' she asked.

'Aye, I reckon he wor.'

'What was the little girl's name?'

'Milly – short for Millicent.'

'Was she a real girl?'

'She wor a lass I loved once long ago, a'fore tha wor born, afore even tha mother wor born.'

'Is gawpin' staring?'

'Aye, it is that.'

'Staring's rude,' Lizzie announced, sententiously.

'It is,' he agreed. And then, gazing above her head, away into the past he added: 'Sometimes it can be a kind of wantin' too.'

Lizzie rested her head against his knee and thought it a shame that the children could never cross the river to play together. She ran her finger down the glossy white waterfall that forever divided them. It was sad; but looking up into his face she knew that Great-uncle Mills was a happy man, so perhaps things which had happened to him long ago stopped being sad when they were old enough to become stories.

Lizzie was seldom sad, not even when she got into trouble with Clara for pestering her after a good Sunday dinner, which made everybody except Lizzie somnolent.

'Just let me have forty winks, will you?' Clara begged. She closed her eyes while Lizzie stood by her chair counting slowly and silently: One, two, three . . . to thirty-nine, before suddenly clapping her hands and shouting: 'Forty!'

Clara jumped. She was cross then, slapping Lizzie and calling her an unfeeling child. 'One day you'll go too far,' she said.

It happened, when Billy Boothby threw the first stone.

A party of boys from Thorpe, a village two miles away, had ventured on to the beach one Saturday afternoon when Billy's gang was collecting coloured pebbles for their catapults. Billy was of the opinion that foreigners from Thorpe had no right to his patch of Robin Hood's Bay.

'Get thee back to Thorpe!' he shouted. And when they began to scramble as fast as they could up the steep hill

21

away from a hail of pebbles, Billy yelled: ''It 'em 'ard, lads! 'It 'em 'ard!'

His lads included Lizzie, her eyes steel-bright and her hair flying as she threw her stone.

It was most unfortunate that just at that moment, Grandma Harrison, carrying a basket of apples given her by a friend, emerged into the street, her mind full of plans for a beautiful apple pie. Lizzie's pebble hit her just where her bustle would have been, had she bothered to wear one. She uttered a squawk, staggered, slipped on the cobbles, and fell, upsetting her basket of apples which rolled and bumped down the hill. Lizzie's hand flew to her mouth when she saw what she'd done, and she cried out: 'Oh!' But Billy's eyes were jumping out of his face with glee as he shouted: 'Good shot Lizzie lass! Let 'em 'ave it!' There was no doubt that Grandma Harrison heard his battle cry.

Next Thursday was memorably bleak. Matilda's smile faded when she heard Clara's story. Lizzie hung her head and felt an outcast from her mother's love. She didn't understand all the ins and outs of the matter, but she knew they were talking about her wickedness as her sister, Katy, led her away to play in the yard behind the shop.

'She's running wild,' said Matilda. 'She's getting into bad company.'

Clara bridled, feeling herself accused. 'She were always a wilful child,' she said.

'It's time she came back to her family in Scarborough. She's allowed too much freedom in the Bay.'

'No more than you and I had, Matilda,' Clara objected, repudiating the blame implied. 'She didn't mean to hit Grandma. She just has too much energy for a girl. She takes after her father in that.'

'It's time she went to a proper school, Clara, time she

was civilised.' Henry had certainly possessed amazing vitality, but he never would have hit his grandmother when aiming at the boys from Thorpe.

In the backyard Lizzie's sister Katy said: 'You're going to come and live with us in Scarborough now.'

'Am I?'

'You're going to be tamed.' Katy was disapproving, but she had an excited glint in her eye. 'What did you *do*?' she asked. 'Was it *very* bad?'

Lizzie made no reply. She was too confused by shame and misery, and was resentful too. She hadn't meant to do it. It was just bad luck. It was only a game that somehow went wrong.

Watching her sister's face, Katy relented. 'You'll go to a big school with me, you know. You'll like it. There are lots of nice girls there.'

'Let's play schools,' said Lizzie.

TWO

Scarborough's streets were full of strangers hurrying about their work, or to and from the many shops, and endlessly moving traffic. Everywhere could be heard the creak and rumble of wheels, the clip-clop of horses' hooves in many rhythmic patterns, the shouts of drivers and the crack of whips. There was an all-pervading smell of horse dung, and at road junctions crossing sweepers were forever sweeping it up. Lizzie was excited by the prospect of walking to school with Katy through this frantic activity and bewildering noise, but what she dreaded was having to dress up in all the strange clothes she would have to wear. At first Katy helped her to dress in the bedroom they shared.

'Stand still!' she commanded. Katy was twelve.

Lizzie was jumping up and down trying to get warm after washing her neck and armpits in the cold water from the flower-printed jug on the corner washstand. She slipped the cotton chemise over her head, and then the stiff calico bodice with many buttons, on which would be attached the cotton drawers. Black stockings had to be rolled up her legs and fixed by tapes buttoned to the bodice. Then came the drawers with frills which had to be smoothed down over each knee.

24

'Do your buttons up properly, Lizzie,' said Katy. 'You don't want your drawers to fall down during morning prayers at school. That would be a horror we can't contemplate.'

But the buttons were so small and Lizzie's fingers so clumsy, it was difficult to manage the horrid little things, and infuriating when they went into the wrong holes. And why should she have to wear all these silly clothes anyway? Her face reddened with rage, she stamped her feet suddenly and shouted: 'I won't! I won't! I hate buttons! I hate tapes!' And before Katy could say another word Lizzie was on her back drumming her heels into the floorboards, rolling about and wailing in a high-pitched scream of helpless fury.

Katy ran out of the room in a fright, calling out: 'Mother! Mother! Come quickly! Lizzie's having a fit!'

By the time Matilda came, Lizzie was sitting up weeping silently.

'Why, Lizzie darling, whatever is the matter?' Matilda asked.

'I want to go home to Robin Hood's Bay!' sobbed Lizzie.

Matilda knelt down beside her youngest daughter and took her in her arms. 'And all because of the new clothes?' she asked, stroking Lizzie's tangled gold curls away from her face and dabbing with her own handkerchief the tears flooding the child's angry blue eyes. Her voice was calm, but she felt Lizzie's words like a whip across her flesh, and was asking herself what had she done, sending her girl away from her mother and the place where she was born, so that now she felt like a stranger in her own real home. She pulled the drawers down over Lizzie's knees, smoothing the frills she herself had gathered, and the feather-stitched edging that her own needle had worked.

'Such pretty stitching, Lizzie!' she crooned, rocking the

child in her embrace. 'I did it for you, you know. And every time I put the needle in the cloth, I thought of Lizzie in Robin Hood's Bay. You can't be a happy savage for ever, my love. These new clothes are for the new growing-up Lizzie. You're going to go to a big school now. You're going to learn to be a big girl with lots of interesting important lessons.' Such was the persuasive power of Matilda's loving voice that Lizzie's sobs were hypnotised away. For years afterwards, she believed that the conversion of herself from unruly savage to civilised, law-abiding woman was somehow dependent on the feather stitching on her drawers. She stood up without another word, sniffed, and picked up her petticoat as Mother kissed her quickly before hurrying off to supervise the family breakfast table; but as Matilda ran downstairs her conscience nagged at her still: What have I done, sending her away so that I couldn't share her childhood, so that now she feels a stranger in my house?

Katy was less forgiving. She liked to see the scales of justice fairly balanced; and in her opinion Lizzie had got off too lightly. 'Happy savage!' she laughed scornfully. 'That's what you are. So pull down those drawers. The embroidery must lie flat below the knees.'

'Nobody sees the embroidery,' said Lizzie. 'So why must it lie flat?'

'God sees it,' said Katy. 'And don't be stubborn. Obstinacy is bad, though not, of course, as bad as temper tantrums before breakfast.' She pursed her lips.

'Does God look at the embroidery on my drawers?' asked Lizzie.

'Of course!' came the reply. 'God sees *everything*.'

There was a long silence. 'It's a queer thing,' Lizzie spoke at last, 'that God sees us all the time and we never get a look at Him.'

Katy's hand flew to her mouth. Would God send a thunderbolt to smash into the roof, scattering the tiles in revenge for her sister's blasphemy? To Lizzie, God's eye was a worrying thought. She just hoped that He might see but, like Mother, be too busy to look too closely.

'You must learn to tie the petticoat yourself,' insisted Katy, as Lizzie fumbled with the tapes behind her waist. 'Tie it firmly. If your petticoat comes adrift in a public place you'll disgrace the family.'

After that there was the underskirt of thick cotton, heavily embroidered round the hem, and after that the dress. And as if all this wasn't enough you had to slip over everything a pinafore adorned at the neck with lace.

'Don't you like your clothes?' asked Katy, seeing Lizzie's unhappy face.

'There are so many of them,' grumbled Lizzie. 'And there are so many fussy fastenings!'

'You should be grateful,' said her sister. 'Cissie and Mother have made them all for you. You're a proper schoolgirl now, so you must dress correctly. And if you grumble, Cissie will be hurt.'

'Well, I do like the sailor suit,' Lizzie admitted. That was her best outfit to be worn on Sundays. 'And I'll tell Cissie so. And I like my buttoned boots too.' What she really loved was the little silver-handled buttonhook Mother had given her. She kept that in her pinafore pocket. She didn't at all mind hooking up the boot buttons.

Although her rebellion was curbed she never liked her clothes as little girls were supposed to do. She often remembered with regret, how she'd run about barefoot in Robin Hood's Bay, when all the clothes she had were a short smock to cover her bare thighs and a pinafore to keep it clean. And now, the older she grew the longer grew her skirts. She chafed and fumed at the silliness of it – all this fuss about covering female legs! When Mother took her to see Lily Langtry at the Spa Theatre, where she was appearing as Rosalind in *As You Like It*, dressed as a boy in cross-gartered tights, the audience fairly buzzed with excitement, not over her acting but over the showing of her legs. 'Why?' Lizzie demanded. 'What's wrong with legs?'

It was not till she was in her teens that she began to think of women's clothes as part of a planned tyranny that made them walk sedately as if trussed up inside their skirts. It was a sort of socially acceptable straitjacket which made normal women avoid any activity that might tear or stain or otherwise spoil their clothes.

Although Lizzie had been a Thursday afternoon visitor to her mother's house in the Newborough End district of the town, she had never before been free to roam through the maze of rooms behind the shop: the office and storerooms, the dining-room and kitchen which led to a warren of lesser rooms, all with rough stone floors – the larder with its cool slate shelves, the lamproom smelling of oil and candle grease, the washroom with its copper boiler belching steam on Mondays, its tub and dolly for pounding dirty clothes in soapsuds, and the mangle for squeezing out excess water. Inside this complicated house lived a complex of human beings with all their rights and hierarchies to understand; and there was a little brown and white King Charles spaniel bitch with soft round eyes called Sukie. Lizzie sometimes smuggled Sukie into her bed at night, which was strictly against the rules. Mother made the rules, but it was Cissie who enforced them. Cissie was the eldest daughter, sixteen and nearly grown-up, and rather bossy about her job as Mother's housekeeper.

George, aged fifteen, was Lizzie's elder brother. He was a tall young man with hair as red as Grandma Harrison's was said to have been in youth, and blue eyes which seemed to dance when he looked at you. The household revolved around him whenever he came home. Mother attached some special importance to him; but when accused by Katy of showing favouritism, she excused herself by saying he was her first boy. The real reason, which she didn't confess to, was because she saw in him a reflection of her lost Henry's glamour. George had his own bedroom on the second floor. To Lizzie it was some sort of bluebeard's sanctum. For one thing, he had forbidden her to enter it; for another she knew it was there that he shaved to prevent his beard growing. She couldn't see any beard on his face, however hard she looked for it; but Flo, the housemaid, who cleaned his room, assured her that he had a razor which he sharpened on a leather strap. 'Like what me Dad used, to beat t' mischief out us lasses with,' she said.

'Did your Dad really beat you?' Lizzie asked, and flinched.

'He did an' all – when he were in his red hot rage. But mostly us knew when to keep out t' way.'

In spite of the still only intermittent growth of George's beard, there was about him a male buccaneering swagger that terrified but also excited Lizzie. She loved to be commanded by him in the occasional game he deigned to play with her; and when his praise or his hand caressed her she was suddenly lifted into joy. She could tell that Flo shared her feelings about George because she did so like talking about him, and sometimes, in the middle of her confidences, she would blush. George had that faculty – impossible to know the how and wherefore of it – for making people of all kinds and ages fall in love with him. He was at a school for sailors, a training ship, the *Conway*, he told her. It was a funny sort of ship because it was on land.

'Well, not really on shore you know,' he explained. 'It's moored off Rock Ferry in Birkenhead. That's in the river Mersey at Liverpool. We're all going to be proper sail sailors.' To learn this he had to be able to furl and reef sails, knot and splice ropes, heave the lead and the log, as well as do all sorts of terrible mathematics much harder than long-division sums, with unheard of names like logarithms and spherical trigonometry, as well as magnetism and deviation of the compass in iron ships, and learning about the stars.

'And Mercator's Projection,' said George, adding loftily: 'but that's only flattening out the atlas of the globe on to a chart.'

'And do you know,' Lizzie later confided to Katy, 'there are ninety guns on the *Conway*!'

'But they don't fire,' said Katy. 'They're only there for show.' This detracted a little from George's prestige, especially as Katy said: 'George is a bit of a show off you know.' She was more impressed when Lizzie told her there were nearly two hundred cadets aboard. 'Really?' she murmured. Then, quickly checking any undeserved enthusiasm, she added dismissively: 'Just boys, of course!'

George, who liked talking to Lizzie because of her uncritical devotion, used to pick up her geography book with its atlases and challenge her to pronounce some difficult names like Popacatapetl, Natashquan and Paleokastrion.

'I'm going to travel all round the world like Captain Cook,' he said. 'One day I shall see all those places.'

When Lizzie repeated this boast to Flo she said: 'And he will, too.' But Katy, annoyed by all this adoration of her elder brother, commented tartly: 'There's no Australia left for him to discover now, you know. And Popacatapetl is a very high mountain. I doubt if he'll get his ship up to the top of that!'

Lizzie's other brother, Edward, who was fourteen, was still at school in Scarborough. He noticed her from time to time, but loftily. Sometimes he gave her a jelly baby or a liquorice bootlace from his Saturday supply of sweets, and occasionally deigned to play with her in the attics where his presence added an exciting warlike element to their games; but at heart he was peace loving, a practical person who was interested in making things work, in making the best of things.

Lizzie's favourite part of the whole day was coming home from school with Katy to a high tea with bacon-and-egg pie. She could smell the warm, pastry-scented air as soon as she ran into the house by the back porch, where she unbuttoned her boots before putting on the slippers that Flo was warming for her by the kitchen range. After tea Cissie played the piano in the parlour, where a fire was burning and the lamps were lit. Sometimes, Mother sang in a steady contralto to Cissie's accompaniment. Lizzie had homework to do, but she waited to hear the generous, happy voice fill the room with the protective feeling engendered by 'Home Sweet Home'. Cissie played softly, striking few wrong notes. The walnut upright piano had two brass candle sconces, but burning candles in them was forbidden for fear the flames might catch some careless singer's hair or clothing. Cissie didn't need extra illumination, since she knew the piece by heart; but Mother lifted the lamp from the central table and placed it on top of the piano, and a circle of amber light fell on her as she stood singing. It shone on Cissie's fair head bent over the keys, crept over a corner of the red Turkey carpet and winked off the brass pedals under Cissie's briskly pressing feet, but left in semi-darkness the lilac-tinted wallpaper and the plush curtains of crimson loaded with shadows which were drawn across the windows to exclude the rude world beyond.

Mother's second song, 'The Lost Chord', instilled an aura of mystery into the silence it left at its ending, a short, solemn silence broken only by the faint crackle of the fire in the big, black grate. Then Lizzie sighed with satisfaction at being part of this magic planetary system of family with Mother as the sun. She used to promise herself: When I'm grown-up I shall have a lot of children.

31

And they'll look at me and smile because I shall give them lovely bacon-and-egg-pie for tea. She wouldn't be able to sing to them like Mother, because she knew she couldn't keep in tune; but perhaps their father might be able to do the singing.

When Cissie moved the lamp back to the middle of the room and opened a thick volume of Samuel Smiles's *Self-Help*, and Mother sat down and began to sew a split seam in one of Edward's shirts, the magic faded. Cissie's voice was clear and precise: 'To secure independence the practice of simple economy is all that is necessary. Economy requires neither superior courage nor eminent virtue, it is satisfied with ordinary energy and the capacity of average minds. Economy is, at bottom, but the spirit of order applied to the administration of domestic affairs; it means management, regularity and the avoidance of waste.'

Lizzie crept quietly out of the parlour and ran to the kitchen where the maids, having removed their starched white aprons, were lolling at ease over the table and their tea.

'It's that dull book again,' Lizzie explained, as she sat down on a stool by the glowing range. 'It's all about helping yourself.'

'There's always some as can't help theirselves,' said Bessie.

'You can help yourself to that, anyroad,' said Flo, handing her a thick slice of bread she'd just cut and spread with dripping.

Lizzie bit into it thoughtfully. 'You don't help yourselves,' she said at last. 'You look after us.'

'We all have to look after one another,' said Flo; but Bessie laughed: 'You'd best be doing your 'omework, Lizzie lass, not wasting your time here with us.'

Bessie was dismissing her from the cosy intimacy of the kitchen; and Lizzie went reluctantly. She turned at the door and looked back at Bessie's tousled hair, at her white cap hanging from the back of her chair and, behind her on the dark wall, a Sunderland pottery plaque. In the firelight, the words of the text blazed out their lustred message: 'Waste Not Want Not'.

Homework was taken seriously at Newborough End – not at all like in Esplanade House where Lizzie used to scribble it off without a thought while listening with half an ear to gossip. Matilda Thorburn believed it was work in which children should not be interrupted if they were to learn how to concentrate. So Edward and Katy did their homework at their desks in their bedrooms, but Lizzie, who had as yet no bedroom of her own, used the small office behind the shop, sitting at the big, battered desk at which, in the old days, her father had done his accounts. There was no fire in the room, and in winter it was cold, but it was quiet, there was always clean blotting paper laid out for her, and clean ink in the sunken inkwells, one filled with blue, one with red ink.

Lizzie undid her satchel and pulled out her exercise books. She slid open the lid of her wooden pencil box with a thumb nail and took out her sharpened pencils: HB for writing and ruling lines, B for Drawing and BB for shading. She loved her pencils. She wasn't so fond of her pen, the twin peaks of whose nib, if she leaned on it too hard, inclined to cross over and bend, which absolutely destroyed the grace of a tall *t* or the neat roundings of an *m*. She opened her arithmetic book and sighed. Long division! What a pest it was! She always seemed to lose the thread of it halfway through the sum.

'I can't get it right!' she wailed.

'Of course you can!' said Mother. 'There's no such word as can't to any girl worth her salt. You must try again.'

'Why is it so important?'

'A girl must be correct over numbers, Alice.' Mother

called her Alice when she was severe, or when she wanted to stress the seriousness of the subject under discussion. 'If you lose numbers from your sums now, you'll lose money from your purse when you're grown-up. And then you'll be poor. Poverty is women's enemy, Alice. And education is their way out of domestic slavery,' she added. She had never enjoyed any formal education herself, which was perhaps why she valued it so much.

Lizzie took longer than usual over her sums that evening, partly because she was thinking of what her mother had said about being poor. She remembered seeing poor boys playing once in Whitby. They were scrambling over boats in the harbour, in and out of the water like naked eels. When she saw that they all had little dangling things, which girls did not possess, she cried out in amazement: 'Oh look! What –?' But Aunt Clara snatched her hand and hurried her away from the scene. 'It's boys' piss-pipes!' she hissed. 'Poor mites! Naked as the day they were born!'

They were poor mites; but Mabel Dorker, who sat next to her in class, and whose mother drove her to school in a smart little carriage with a liveried Tiger standing on the step behind, ready to jump down and open the door for her, was rich. Then again, everybody was richer than the widow and her swarming family in Boreman's Yard at the back of Newborough. In Boreman's Yard, twenty families huddled round a central area into which they threw rubbish and slops, and even (so Flo said) emptied chamber pots; and all the filth piled up making a horrible smell till the town cart came in by a narrow alley and shovelled it all up before taking it to some dump far away.

The youngest child of one of those Boreman's Yard families was a little barefoot urchin who came round to the kitchen door each evening to collect the scraps left over from Thorburn meals. He was referred to as

34

a 'poor mite' by Bessie, but he wore clothes of a sort, chiefly old and often incongruous hand-me-downs from Thorburn wardrobes: trousers worn and grown out of long ago by Edward, and over them a pinafore which was once Katy's. He never wore stockings, and his feet, even in the coldest weather, were bare. The boys from Boreman's Yard were certainly very poor, although their dangling things were covered up. With an effort of will she pulled her thoughts back to long division and tried again to do the sum.

Dr Beverley, Mother said, was a very important man; but he looked ordinary and insignificant and quite small without his tall top hat, which Mother had taken from him and was carrying when they entered the bedroom. Lizzie, who had been curled up in bed as tightly as she could make herself, peeped at him over the sheet. Her eyelids were red with crying. The pain in her ear was so bad that the tears just keep oozing out of her eyes in spite of all her efforts to be brave. But now that Dr Beverley had come to take away the horrid ache, she already felt better. He didn't say much, but he popped a cold little tube into her ear and, using a light, he bent down and peered inside. Then he gave a grunt and stood up. He stroked the hair away from her damp forehead.

'You must be a brave little soldier,' he said.

Lizzie turned her head on the pillow to look at him. 'I think I'd rather be a sailor,' she said.

That made both Mother and Dr Beverley laugh as he wrote a prescription for some medicine, which sent Edward running to the chemist's shop to get the precious stuff put into a bottle. It was magic, Lizzie declared, as the pain grew less fierce.

Mother put a few drops of olive oil on to a spoon and warmed it over a lighted match before pouring it into Lizzie's poorly ear.

'That's nice,' sighed Lizzie. Mother sat by her bed and held her hand. 'When I grow up I shall be a doctor,' declared Lizzie. 'And then I can do all that magic for poorly people.'

'You will?' Matilda smiled. 'There aren't many women doctors, you know.' In her own youth she had sometimes dreamed similar impossible dreams. When she was first married she used to read the *Englishwoman's Journal*, which gave all the news about the women's movement, and had followed Elizabeth Garrett Anderson's progress as she struggled to become England's first woman doctor. Matilda had admired her from afar. She thought of her as being like a Whitby-built ship, elegant, but strong enough to sail through all the buffetings, the storms of hostility and derision that assailed her. She was no intellectual giant; her genius was a talent for common sense. Where more strident 'strong-minded' feminists had aroused anger and even hatred, her good manners, inoffensive dress and quiet, reasonable voice had, in the end, prevailed. She was the kind of New Woman Matilda, in different circumstances, in another life perhaps, would have liked to follow. She smiled, remembering Henry's reaction when she had confessed to him these secret daydreams. They were lying in the great oak bed she still slept in, but then it stood in Trafalgar House, in a room overlooking St Mary's church. It was a Sunday evening, and they had attended Evensong that day.

'Good God, woman!' he cried in mock horror. 'If you were a barber-surgeon I'd be afraid of going to bed with you! I'd be afraid you might cut off more than my beard!' And then he rolled over her and covered her with laughter and blustery kisses.

But in spite of the impossibility of it, she used to think sometimes when she sat breastfeeding the latest baby: In another time, in another life I might have been . . . The best she could do was to put flowers on the grave of

Anne Brontë, who (poor soul!) came to Scarborough to cure her consumption but died instead, and was buried in St Mary's churchyard opposite the house. In that way she could, at least, commemorate another brave girl who tried to push forward the pioneering frontiers for women in a previous age.

'Elizabeth Garrett Anderson was the first,' Matilda said. She tucked the bedclothes round Lizzie and added judiciously: 'But I don't believe she could have done it without the backing of a wealthy father and the support of a rich husband.' It was not, after all, the sort of thing a woman of no means and no importance could do.

'Mm . . . mm . . .' sighed Lizzie. Dr Beverley's medicine was making her sleepy.

Lizzie overcame her difficulties with long division at about the same time as she was cured of her earache. She was soon eager to go back to school, and often ran along the pavement so that Katy had to run, too, to keep up with her. She began to enjoy learning so much, grabbing at scraps of new knowledge and turning them over in her imagination with such pleasure that her teacher declared she was positively a glutton for facts. She was learning fast, so fast that by the time she was fourteen the headmistress wrote to Matilda inviting her to come to the school to discuss her daughter's progress. 'Lizzie needs more than we can teach her here,' she said. She even suggested that Lizzie might, if her mother approved, try to win a place at one of the universities now open to women, but would need extra coaching to pass the entrance exam, or matriculation. She suggested as tutor, Samuel Bodkin, who taught political economy to the girls in their last year at school.

He was a Quaker, a small, unassuming man of great intelligence but no aptitude as a disciplinarian. The girls called him Bodykins. During his classes they lolled about on their desks, laughed openly, and threw each other scribbled missives torn out of exercise books. He never questioned his teaching method, nor the content of his discourse, but simply presumed that girls' brains were incapable of understanding abstract concepts and all the interesting speculation and logical argument that might arise from these.

Lizzie ran with the hounds while at school, and was prepared to ridicule him with the rest, so it came as a surprise to have to admit, when she sat opposite him at a table in the front parlour of his own home, that this small man contained inside his large head all that she needed to know to gain entrance to London University and to what she and Mother were beginning to regard as the Golden Jerusalem beyond. She was actually enjoying his elegant demonstration, with triangles and parallelograms drawn on paper, of the rightness of Pythagoras's theorem.

She was momentarily distracted by the sight of black hairs on the backs of his hands, and wondered if even Bodykins hid some secret beastliness under his frock coat. Looking up she met his steady, reasonable gaze.

'It's very interesting,' she said. 'Pythagoras, I mean . . . Why don't we learn this at school?'

'Why not, indeed?' he murmured.

Mechanics was another matter. She found that very hard to battle with: all those weights and masses and levers and resolution of forces.

'Why must I do all this?' she demanded. 'I don't want to be a railway engineer!'

At the end of the lesson, Mrs Bodkin, with a great rustle of skirts and an agitated flurry of movements, brought in a tray of tea. She placed it on the table, sweeping aside their books and papers, some of which fluttered to the floor and were not picked up, and sat down to preside over the teapot, while her inadequately-put-together hair flopped about her face. As she poured the first cup, a hairpin fell out and hit the saucer with a frivolous ping. The tea was served with very hard rock cakes that left showers of crumbs. It was then that Lizzie realised Samuel Bodkin was human after all, for he rose from the table and solemnly taking his plate to the window, he opened it and threw his crumbs to a crowd of expectant sparrows perched on a privet hedge outside.

'They get rather peckish at this time of year,' he explained. 'Birds die off in the winter, you know. Hunger and cold keep down their population in accordance with Malthusian principles.'

'And he's trying to prove Malthus wrong!' laughed his wife. 'Aren't you, pet?'

Lizzie looked from one to the other. Who on earth was Malthus?

'He was wrong, my dear,' he said mildly. 'Certainly in rich industrial countries, where excessive population growth can be maintained because the food needed can be brought in through trade. In a more natural agricultural setting his law does, of course, operate.'

'He believes in Malthus, but he doesn't like him,' said Mrs Bodkin. She shook her head, smiling indulgently, and a hailstorm of hairpins fell upon the plates.

'And so the sparrows get fed in winter,' said Lizzie.

'Even political economists are illogical at times,' he admitted.

'He likes Godwin better than Malthus,' said Mrs Bodkin.

'Of course I like Godwin,' he agreed. 'He was an optimist. He believed in the perfectibility of man. He thought man's natural intelligence and goodness—'

'Woman's goodness,' interrupted his wife.

'– would eventually put right all the world's troubles.'

'I've heard of Godwin,' said Lizzie. 'Wasn't he the father of Mary Shelley, who wrote *Frankenstein*?'

'Such a horrible story!' declared Mrs B. 'And she, only nineteen when she wrote it!'

'But I fear' – Mr B. was pursuing his own train of thought – 'I fear he may be wrong in his reasoning – or at least in his first premise.'

Mrs Bodkin smiled conspiratorially at Lizzie as she offered her another cake. 'I expect you think we're slightly mad,' she said.

'Other people may be mad,' he corrected her, 'but we are idiosyncratic.'

In spite of his idiosyncrasies he was able to prepare Lizzie by the time she was seventeen to sit for the College of Preceptors' exam, which would provide her with a certificate qualifying her at least for the position of governess. The exam was held in Scarborough in the Pavilion Hotel.

'Are you ready for the high jump?' asked Edward at breakfast on the morning of the event. He didn't think much of this education-for-women lark. It seemed to him that women had enough to do looking after their own business, without filling their heads full of ideas they couldn't cope with. He was, by now, a partner in Messrs Thorburn and Son, and intended to take over the business entirely, as soon as Mother thought fit to retire. He wouldn't in the least object to her indulging her Women's Rights notions then, when she had nothing better to do.

If looks could kill, Lizzie would have felled him then and there; but she said nothing. She wasn't feeling very well. She couldn't swallow her porridge, but managed to drink a cup of tea.

'When it's all over, treat yourself to a nice tea in the hotel,' said Mother, helping her to put on her coat. Lizzie was rather young to order tea in a hotel for herself, but there would be other examinees there whom she might join.

The dining-room of the Pavilion Hotel was laid out that morning in June, not for diners but for nervous pupils. Lizzie counted half a dozen girls among the crowd of boys. She sat at a small table facing a long window that overlooked the railway station, and was aware, as she read the instructions heading the English paper, of muffled clangings and the shunting of an engine. She had two-and-a-half hours to answer the questions in the morning, and another two-and-a-half hours to deal with history in the afternoon. Tomorrow it would be scripture and German.

She was reading a piece of prose full of long sentences and complicated grammar, which she had to précis into a single short paragraph, when she heard a thump behind her and, glancing back, she saw that one of the girls had fainted and fallen into the aisle between the rows of desks. Two invigilators rushed forward to pick up the limp body and carry it out. Lizzie thought no more of the incident till she'd finished her paper when, feeling no longer ill, but relieved and elated and rather hungry she walked into the hotel tea-room.

A pianist sat on a dais flanked by palms in pots, and just below, at a little round table covered by a white tablecloth, sat the girl who had fainted. She was alone, and Lizzie saw at once that she'd been crying.

'May I join you?' Lizzie asked. 'Are you all right now? I'm awfully sorry you were ill.' She couldn't help noticing that the stranger was expensively dressed.

The girl glanced at her without smiling, but nodded. Scornfully she jerked her head towards the pianist playing above them. 'Mendelssohn,' she murmured under her breath. 'One of his songs without words. Thank heaven! The words would almost certainly be silly and sentimental!' She stopped talking and her face relaxed its sharpness as she listened. 'Rather nice that, though . . .' she conceded. In spite of her desire to mock, her attention was held by the melody rippling down the keys. She said no more till Lizzie's tea arrived, and then, as Lizzie was pouring it out, she began to speak in quick, excited bursts.

'I envy you your health and strength,' she said, glancing not altogether kindly at Lizzie's bright eyes and flushed cheeks. 'I expect you've passed the exam. I shall never have another chance.'

'Why not? Surely . . .'

'Because my parents won't allow it. I've always been delicate, you see. They think higher education will warp my character and make me ill. And anyway I shall soon be too old.'

'Oh, no. Surely not,' Lizzie protested, guessing her age at around nineteen.

'Elizabeth Garrett Anderson was older than me when she took up her studies. You've heard of her I suppose?'

'Of course. And of her sister Millicent Fawcett, who's been trying to get the Vote for us.'

'Elizabeth Garrett was no thick-skinned peasant either, you know,' said the girl. 'She was a lady. Everything she did, she did gently, with good manners. So why shouldn't I?'

'You mean you want to be a doctor? That's awfully ambitious!'

'Yes. I want to go to India to help those poor Indian ladies who have no doctors to look after them. India is so romantic: the jungle full of tigers and chattering monkeys, the zenanas screened from men, the bright silk saris. And the perfumes . . . ! I've read a lot about it.'

'It's a long training I believe,' said Lizzie.

'Well, I wouldn't mind that.'

'You've left school, I suppose?' Lizzie looked over the rim of her teacup, sipping thoughtfully.

'I never went to school. Mama thought it too common. I had governesses, then tutors. They all seemed to think

I was clever enough to do it. And I was always happy caring for the sick poor on Papa's estate. This College of Preceptors exam is only a trial run. And now they'll never allow me to matriculate!'

'You must try again. You must insist.'

'I don't think they'll let me. I know what they'll say. Mama will declare that my nervous system is too finely tuned for the low class of patients I would have to meet; and Papa will say that all that blood and guts and saw-bones surgery (men are so coarse in their language, aren't they?) would drive me into an asylum for the insane. But look at Florence Nightingale! She has suffered years of ill health but still works wonders from her bed!'

'What do your parents say to that?'

'It was all those horrors at Scutari which have undermined her health, is what they say.'

The pianist stopped playing. He rose and bowed gravely to scattered clapping. At this moment the unhappy girl stood up and turned towards the door where a tall man with drooping black moustaches was searching the faces of the seated crowd.

'There's Papa,' said his daughter. 'He's come to take me home. And I'll have to tell him what happened. He'll pretend to sympathise, of course, but they'll all be secretly delighted.' She added bitterly: 'Believing they've been proved right.'

'I'm so sorry,' said Lizzie. 'I wish . . .'

'You could be a doctor,' said the girl, suddenly offering her hand. Lizzie noticed that it was trembling as she shook it. 'You have the health and strength for it.' And, picking up her gloves from the table, she hurried away to her Papa.

Lizzie did well in the exam and was awarded a prize by the College of Preceptors: ten volumes of *Chambers Encyclopaedia* bound in gilded yellow calf. Her new books, precious to her because they contained so much of all that knowledge she wanted to acquire, she stacked in a small bookcase left behind by George, in the bedroom she now occupied alone.

She often read in bed late at night by the light of her candle. She read any book she could lay hands on, borrowing novels, histories, essays, travellers' tales, and accounts of local lore from the subscription library, or the bookshelves of friends; and on the Saturday, when the *Strand Magazine* came out, she used to run down to the Mechanics' Institute, as soon as she could get away from the house, to read the latest of Conan Doyle's Sherlock Holmes stories. There she stood among all the men, a few in top hats, more in bowlers, but most of them wearing the flat cloth caps of artisans and labourers, all jostling to get a glimpse of the newspapers and journals displayed free on eye-level stands.

To her mother, who was beginning to worry that all this reading was abnormal in a girl of her age, her curiosity seemed insatiable. It seemed to Matilda strange, too, that Lizzie took no interest in her clothes or her appearance. Once, when it was suggested that she should make an effort to look 'nice' she asked 'Why?' And when her mother pursued: 'Most girls take notice of fashions, or at least try to look attractive,' Lizzie said: 'Those things are too trivial to bother about.' She spoke in an abstracted way, gazing out of the window, and feeling trapped, like Eve, longing for the fruit of that forbidden tree – forbidden, especially to women – the tree of knowledge.

Matilda was not the only member of the household who was aware of Lizzie's withdrawn mood. Flo, who was gentle with her when everyone else was irritated and impatient, declared in confidence to Bessie: 'It's love she's wanting. She's yearning for it, poor duck! I know just how she feels.'

'You be careful, my lass!' warned Bessie sharply. 'Don't you be too quick to tumble into that marriage bed. 'Tis not one can be tumbled out of once you're in!'

Flo now had a constant follower in the postman; but their engagement would be a long one, since their combined savings were not, and wouldn't be for years, enough to set up house together.

Lizzie became more and more silent at mealtimes, till at last her mother could bear it no longer and decided to speak about her fears to Dr Beverley who, as the family doctor and a friend of long standing might be able to help.

'She's becoming a blue-stocking,' said Matilda.

'Well, what of it?'

'But you know, Frank, as well as I do, that men dislike that sort of woman. She might never marry, and what will happen to her then?' Matilda thought of her own sister Clara's lonely and, she thought, wasted life. To her way of thinking, any woman without children suffered a terrible loss.

'There's many a married woman I know who wishes she were single,' he said.

'Oh, Frank!' sighed Matilda. 'I don't mind so much her being a blue-stocking; but I don't want her to be a freak condemned by her oddity to isolation. A girl should be a woman still, even though she's clever and educated.'

'I don't think she's a freak. To me she just seems a jolly girl.'

After a pause she said: 'I suppose she's starving for knowledge. That's all she seems to want. Anyone would think she had a tapeworm in her mind.'

'She's growing up, that's all,' he said. 'It takes young people differently. It's just the pains of adolescence she's going through in her own way.' If he'd been talking to a male colleague he would have said: 'The girl's on heat, but doesn't know it.' But, of course, he couldn't say that

45

sort of thing to a lady even if she was the girl's mother and an old friend. 'It can be misery, you know – growing up,' was what he said instead. 'It's nearly as bad as going through the Valley of Death in the psalm, except that you do come out of adolescence at last, and in the psalm you don't.'

'She's so silent sometimes I wonder what on earth she's thinking about,' grumbled Matilda.

'She's probably not thinking at all,' he said; but there he was wrong. 'I remember my own boyhood. A pretty good hell it was.'

'How did you come out of it?'

'Exercise, Matilda. That's the cure for mental derangements. Exercise and cold baths. She shouldn't read so much, I agree. That can't be good for a girl. She should walk more.'

'Well, she does wash in cold water. And she does walk a lot. She walks with Dax, all afternoon sometimes, now that the summer holidays are here.' Sukie had moved on into whatever Elysian fields are reserved for pretty King Charles spaniel bitches with pop eyes, and Dax, a smooth-haired, black Dachshund with a white stripe down his nose, had taken her place. Dr Beverley remembered the Dachshund he'd tripped over as he'd entered the house, and the shockingly loud squeals of protest uttered by that small dog.

'Do you think she should go in for the Matriculation and leave home to go to a university afterwards?' Matilda spoke doubtfully.

'Why not? Why not? She's done so well in her first exam. She'll do it all easily.'

'I suppose – if she didn't marry – she might one day be a teacher, perhaps even a headmistress, in one of these new, independent schools for girls?'

'And meanwhile,' said the doctor, as if it had all been decided, 'send her on errands across town with her dog.

46

No need to worry. She's a big strong girl. No anaemia there. She'll come through.'

So Lizzie walked daily for miles that summer with little Dax trotting at her heels, along the beaches of Scarborough's two bays, across the town and out into the countryside. But all this exercise didn't curb what, to her mother, was an excessive and unnatural desire for books, and to Lizzie was the gateway to a fuller, richer life. She was always happy when she was reading; but when she wasn't, she had to admit she was worried. She had now left school. She seemed to have very little to do at home. What was there in the future for her? Edward was gradually becoming the boss in the grocery business, and she certainly had no intention of working in the shop under him. And his friends, too, were bores. All they talked about was pounds, shillings and pence, and the price of cheese. Much as she loved her mother and her home in Scarborough, she wanted to get away from them; she felt imprisoned – almost, she thought, as much as that poor highly-strung girl in the Pavilion Hotel, who dreamed of romance in distant exotic lands but was caged by her parents and their wealth.

That girl had planted a seed in Lizzie's mind. To be a doctor . . . Now that would be something. Perhaps if she were a doctor she could help the women whose enemy was poverty. To go to London to study . . . The very thought of it quickened her pulse. London: the throbbing heart of the Empire, of the world, the great capital with its trade sliding in and out of its railway terminals and port; the mysterious city containing five million souls and the ghosts of centuries was beckoning her. Why not a doctor? It would be a hard, daunting, perhaps impossible struggle. It would be like embarking on almost uncharted seas, and would need all the courage and endurance of her seafaring ancestors; but it would be terribly exciting. So her secret ambition began to grow. She made a few enquiries; she wrote letters to London, one to the Secretary of the new London School of Medicine for Women where Elizabeth Garrett Anderson was Dean of Studies. She discovered that there were nearly fifty students there now, and that the school had become amalgamated to the neighbouring Royal Free Hospital, so that female students debarred from all other London Teaching Hospitals now had access to wards where they could do their clinical work.

To Flo, who always picked up letters from the postman first thing in the morning, Lizzie said: 'If there's a letter for me with a London postmark, will you give it to me direct? Not leave it on the breakfast table, I mean . . .'

Flo was pleased and excited, imagining a romance, picturing some dashing young man Lizzie had met and was now secretly corresponding with.

Lizzie couldn't discuss her dreams with anyone. She knew Edward would consider it a mad idea, and Katy would laugh when she heard about it: 'You want to do what's impossible! You want to sail to the top of Popacatapetl!' And Mother would be worried to death by the prospect of letting her daughter go south to live in a place reputed to be full of luxury and wickedness and terrible dangers for young girls. Moreover, the enterprise would cost money. Lizzie had no idea how much, but she guessed it would be too much. So she kept silent and continued reading far into the night and going for long solitary walks by day.

The autumn brought many changes to Newborough End. George, who was sailing on foreign-going vessels, was seldom at home. After being apprenticed for four years to ships of the Allan Line, which plied for trade across the Atlantic to and from Canadian and North American ports, he passed all the Board of Trade exams for Third, Second and First Mate, and now, at last, his Master's certificate was in his pocket too. He was not yet, but hoped to be soon, in command of his own ship. Cissie was also sailing on the high seas in a rather different capacity. She had undertaken to act as paid companion and nurse on a long voyage to Australia to a very sick young woman, whose parents believed the change of air and sea travel would benefit her health. Perhaps they knew that whatever they did for her nothing could stop the destruction of her consumptive lungs. Perhaps it was because they were unable to bear the prospect of watching her die, that they shovelled her into that small cabin with Cissie on a pitching steamer and pushed her off out of sight. It was Cissie, all unknowing when, with her frail charge, she boarded the ship in Tilbury Docks, who would see her die and be cast with a few perfunctory prayers into the Indian Ocean.

Katy was a governess to two little girls in a big house down south, in Surrey. She wrote happy letters home. She was not unduly put upon, she said; her children were bright and full of fun, and seemed to enjoy their lessons; and the woods round Hindhead were spectacularly beautiful in their autumn colour.

There was no one now to play the piano for Mother's songs; but reading aloud still continued in the evenings. When Edward found time to join them, he took his turn, but it was usually Lizzie who read to Mother the weekly novel sent through the post by Mudie's Circulating Library. In spite of the recent attack on Mr Mudie in a literary journal, for circulating morals rather than literature, the books read at Newborough End were a good deal more entertaining than the heavy volumes of Samuel Smiles's advice of a decade earlier. Edward's favourite was the *Diary of a Nobody*, and *The Strange Case of Dr Jekyll and Mr Hyde* filled Lizzie with gleeful horror.

For Matilda it was the best part of the day. She clung to the habit of this happy hour, though it was no longer what it was when all her children were still pressing round her, dependent, confiding and demanding love. There was a shadow of sadness in it now, which she could not dispel. Three of her children had left their home; Edward was, she knew, itching to push her out of the business she had made so successful; and Lizzie, her last and best-loved baby, was drifting away from her into some secret, solitary world of her own. For reasons which she could not fathom, this little daughter, who used to delight her with her carefree talk and funny observations, no longer shared her thoughts; but at least when she sat there reading aloud in a steady voice, she did seem to come back briefly into the family circle, and sometimes she even laughed. Matilda could only hope that Dr Beverley was right, and that this estranged Lizzie would somehow come through her Valley of the Shadow of Adolescence, and return to her old self, happy and cheerful as she used to be.

THREE

Clara seldom visited nowadays. All her time and energy were devoted to the care of the old people in Robin Hood's Bay; but one Thursday she did travel across the moor in the carter's van, with news of Grandma Harrison. For some years now, she had been lame with rheumatics in her knees, and last week had fallen as she hobbled uphill from Fletcher's bakery with a loaf under her arm. She fell on the cobbles and the loaf skidded down the hill till it was stopped by a boy running home from school. The whole episode was so reminiscent of Lizzie's fateful day with Billy Boothby's warring gang, that she couldn't help laughing.

'There's nowt to laugh at,' said Clara.

'I was remembering something else,' said Lizzie. 'What happened to Billy Boothby?'

'He's gone to sea,' said Clara. 'What else?'

Lizzie was still smiling, as into her mind came the words of the old song: 'Bobby Shafto's gone to sea./ Silver buckles on his knee./ He'll come home and marry me./ Bonny Bobby Shafto!' Billy Boothby certainly would have had no silver buckles on his knee, and even more certainly would never come back to marry her, but she couldn't help smiling when she thought of him. Wild and wicked he might have been, but he did make things come alive.

Not long after Clara's visit Grandma Harrison had a stroke. She didn't survive more than a few weeks, though Clara washed her and fed her, and plumped her pillows so that she could sit up and look out of the windows.

'Not a reet lot o' pomp,' she managed to utter before she died. 'Nor none o' them hymns wi' daft words neither.' All she wanted was to sing for those in peril on the sea. So her funeral at St Stephen's church was a quiet affair.

Great-uncle Mills, though not exactly going strong, was still going. He was very old and forgetful, not always knowing where he was, sometimes thinking he was still a sailor. He used to totter down to the Bay whenever he could escape Clara's vigilance, and if a boat was anchored within reach he would wade out to it and try to clamber aboard. Of course he fell in the water more than once, which caused Clara to fear he'd drown himself one day. Dying at sea might be a proper thing for a man and a sailor, but doing it in two feet of water would be ignominious. When he finally died he was in bed. Nobody knew what he died of, he wasn't ill, but simply shuffled off his mortal coil while he slept. Clara, wishing to make more fuss of his going than he had, arranged an elaborate funeral. He had many friends in Robin Hood's Bay, but Clara knew he'd wanted to be buried in Whitby among his ancestors.

'It's more than a stone's throw from Scarborough to Whitby,' said Edward. 'We'll need a closed carriage.' The old wagonette which had been used for many outings, for visits to friends and picnics in the country, rested on its shafts in the coach house, but having no roof would give no protection from chilly winds and rain on the long drive. Matilda, as her fortunes improved, had indulged her desire to possess her own dogcart, the capital expense of which made Edward frown, especially as there was also an annual tax of one guinea to pay on it. It was a smart little buggy for the women to drive on a fine day, but quite unsuitable for the funeral. So, while Matilda and Lizzie were being fitted for their black clothes by the local dressmaker he took his uncle, Wallace Thorburn, to visit a coach builder who, besides selling vehicles, also hired them out.

'It's going to be an occasion for pomp then,' was Wallace's comment, as they stood admiring a beautiful landau in shining green paint, with a pair of hoods which could be opened or shut at will, a door at the side, a low step for easy entrance, and curved anti-mud splashboards over the wheels.

'Do you want to come?' asked Edward. And Wallace, who dearly loved the solemn ritual of funerals with a crowd of folk to celebrate them, especially when there was no expense to be incurred by himself, assented. 'I think I should put in an appearance, don't you? Stand by you, and support the women?'

Matilda had been on terms of very cool courtesy with Wallace since the time of his attempt to take over the management of her business, but she agreed that it would be proper to be accompanied by another male mourner besides Edward, who still looked so young – too young to manage their part in the affair, though she knew he was perfectly capable of doing so. Mercifully, her mother-in-law could be left out of it, since she was now too old and frail to travel.

Tom, the groom, with Davy from Boreham's Yard who helped him in the stables, harnessed two horses to the hired carriage and then climbed up on the coachman's box. Lizzie had been squeezed, much against her will, into a black bombazine dress with leg-o'-mutton sleeves, so tight at the waist that her breathing was constricted. She sat beside Mother, also in deepest mourning, facing the men in their black frock coats. They drove with the heads folded back, as it was a warm October morning, though the sky was overcast. When the carriage moved off, the black voile scarves tied about the men's top hats fluttered in the breeze, dancing on the air with the black feathers and netting swathed around the headgear of the ladies. For the first quarter of an hour nobody spoke.

'I suppose it was his wish to be buried in Whitby so that he might join his forefathers?' Wallace broke the silence. He wanted to roll the conversational ball a bit, to lift the atmosphere out of the lugubrious, but without introducing any unseemly levity.

'I suppose so,' said Edward. 'There are a great many of us buried there. And they go back a long way.'

Lizzie listened to the men's voices above the sounds of wheels and hooves. She thought of Great-uncle Mills and the little girl he had loved on the other side of the river. Millicent, that was her name. 'He spent his childhood there, you see,' she prompted.

'What's that?' from Wallace. 'Oh, yes! And went to school there too I suppose?'

'But it's more than those things, which attached him to the place,' Edward explained. 'His father sailed whaling ships out of Whitby to catch whales east of Greenland; and as a boy he must have sailed with him.' And dragged the poor beasts back through ice floes before cutting them up for oil and blubber and fishy-tasting meat, Lizzie reflected. 'And before that,' Edward was expounding, 'the Mills forefathers built Whitby ships. I wouldn't be surprised if they didn't help build Captain Cook's *Endeavour*.'

Silence fell again.

'We've got to go to the Angel to meet the funeral cortege,' said Matilda. 'Does Tom know?'

'Don't worry so, Mother,' said Edward. 'I've told him all.'

54

At the Angel they dismounted, glad to stretch their legs and glad to see Clara, who had driven over from Robin Hood's Bay with a friend. After some delay the family climbed into the undertaker's black coach, which was to ride immediately behind the hearse.

A long procession of carriages of all sorts followed behind the great glass box mounted on a black cart. High above it sat the coachman and his boy, black-coated and top-hatted, ready to drive the four heavy black Belgian horses known as the Black Brigade. Black ostrich plumes attached to their heads began nodding as soon as the slow and stately cortege moved through the town. The undertaker's mutes, dressed all in black, walked two on each side of the hearse, the gossamer-thin black scarves tied round their top hats floating out behind them. People in the street stood still, and men doffed their caps as they watched. Through the moving bodies of the mutes, and in between the ferns and grasses engraved on the glass walls of the hearse, spectators could catch glimpses of the coffin, almost entirely submerged under floral wreaths. This was the first funeral Lizzie had attended. It was horrid to think of Great-uncle Mills suffocated by all those flowers. She felt that she, too, was being smothered by the weight of them, and that her grief was being squeezed out of her by the solemn ceremonies. The service and the long sermon in the crowded church were hard enough to bear without having to endure the tightness of her waistband; but when they reached the graveyard she forgot all her discomfort at the sight of the mutes lowering the coffin into the grave; and when Mother and Clara threw lumps of clay, which hit the coffin lid with a thud, Lizzie sobbed loudly. *Dust to dust, ashes to ashes* . . . Was this, then, the end of us all?

Rain began to fall as the mourners clambered hastily into their carriages for the drive back to the Angel and the funeral baked meats. The ladies drank tea and spoke quietly together, but a lot of the men swallowed quarts of beer, and after half an hour or so there was some noisy laughter.

Edward had to give up his seat inside the landau to Clara for the ride back to Robin Hood's Bay, and join Tom outside. By now it was raining steadily. The travellers inside were dry and snug enough, but Tom and Edward on the coachman's box had only a leather apron to cover their knees, so when they reached Esplanade House they were thoroughly wet and chilled, and very glad to stable the horses and to go at last into Clara's warm kitchen. The maidservant had kept the range burning all day to welcome the party home with hot tea to drink and hot water to wash in.

Lizzie stood for a moment by the range and thought of Great-uncle Mills. He had drifted away from her on the sea of years, out of sight, out of mind; but now, standing once more in the kitchen of the old house, she felt his powerful presence enveloping her as when, in childhood, she had sat on the floor between his knees. She could hear his voice, his ready laugh, and feel his hand on her shoulder. It was almost as if he were directing her with that skill and sureness that had steered so many rudders in his sailing days.

Lizzie ran upstairs to her attic window, where she stood staring out through the twilight at the North Sea. No. She wouldn't think of him slowly decaying in that damp, cold cemetery. He had heaved up his anchor. His spirit had slipped its moorings and drifted out of harbour on the ebb. *Blow the wind southerly, southerly, southerly* . . . let his sails fill and carry him all the way to east of Greenland, into long, northern summer days to leap and dive and wallow with spouting whales among icebergs, among fathoms of dark, dangerous, underwater ice-mountains, whose white-crested tips flashed blue and rose and gold under the Aurora Borealis as it broke into fireworks to celebrate their sport. Then Lizzie wept freely, without shame.

When she lay down that night in what now seemed a very old, very narrow, creaking bed, Clara sat on the edge of it as she used to do in the old days when Lizzie was a child.

'You and he were best friends when you were little, Lizzie,' she said. 'I think he'd like you to have something out of the old house as a keepsake – something to remember him by.'

Lizzie buried her face in the pillow and sobbed, while Clara stroked her hair, till Lizzie lifted her head and sniffed: 'I'm sorry I'm such a crybaby. Yes. I'd like to keep that Staffordshire flatback of the boy and girl beside the waterfall. He used to tell me stories about it.'

'You shall have it then,' said Clara, kissing her goodnight.

Lizzie woke next morning and, stripping to the waist to wash in the cold water provided, she felt remarkably fresh, as if she'd been for a swim in the sea and emerged newly born. Her thoughts and feelings seemed to have settled into limpid rock pools, and all the geography of her shorelife was clearly mapped out. A tide had ebbed; and she had made up her mind.

Silence presided over breakfast. Clara was pouring tea from the tap on Grandma Harrison's old urn, Mother was cracking the top of a boiled egg, and Edward and Wallace were helping themselves to grilled bacon and kidneys from a hotplate, when Lizzie announced. 'I've decided I'm going to be a doctor.'

Clara's cup remained suspended for several seconds, Mother's egg spoon stuck in solid-seeming air, the silver-plated servers in Edward's hand clattered onto the hotplate, and Wallace quietly lowered his fork.

Mother spoke first, angrily, her face flushed: 'You're

much too young to make any such decision. Whoever put such nonsense into your head?'

'How could you go so far away from us to a hospital full of terrible diseases – and all those people dying?' asked Clara plaintively.

Edward grimaced in disgust. 'You'd have to chop up corpses, you know, to do anatomy. A girl couldn't do that!'

'It would cost too much,' said Wallace Thorburn. 'We couldn't afford it.'

Matilda cast him a sharp glance across the table. 'We' indeed! What was it to do with him? For a few moments nobody spoke, all reviewing their armaments for the next assault, while the men munched their grilled kidneys and bacon rashers.

'The London School of Medicine for Women wouldn't take me yet. I am too young,' said Lizzie. 'I could work for a whole year to earn money,' she suggested.

'What you'd earn in a year as a governess would be only a pittance,' said her mother; but she was thinking: to be a blue-stocking would be no embarrassment in a woman doctor. The few women who were doctors didn't marry, did they? And if the blueness of Lizzie's stockings was destined to be an abiding and incurable affliction . . . ?

'London is a great city full of criminals,' said Clara. 'And terrible perils for a lonely girl. Who would you turn to for help, with your own family so far away?' They fell silent again then.

Lizzie cried a little when they parted from Clara. Matilda wished her sister would return with them to Scarborough; but Clara had too much work to do clearing up Esplanade House and her Uncle Mills's affairs. She walked beside the landau to the top of the hill, and stood by the road, waving till it was out of sight.

There was very little conversation in the carriage on the

way home. Matilda was melancholy, filled with uncertainties and gloomy forebodings about Lizzie's future. Edward was anxious, too. If Lizzie were to be permitted to train as a doctor, the cost of it all would have to come out of the shop's profits. That would, in the long run, mean less for himself, and for any future wife and family he had to support. Why couldn't she be like other girls? he asked himself impatiently. Why couldn't she be satisfied with the prospect of marriage to some acceptable young man with adequate expectations who would be willing to support her in return for bearing him children and looking after him and his home?

Her Uncle Wallace, stealing a look at Lizzie as she sat staring out of the carriage window, thought: Aye. She's a right self-willed lass. Just like her mother. But turning to Matilda he asked: 'Will you be giving that young assistant a bonus for looking after shop while we're away?'

'I shall certainly give him a bonus,' said Matilda. The impertinence! she thought.

'I should think two shillings would do,' he said. 'We've been away two days. That would be a shilling a day.'

'I shall give him five shillings,' said Matilda, her face red with anger. It was too much, she knew; but Wallace's meanness, and his attempts to control her affairs, drove her to extravagance. If Wallace had been in charge of Thorburns all these years, she thought, it would never have burgeoned into the cornucopia of plenty it had become in her hands, with customers from all over town, and all the gentry coming in from the surrounding countryside as well. His small-mindedness would have estranged his best workers; he'd have been too niggardly to spend money on any new venture; he would have ended up with a sulky staff and a small, old-fashioned shop.

Her anger with Wallace jolted her mind out of its

accustomed ruts. He was incapable of imaginative innovation, was the sort of man who would always stick in the safe familiar ways. Lizzie was not like him, had never been like that. And was she now trying to make an imaginative leap into another life, another way of living and working, undreamt of by her mother's generation? And was she, Matilda asked herself, being as niggardly and old-fashioned as her brother-in-law, as stuck in the mud of her own time, while Lizzie was burning with desire for adventure, for the kind of thing that had never been done before? But then, this desire of hers was probably only some foolish adolescent fancy that, if pursued, might carry her to disaster, but if ignored would, in time, be forgotten, even laughed at in the years ahead, when she met Mr Right and began having babies.

Lizzie's own thoughts and feelings were in a turmoil of silent but furious rebellion. She was filled with resentment against her family's lack of sympathy with her wishes, and rage against society, which allowed George to be free to roam the world while she, although she could, she believed, pass the necessary exams if she worked hard enough, was forbidden to do the work she wanted to do. She had often suffered twinges of jealousy over George, who was her mother's favourite, her first son, the apple of her eye because of his resemblance, in voice as well as looks, to her lost Henry. Now Lizzie felt a sudden, unreasonable hatred of him. She knew she was strong and healthy enough to survive the training for medical work, but she was penned up, imprisoned inside Newborough End, her stride hampered by long skirts whose hems picked up dust indoors and got wet when she walked across fields. Her speech had to be trimmed to express sentiments colourless and inoffensive enough to be ladylike, even her thoughts must be censored and cut down to sweet banalities. She would, undoubtedly, be pushed into some dull family rich enough to afford her services as a governess to stupid children unwilling to learn anything, and have to endure the unfriendliness of servants who were of a lower class, the contempt of some silly lady's maid who would despise her unfashionable clothes, and the cold indifference of an employer of a higher class, who would be interested only in her own social life, and who probably never opened a book other than the *Book of Common Prayer* pushed into her hands on Sundays. Worse than the loneliness of such a life would be the boredom, long years of boredom, wasted years full of unsatisfied longings. The world and her own family would never allow her to be a doctor. And all because her sex was female! She bit the forefinger of a new black kid glove into a hole thinking about the injustice of it all.

Matilda's distress over the whole matter was such that she couldn't sleep. During the rest of the week, a silent truce in hostilities lay between mother and daughter. The only relevant comment made by Matilda, was about Katy: 'I know she's happy living down south. But it's not in London. It's in the country – and safe with a good family, too.' Worrying made Matilda feel so ill that eventually she sent Davy with a message to Dr Beverley asking him to tea with her on Sunday, when she knew she'd be alone.

The house, in its Sunday somnolence, was very quiet when he arrived. His coachman drove the brougham into the coach-house yard and dismounted to open the carriage door. As Dr Beverley squeezed himself out he shouted to Davy, who was keeping an eye on things for Tom: 'Look after my pill box, will you? And help Walter with the pony. I'll be about an hour, I suppose.'

'Pill box is it?' The lad laughed. 'Smells more of tobacco than pills to me!'

Dr Beverley thought him a cheeky young whipper-snapper, but agreed sheepishly: 'Well, I do like a small cigar when I'm driving. And there's not much ventilation inside I must admit.'

Lizzie was out walking with her dog; Edward had saddled one of the delivery van horses and ridden off for the day, across the moor. Flo was out with her postman, and Bessie, having cooked Sunday dinner, had retired with her copy of the *News of the World*, to bed, where she felt safer with it. Mrs Thorburn would be unlikely to barge in here, and if she did Bessie could hide the paper under the bedclothes. Its lurid contents, so disapproved of by Matilda, never gave Bessie the bad dreams her mistress promised they would. All the murders and the lawcourt reports only added to Bessie's satisfaction with her own safe life and comfortable self, reassuring her about the horrors she had been spared.

So it was Mrs Thorburn herself who answered the doorbell to admit Dr Beverley that afternoon. He noticed that the best china teacups were laid out on the tea table, and the silver-plated teapot was partnered by the silver-plated spirit kettle standing at her elbow.

'It's excellent China tea,' he said. 'My favourite, I think?'

'Lapsang Suchong. I know you like it. A little lemon?'

'Such fragrance!' He breathed in the scent from his cup before sipping contentedly. He liked talking to Matilda; she was a woman you could be comfortable with. It had crossed his mind more than once in the years since he'd been widowed that she'd make an excellent wife. If only she hadn't had all those children, and all that business to be a millstone round her neck! Lucrative, of course, the shop was reputed to be. There was a bit of brass tied up there.

'What's the trouble, Matilda?' he asked.

'I've not been sleeping well.'

'Is something worrying you?'

'It's about Lizzie,' she blurted out. 'I don't know what

to do, what to say. She wants to be a doctor. I can see she's made up her mind, too. And won't be held at home for long. I'm even afraid she might run away to London. She's so impetuous – indeed, wilful at times.'

'Some boys run away to sea . . .' he said, taking a buttered scone. 'Well, she's got the brains for it I suppose, since she did so well in that College of Preceptors exam. You were adventurous yourself, Matilda, when you took on Thorburns without a man to help you. And five young children, too, if I remember rightly.' He chewed appreciatively. 'Scones are good today. But then, they always are, aren't they?' And after the briefest of pauses: 'Why not let her try?'

Matilda put down her cup and stared incredulously at him as he continued: 'The first three years she'll spend studying hard at science subjects, and won't get anywhere near the hospital. It'll be just like boarding school with a bit more freedom, quite proper for her age, and a lot more work. She might not finish the course. She might fall in love and throw it all up to follow some young man.'

'Some young man we don't know at all, who might be a criminal . . .'

'Come now, Matilda!' Dr Beverley was coaxing. 'Most young men are not as bad as that – even if they are so unlucky as to have been born south of York.'

She laughed then; and he was glad to see the lines smoothed away by laughter from her eyes and mouth. Even in middle age she could still look beautiful. He smiled at her affectionately, thinking that without Lizzie she would be lonely, and that might make her lean more on him. It could make the wooing of her easier for him – if he were ever to pursue that course . . .

'All the same,' she said. 'I'm afraid the South will seduce her, and she won't come back home.' She would be so engrossed in her studies, so involved with her new friends and their new ideas that she would begin to look upon her own mother as a stranger from another world. Edward would be a companion of a sort till he got married, but Lizzie would come less and less often to Scarborough, and Matilda would be left to grow old alone.

'You'll have to travel down to London yourself then, to visit her. It's less than a five-hour journey from York to King's Cross station you know. I was down there myself a fortnight ago, to attend a reunion dinner of fellows from my year at Barts.'

Matilda admitted that she now had more leisure and could find the time to travel, if need be, even such a long distance. 'But the expense?' she argued. 'The long training surely must be a very great expense?'

'It doesn't come all at once,' he said. 'It would be spread over five or six years.' He drank his now cooling tea. 'Women can be mighty sometimes,' he said thoughtfully. 'Look at Grace Darling, and what she did: rescuing sailors from a wreck and rowing them back to safety through huge waves . . . Lizzie is a strong girl. And doesn't she come from adventurous seafaring stock?'

Matilda was silent, so he pursued his argument. 'She will never be content to spend her years running after snivelling brats with handkerchiefs and exercise books,' he said. And he added the warning: 'If you don't let her go, you'll have a discontented spinster left on your hands.'

'Well, I'll have to think about it,' she said.

When he was about to leave, he picked up his top hat from the hall table, just as Lizzie rushed in through the front door with Dax at her heels. The wretched little dog scampered over his feet and jumped up with muddy paws on his trousers, and Lizzie, stooping to catch Dax's collar, knocked the doctor's top hat to the floor. She scrambled after it, blushing furiously and uttering apologies, finally dusting it with her elbow, and then with her handkerchief. He was laughing by the time he took it from her.

'What a great clumsy girl you are!' he said. 'Five foot ten I do believe, and taller than I am! Taller than your brother Edward, are you?'

'But not as tall as George,' she replied breathlessly. 'He's six foot.' Disgracefully untidy you are, too, was what he thought, his clinical eye observing all the burrs stuck to her skirt, gathered there, no doubt, in crossing some field full of tares. And her hair! The combined forces of the wind and her own energetic movements had loosened the schoolgirl plait, and her tangled hair fell about her shoulders. But he couldn't help smiling as he remembered that old poem about the girl with sweet disorder in her dress. There was something so innocent about Lizzie . . . No trace of coquetry, no female wile colouring those cheeks, made rosy with exercise, nor could she ever be guilty of deceit. He bent towards her and whispered in her ear: 'I think you'll find that some of your dreams of adventure might come true after all.'

Lizzie's heart began to race, and her cheeks grew redder than ever. What could he mean? What had he been saying to Mother?

She took off her coat, snatched a comb from its pocket and, standing in front of the mirror framed in the hall stand, she combed her hair smoother and plaited it again as neatly as she could before going into the sitting-room.

'Sit down, Lizzie dear,' said Mother. It was obvious from her slightly guilty expression that they'd been talking about her. 'The tea's still fresh enough.' She refilled the teapot from the spirit kettle simmering above its flame. 'Did you enjoy your walk?'

Neither of them mentioned the subject uppermost in their thoughts, but Lizzie knew from her mother's tone of voice that the direction of the wind had altered.

On Monday morning, Flo answered the postman's knock.

'There's an interesting letter for Miss Lizzie this morning,' said the postman, dumping his sack and using his freed arm to squeeze Flo round the waist.

'Be careful! You'll crumple my starched apron!' she cried, taking the letter. It was a big envelope, the flap stuck down with a crimson ribbon and sealed with crimson wax on which was impressed a design of an anchor entwined with seaweed. Flo thought it must be a very important letter. The postmark said Whitby, not London, so she guessed it would be all right to display the beautiful seal on Lizzie's plate at the breakfast table. Lizzie, too, thought it so beautiful that it was a shame to break it. She turned the letter over and saw the postmark, Whitby. She read the letter and grew so remarkably pale that Mother asked: 'What is it Lizzie? It can't be bad news – addressed to you?'

Lizzie handed her the letter without a word. She had no need to read it again: the words were branded indelibly into her memory.

'Five hundred pounds! Your Great-uncle Mills has left you five hundred pounds? It says here that in his Will he asked "that the money be kept until such time as it be required for her further education . . ."'

Lizzie stared out of the window, not at the garden and the clothesline ready for its load of Monday washing, but at whales blowing out of an enormous expanse of ice-blue sea. Great-uncle Mills's spirit was calling to her from Greenland. Ghosts were nothing to be afraid of, she told herself. Her own special ghost was going to remain with her, was going to haunt her with happiness.

PART TWO

Medical Student in London

FOUR

'I was bowled over,' Lizzie used to say in later life, when speaking of her first weeks in London. Those were her rites of passage days, so filled with strange new sights and sounds that her feelings on parting with her familiar faces were all but expunged from memory. There were some sharp images of leaving home: Edward rushing out from the shop in his grocer's striped navy and white apron, just as the cab was about to leave for the station, pushing a packet of warm, newly-baked Yorkshire parkin into her hands, and Flo, upstairs in Lizzie's bedroom, dressing her hair.

'It's so untidy, Flo. What can I do with it?' She didn't want to be like Mrs Bodkin showering hairpins everywhere.

'You don't want to scrape the hair back so,' said Flo. 'It makes you look like a prison wardress.'

'You do it for me, then.'

Flo took a handful of tresses, looping them over the side of Lizzie's face and up at the back, admiring the effect. She parted the hair deftly down the middle and plaited it loosely into two ropes which she twisted together and fixed with pins on the nape of the neck.

'There now! What about that?'

Examining her head from all angles with the help of a small hand mirror, Lizzie hardly knew herself.

'You'll have to practise doing it yourself, mind!'

'You could have been a lady's maid and earned yourself a higher salary than you get here.'

'Money isn't everything,' said Flo, though she knew that if she had more of it she could marry her postman sooner.

Lizzie's heart beat faster as she approached the mainline railway station of York and gazed upwards at its great glass roof supported by ornamental iron pillars. She didn't have much time to admire it because, almost immediately, the express train drew up at the platform, with a hiss of steam and a clatter of iron that made her snatch up Dax and run towards a carriage door; Matilda followed close behind, her mouth dry with anxiety. The porter, pulling a trolley loaded with Lizzie's trunk, trundled after them.

That first journey to London seemed to pass in a series of brightly-flashing images: glimpses of green fields seen through the carriage window; Dax as good as gold sleeping on her lap; Mother sitting opposite, upright and tidy, her hat pinned firmly on her hair by two hatpins embellished with pink enamelled finials, clutching her canvas bag on her knees; the light luggage in a rack resembling a cat's cradle of string above her head; and on the wall of the compartment a little oval mirror framed in tin, on which was printed, in a black wreath around the glass: 'STEPHEN'S WRITING AND COPYING INKS'. At King's Cross, where Katy met them, there was a bewildering confusion of noise and bustle, but somehow they managed to get outside and, ignoring the line of smart hansom cabs, they found an old-fashioned growler whose four-seater box was roomy enough to seat them all as well as take Lizzie's trunk on its roof.

They were all happy and excited as they settled down inside. It was a year since they had seen Katy, who had a great deal to tell them. The creaking, groaning and occasional lurching of the battered cab didn't stop their talk and laughter as the driver persuaded his old horse slowly through the traffic towards their hotel. Eager conversation continued over high tea, which they took in the comfortable dining-room on the ground floor, and went on far into the night in the bedroom that the three of them shared, Lizzie in the big double bed with her mother, Katy in a small bed alongside, provided for a child.

The next day was spent exploring the streets and squares round Bloomsbury as, with Dax trotting happily at their heels, they searched for suitable lodgings for Lizzie.

One landlady disliked the look of Dax. 'I don't take dogs as paying guests,' she said. Another objected to Lizzie. 'A single young lady student would be too great a responsibility for me, ma'am.' But at last they found a pleasant room at the top of a tall house in Doughty Street, where the landlady, Mrs Plumm, promised to provide breakfast and an evening meal as well as a furnished room for one pound a week.

'What about my dog, Dax?' asked Lizzie.

'So long as he's a perfect gentleman he can stay,' said Mrs Plumm. 'But if he don't behave himself he'll have to go.'

Dax cast one mournful, upward glance at her, which said he knew when to keep silent, and immediately took refuge under Lizzie's skirt.

When they parted the next day, there were a few tears, but many smiles and good wishes, too, as the sisters waved to their mother's train steaming away from the platform at King's Cross, and again on Waterloo Station as Katy kissed Lizzie goodbye before she caught her train to Guildford. Then Lizzie was left alone.

When she stood at the dormer window of her little room, which she thought of as her fortress, and contemplated her new, independent life, feelings of elation, hope and triumph jostled inside her with fears of the unknown. She gazed down at an expanse of London roofs glistening in the evening rain. Here she was in Doughty Street, only a few doors away from No. 48, where the great Dickens himself had once lived, in the very heart of London. In the middle of the world. This was where things happened, where it was possible to move forward into a new philosophy, into new ways of thinking, where the New Woman was being born. Dax stood at her elbow on the wide sill and sniffed the air.

'Lord of all you survey,' she said, tickling his ears. 'Aren't you?'

Lizzie enrolled as a student for the matriculation course at the University Tutorial College; but so excellent had been Samuel Bodkin's coaching that she found she already knew most of what the tutors were trying to teach her, and was able to spend many leisure hours exploring the great city. She often spent the whole of Sunday, with no more sustenance than a couple of oranges in a string bag, walking about the streets and parks with Dax at her heels. She did not mind being alone at all. Her hungry curiosity was being fed, daily, by the inexhaustible spectacle of London life. In retrospect, when she was old, she saw those first few months in London as a long, glorious summer when her own happiness surrounded her like a wall of light. Perhaps it protected her, too, because she was never accosted nor followed in the streets, though she saw many drunks, both male and female, reeling along the pavements.

Policemen stood at certain road junctions directing the steady flow of noisy vehicles: horse-drawn buses, carts, vans, cabs and carriages, which creaked and rumbled by, accompanied by the shouts of drivers, jingle of horse brasses shaken by the great heads and flanks of powerful drays, and the interwoven rhythms of innumerable metal shoes, some heavy and slow, some light and quick, clip-clopping on the hard roads; but the continuous murmur of thousands of internal combustion engines was not yet heard. The air was smoky, filled with the sharp smell of coal fires and steaming horse dung; but petrol fumes had not yet invaded the city.

The streets in the West End displayed wealth and elegance. Here, shop windows were crammed full of every article anyone could want to buy. Splendid carriages rolled past with liveried servants outside and well-dressed owners within, and on the pavements shoppers strolled, happily considering the choices they might make with the help of well-filled purses. Here, at evening, the still new-enough-to-be-wondered-at electric light blazed from street lamps; but in the narrow, cobbled alleys of the East End, only dimly lit at dusk by gaslight, it was a different scene, crowded with ragged life, swarming with children, and full of the hoarse cries of costermongers around whose barrows, laden with fruit and vegetables, meat pies, or whelks and jellied eels, chickens pecked the littered ground. Here, overflowing dustbins were besieged by hungry urchins scavenging for discarded crusts of bread or fruit not yet quite rotten. Sometimes a young mother, her baby bound to her back with a grimy tattered shawl, staggered drunkenly, bumping into Lizzie as she walked; and skinny, pallid children playing marbles ran barefoot along the gutters, stopping sometimes to fondle Dax and talk about the ways of dogs in accents that Lizzie's Yorkshire ears took time to get accustomed to.

Carrying Dax under one arm, she climbed the narrow spiral stair to the top of a horse-drawn omnibus and sat down in the open with Dax sprawled happily across her knees. The conductor, gazing down as he sold her

73

a halfpenny ticket sighed and murmured: 'Wish I was a dawg!'

Travelling on the tops of omnibuses was a lark; but going down into the London Underground railway filled her, at first, with trepidation. It reminded her of old Sunday School pictures of hell. The Inner Circle had been built thirty years before, and was so filled with steam and smoke from the engines that passengers choked and spluttered as they were carried along the line; but the new electric extension to Hampstead, clean and smoke-less, was a joy to ride on. You knew then that the world was really making progress.

One fine Sunday afternoon, when she was walking with Dax in Hyde park, she noticed a sudden commotion. People were running towards the roadway to watch an open victoria pulled by two bay horses. Its sides were emblazoned with gilded crests, and two splendidly-attired grooms hung on at the back. The long yellow spokes of the wheels flickered in the sunlight as the carriage passed by.

'Did you see?' shouted a man in the crowd. 'It's the Queen. God bless her!'

Lizzie had seen: the old pop-eyed Queen was hud-dled in black beside her granddaughter, Alix of Hesse-Darmstadt. They were taking the air. Only a few months later the young princess would marry the last Czar of Russia. As she rolled past Lizzie, the charming girl looked like a painting by Renoir; the casual onlooker could never have foreseen the menace of her bad angel Rasputin, nor her own folly, nor the terrible end which would overtake her twenty-four years later, in captivity in Ekaterinberg – her dress splashed, not as now with the laced intricacies of light and shade thrown by summer sunshine through overarching trees, but by her own hot, spurting blood.

That Sunday was one Lizzie long remembered because, on her way home, as she stood for a moment on the

74

corner of Brunswick Square, an open hansom cab swung round at great speed, and the centrifugal force engendered by its swing, flung the passenger, a frail old lady, through the door she had forgotten to fasten, and straight into Lizzie's arms.

'What a mercy I was standing here!' gasped Lizzie.

'Dear, dear! Dear, dear!' was all the poor old lady could manage in her agitation, while Dax yapped excitedly round their skirts.

The cab driver, realising what had happened, tied his horse to a lamppost and walked back towards them.

'All in one piece, are you, ma'am?' he asked.

'This young lady caught me in her arms.'

'Blimey! No bones broken then? That's a bit o' luck, ain't it?' He looked them both up and down, Lizzie still holding his trembling customer, she rather dishevelled with her black straw bonnet pushed awry over one ear. 'Must 'ave bin a bit of a shock. Get in, the two of you, and I'll drive you 'ome.' And before Lizzie knew what was happening she was seated inside the hansom holding a small trembling hand, Dax was hiding between her feet, and the cabby was driving at a smart trot to a house in Rocket Street.

Here, they were met at the door by a spruce young maidservant in starched white cap and apron, and a very old man with shaky limbs, and, a moment later, by a thin young man, who joined them for tea. A fire was burning in the drawing-room grate although it was a warm day in June. It was a large room but so stuffed with furniture (big chairs, little chairs, ladies' worktables, jardinières sprouting ferns and ivy, whatnots displaying all sorts of bric-à-brac) that Lizzie had difficulty walking through it without bumping into things. When she did manage to reach the tea-table in front of the fire she remained standing because nobody offered her a seat. She was rescued by the thin young man who addressed her.

'Sit down, do, Miss – Miss –?'

'Thorburn, Lizzie Thorburn.'

'And these are my grandparents, Mr and Mrs Ashwolde. And I'm Tob.'

She was plied with cups of tea and shortbread biscuits; she was made to sit down and tell her story several times, and each time she was praised for her courage and presence of mind.

'Not really presence of mind,' she said. 'Rather presence of body. I just happened to be standing there.' And the young man called Tob laughed.

The maid was still in the room, pouring out tea, (which her mistress seemed unable to do), popping sugar lumps into the old people's cups and even stirring for them. She tucked a napkin under the grandfather's chin and lifted his cup to his lips.

'Do you know *The Ring*?' he asked Lizzie between gulps. 'Wagner . . . What genius! Four days it takes to hear it all.' His voice was creaky like a wheel needing oiling. Then he said again: 'Do you know *The Ring*?'

'I'm afraid . . .' said Lizzie; but he didn't hear her and began his rigmarole all over again: '*The Ring* . . . Marvellous . . . Wagner, you know . . . It takes four days . . .'

'I'm afraid I'm not at all musical,' said Lizzie. 'I only know it's Wagner when I hear the sopranos shrieking.'

The thin young man laughed aloud, and Lizzie looked at him, noticing for the first time, with a slight shock, how beautiful he was, too beautiful for a man, Katy would have said, with finely-shaped nose, full lips and large eyes – steady and dark blue – and hair the colour of polished ebony. Rather delicate, Mother would have said. A look of horror momentarily overtook the old man's face till he forgot what she'd said, and his usual benevolence was restored as he murmured: 'Ah Wagner! *The Ring*! Four days of heavenly bliss! D'you know it, my dear?'

The young man insisted on accompanying Lizzie home.

'But I walk everywhere in London alone,' she remonstrated. 'I'm perfectly well able to look after myself.'

'Are you?' he asked, his great, deep eyes resting for a moment on hers. 'Isn't that rather brave?'

'Well, it's still daylight. And it's not very far from here to Doughty Street.'

He laughed again. 'Of course. It's absurd. But we're forced to accept so many absurdities, aren't we? So I'll walk with you. If I may. Just think of my name: Tob. Did you ever hear anything more absurd?'

'It must be short for Toby.'

'Tobias, if the truth be told. Tobias was the son of Tobit who was blinded by sparrows which "muted warm dung in his eyes". An unpleasant story, even for the Bible. However his son very cleverly cured him by wiping his eyes with some equally nasty part of a fish. All most unlikely. I had a great-uncle called Tobias, you see. And he was named after that high-spirited bawdy writer, Smollett. Anyway, Uncle Toby was a rich bachelor. He consented to being my godfather, so my parents presumed that if they christened me after him he'd leave his fortune to me. I used to have to dress up tidily and go to visit him at regular intervals while I was at school. But the old blackguard –' He laughed, stopped as if the effort of laughing was too much for him, and coughed before resuming: '. . . the old blackguard left it all to the Salvation Army. He never thought of my salvation, did he?'

'I expect the Salvation Army needed it more than you,' she said.

'Oh, no doubt, no doubt.' And, as he resumed walking, 'I walk a lot in London myself, mostly in the East End. My Mater calls it slumming for Art. I find it enormously interesting – the great canvas of London life.'

'Do you?' Lizzie glanced at him sideways as they walked, noting that he must be five foot ten, since his head was on a level with her own. 'So do I.'

'Have you seen Sickert's work? I admire him – his painting I mean, of course, not his way of living.' He laughed again. 'That's where he gets the material for his painting: the East End.' He then told Lizzie he was a student at the Slade, that his parents lived beyond suburbia, near Hampton Court, that he was lodging with his grandparents in order to be near the art school. 'And what, if I may ask, are you doing all alone in London, Miss Thorburn?'

'I'm going to be a doctor,' she replied. 'At present I'm studying for my matric. I can't get into medical school without it.'

He stopped to stare at her, quite rudely, she thought. 'My word! You *are* a New Woman, and no mistake!' When he caught up with her he said: 'I have a sister, Aurora, who is a better painter than I am as a matter of fact, though I don't admit it to her. They won't let her into life classes at the Slade because they say a woman can't study anatomy and paint the nude form alongside men.'

'They said the same about women medical students studying anatomy not so very long ago,' said Lizzie. 'Did you know that in Cork some brave woman medical student was refused the Sacrament by her priest because she'd dissected a naked corpse in the presence of men?'

He made a face. 'Oh! Ireland . . .' he said. 'Anyone would think that the good Lord had Himself blindfolded before creating Adam and Eve.'

'Well, no,' said Lizzie judiciously, 'it was only after they ate the apple that all the fuss was made about nakedness.'

'How are you going to get over this barrier anyway?' he asked.

'There's the London School of Medicine for Women now, where we can study and qualify in peace. That's what I'm in London for. I come from Scarborough.'

He stopped again, and stood still for a moment. 'The

78

only thing I know about Scarborough is that lovely folk song: "Scarborough Fair".'

Lizzie nodded. 'My mother used to sing it sometimes.' Then she told him how Cissie used to play the piano and sing. 'She practised a lot. She persevered. Purcell's "Nymphs and Shepherds", over and over again. "Nymphs and Shepherds come away, come away, come, come, come away . . ." But they never seemed to come when they were called. I think that's what turned me against sopranos.'

He laughed again, delightedly. In his own family such irreverence about music was unheard of. Lizzie added that her brother, George, was First Mate on a merchant ship now on its way to Buenos Aires, and Tob sighed: 'How I envy him!'

They reached her lodgings in no time at all. He bowed in mock solemnity, thanking her for saving his grandmother's life. 'Though no doubt she'll be in need of saving again pretty soon. She's tottering – they both are, poor old dears! – on the brink of eternity . . .' He took her hand and shook it absentmindedly.

'Goodbye,' said Lizzie. 'And thank you for walking back with me.'

His eyes suddenly focused on her. 'What an extraordinary girl you are!' he said. 'And what a pity more girls aren't like you!' But he didn't suggest any further meeting; and Lizzie felt a pang of disappointment to see him go. She wanted to ask if she might accompany him on some of those slumming expeditions in the cause of Art; but she knew that was something a young lady should not do.

The following week she visited Swan and Edgar's department store in Piccadilly Circus. All the girls in London were wearing straw boaters, having discarded their heavier winter headgear, which Lizzie hated anyway, what with all those feather decorations like birds' nests, or bunches of artificial flowers, or even (most absurd of all) bowls of fruit. She did, however, like the new straw boater. Simple, cool and clean, she thought, as she tried one on in front of a mirror in the shop. She was tempted then, by a display of blouses with big leg-o'-mutton sleeves. She particularly liked the new masculine look of high collar complete with tie, and decided to buy two: one plain white shirt with navy blue tie, the other striped blue and white with a plain white tie. It was the first time she had ever bought a garment ready made. As she examined her reflection, outfitted in the latest fashion, she thought: I do look rather like the New Woman now.

She didn't hear from Tob again, until autumn winds were shaking shrivelled leaves from plane trees in the residential squares, and the infamous pea-soup London fog was beginning to settle in the streets. By the time she got his letter she had passed her matric. The question on levers in the applied maths paper, she'd been able to avoid, and her Latin grammar had proved sufficient to push her through the exam. Now, as she started her preliminary medical studies she felt she was really on her way. She concentrated her attention on her physics textbook, which thrilled and satisfied her with its inevitable laws; chemistry became an exciting hazard when, during afternoon practicals, her impatient fingers mixed explosive powders or tried to filter substances through funnels without knocking over the glass jars or cracking glass tubes in the flame of her Bunsen burner; biology enthralled her by providing as many puzzles as its study solved.

During the week her mind and body were fully occupied with her work; on Sundays she still strolled about the city with Dax at her heels, still watched and learned with avid curiosity about the infinite variety of London life. She had almost forgotten Tob when an envelope addressed in an unknown hand was delivered to her in Doughty Street.

'Dear Lizzie,' Tob wrote. She noted with interest his clear, elegant, if somewhat spidery writing with its long downward strokes, elaborate spirals and the sudden flamboyant scrawl of his signature. 'I saw your name in *The Times*, with other successful matriculation candidates, and write – much too late I know – to congratulate you. The fact is I have been out of the country, in France, enjoying the clean air of the French Alps, and have only just returned to dear old dirty London. I wonder if you could forgive my tardiness enough to allow me to take you out to lunch next Sunday? It could be a somewhat delayed celebration of your triumph. It would certainly be a great pleasure for me.'

It was not at all foggy on that Sunday noon when they met again. The air was clear and crisp with a promise of frost to come as they walked up the Strand towards Covent Garden, turned into Maiden Lane and entered Rules restaurant. Lizzie felt a keen rush of pleasure as she was engulfed in warm air made rosy by the crimson plush upholstery covering all the two-seater benches which lined the walls. She noted approvingly the tables spread with immaculate white cloths, and the glass and cutlery which sparkled from zealous polishing.

'Oscar Wilde comes here to dine sometimes,' said Tob. 'The place has a certain upper-class Bohemian charm, and is often full; but I've booked a table.'

A waiter took their coats and Tob's hat, which he twirled cheekily on Tob's silver-topped cane.

Lizzie sat on the double seat against the wall, but Tob took the chair opposite. For a moment her eye was caught by a pair of Spy cartoons on the other side of the room, then she glanced across the table at Tob. He looked happy, smiling, as if he hadn't a care in the world.

'All that study doesn't seem to be exhausting you, Lizzie,' he said. 'You look the picture of health and vitality.' He thought: She is an Amazon, the New Woman, braver and stronger than half a dozen men. He had been afraid when he wrote to her that she might prove disappointing at second meeting, that absence might have magnified, perhaps romanticised her image in his memory: but he found this was not so. He was intrigued, making guesses about her because she was so unlike other girls he knew. 'What can it be in all that poring over books that exhilarates you so?'

'It's not only reading books, you know,' she explained. 'I have to make chemical experiments, and examine the anatomy of creatures. I'm dissecting a dogfish at present.'

'How revolting!' he cried. 'Well, I do hope they have something better than dogfish to serve up here today. Let's study the menu. That's more in my line.' And as his eye scanned the day's list of dishes, he thought: She's really not like *any* other woman. She seems to have no interest in what most girls want – pretty clothes and parties and love tokens from young men they've rendered helpless by flirtation, those little gold or silver amulets to wear on a scalp-chain round the neck, like the one my sister Maisie wears. Lizzie's tokens of triumph were pieces of knowledge gained and exams passed. These were the scalps she wanted to add to her chain.

'And what have you been doing all these months?' she asked, when the waiter had taken their order. She imagined him sitting at a high window painting a landscape of snow-capped mountains seen through a gap in a forest of conifers.

'Reading, reading, reading . . .' he replied. 'Books that take ages to finish are best when you have all the time in the world to fill. *Little Dorrit* – so funny, some of it, and so haunting too . . . What have you been reading Lizzie, what literature apart from dogfish tales?'

'I've just finished Rider Haggards's *King Solomon's Mines*. It was so exciting I couldn't put it down.'

'I rather like the kind of book you can put down – must put down now and again, in order to think about what you've just read.'

The waiter placed warmed plates before them and began to serve their Dover sole. Tob fell silent and watched Lizzie, thinking: She has been dealt a good hand by fate. Although it was obvious she didn't come from a wealthy family, he guessed she'd enjoyed a happy childhood. To be as trusting and confident as she was, without the least tendency to boasting or bravado, she must have been surrounded, in infancy, by affection from people sure of their position and direction in life – with all too simple views of morality, no doubt, but of unwavering goodwill. That she was enormously happy could not be doubted. Happiness literally shone out of her. It was what he most liked about her. She didn't grumble at small discomforts, or pout and sulk if she didn't get her own way. She had, too, he decided, the insatiable curiosity of a small boy, and it was this which drove her through all difficulties. It was also what made her such a good companion.

'Are you still walking all over London by yourself?' he asked.

'Sometimes on Sundays, when the weather's fine.'

'Do you brave slumming in the East End too?'

'Well yes, in daylight. Not after dark, of course.' She had not forgotten her mother's warnings. 'I do think of Jack the Ripper when it gets dark.' She shuddered, imagining the mutilations done on the five known and who knows how many unknown victims he had murdered in Whitechapel not so long ago. 'He's probably still alive somewhere.'

He laughed. 'Well, I don't see you getting into his clutches! His victims were all ladies of the night; and violent death is almost a calculated risk they take in that profession.' While she, he thought, walks protected by the armour of innocence. He glanced at her over the top of his fork to admire her straw boater, and her mannish, high collar and tie, and smiled with pleasure to see that even that straight strict shirt could not subdue the glorious swell of her breasts beneath. How he would love to paint her naked! But, of course, that would be impossible. Simply not done. 'Any study of London is incomplete without a view of London's night life,' he said. After another mouthful of fish he added: 'I could show you some of it, if you'd come with me to a music hall. I could take you to the Queen's in Poplar. Plenty of low-life there. It's the sort of scene that Sickert loves to paint: a crowd of grey men in cloth caps, a crimson curtain across the stage, and a brilliant Cockney butterfly screeching and kicking up her legs.' He laughed again, and Lizzie noticed how his eyes glittered with delight.

'Oh, Tob! I'd love that!'

'It would have to be on Saturday, Lizzie. I can't see you next Sunday because I've promised to accompany my grandmother to church. And it takes me the rest of the day to recover from that exercise. My grandfather – poor old chap! – is no longer *compos mentis*, and so can't go with her. Last time he attended divine service he left his pew in the middle of the sermon and went searching along the aisle for the Valkyrie, or his lost ticket for the opera, or some such. No doubt the sermon was tedious. I often make up on lost sleep myself during sermons.'

He watched her closely as she sipped her dry white Bordeaux.

'D'you like it?'

'Hmm. Flavoursome,' she said. She knew nothing about wine although her father had once imported large

84

quantities of it into Scarborough and her mother still sold it over the counter at the shop. At home, drinking wine had been limited to a glass for Christmas dinner, and whenever George came home from sea. Her appreciation pleased Tob, and that pleased her.

While they waited for their coats to be handed to them as they were about to leave the restaurant, he drew her attention to a narrow staircase near the entrance; he dropped his voice conspiratorially: 'There's a private room upstairs reserved for the Prince of Wales, you know.'

'Really?'

'He used to bring the Jersey Lily here for dinner.' Tob confided, and gave a large wink so outrageously vulgar that she was reminded of common street urchins at Newborough End.

'I saw Lily Langtry once on the stage,' she said. 'It was at the theatre in Scarborough. *As You Like It*, it was. She played Rosalind, dressed as a boy in tights. I was about ten at the time, and I couldn't understand why all the grown-ups got so excited about her legs.'

'Ah! You weren't so wicked then as they were.' He gave her his arm. They walked up towards the Strand, he humming the tune of 'Lily of Laguna' and she, knowing she couldn't sing in tune, simply speaking the words here and there.

They walked all the way to Doughty Street, some of the way with linked arms, and now and again swinging their arms in carefree abandon.

'Till Saturday then!' said Tob as he left her on her doorstep.

'Till Saturday!'

It wasn't until she was climbing the stairs to her attic room that she realised he hadn't told her what he'd been up to all the summer months in France.

FIVE

A peculiar smell pervaded the biology lab. The dogfish carcases, cut open and displayed upon the dissection tables, had all been preserved in formaldehyde. It was a powerful, persistent smell which Lizzie found almost impossible to wash off her hands and scrub out from under her nails at the end of a dissecting afternoon. She sat beside Miss Watkins. Although there was a more relaxed atmosphere in the labs than in the lecture room, the students still addressed each other formally.

'Oh, heavens!' cried Lizzie. 'Whatever have I done, Miss Watkins?' She was trying to free the heart and aorta from its surrounding fibrous tissue as it lay on the anterior aspect of the dorsal spine. The other girl leaned over to peer inside the fish.

'You've cut the dorsal vein by mistake, Miss Thorburn,' she said. 'I can see you'll never make a surgeon.'

'What a mercy my patient isn't alive, Miss Watkins!' said Lizzie.

The girls looked at each other and began to laugh.

'I do think "Miss Watkins" is a bit stiff,' said Lizzie. 'Don't you? I'd much rather call you Primrose.' Though that was, Lizzie couldn't help thinking, an unsuitable name for such a tall, ungainly girl with big red hands.

She was the daughter of a clergyman who had three sons with acceptable names and four other daughters all called after flowers. If they were anything like her, Lizzie thought, when she heard Primrose refer to her sisters as Rose, Violet, Iris and May, there had been some unseemly christenings. Perhaps her father was a botanist with a passion for collecting wild flowers, and her poor mother, too busy with domestic and parish duties and with child-bearing, had no breath left to voice objections. But Primrose didn't stick for long. Next day when they were peering down microscopes at slides showing specimens of amoeba, Lizzie, seeing strange one-celled creatures moving about on the glass, cried out: 'Whatever are these things doing?'

Miss Watkins's approach to learning was more measured. She stopped Mr Brown as he walked past with head bent, and asked: 'If I may be so bold as to enquire, Mr Brown, what activity are those cells displaying?'

Poor Mr Brown, who was a junior demonstrator in biology, new to his job, was a shy young man, quite unaccustomed to dealing with a crowd of earnest lady students. He blushed whenever he was asked a question, and positively hated coming near enough to any of them to help with dissection. He blushed now, as he replied to Primrose: 'It is the simple division of asexual reproduction, Miss Watkins.'

'What a great pity, if I may say so, what a misfortune that the human race has not evolved so easy and so chaste a method for multiplication, Mr Brown!'

His blush deepened to a purple hue as he fled from her.

'Prosy is what you are, Miss Watkins,' said Lizzie. And Prosy was what she became for everybody in the biology department.

Laughter, as well as dissection, cemented the girls' friendship so that later, when they came to anatomy and had to dissect a human corpse, they decided to do it together. But on this afternoon, anatomy was still far away.

When Lizzie got back to Doughty Street she demanded a bath. One of the maids carried a big hip bath upstairs to Lizzie's room, rather unwillingly, and no wonder, since she lived at the top of the house; another carried cans of hot water that had been heated on the coal range in the basement. Lizzie added a little cold water from the jug on her washstand and was soon enjoying a warm bath, which at last banished that dogfish smell. Tomorrow, she told herself, I'm going with Tob to the Queen's in Poplar.

A damp November day had faded by the time their cab deposited them in the Mile End Road, and drizzle was falling as they began to walk. Tob pulled up the collar of his coat, taking care not to crush the hothouse rosebud in the buttonhole of his jacket. Lizzie picked her way carefully between the gobs of spittle on the pavement. She could see a crowd of people standing in a queue beneath a great, bleak building that looked to her like a prison, and wondered what they were all waiting for.

'It's the Poplar Workhouse,' Tob explained. 'They have to queue early to get a bed for the night.'

'I do hope they'll be let in soon,' said Lizzie. 'It must be very cold standing there.' She could see, as they approached, that many of the men and women were dressed in little more than rags.

'They're the lucky ones,' said Tob. 'They'll have a bath and be deloused, and given some sort of a meal before they lie down to sleep. But they'll not all get in tonight. There are too many of them. A lot will be turned away.'

'What happens to them if they can't get a bed?'

'They have to keep walking, Lizzie, my dear. Maybe

some will find shelter in doorways; but if the policeman with his lantern finds them sleeping there, he'll move them on.'

'You mean to say they're absolutely homeless?'

'Thousands of them . . . They walk about all night – lucky if they can find a bench to sit on. They sometimes bump into you if you're out on the street after a concert or a play. They're the sleep-walking poor.'

'But that's dreadful! Isn't there anywhere they can go to in this cold?'

'The parks are locked up for the night, but they open at about four to five a.m. and then they can go in there. There are some empty benches in the parks at that hour in the morning. I once saw some sleepers stretched out on the grass when I went through Green Park. The rain was falling on them steadily, and they must have been wet through; but – do you know? – they didn't stir, they were so dog tired.'

'But this is awful!' Lizzie was horrified. Here we are, she thought, in the middle of the capital of the greatest empire, made rich by the labour, and by the inventiveness of the cleverest people in the world, and we let thousands of sleepless waifs flit through the city streets at night searching for food and shelter. That's not very clever. In fact it seemed to her downright stupid, since all those poor wanderers would get sick from hunger and the cold, and doubtless die before their time. She shivered not only for them but for herself, feeling suddenly a stranger in the country which was her own.

She was glad when they reached the Queen's. It was brightly lit, warm and welcoming, the odour of human bodies mingling with the smell of beer being served. The bar, which stood along one side, was separated from the main body of the theatre by a brass rail. The hum of conversation, punctuated by the high-pitched laughter of women, filled her ears. People were happy here. She sat down on a plush-covered seat while Tob went to the bar for drinks. There, crowds of working men, still wearing their cloth caps, jostled with matrons dressed in drab colours but sporting big hats with exotic decorations of flowers, feathers or fruit. Between Lizzie and the stage, crimson velvet curtains had been parted to reveal a canvas screen, white-washed and scribbled over with what she thought at first were graffiti but on closer inspection proved to be advertisements for local traders, one of whom, a furniture remover, promised: 'Pianos handled like children!'

There was a group of pretty girls inside the bar area who were very young – fifteen or sixteen at most. Their gorgeous hats of crimson or scarlet plush displayed enormous ostrich plumes in matching colours. They talked in loud, excited voices, made quick, exaggerated gestures, and laughed inordinately. To Lizzie they seemed like tropical birds.

'They're East End factory girls,' Tob explained, when Lizzie commented on them. 'I've got you a port and lemon, my dear. That's what women drink in these parts.' He himself preferred beer. 'Birds of bright plumage,' he added, 'as long as they're in work. They go in for ostrich plumes. Marvellous to paint, those feathers – the texture, don't you know. It seems to be their Saturday night regalia. But brief is their gaudy youth, their glory transitory.'

'You sound like Gibbon's *Decline and Fall*,' said Lizzie.

'Well, that's what it is: decline and fall of the factory girl. As soon as they marry they're finished.'

'What do you mean, Tob?'

He swallowed a large mouthful of beer. 'Once they've had a few kids and can't go out to work, their freedom is gone.'

Why ever do they marry? Lizzie wondered. She supposed the biological urge to mate and have children was too strong to resist. Their own nature, perhaps a hope for love, betrayed them into a sort of slavery, and yes (since life expectancy in the East End was much lower than in the West End of London), an early death.

'And when they have hordes of children,' he continued remorselessly, 'with nothing to eat, they have to send them out on the streets to earn money by begging or prostitution. In the alleys around Spitalfields, girls will sell themselves after dark for a loaf of bread.'

The word 'prostitution' was never mentioned at Newborough End, never hung in the air at home as it did now above their seats in the pit.

'They're hungry, pool souls!' she said.

'Do I shock you, Lizzie?'

'A little – yes,' she admitted.

He smiled. That was, after all, what he intended. 'I rather like looking into the abyss as long as I know I can't fall into it myself,' he said.

She asked him how he knew so much about the way these people lived.

'Only second-hand, you know,' he explained. 'I'm not one of your heroic field workers who go and live in dosshouses to learn what's going on. I went to hear a speaker at a Fabian Society meeting who gave a sermon that wasn't at all boring, so I stayed awake. He was talking about this new book: *Life and Labour of the People of London*. It's by a man named Booth. He took years to write it. You wonder what made him do it – a rich Liverpool shipowner. I suppose he felt guilty, sitting in his club in a comfortable armchair. His revelations have been a bit of a shock to the rest of us. Things are not much better than in Dickens's day, it seems.'

As soon as the curtain rose, any apprehensions of misery were forgotten as gales of laughter swept across the auditorium at the comic turns and naughty songs peppered with *doubles entendres*, some of which Lizzie didn't understand. Marie Lloyd was billed to make a brief, guest appearance halfway through the programme as a 'Prime Performer', a description which made Lizzie think of a joint of beef. When the star did appear, she was anything but beefy. She was a tiny little creature, not much to look at, Lizzie thought, although she had wide blue eyes and a big, friendly smile. The audience went wild at the sight of her. Never before had Lizzie heard such clapping and cheering, such whistling and stamping of feet. An old woman on her right turned to shout in her ear: 'She's the darling of the 'alls, is our Marie! Our little cockney sparrer. Such a card, ain't she?'

A sudden profound silence fell on the crowd as, looking up towards the gods and waving, she began to sing:

'The boy I love is up in the gallery.'

Then she broke into a dance routine, allowing her legs in their yellow satin drawers to flash skittishly from under her skirt to gasps of 'Ooh!' and 'Aah!' and shrill whistles. Her final bow released such a mayhem of rapture that for a moment Lizzie thought the whole audience would rise up and throw itself on the stage. Instead, they threw flowers, nosegays of mixed blooms, bunches of violets and single stems of hothouse lilies and roses; and Tob, too, pulled the rosebud from his buttonhole and threw it over the footlights. Of course she had to give an encore, and then another, till at last, reluctantly, her admirers let her go.

'She's making a fortune!' shouted Tob above the din.

'And gives it all away!' shouted the woman on Lizzie's right. Her eyes were shining. 'And did you know, she once 'elped 'er old Dad makin' hartificial flowers? They say she 'ates 'em. Hartificial. That's why all 'er fans 'as to throw real ones!'

Marie Lloyd was followed by an act calculated to calm them down. There was a quick shift of scene to a backcloth painted to represent a country lane with a hedge smothered by honeysuckle and wild roses. A pair of young lovers sauntered by singing, first by turns and then together, a sweet, sentimental, popular song, 'The Honeysuckle and the Bee', in which the audience joined, swaying rhythmically in their seats, or as they stood, still at the bar, with glasses in their hands.

And Lizzie, not singing but watching the people around her, was thinking: There's something about these cockneys. Her belief in the superiority of Yorkshire men and women over all southerners was beginning to melt at the edges. These Londoners have got something . . .

Lizzie packed her biology textbook at the bottom of her holdall. There would be time, she felt sure, sometime during the Christmas holidays at home, to read and try to understand the chapter on the differences between Lamarck's and Darwin's theories of evolution. She folded clothes over the book, added her sponge bag and soap, and pushed down, into all available spaces, the presents she had bought and wrapped into small brown paper parcels. She did not pack (because she intended reading it on the train) her library copy of Anthony Hope's *The Prisoner of Zenda*. She'd had to wait some time for it. It had been the bestseller of the year, and the list of would-be readers had been long. She dropped the book into her large handbag along with some dog biscuits for Dax, who seemed as eager as she was to get to the station. The journey would have been tedious and uncomfortable if it hadn't been for the dangerous adventures of the swashbuckling hero, and the comfort derived from a footwarmer under the seat. It emitted a strange smell, but Lizzie didn't mind that; she was just grateful for the warmth on the soles of her boots.

It was good to be home, at last, in Newborough End where life went on as usual, where all problems seemed to have been solved, or at least contentedly shelved, where the scent of Bessie's pastry still wafted upstairs and around the landings promising blissful eating to come. Cissie and Katy, who had arrived the day before, kept running in and out of each other's rooms to exchange titbits of information and little confidences in excited voices, Edward came out of the shop to show off his new magnificent moustache, and Mother, looking rather harassed, managed to snatch a moment every now and then from behind the counter to run into the kitchen, where Lizzie had installed herself, to embrace her daughter and to ask, peering into her face: 'Are you eating properly?' and 'Do your shoes need mending?' and 'Are you really happy, dear?' before being summoned by the sound of the shop's bell back to business.

'We're all pleased to see you home, Miss Thorburn,' said Bessie. She had never before addressed Lizzie as Miss. 'And I'm glad to be home,' said Lizzie. She took an apron hanging on a hook on the back of the door and, tying it round her waist, she walked into the back scullery and began to scrub the pans Bessie had been using, with copper wire and a bit of soap.

'Wait a bit lass!' shouted Bessie from the kitchen. 'Wait till I get some more warm water for them pots!'

It wasn't till they were all seated at table for high tea, and Edward was showing off his special china tea cup with a shelf above the rim to keep his moustache out of the liquid, that George arrived. He burst into the dining-room and stood there suntanned and bearded, his massive bulk filling the doorway, blue eyes flashing and his great smile embracing the whole room. Lizzie thought: He really is the answer to every maiden's prayer; but Katy chanted: '"Home is the sailor, home from sea. And the hunter home from the hill."' Her little song was not without a sardonic note.

Mother rose from the table and flung herself into his arms, from which, laughing, he disengaged her. But he made Cissie give up her place so that he could sit beside his mother. He was in high spirits and hungry, devouring several of Bessie's toasts spread with Gentleman's Relish, and three, if not four, of her excellent mince pies, amusing them all, between mouthfuls, with his tales of voyages to far-off, exotic places, and his jokes. Mother hung on his every word, and sometimes on his shoulder too. She is happy, Lizzie thought, the happiness of having us around her shines through the shadows under her eyes and smooths out the wrinkles of anxiety on her forehead.

It was lovely to be home; but Lizzie soon became aware that things were somehow different. 'Love is not love which alters when it alteration finds,' she remembered. Of course, love still filled her heart for everything at home, especially her mother; but she recognised that she herself no longer belonged in quite the same way. The old bonds were loosening; she was standing on the edge and looking inwards at the scene; she was no longer an active participant. She told herself she felt no less love for them all, but it was, if she were to be truthful, of a different, more distanced kind. It was not 'home' which had altered, but something inside herself. This was partly because she knew that none of them, not even Mother, could ever understand her passion for her studies, for the thrills of London, and, last but not least, her friendship with Tob. That was something she simply could not talk about. If she did, they wouldn't give her a moment's peace. They would all bombard her with questions, pushing her into a corner, tying her up in matrimony within minutes of her mentioning his name.

And then, as she sat in Mother's sitting-room after tea, surrounded by the lilac wallpaper and shut in by thick crimson curtains with their tasselled cords, and listened with half an ear to her brothers and sisters talking, while glancing occasionally at the textbook open on her knees, her attention began to wander through mazes in which the sleep-walking homeless flitted like ghosts and Marie Lloyd screeched and kicked up her legs to let the pit catch a glimpse of her yellow drawers, and Darwin tugged at his beard and ordered all inefficient and ill-adapted species to drop out of the three-legged race, and Lizzie tripped and fell on the grass. She woke with a start to the sound of laughter, and found she'd slipped to the floor from her chair.

'Just like poor Shelley when he had to listen to Southey reading aloud one of his epic poems!' laughed Katy.

Mother said: 'You're tired, Lizzie dear, after your long train journey. Just you go to bed now. And don't try to do any more reading tonight.'

But Lizzie didn't heed her mother's advice. As soon as she was in bed she opened her textbook of biology and began to read: 'We stand at the door opening on discovery in the study of heredity. Perhaps the coming century will reveal how characteristics are transmitted. At present we can only guess; but that there is, within the protoplasm which is the body substance of all living animals and plants, some matter which specifically carries inheritance, and that this matter is enclosed in the gametes or germ cells, is certain. In mating there is a mingling of the gametes so that the offspring receives from both parents all that has been inherited from the many preceding ancestors of two separate lines of descent.'

The author was as prosy as Primrose Watkins. It was hard to concentrate because her thoughts were, against her will, being tugged back to Tob. There was, she had to admit, hardly an hour of her waking day into which his image didn't intrude. Was it an intrusion then? If so, it was a welcome one, for she revelled in these daydreams. It wasn't really thinking at all; it was a trance-like state in which she imagined meetings and conversations with him, and exchanged glances, and even touchings. Could this possibly be love? And was she, after all, no different from those factory girls whose biological urges drove them towards marriage and the sacrifice of brief and precious freedom? Lizzie believed she might marry one day in the far distant future, but she pleaded, like St Augustine when he knew he must give up his sins: Not yet, please God! Not yet! She had too much to accomplish first. In any case, she was uncertain as to Tob's feelings towards herself. She felt confused when she thought about the matter. He behaved towards her like an old friend, treating her with frankness and even, occasionally, with an affection perhaps more than should be expected from a man who was not a fiancé; but he kept a certain distance between them. For one thing he had told her very little about himself. She guessed he had been unhappy at school when he told her: 'I was rather small for my age till I was thirteen when I suddenly grew into a beanpole. You have to be quick on your feet, or funny, to survive, if you're small at school.' She supposed he had been both. But she knew nothing of his parents, and only that his sister, Aurora, was a better painter than himself.

Tob had given her a Christmas present, a parcel whose brown paper wrapping she had torn open on the train. It contained a book, *The Egoist* by George Meredith. While she had been reading it in the sitting-room on her first evening at home, Katy, had peeped over her shoulder at the title and asked: 'Do you like it, Lizzie?'

'I'll tell you when I've finished it,' she replied.

'Meredith writes such complicated prose,' said her sister. 'Trollope described it as "twisted in curl-papers".'

Lizzie had closed the book with a snap of annoyance. It was no ordinary novel, borrowed from Mudie's Circulating Library, but a special gift stamped with Tob's personality, and so had to be protected from Katy's derision. She had removed Tob's card from between the covers of the book, and was glad that her sister couldn't scrutinise, in his elegant spidery hand, the quotation from Meredith's poem 'Modern Love':

> Then each applied to each that fatal knife
> Deep questioning, which probes to endless dole.
> Ah! What a dusty answer gets the soul
> When hot for certainties in this our life!

She could imagine Tob's full, beautiful lips reciting that poem. It was a message, all at once clear, and yet asking so many questions that it was no wonder Lizzie couldn't concentrate on the mechanisms of heredity. It was about lovers. *Does he love me then*? It suggested a longing for love, but also that love's fulfilment was somehow impossible to achieve. It recognised the fear that love demands too much of human nature; it expressed disappointment and even cynicism. *Is it some form of confession*? Perhaps he was trying to tell her that he had sown his wild oats, had known love and been too hurt by the experience to risk losing his heart again. Or was he trying to warn her that, like other men he, too, was an egoist, and would demand of her all that she had to give and more besides? That thought was alarming. The friendship she had with Tob was, she believed, of a Platonic kind, a meeting of mind and spirit, not a vulgar flirtation, nor a common love affair, and certainly not an all-devouring romantic passion. That image filled her with fear. She was making no demands of him, nor he of her. She had no desire to tie him down in any way. All she wanted was the free exchange of ideas and confidences, an equal companionship, a happy, mutual trust. She shut her eyes and tried to think about it more clearly; but at last, even Tob and his Christmas present were washed out of her thoughts as sleep flooded over them like a tide obliterating all marks on a sandy shore.

*   *   *

Lizzie took the telegram and thanked the postman and, holding the flimsy piece of paper in her hand, she stood quite still. Her mouth felt dry and she feared the worst. *Her mother must be dead.* She knew that couldn't possibly be the case because only that morning she'd received a cheerful letter from her with no hint of sickness or misfortune in it. *Tob had been killed in a railway accident.* This vision didn't strike her as at all incongruous, nor did she ask herself why, since she had no ties whatever with him, and had never even met his parents, a telegram should be sent to her to inform her of his death.

'It's reply paid, Miss,' said the postman. 'Do you want to reply?'

'Yes. Oh, yes. I'm so sorry,' she replied, and tore open the envelope.

She was surprised when she read it. It was from Tob's sister. 'DO COME FOR LUNCH SUNDAY. STAYING WITH GRANDMOTHER. DO SO WANT TO MEET YOU. AURORA ASHWOLDE.' There was no mention of Tob. Lizzie wrote her reply in pencil: 'LOOK FORWARD TO MEETING SUNDAY. THANKS. LIZZIE THORBURN.' She was pleased and excited at the prospect of meeting Aurora. She supposed that Tob would be there too. She had heard nothing from him for nearly twelve weeks, although she had written to thank him for his Christmas gift, to say how much she'd enjoyed reading *The Egoist*, and to hope they'd meet again soon. As January passed, she mourned his absence, ate with a little less appetite, and began to be so absent-minded in the lab that Prosy protested: 'You're stargazing again, Lizzie. What's the matter? Are you in love?'

'Certainly not!' Lizzie blushed with indignation.

Prosy's rebuke, for that's what it was, made her throw herself into her work once more, helping her to dissect conscientiously, in spite of the smell, the open carcase of a rabbit.

'Mammalia,' Prosy pronounced. 'The rabbit is higher up the evolutionary scale than the dogfish. It's important to understand the differences in the respiratory systems of fishes and mammals. The rabbit breathes from lungs inside the thorax; fishes breathe through lungs spread out over the gills in the neck.'

Mr Brown, who was beginning to overcome his shyness, stopped by their table when he heard what Prosy said. 'The human embryo, you know, in its development, passes through all the evolutionary stages of its ancestors. And at one time, when it's still very small, the human embryo actually has gills, which later disappear. We call this process recapitulation, that is, a working through of our evolutionary history.' His eye was held by the expression on Lizzie's face as he continued: 'But occasionally, the gills don't entirely close up, and a remnant of a gill slit is left, producing, in the human animal, what's known as a branchial cyst of the neck.'

Lizzie was entranced. To think that we reproduce in our developing bodies the physical history of our ancestors! She remembered the arguments at home during her adolescence, all the talk about Darwin voting for apes and Disraeli being on the side of the angels. It was a bit of a joke, but she remembered, too, her mother's thinking silences, as well as Edward's scornful laughter at the notion of having monkey forbears. Lizzie had never taken it very seriously; she had had other more pressing personal concerns while she was growing up. But now, here was this 'recapitulation', revealing that our ancestors were far more primitive even than apes, that our line of descent could be traced backwards through millions of years, to a time when some fishlike creatures were trying to emerge onto dry land, to an era, even before that, when living organisms were just bits of protoplasm floating about in the sea. The shock of the very idea made her gasp. It was like a firework exploding in her brain, the shooting sparks expanding to light up a firmament of interrelated meanings. She began to understand, for the first time, why the whole country had been split by the controversy which followed the publication of Darwin's books and why such heated arguments between Creationists and Evolutionists echoed down subsequent decades, and still continued to reverberate in private homes.

It was because doubt threatened to corrode the iron of long-held belief in the authenticity of the Bible. For all honest Christians, and for all those who thought at all about the meaning of life, it had been a time for deep heart and soul searching. Many must have been seized by feelings almost of panic when they began to consider the possibility that the survival of the fittest, perhaps by chance, and not the careful hand of a loving God, might be controlling our living world. For many, the whole religious system they had been happy to trust must have been suddenly turned upside down. Some, no doubt, were unable to face the fears engendered in their minds by Darwin's theory, and simply shut the door on him in obstinate anger; but many others, believers in scientific progress, if not always very well informed scientists, fought eagerly to spread a new religion of Darwinism – to them the truth, to their opponents a gospel of materialistic determinism that attacked the very roots of human responsibility for good and evil.

Lizzie wondered what Prosy, with her vicarage background, would make of all this. At what point in the development of our ape-like ancestor (when he stood upright, or when he first used his finger and thumb to scratch a sign on a rock, or daub a cave with coloured clay, or make a simple tool) did God insert the soul into him? It must have been done into the brain, Lizzie thought, for that's the seat of intelligence; and here she already

101

disagreed with the Bible according to Leviticus when he declared: 'Blood is the vessel of the soul.' Blood was something we shared with animals – mammals, birds, reptiles, and fishes. Was man but a cleverer mammal with no substance in him that might survive death? Or could it be that all animals possessed some eternal substance that you might call the soul? Lizzie thought of Dax. Perhaps there was a heaven for little dogs after all . . .

She had so much to ponder on that by the end of February even Tob was being dismissed from her thoughts for several hours a day. And now, here he was interrupting her life again, indirectly, through his sister's telegram.

A trim maid opened the door, but it was Aurora who ran forward into the hall to greet Lizzie with outstretched hands.

'I've heard such a lot about you!' she cried eagerly, her words tripping over each other in their speed of utterance. 'Grandmama still tells the tale of how you rescued her, you know.'

The old couple sat by the fire in the drawing-room on the first floor. The old man tried to rise to his feet with the aid of a silver-topped cane. He bowed formally. 'At your service marm,' he said, his accent and manners seeming to come from a distant past. He then addressed his granddaughter: 'Pleased to make your acquaintance, marm.' He waited, bent over his stick, till the ladies were seated, each holding the small glasses of sherry Aurora had poured out from a cut-glass decanter. 'Are you fond of opera, ladies?' he pursued between sips. 'Jenny Lind now, at Convent Garden last week . . . What a voice! Like a bird!'

Aurora and Lizzie exchanged smiles. He must have been remembering an event in his youth, for the Swedish Nightingale had been silent for years, and, indeed, had died some time ago.

'You're getting mixed up again over dates, Archie,' said his wife crossly.

'Oh, am I my dear?' he asked amiably. 'Well, I've seen a few dates in my time, I suppose. . . . Sings like a bird!'

Lunch was served in the dining-room on the ground floor. The dishes rose from the basement kitchen on a food lift in the wall. The maid transferred the dishes to the table, removed the silver-plated covers from boiled chicken, from carrots tossed in butter and potatoes baked whole in their jackets, and then left the room. It was Aurora who presided over the carving.

She was not as handsome as her brother, Lizzie judged, but she was someone who would be noticed in a crowd. She was nearly as tall as herself and had large, deep blue eyes like Tob's, but her nose was prominent and aquiline, and her lips firmer and more purposeful. She reminded Lizzie of a portrait she'd seen in some art gallery, of a Renaissance cardinal. Lizzie thought she must be older than Tob, twenty-six perhaps. Throughout the meal she talked easily and volubly, telling Lizzie more about Tob's background, without mentioning his name, than he had ever told her himself.

'I'm up at the Slade, at last! I've been there a week now, just settling in. I'm so happy! They accepted me as a student, and the parents have agreed to pay the fees. So I'm to live here with Grandmama and Grandpapa, and keep an eye on them at the same time. I've heard about you, of course – that you're a New Woman, independent and all the rest, and I rather hoped you'd be able to show me the ropes.'

'Medicine may not have quite the same ropes as art,' said Lizzie, cautiously.

Aurora laughed. 'No, I suppose not. But do you know? Our professor at the Slade is a surgeon. Yes, would you believe it? He learned his anatomy from corpses in the dissecting room. But he's given up surgery now for art's sake. Henry Tonks. He's terribly severe. 'Drawing first, painting second', is what he teaches. Slapdash drawing is his bugbear. They say he can reduce a girl student to tears in no time. But he really can draw.' There was a short silence while she swallowed a mouthful of chicken. 'He hasn't made me cry yet. He stopped behind me and looked over my shoulder, but said nothing. He nodded, and then passed on. I expect that's a good sign.' She picked up a piece of carrot with her fork. 'But the great thing is to be free at last. Although there are still lots of old-fashioned rules at the Slade. Girls are only allowed to mix with male students while drawing the antique: busts of Nero, the torso of Hercules, that sort of thing . . . The sexes are entirely separated for painting the nude form.'

'I should hope so too!' exclaimed her grandmother.

'But I'm so excited about my freedom! It's taken me so long to persuade the parents to let me go; but they've agreed, at last, that I'm old enough to be released into the big, bad city.' She laughed, before popping the piece of carrot into her mouth.

'I know how you feel,' said Lizzie.

'I hear you walk about the streets alone, Lizzie. May I call you Lizzie? I do so hope we shall be friends. There are so many things I want to see and do in London. I thought, perhaps, you might be able to show me the way.'

'I should be pleased to do so,' said Lizzie, and managed to ask at last: 'How is Tob?'

'Quite well now, I'm thankful to say,' said Aurora. 'He caught a cold over the New Year holiday, and the chill went down on his chest. A sort of pneumonia, the doctor said it was, so it took a little while for him to shake it off; but he'll be back at his easel next week I hope. Tob's very strong, really, but he has got rather thin, and needs feeding up still. So I daresay I shall have to keep an eye on him as well as the old folks.'

104

'Pneumonia's rather serious, isn't it?' asked Lizzie, spooning out her pudding from a custard glass.

Aurora was more interested in her new-found freedom and in women's rights than in her brother's health. 'Oh, Tob recovers quickly from these setbacks,' she said dismissively, and immediately asked: 'Do you belong to any group working for the Women's Movement, Lizzie – fighting for representation of women in parliament, getting votes for women – that sort of thing? Women got the vote in New Zealand last year. That was a historic triumph for the Cause on the other side of the world. We've got to win that battle over here. It can be won; it will be won!'

The maid came in to announce that coffee was served in the drawing-room, and they all rose from the table and went upstairs. Quite soon after sitting down in his armchair by the fire, old Mr Ashwolde began to nod, which encouraged Aurora to speak freely about him. She lowered her voice in order not to disturb him and, perhaps, because her grandmother, though rather deaf, was still awake.

'He's an old India hand, you know. Went out in the thirties to work for the East India Company, shipping teas. He knew a lot about teas; and then, when he came home from the East in the fifties, when the whole population of Britain seemed to want to drink tea, gallons of it, he went into business importing it. Dowling and Ashwolde – a household name really. Made money, of course. Lots of it. Sadly, there's not much of it left now.' She fell silent and looked sad. Lizzie was wondering how she could bring the conversation back to Tob without revealing too great an interest in him, when Aurora spoke again: 'Pandering to national addictions, that's what his life's work has been – though of course he'd never admit it. Selling opium to the Chinese in exchange for tea to the British . . . He used to say that was before his time, when the big broad-bottomed East Indiamen used to sail into East India docks with their cargoes of tea and porcelain. Floating warehouses, people used to call them – overtaken now by faster steam-ships.'

'Is the business still in family hands?' Lizzie asked.

'No, I'm afraid not. Papa never liked the trade. While he was growing up there was always plenty of money for him to live like a gentleman with no occupation. And then Grandpapa lost a lot of capital.'

'Speculating,' Mrs Ashwolde interrupted suddenly. 'Railway fever – building South American railways which were never built.'

'So that's how the old firm went broke,' said Aurora.

'And all my dowry went with it,' added the old lady. 'That law that was passed allowing married women to keep their own property was too late for mine. My money disappeared with the rest. Overnight it happened.'

Lizzie noticed that Mrs Ashwolde seemed well able to hear what she wanted to. She remembered her own mother speaking of that Married Women's Property Act as a great step in the right direction.

'The old firm was bought up by Lewton's, and Grandpapa retired after that; Papa was made a director on the new board.'

'But, of course, he doesn't have to work,' Mrs Ashwolde hastened to explain. 'He just has to show up once or twice a year to meet the other directors.' It amazed Lizzie that the old lady, without a trace of irony, was trying to reassure her that Papa was doing the gentlemanly thing.

It was only later, after Tob's return to London, that Lizzie learned how the family fortunes were rescued by the marriage of Papa to Miss Tarbutt, an Anglo-Irish heiress from Mayo. Luckily, her fortune was protected by the new Act, and as Lizzie was soon to discover it was Mama who held the purse strings and who managed their affairs.

SIX

St James's theatre was packed. Lizzie, scanning the auditorium, couldn't see a single empty seat. They had, all three, felt the excitement earlier in the street outside where two newsboys paraded, shouting hoarsely: 'News! News! All the latest on the Queensberry trial!' A theatregoer, stopping to buy an evening paper and reading the headlines feverishly as if his life depended on it, was reassured by the seller: 'Trial's been dropped, Sir.' And then he shouted again: 'Libel charges dropped! Queensberry jubilant!'

Tob, looking anxiously around at the crowd, muttered: 'And what will happen now?'

'Why is Queensberry being tried?' asked Lizzie. She knew he was a patron of the boxing ring and the originator of the rules for the game, but what all this fuss was about she had no idea.

'He's the father of Oscar's paramour,' Tob explained. 'And he objects to his pretty little son being seduced.'

The Importance of Being Earnest was playing, night after night, to full houses, but the placards advertising the production had been defaced by large white stickers obliterating Oscar Wilde's name. Lizzie was indignant that the theatre management could be so two-faced. With such a successful play on their hands they must have been coining money out of the disgraced playwright. It was Saturday, 6 April. The trial of the Marquis of Queensberry, accused by Wilde of libel, which had begun on 3 April, had just been abandoned on the advice of Wilde's lawyers. Public interest in the trial was intense; the whole of London was talking about it; everybody, it seemed to Lizzie, except herself. She never read the daily papers, was innocent to the point of ignorance on the subject of poor Oscar's amorous tendencies, and mystified over the whole affair.

Inside the theatre, the excitement was almost palpable. The atmosphere was alert, expectant, as if charged by an electric current sparking across the pit, from box to box and running along the rows of stalls and the edge of the dress circle, setting alight the eyes of the audience, until they seemed to reflect the cruel glitter of watchers at a Roman circus hoping for the sight and smell of blood.

'What on earth is it all about?' she asked, when they were seated. Aurora and Tob on either side talked animatedly across her.

'It all began,' he explained, 'because Queensberry objected to the friendship – call it affection, if you like – between his son and Oscar.'

'You know he arrived – the Marquis, I mean – on the first night, armed with a bunch of carrots and turnips to throw at Oscar when he took his curtain call at the end of the play?'

'Did he throw them onto the stage?' asked Lizzie.

'No. He was turned away by vigilant doormen who were waiting for him at every entrance.'

'So then he went to Oscar's club, the Albemarle, and handed in an offensive card. And then Oscar decided to sue him for libel.'

'They say it was Alfred Douglas who egged Oscar on to taking legal action.'

'Whoever made the decision, it was a great mistake,' said Tob.

'What was so insulting about that card?' asked Lizzie.

'It called him a somdomite.' Tob laughed. 'Queensberry's such a philistine he couldn't even spell it right!'

'What's a somdomite?' Lizzie persisted.

There was an awkward silence, which Aurora broke: 'Well, you know . . . the cities of the plain in the Bible . . . destroyed by God for their wickedness. Sodom and Gomorrah.'

To cover his embarrassment, Tob took from his pocket a pencil and a drawing-pad and began to sketch Lizzie's head in profile. Aurora, pulling a smaller pad and pencil from her reticule drew Lizzie from the other side. 'Race you to it!' she laughed.

While they were drawing her, Lizzie held her head up and gazed around at the crowd. She noted the gleaming white shirts and long black tail coats of well-dressed men in the tiers of boxes, where they stood behind bare-shouldered women in silks and velvets of blue, green and amber. White-gloved arms leaned on the edge of the dress circle as they moved opera glasses or lorgnettes the better to survey the scene or to study their programmes. She was thankful to have a seat in the pit where nobody needed to dress up for the occasion.

The lights dimmed and the curtain went up before the drawings were finished, but Lizzie studied them during the interval. She was interested to see how different they were. Tob's was a scrawl, a bird's nest of criss-crossed lines out of which emerged two large eyes and a vague outline of a face in which Lizzie could see no resemblance to herself; Aurora's consisted of a few strong curves that immediately conveyed a good likeness, though perhaps caricatured.

Lizzie, looking at Tob's drawing asked: 'Am I really as untidy as that?'

'Yes, of course you are, Lizzie. You're a whirlwind,' he said.

'Tonks wouldn't like it,' said Aurora. 'He'd stand behind you as you're drawing, and demand: "What is it? What *is* it?"'

'I'm not too keen to have Tonks standing behind me smelling of carbolic from the operating theatre and using his pencil like a surgeon's scalpel to make cuts on the paper.'

'I've never smelt carbolic on him,' protested his sister. 'I think that's a myth he brought with him from the London Hospital.'

'Well, your sense of smell is not well developed, Aurora. And anyway, I prefer Steer for a teacher. Tonks is all for the Pre-Raphaelites – accurate details observed and carefully painted. It's a good way to start, I suppose; but it's not enough, is it?'

'Why not?'

'Imagination has to rise above all that copying, that certainty. It's ambiguity that makes a picture interesting.'

Aurora laughed. 'You should have been a poet, Tob, not a painter.'

'Dozy old Wilson Steer is trying out a new technique with his paintings of pretty girls in fluffy blots. He'll take to my sketch.'

'If he can keep awake long enough to see you finish it,' said Aurora. 'Mary Blake told me he fell asleep sitting behind her chair as she was drawing.'

Lizzie interrupted their sparring: 'Can I keep the sketches?'

Aurora immediately gave Lizzie hers; but Tob crammed his into a pocket. 'No. It's not good enough,' he said.

'Mama was dying to see the play,' Aurora confided to Lizzie, 'especially since all the scandal broke; but she's still religious enough to consider it improper to go the theatre during Lent.'

'Well, at least she's not such a hypocrite as all this crowd,' said Tob, 'scandalised by Oscar, but flocking in droves to laugh at his witticisms.'

Lizzie was secretly glad Mama had not come up to town to see the play. If she had, seats would have been booked in a box, or in the stalls, where everybody wore evening dress, of which Lizzie possessed not one item. In any case, she felt much happier in the pit, in what she regarded as the slightly Bohemian, and certainly less demanding company of Tob and Aurora. If she had been alone, or with Prosy, she would have endured the wooden benches and the neck craning necessary in the gallery, so that for her, even the pit was a rise in theatre-going status.

'I daresay the parents will see the play after Easter,' said Aurora. 'In spite of all the scandal, Mama has a certain respect for Oscar. She looks upon the Wilde family as a lot of scallywags, really. Oscar's mother is so eccentric as to be almost crazy. But in Ireland they were always staunch Home Rulers, you know.'

The animated crowd spilled out of the theatre on the pavement after the play was over, and broke into groups, waiting for cabs and chattering happily as they did so. They seemed to have forgotten Oscar's unspeakable crimes, revealed by witnesses in that week's trial, and remembered only that he had made them laugh.

'What I liked best was Miss Prism's definition of fiction,' said Lizzie. 'According to her, the good end happily and the bad unhappily.'

'You think justice should be done and should be seen to be done?' Tob's voice was teasing.

She recognised, uneasily, that life was not like that, but she considered it was the novelist's job to make it so.

They managed to get a cab at last.

'We'll see you at Easter down at Hampton Court, won't we?' asked Tob, as they approached Lizzie's digs in Doughty Street. 'I shall look forward to it,' said Lizzie. 'Greatly.'

The cab stopped under a street lamp.

'I'm looking forward to showing you our willow trees,' he said. 'They're just putting on their first green bridal veils.' She couldn't see his face in the dimly-lit interior of the cab, but she felt his hand reach out for hers and squeeze it lightly. She didn't look back, but as she clambered out she murmured: 'I shall look forward to that too.'

As Lizzie stepped down from the footplate, Aurora caught her arm and spoke hurriedly in a low voice: 'I think it best not to let the parents know you were Tob's friend before you met me. Make out you're my friend, don't you know.'

Lizzie nodded: 'Well, so I am.' Her mind was still in the gilded theatre, her ears full of the sound of laughter.

'The parents are rather old-fashioned and formal,' Aurora added. 'They like proper introductions, families they know of – that sort of thing.'

Tob, leaning back in his corner of the cab, could not hear her. He was watching the lamplight fall on Lizzie's upturned face. If only . . . he thought, if only I could paint her – not as Botticelli's Venus rising naked from the waves, but as some earth goddess emerging from the bole of a willow, with the first green flames of the fire of spring flickering over her skin . . .

Then, with a crack of his whip and a sharp command, the cabby drove his horse into a canter, while Lizzie stood on the pavement waving till they were out of sight.

'You're not too tired, Tob?' asked Aurora; and when he made no reply she continued: 'I do believe you should have been a poet, Tob. Yes. Those willows at the end of the garden are lovely in spring.'

Meanwhile, Lizzie let herself in with her own front door key. As she climbed the stairs she considered the prospect of Easter with some dread. In her meetings with Aurora, and especially on last Sunday, when the three of them had walked through Hyde Park after lunch in order to enjoy the free entertainment provided at Speakers' Corner, Lizzie had picked up certain hints about the younger Mrs Ashwolde which made her think of Mama as rather a formidable person.

They had listened to the tub-thumpers, wild prophets promising the dooms of hell for sinners, eccentrics hurling imprecations at the human condition, and would-be politicians blaming the government for this or that economic theory, or whatever was their chosen scapegoat for all the ills of humanity. As they had turned away, Tob had remarked that in Ireland every other man saw himself as a politician.

'Oh, Ireland . . .' said Aurora. 'Over there, murder is a political manoeuvre, you know.' She was thinking of the recent assassination in Dublin of Lord Frederick Cavendish, the Chief Secretary, and his permanent undersecretary, as they walked to take the air in Phoenix Park.

Tob then began to talk about his mother's home in Ireland, where he and his sisters had spent many childhood holidays: a great dark, stone-walled castle with crenellated turrets perched on the wild coast of Mayo, on the western-most edge of Europe, facing the Atlantic.

'It was whistled through by gales in winter,' he said. 'And flocks of seabirds crying like souls in purgatory swirled round it.'

That seemed, to Lizzie, a very papistical idea, though she knew the Ashwoldes were not papists.

'And the land so poor and stony, very little food could be grown by the peasants, and very few rents collected from them,' added Aurora.

Before Mama married and came to live in England she had, in common with the rest of her family, 'lived for the hunting'. They kept their hunters, not in Mayo, but on the more fertile land of a cousin in Galway, where they spent most of the winters hunting with the Galway Blazers. In their own estimation they were not rich, but they claimed descent from an ancient lineage of earls who ruled Ireland long before even the Normans had invaded the country. Mama, though not an heiress, was forthright and bold to the point of recklessness while hunting, jumping the worst fences without a tumble, and racing away from the field. It was her prowess and her love of the sport that endeared her to an English uncle on her mother's side who died without issue, leaving her the 'small fortune' which had rescued the Ashwoldes.

Papa, Lizzie was given to understand, was a genial, unimportant sort of chap; but Mama, although no doubt hidebound by some old-fashioned prejudices, was a person to be reckoned with. She would, Lizzie guessed, look down on her unfashionable clothes, would be suspicious of her independence, and not quite certain about her morals, would regard her as 'not one of us' because her family could not be traced in Mama's *Debrett* or even in *Who's Who*.

'Oh, well!' sighed Lizzie philosophically. 'What will be, will be.'

Mrs Plumm was already in bed, but Dax uncurled himself from his cushion and hurled himself at her. She caught him in her arms and spoke soothingly: 'Even if she is a terrible snob it won't kill us, will it Dax? You and I can stand up to a bit of cold shoulder and a withering glance or two, can't we, old boy, what?' And laughing, she chased him downstairs and out into the street for his last run around before they settled down for the night.

Lizzie forgot her feelings of apprehension about Mama in the excitement of her first visit to 'Green Arbour', and Dax, who had been invited to accompany her, as soon as he saw the extent of the garden and the shrubberies beyond, was delighted with the place. Aurora had spoken of it as their house in the country. It was not really in the country but on the edge of an expanding town which seemed to stop expanding at the banks of the river Mole, on the far side of which were green fields. Built of brick about fifty years ago, the house had a pantiled roof and deep, sloping gables. A frieze of decorative woodwork, painted white, hung below the eaves like a lace edging; and big sash windows glared in the sun from both storeys, letting in plenty of light to the rooms inside. It was a very sunny house, aptly named, surrounded as it was by lawns, and around them by flowerbeds at present full of daffodils but planted with numerous other blooms for later in the year, in herbaceous borders, as Maisie, Tob's younger sister, who was twenty, explained as she took Lizzie round the garden: 'It's a sort of orderly disorder. The house must flow out into the garden, and the garden must be part of the house. That's the latest horticultural fashion. And Mama goes along with it.'

Since Lizzie confessed to knowing nothing about horticultural fashions, Maisie was able to feel just a little patronising towards this big girl who, from what she'd heard Rory say, was very clever and altogether the New Woman. Maisie went on to reveal that Mama had given up hunting for horticulture. Gardening was her passion now. Lizzie took the opportunity to remark that it was doubtless due to Mama that the garden was such a delight.

Beyond the shrubberies there was a vegetable patch with rows of young onions and feathery carrot leaves, and potatoes in ridges beginning to push through the heaped-up earth; and there was a netted cage for soft fruit, the bushes, as yet, only in bud.

'The naughty blackbirds do get in to steal the raspberries in summer,' said Maisie, 'in spite of the risk of tangling their wings in the nets – poor, silly things!'

At the end of the garden stood a rank of weeping willow trees leaning over the idle river. When Dax began to explore the banks, a gardener appeared, his arms full of daffodils for his missus. He was about to go off for his Easter holiday when he saw the dog, and immediately, fearing the destructive potential of the whole canine species, he advanced trying to look menacing. Lizzie, reading the expression on his face, called out: 'Dax! Daxie! Come here,' and soon slipped the leash over his collar.

'It's a lazy little river you have here,' she said.

'But 'e can be the very devil when 'e fancies,' the gardener replied, pleased to be able to contradict the lady dog-owner, ''E can creep over my carrot seedlings and push 'em up by the roots when it's rained special 'ard like. Even been known to flood the cellars of the 'ouse.'

'Good gracious!' Lizzie was properly impressed. 'Who would have thought it possible?' He nodded with solemn satisfaction but stood watching them and the dangerous dog till they were safely back inside the house, before leaving the premises himself.

Lizzie's cloak was taken from her by a pretty young Irish maid whose spirit seemed not entirely subdued by her black uniform and white apron, for her stare was bold, and her richly-curled red hair sprouted rebelliously from under the confines of her starched white cap.

'Maisie said: 'This is Anastasia, Lizzie,' and to the maid: 'Miss Thorburn is going to be a doctor.' Anastasia's surprise at this statement knocked away any semblance she had to a properly trained servant. Her hand shot up to her mouth to stop a laugh and she cried out: 'A doctor is it? Holy Moses! A lady doctor? God help us all!' But she put the cloak over her arm and smiled encouragingly as Lizzie was led by Maisie into the drawing-room to meet Mama and Papa.

Muriel Ashwolde was a stately, unsmiling woman with

a fine head of dark hair only very lightly streaked with grey and piled up into a loose bun, kept in place by two long, ornamental pins. 'How do you *do*?' She trumpeted forth her greeting through a nose even more formidable than Aurora's, and lifted a condescending hand to Lizzie's as if she found the formality distasteful.

Papa, who was more genial, smiled a slow, lazy smile at her and asked her how she liked London after the wilds of Yorkshire. 'Less bracing, perhaps, than the air up there?' he asked, smoothing his waistcoat down over a plump girth.

Lunch was served in the dining-room; and here Anastasia struggled to maintain dignity, standing like a soldier on sentry by the sideboard between courses. The window was open to allow currents of air to carry into the room, bursts of birdsong from the garden and a scent of hyacinths from bulbs planted in a Minton pottery jardinière. It was too warm for a fire, but in the fireplace stood a handsome firescreen of beaten brass in the fashionable Art Nouveau manner, spread out into a fan shape and patterned with eyes like a peacock's tail. In the centre of the table there shone a silver and glass epergne, its five flutes holding feathery ferns and hothouse orchids, a floral display that Lizzie thought very grand.

The talk was all of Oscar Wilde. Within a few hours of the collapse of the libel trial, he had been arrested and taken to Bow Street police station where he had been charged.

'What is he accused of?' asked Lizzie, crumbling bread beside her soup plate. There was a short silence.

'Well, he's a pervert, isn't he?' asked Maisie.

'What's wrong with that?' asked Lizzie. 'I mean, it may be a religious mistake, but surely not criminal, is it? Wasn't Cardinal Newman a pervert when he went over to Rome?'

Amid the laughter that followed, which made Lizzie

blush with shame because even the maid standing at the sideboard was laughing at her, Mr Ashwolde leaned towards her kindly. 'I think the meaning of the word has altered considerably over the years, Miss Thorburn. Certainly "pervert" was once used in some quarters to mean "convert", but nowadays it carries a more sinister connotation.'

'Oscar's crime is that he perverts the young from the straight and narrow path,' said Mrs Ashwolde severely. 'Especially young men.'

There was another short silence.

'He'll not get a fair trial, though,' said her husband. 'He's already been condemned by the press and the British public.'

'In one of its fits of moral indignation,' said Tob.' When everyone knows the public schools are full of Oscar's offence.'

'Oh, come now, Tob!' his father protested. 'That surely is an exaggeration.'

'Public schoolboys certainly don't look like Oscar,' said Muriel.

'And do you know?' put in Maisie excitedly, 'even quite moral men, who are well dressed but happen to wear their hair long, are being booed in the street by strangers – laughed at for being "Oscars"! Rather comical, isn't it?'

'I do believe none of this would have happened if it hadn't been for that book.' said Papa. 'We all know this sort of thing goes on – has gone on, throughout history. Most of us have had a classical education, so we've heard of Plato and his pals. They all accepted it as normal then. If it hadn't been for the publication last year of that book . . . Have you read the *Green Carnation*, Miss Thorburn? It seems the author, anonymous you understand, met Wilde and Lord Alfred Douglas in Cairo when they were guests of Lord and Lady Cromer, who took them up the

Nile on a river steamer. The author calls Wilde Esme Amarinth in the book, and gives him some witticisms that must have come straight out of Oscar's mouth.' Ashwolde patted his lips with his napkin, and looked at the expectant faces round the table. 'Such as: "She lives in Canterbury and does a lot of good among the rich."'

'Oh, that's nice,' said Aurora. 'Have you any more?'

'The character, Amarinth, also suggests that the lady in question actually converted one of the canons to a belief in the Thirty-nine Articles.'

'It's all very well to laugh, Alex,' his wife reproved him, 'but that's just the sort of thing that will go against him at his trial.'

'I've heard his poor wife has had to run away from her own home to escape the press,' said Aurora.

'And his innocent sons will no doubt be expelled from school,' said Tob.

'Justice will be seen to be done all right,' said Aurora, 'even before he's proved guilty.'

'I'm afraid people do like to see the proud fall,' said her father.

'I don't,' Lizzie spoke up suddenly. 'I think it's sad – especially for those little boys.'

'You mean his sons, I suppose?' came from Muriel. Lizzie met her steady gaze. Under the vast white damask cloth Tob's knee touched hers in a gesture of sympathy.

After lunch, Papa retired to his study to smoke and read the papers, Mama to the drawing-room and her embroidery frame. Maisie sat with her, reading a new novel from Mudie's, but Tob and the other two decided to walk to Hampton Court where the gardens had been opened to the public by the Queen.

As they walked across the bridge, Lizzie called out: 'Oh, look, look! The first swallows!'

Above the Thames, swallows swooped and soared untroubled by the passengers disembarking nearby from a steamer that had chugged its way upstream all morning from Westminster Bridge, carrying its cargo of Sunday trippers. The courtyard in front of the palace was full of carriages and happy family groups stepping down and wandering off into the gardens. As might have been expected on a fine Easter Sunday afternoon, the place was crowded, and Aurora, who didn't like crowds, hurried through the formal gardens with their clipped yews and trim box hedges and pushed on towards a meadow of mown grass beside the famous Long Water. Here, thousands of orange crocuses sprang up at their feet like flames, so many that Lizzie imagined that the ground they walked on was on fire.

When they'd had enough of strolling about beside the Long Water, Tob and Aurora escorted Lizzie to the railway station and put her on the London train. By the time they reached home, a late tea was being served in the drawing-room. Tob drank a cup with his mother, and then retired to the study with Papa, but Aurora remained. 'Tob looks tired,' said Mama. 'I do hope you didn't let him walk too far, Rory.'

'I can't make him sit down, Mama. He does what he likes. You know that.'

'You put Miss Thorburn on her train?'

Rory nodded.

'She's certainly a very independent young woman. Wherever did Tob pick her up?' asked Maisie with a sharp glance of triumph at her sister. Although Tob and Lizzie had spoken hardly a word to each other in her presence, Maisie had guessed that there was a hidden bond between them. She prided herself on her feminine intuition, which Rory, she believed, in spite of all her cleverness and her devotion to high ideals and higher thinking, lacked.

'Nobody picked her up,' said Rory crossly. 'It was she who picked Grandmama up. Literally. Saved her from crashing to the pavement out of a hansom cab, as you well know.'

'Oh! I'm sure she's as strong as a horse and could carry a hundredweight!' said Maisie.

'She's a strapping gel all right,' her mother agreed, 'but rather *gauche*, I think.'

'She refuses to wear corsets, you know,' Maisie continued. 'She says they give her indigestion.'

'It's rather an indelicate subject for conversation between mere acquaintances, isn't it?'

'Well, you know Maisie, Mama,' said Aurora. 'You know how she worms things out of people, makes them say more than they mean to – just for her own excitement.'

'We were talking about the fashions,' Maisie defended herself.

'What Lizzie actually said was that her ancestors had hunted whales, but she herself couldn't bear to have her breathing choked by whalebone stays.'

'Women must expect to suffer for the sake of elegance,' said Mama.

'And her clothes are terrible!' declared Maisie.

Aurora was nettled. 'There are other things in life, you know. Lizzie has a great many more important things to think about besides the fashions. And in any case she hasn't much money. She has to keep herself as a student. She is really and actually independent of her family; but she has to be very careful what she spends.'

'Surely her mother must make her an allowance for dress?' asked Muriel.

'I don't think she does, Mama. And I don't suppose Lizzie spends more than twenty pounds a year on dress.'

'You cannot *dress* on twenty pounds a year!' declared Muriel;. 'You can merely clothe yourself.'

'I don't think she cares about it much.'

'The more fool she!' was Maisie's comment. She thought,

but did not say so aloud, that Tob didn't care much about fashions either. But then, he was an artist, and artists did have such strange ideas about things . . . To be able to find a frump attractive was quite beyond Maisie's comprehension.

'She's not quite a lady, is she?' Muriel fixed her needle in the cloth as she spoke. 'Her family is something in trade, I believe?'

'So was Grandpapa,' Rory reminded her sharply.

'The Tarbutts have never been in trade,' Muriel said serenely. 'And your grandfather Ashwolde was hardly in business of the lower sort. He was an importer of commodities. He never dealt in cash, only in accounts. And in any case, my dear, that was a very long time ago.' She smiled tolerantly at Rory over the tops of her spectacles.

But Aurora was not tolerant. 'The Tarbutts dealt in cash all right,' she accused her mother. 'They collected it from starving tenants in the stonier parts of County Mayo.'

'If you refer to the ghastly disaster of the famine years I can assure you the Tarbutts were always merciful landlords in those times. It was just unfortunate that that rabble-rouser led a boycott on us.'

Aurora said no more. Her face was stern, but her mother continued heatedly: 'It was none of our fault that we were subjected to all that trouble. That agitator knew nothing of our ways; he didn't even come from Mayo, but was sent down from some Dublin newspaper to create insurrection in the West.' It was difficult to remain calm when talking about that affair, doubly difficult when one was blamed for it, quite unjustly, by a daughter whose opinions were formed by reading inaccurate information culled, no doubt, from those Fabian tracts she read, and which were, Muriel considered, dangerously near to sedition. 'It all came out in the courts later when he was arrested after trying to set fire to a wing of my

122

cousin's house in Galway. So I know what I'm talking about.' She put aside her embroidery frame. 'And as for your Tarbutt grandfather, he never soiled his fingers with coins. He had a rent-collector to do all that sort of thing.' She took off her glasses, and tried to change the direction of her thoughts. Anger and agitation did her no good, she knew, so she held the handle of the tea kettle firmly, although it was very hot from long simmering above its spirit lamp, and she tipped it, refilling the teapot before offering Rory another cup. She thought about Miss Thorburn. There were some things about that young woman that were interesting. She was going to be a doctor, a lady doctor. That might be almost as good as a nurse in the event of real sickness. And if, indeed, the girl was sweet on Tob, as Maisie had been insinuating, her devotion might, one day, prove useful. Any hint of marriage was, of course, absolutely out of the question. The girl herself, who seemed sensible enough, would have the wisdom to understand that; but if she was of the idealistic, self-sacrificing kind, she might, when the need arose, be made to serve him, to serve them all.

Lizzie leaned back in her corner seat as soon as the train moved. She didn't pick up the book she carried in her handbag; instead, she gazed out of the window, blind to the passing scene. She had no need of a book to entertain her when images as brightly coloured as magic lantern slides were scudding past the eyes of her memory, and the clearly enunciated speech of the Anglo-Irish Ascendancy echoed in her ears with an undeniable urgency. 'Green Arbour' was not like her own home; and the lives lived by the Ashwoldes were utterly different from the lives of people she knew in Scarborough and Robin Hood's Bay. The Ashwoldes seemed to Lizzie to live very comfortably, if not luxuriously, though Aurora had given her to understand that they considered themselves rather badly off, having come down in the world from some previously exalted level of wealth unimaginable to Lizzie. And Papa, it seemed, did no work at all. She had once, in all innocence, asked Aurora what he did for a living, and had received the reply: 'He's a gentleman.' It was taken for granted that he had no other occupation. Theirs was a world far removed from the lab smelling of formaldehyde, from dogfish dissection and talking about comparative anatomy with Prosy, from arguing about Darwin and wondering what her parents and all her floral sisters at the vicarage would say to his disturbing ideas. She thought rather wistfully about Tob. Dear Tob had had very little chance to talk to her. They never seemed to be alone nowadays. There was always Aurora between them. It occurred to Lizzie that in this threesome of friends Aurora was pushing Tob out.

She considered Alex Ashwolde's words: 'We all like to see the proud fall,' and wondered if they thought of her as proud. Probably not, she decided. She had noted Maisie's quick appraisal of her unfashionable clothes, and guessed her reaction: 'Clever, of course, but dowdy.' Probably, she had been pigeon-holed by Tob's mother as rather like Lady Wilde, not perhaps 'a vulgar Bohemian', but 'wrong-headed' and certainly 'not one of us.' Lizzie imagined they had placed her like a governess, suspended in a social limbo, belonging neither to her employers' class nor to the servants' hall, a shadowy figure but a necessary one in all good families, and lonely, standing always in the background, soberly dressed, restrained and restraining, solitary and unfulfilled. A flush of indignation for the fate of governesses spread through her: poor dedicated women, educated beyond the average for their sex, but doomed only to forcing some knowledge, and manners too, into moneyed little savages. It must often be a thankless task, she reflected. Very few were as lucky as Jane Eyre in netting romantic Mr Rochesters. She was suddenly thankful to whatever gods there might be for Great-uncle Mills's legacy, which had granted her independence and freed her from a governess's lot. She asked herself: Am I proud? Perhaps, in a way. And then she made a resolution: But I'm not going to fall – not to satisfy anybody – not for any reason.

Lizzie spent the rest of the Easter holiday swotting. Lectures and demonstrations had ceased at the end of term, but the library remained open, and there Lizzie and Prosy sat all morning and all afternoon, side by side at a small table, reading their textbooks and making notes. Occasionally, they exchanged whispered comments. When they emerged from this silent tomb-like atmosphere they blinked in the sunlight, blinked, too, at the news placards in the street and the hoarse shouts of urchin newsvendors. The trial of Oscar Wilde began on 26 April and continued till 1 May, when he was released on bail, the jury having been unable to agree on their verdict.

'What is the "Love that dare not speak its name?"' asked Lizzie, as she bought a paper and scanned the headlines. 'Nobody will tell me.'

'Well, you know – David and Jonathon – men loving men. It was quite accepted in ancient Greece, so my father says,' said Prosy.

The second trial began on 20 May while the girls were sitting their first medical exam, and like the exam it lasted for four days. When, exhausted by her efforts at concentrated thought, her attempts to abbreviate complicated arguments and write it all down neatly, Lizzie came out of the examination hall and into the light of ordinary day, she read the placards: 'WILDE TRIAL. GUILTY VERDICT.' People were actually running to buy the papers. They stood in the street and read them there and then, greedily. There was something horrible in their eagerness to learn of Oscar's downfall.

'Poor Oscar!' she murmured. 'Poor hunted man!' She thought of his recent, and often-quoted description of the sport of hunting: 'The unspeakable in full pursuit of the uneatable.' The unspeakable were hunting him now.

'Two years' hard labour,' said Prosy. 'Will he survive it?'

By the time their exam results were pinned up on the wall of the college corridor the world was already forgetting Oscar, and so too were the girls, such was their relief and jubilation when they learned that they had both passed. Now they could put behind them all those preliminaries which had been but a preparation for real life; now they could, at last, enter the London School of Medicine for Women: the Real Thing, was within their grasp.

SEVEN

They sat in the lecture theatre listening attentively to Dr Starling, famous pioneer in human physiology, and enjoying every word he said. He was a good speaker, and a warm-hearted man with the talent to distil his complex subject into terms simple enough for his students to understand. He would divide his programme into six parts: the musculo-skeletal system, the digestive system, the respiratory and circulatory systems, the brain and nervous systems, and finally, reproduction, which he would deal with plainly but delicately so that any mysteries remaining in these young ladies' minds about human sex would be uncovered and explained. They were to begin with the musculo-skeletal system, and during the afternoon practical session, they were expected to set up their own experiments to show how muscles contracted.

'I don't like these awful things you have to do with frogs,' Lizzie grumbled.

Prosy, who was neat-fingered, dissected out the little thigh muscle easily, but Lizzie's large impatient fingers found it difficult to do, and even more awkward to tie the tendon with a tiny cotton ligature to a wire lever, and to make the muscle, already drying and dying in the warm air, respond. It was supposed to contract when stimulated by electrical impulses, and, by a series of jerks, mark a tracing on a rotating drum, previously blackened by smoke from a candle flame. In the process, Lizzie's nose and chin gained quantities of soot.

A fortnight later, however, she found Dr Starling's lecture on the circulation of the blood as exciting as a novel. 'It's as good as a detective story by Conan Doyle, Prosy!' she declared. 'All that stuff Harvey discovered and worked out.' She was filled with wonder over what she considered a miracle: the thick muscle of the left chamber of the heart pumping fresh, red, oxygenated blood with great force into all parts of the body through muscular arteries capable of standing up to great pressure, and then the sucking back of the dark, used-up, deoxygenated blood through thin-walled veins to be recycled. She understood, with a sudden thrill, why the right chamber of the heart was smaller and less muscular than its left neighbour – the economy of it! – since it had only to push its blood through a short distance into expanding elastic lungs.

'William Harvey was one of the great physicians of all time,' she confided to Prosy as they walked back to their digs. Through careful observation and animal experiments he had dragged his subject out of the medieval obscurity of belief in theories, into the modern world of factual knowledge.

'Before him they didn't really understand the difference between arterial and venous blood,' said Prosy. 'And I suppose they didn't know about the valves inside the veins helping to return blood to the heart.'

'Starling said Harvey was quite a small man,' said Lizzie. 'And do you know? So was Hippocrates.' She remembered reading somewhere, years ago, that Aristotle had written of Hippocrates: 'He was a man of small stature, but a Great Physician.'

'Dr Harvey said the heart makes more than a thousand pulses in half an hour,' said Prosy. 'If he'd been counting his own he must have had a very slow heart. I counted mine while Dr Starling was lecturing and found it to be seventy per minute. That makes 2100 in half an hour.'

'Think what that means, Prosy! It's 100,000 in a day!'

'And that means about 36 million times a year!' said Prosy, who was quick at mental arithmetic.

It *was* a miracle, Lizzie thought, that a pump made of living muscle could be so efficient for so long. No humanly-manufactured pump could stand up to the same degree of wear and tear. The heart had some way of renewing and maintaining itself. It was a thrilling thought.

But anatomy was another matter. The first time they entered the dissecting room had been a solemn moment for all the girls. Nobody had fainted on seeing the corpses laid out on the tables; but they had been subdued and serious in the presence of death. Lizzie had comforted herself with the thought that these human remains hardly looked like human beings any more, they were so yellow and shrivelled, and absolutely cold, and smelling dreadfully of formaldehyde; but she couldn't help reflecting that they had probably once been hungry paupers dying in the workhouse, whose bodies were unclaimed by any relatives.

The students wore coarse, calico aprons to cover their dresses, and rolled their sleeves up to the elbow. Lizzie and Prosy sat opposite each other with a human arm between them; and at one end of their table, Lizzie's textbook, *Gray's Anatomy*, was propped open to display the appropriate page. It was an enormous book, more than a thousand pages long, and so full of Latin names that Lizzie was dismayed.

'Where on earth do we begin?' she demanded. 'This book is like ten Latin dictionaries rolled into one. There doesn't seem to be any rhyme or reason in the subject at all.'

A young woman demonstrator showed them how to start; and soon they had cut open the skin and laid bare the muscles of the shoulder, the deltoid fitting like a neat cap over the ball of the joint and, peeping out from under it, the biceps muscle, which everybody had heard of as being the one prize fighters developed to such gigantic size. It was, they discovered, attached above to the globular head of the humerus bone, and below the elbow joint to the head of the radius, so that when it contracted the hand could be brought close to the mouth. And there, when they carefully teased away the fine tissue, tucked into a groove between the biceps on the front and the triceps on the back of the bone, lay the main blood vessels and the two nerves carrying life and activity to the arm and hand.

'It's all so very neat, really, when you come to think of it,' said Lizzie as they soaped their hands, and scrubbed and scrubbed again in cold water after the session.

'What I want is a cup of tea,' said Prosy, fatigue for once cutting short her speech.

Tob was silent, watching Lizzie's face with joyful anticipation as she read the gilt-edged invitation card. Mr and Mrs Alexander Ashwolde requested the pleasure of her company on the occasion of their daughter, Maisie's, coming of age. In the left-hand bottom corner was printed RSVP and on the right was the word DANCING. He was thinking: She'll be with us for the whole weekend.

'But I can't dance!' she confessed.

'Oh, Lizzie, you should! You don't know what you're missing!' he cried. 'Dancing's such a liberation of the spirit!'

'And I haven't got a ballgown, either.' It was not the sort of thing you were expected to possess at medical school. Nor did she have the pair of white kid gloves that she believed were essential for such occasions. These difficulties were partly overcome by the offer of a blue-and-white-striped taffeta skirt from Aurora. To go with this Lizzie bought, with mixed feelings of pleasure and guilt, a beautiful Honiton lace blouse. She knew she looked well in it, but it was a terrible extravagance. She dismissed the kid gloves as unnecessary since she would not be dancing.

'I shall have to sit out on the edge of the dance floor with all the middle-aged chaperons,' she grumbled. 'But I expect I shall enjoy the fun.'

She was to remember the vivid colours of that weekend, the bright and dark shadows of it, all her life. The perfect English garden on that brightest and longest day of the year, the lawn mown smooth as a billiard table and spiked with white croquet hoops; the flowerbeds banked with roses and peonies, and behind them tall delphiniums of an intense blue; the scented archway covered with interwined jasmine and roses where a loose trailing branch caught at the silk shawl she'd thrown over her shoulders. The archway led to a walk down to the willows bordering the river, and here Tob's footsteps sounded heavy on the muddy bank because of the waders he was wearing. He took her hand, and she felt the heat of his palm, watched his eyes glitter with some inner excitement, and his face flush with joy. Lizzie knew he shared her feelings of elation on this magical midsummer's day.

'I may have to jump in to push us off the mudbanks,' he said as he untied the punt, 'but you can rest on the cushions, Lizzie.'

The other ladies of the house had retired before the exertions of the evening to come, but Lizzie had no need to rest. She had never felt so full of energy and happiness in her life before. He took the pole when

131

she was seated, and pushed the boat out into faster flowing water.

It was cool and calm on the river, so quiet that Lizzie could hear the rustle of water through her dabbling fingers, and the rhythmic plop and splash of Tob's pole seemed loud. They didn't speak. Tob concentrated on navigating his way through clumps of reeds, finding a channel through the shallows, and Lizzie idly watched a pair of wagtails running along the bank, saucily flaunting their fine feathers.

Ringing in her memory, she could still hear the game of croquet they had all been playing: the click of mallet on ball, the cries of dismay when a player missed a good shot, and Maisie's triumphant shouts whenever she hit her ball through a hoop. What Lizzie didn't hear was the exchange between Maisie and Tob when he croquetted Lizzie's ball right off the lawn into a flowerbed, and she had to run after it.

'Are you serious about this girl, Tob?'

'Good heavens! Are you thinking of wedding bells?'

'Naturally.'

'In that case, no. She's tone deaf, Maisie.'

'Does that matter so much?'

'It would be like building a house with one wall missing,' he'd said, watching Lizzie retrieve her ball from among the peonies. 'Do you know what, Maisie? She only knows it's Wagner when she hears the sopranos shrieking!' He had burst out laughing and ended up coughing, and had to support himself on the handle of his mallet while his shoulders heaved.

When they returned to the bank, Tob tied the punt to a fencing post before taking Lizzie's hand and pulling her through a curtain of drooping branches into the dome of green shade beneath a willow tree.

'It's just like a house inside,' she said.

'It's our sacred temple.' He held both her hands and

met her questioning look with steady, solemn eyes. 'It's where we must make our secret vows.' He leaned forward and kissed her forehead. 'I hope you won't give me a dusty answer, Lizzie.'

She was silent for a moment. Then, gently and deliberately, she kissed him on his lips that she had always thought of as so full and beautiful.

He pulled her towards him then, roughly and joyfully, crying: 'Oh Lizzie, Lizzie! My generous, undemanding – my gorgeous girl!' He smoothed away the hair from her temples and kissed her forhead, her eyelids, her mouth, and as she bent towards him, her ears and neck as well; and the shawl over her arm fell unheeded to the ground.

'Lizzie,' he said, suddenly, coming back to earth, 'I shall have to do my duty tonight as son of the house, you know, and dance with all the boring girls; but will you save the last dance for me?'

'You know I can't dance, Tob.'

'No, no. What I mean is, come out when the party's ending and walk with me in the garden under the stars. And then we can hide together in our sacred temple.'

What a child he is! she thought, as she stooped to pick up her shawl. 'Of course I will, Tob.'

They walked back through the vegetable garden hand in hand towards the lawn, and Lizzie, remembering Christina Rosetti's love poem began to recite it: '"My heart is like a singing bird / Whose nest is in watered shoot."' He stopped to embrace her on the path, murmuring: 'I think I shall die of happiness, my love.'

He left her when they reached the house. 'You go in through the conservatory,' he suggested. 'I'll have to go round the back to leave my waders in the shed; but I'll meet you in the kitchen for a cup of tea.'

Lizzie walked through the conservatory, which seemed excessively hot, although the doors were wide open and the glass roof thickly shaded by a climbing plant, and stood still for a moment in the drawing-room beyond. It was a large, L-shaped room. Chairs and music stands were arranged, awaiting the musicians in the smaller compartment of the L where Aurora's upright piano stood; armchairs had been pushed to the other end, no doubt to seat chaperons and mothers and other spectators. The carpet had been rolled back and the exposed floor sprinkled with Fullers' earth and polished to a smooth, slightly slippery surface for the dancers' feet. Some of the remaining small chairs had been removed, and ranged round the walls of the dining-room, where the table, pushed to one side, was laid ready to receive the food. A cold buffet supper would be served between nine and ten p.m. that evening. The rooms were empty; the whole house seemed to be asleep, but as Lizzie entered the hall Alex Ashwolde emerged from his study on a puff of cigar smoke.

'I thought I heard someone come in from the garden,' he said. He smiled sleepily at her. 'Let me take your shawl.' He took it from her with one hand, and as he did so his other hand slid down her back and gave her buttocks a smart pinch. She was too surprised to be as angry as he'd expected.

'Mr Ashwolde,' she said. 'I allowed you to take my shawl from me, not my gluteus maximus muscle as well.'

'Is that what you medicos call it?' he asked, quite unabashed. 'Whatever its anatomical name it's very well developed in your case, Miss Thorburn, if I may say so.'

She made no further comment because just then Tob appeared at the green baize-covered door that separated the hall corridor from the kitchen quarters.

'Anastasia has a cup of tea ready for us,' he said. 'Do you want one too, Papa?' But Ashwolde senior did not. Instead, he walked out of the front door, leaving it open in order to increase the draught of air through the house, and went to the stables to talk to Duffy about the horses. Several guests were to arrive that evening by train from London, and arrangements had to be made for Duffy to meet them at the station. Their discussion could not have lasted long, however, because very soon after Lizzie and Tob were seated in the kitchen drinking tea, Duffy came in and stood, silent and shy, by the door. Anastasia spoke without looking at him. 'Will you leave the door open, Duffy? For 'tis as hot as hell in here.' The range, though banked down to burn more slowly, was still alight. It was needed to provide hot water later for the guests who would be staying overnight.

Duffy, like the other servants in the house, was Irish, but unrelated to the others, who all belonged to the same family. Anastasia was parlourmaid, the cook her aunt, the housemaid Anastasia's cousin. Mrs Ashwolde had dispensed with ladies' maids for the sake of economy, using, instead, the services of a visiting seamstress once a week to repair and iron their dresses, collars and so on; her more essential servants she had imported, untrained, from Ireland after they had been rigorously interviewed and recommended by reliable opinions from across the water.

Anastasia poured out a cup of tea for Duffy and handed it to him without a word, but Lizzie guessed from the way the poor young man blushed and the way he gazed at Anastasia's pretty red curls, that he was hopelessly in love with her.

'Anastasia,' said Tob (rather arrogantly, Lizzie thought), 'You'll dance for us, won't you? Miss Thorburn is all agog to see an Irish jig, and I want to make another sketch of you doing it.'

Lizzie had heard nothing of this Irish jig before, and certainly had never expressed a wish to see it. This time it was Anastasia who blushed, demurring: 'Oh, Mr Tob –

Oh, Miss Lizzie – Miss Doctor Thorburn, sure 'tis nothing to write home about. He does go on about it so!'

'Why, Anastasia, you know you're a wonderful dancer! She won a medal for her dancing at a grand festival in Ireland last year,' he explained to Lizzie.

The girl climbed up on the scrubbed deal table, and lifting her black skirt above her neat ankles and her small black-shod feet, she began to dance, singing a few bars of 'Phil the Fluter' to give herself the rhythm. Tob took it up, clapping his hands and stamping on the stone floor. After a minute or so young Duffy took a mouth organ out of his pocket and blew the tune to Tob's words:

> With a toot on the flute
> And a twiddle on the fiddle-o
> Hoppin' up and down like
> A herrin' on the griddle-o

Lizzie was amazed at the speed of Anastasia's feet, entranced and captivated by the complicated rhythmic patterns they performed on a space no bigger than a square yard. And all the time her heels and toes were moving, the rest of her body was so marvellously balanced that her black frock and white apron remained unruffled and her white maid's cap still sat snugly over her curls. Lizzie clapped enthusiastically when the dance ended. Tob, who by this time was scribbling wildly on his sketch-pad, demanded: '*Encore*! *Encore*!'

But Anastasia spoke primly. 'I must get on with me work now, sir.' And turning to Lizzie she added: 'I'll bring you some warm water up to your room, Miss.'

As Lizzie went upstairs, Muriel Ashwolde opened the door of her own room. She was wearing a dressing-gown, and her hair hung loosely around her shoulders.

'Have the musicians arrived already?' she asked.

'Oh, no,' said Lizzie, glancing at her wristwatch. 'It's only half-past five.'

'I thought I heard music,' said her hostess. 'Tuning up . . .' She went back into her room, and Lizzie walked on to hers, which was a small dressing-room beside Aurora's. Maisie had moved in with her sister for the night, and her bedroom, along with all the spare rooms in the house, was ready to receive London visitors.

When Anastasia arrived with the water in a copper can Lizzie thanked her. 'I wish I could dance like you, Anastasia,' she said.

'What would you be wantin' that for, Miss?'

'You won't see me on the dance floor tonight, you know. I simply have no idea how to do it.'

Anastasia had never before heard of a girl who couldn't dance, and pitying her for such a lack of grace, she tried to console her. 'But Doctor Miss Thorburn,' she said gently, 'what use is any of them old jigs to you, a great doctor and all?'

'I'm not a doctor yet, you know.'

'Sure, think of the grand day when you'll be making all them miracle cures, and comforting the sick and dying now, will you? What will dancing be to you then, but worldly vanities – glory be to God!'

'I suppose so,' said Lizzie, rather half-heartedly to Anastasia's way of thinking.

No lamps were lit, it was not yet dark, that long day's night had not yet descended when the guests arrived. Maisie, as pretty as a china doll in her dress made of layer upon layer of pink tulle, stood in the middle of the drawing-room surrounded by girls in many-coloured silks who fluttered, uttering parakeet cries of greeting and congratulations in high excited voices, while the men stood in a more sober outer ring like magpies in their evening clothes. Purposefully above the noise, the

137

musicians played selections from 'The Gaiety Girl'. Muriel Ashwolde, majestic in dark blue velvet, her splendid shoulders startlingly white above the low-necked gown, stood in the hall to greet late arrivals, but her husband, tightly strapped together by a red cummerbund round his too-ample middle, had tired of standing to formal attention with her, and was drifting round the edge of all the activity, awaiting the moment when he could assert his authority as master of ceremonies, and the dancing would commence.

Lizzie thought Aurora, dressed in amber silk and wearing a red rose threaded through her hair, looked like a goddess. She had cut a few sprays of jasmine and tied them together into a nosegay for Lizzie, who pinned it to her blouse. As she came downstairs she caught sight of herself in a gilded mirror and was surprised by the image of a young, unsophisticated person, who might have been a schoolgirl still, with her shining apple cheeks, her eager blue eyes, and her fair hair piled on top of her head, but always threatening to tumble down. She thought: I suppose I'll do.

Knowing none of the guests, although Aurora made an attempt to introduce her to one or two of them, Lizzie kept herself in the background, a watcher on the edge of things. Once, she caught Tob's eye, and he flashed a smile at her above the crowd; but she knew she could expect to see very little of him till much later in the evening.

The music stopped, the hubbub of talk ceased, and Alex Ashwolde cleared the floor; the elder ladies took their seats, and Lizzie joined them while the younger people stood around the walls. After the dancing began, Lizzie was attentive for a time, watching as a waltz followed the lancers and a polka followed the waltz; but after an hour or so the spectacle became monotonous, and she began to look forward to the supper interval. Behind the green baize door, Duffy, whose job it was to trim and polish and light the lamps in his little lamp room beyond the scullery, signalled to the maids to carry them one by one into their appointed places. Lizzie caught Anastasia's eye and smiled as she advanced into the drawing-room proudly carrying her oil lamp, its soft light glowing on her face and the long white trailers she'd attached to her cap for this splendid occasion. The dancers were performing a 'Roger de Coverley' skipping in pairs under an archway of raised arms. It was a communal dance, which Lizzie recognised as one she'd taken part in at a children's Christmas party once, in Scarborough. She thought: Anastasia's a better dancer than all these jogging donkeys, and prettier, too, than any other girl in the room, except Maisie, the birthday girl in her pink cloud, or, perhaps, that young stranger who stood beside the conservatory door fanning herself with an ivory and lace fan, her cheeks flushed and her eyes bright with exercise and expectation. But then, it might have been her dress which made the girl look so lovely, in billowing white taffeta, the skirt embroidered with scarlet poppies. As the orchestra began a very lively waltz, Lizzie watched with a revival of interest as Tob came eagerly towards the girl and grasped her hand. It seemed to Lizzie on the other side of the floor that they took off with frightening speed. She saw Muriel look up for a moment, anxiously, as Tob and the girl in white flew by her in a mad whirl. They passed Lizzie several times without noticing her in their circling, the girl laughing up into Tob's eyes, her left hand resting on his shoulder, the fingers still holding the fan which lay starkly in an oblique line across the black cloth below his collar. He was smiling down at her. He was oblivious of Lizzie, oblivious of all but the joy of the passing moment. He looks like the god Pan, a smiling happy pagan, Lizzie thought, as jealousy darted painfully through her. He is a Greek pagan, wanting pleasure only.

Just as they passed the conservatory door, on what was to be their last circuit of the room, he bent his head close to the girl's neck. He was coughing violently, and a fresh poppy suddenly burst into bloom on her shoulder, expanding and shedding its petals down the back of her dress. Tob seemed to crumple as he fell away from her. As he leaned against the door the girl, touching her shoulder and looking at her fingers, saw the blood. For a moment Lizzie could see her face. The mouth, open in horror, must have cried out, although it was impossible to hear the sound above the music as, skirting the empty chairs along the wall, she fled from Tob towards her mother. Muriel, talking behind her fan to a friend, had seen nothing. When Lizzie glanced back towards the conservatory, Tob had disappeared into it. Nobody seemed to have noticed the manner of his going: the music didn't stop, the dancers still danced on as Lizzie slipped out of the room and came face to face with Anastasia standing in the hall like one entranced, her ears full of music, her eyes wide with wonder.

'Mr Tob's been taken ill, Anastasia,' said Lizzie. 'Please bring some hot water and a basin with towels to the conservatory. But mind you go round the outside of the house.' She was thinking: It was arterial blood, bright red and oxygenated, straight from the lungs.

Anastasia shook herself as if coming out of a dream, but she ran without a word into the kitchen while Lizzie made her way through the front door and round the side of the house to the conservatory. At its entrance grew a clump of white marguerites that gleamed like lamps. They seemed to have absorbed the sun's energy throughout that long midsummer's day, and were now reflecting it into the gathering darkness. The only light in the conservatory was from the fading twilight and a beam from the door open to the drawing-room. Lizzie walked across the tiled floor to shut it, blocking out the noise of music and laughter.

Tob sat crouched in a cane chair backed by dark palms in tubs, and bougainvillaea made a green gloom above his head; but even in the poor light Lizzie could see how white his face was. A streak of dried blood stuck to his chin and stained the front of his white shirt; and with his left hand he grasped his chest as if his ribs hurt. She knelt down on the tiles beside him and took his other hand. He opened his eyes and grasped her fingers with desperation. 'Lizzie – dear Lizzie – don't leave me,' he gasped, and immediately began to cough again. A fresh spurt of blood came into his mouth. He leaned forward and let it spill on to the floor.

'Don't try to talk Tob,' she said. 'I'll get help.' She felt him shivering. 'You're cold, my dear.' She guessed he must have a fever to make him shiver so, when under the glass it was still uncomfortably hot.

Anastasia arrived with the water and towels and stood quietly by while Lizzie bathed Tob's face and gave him a towel to blot any more bleeding that might occur. Looking up at the maid's figure Lizzie thought: Anastasia's no fool. She's got quite as much wit inside her head as in those jigging feet of hers. She said: 'Find the master, Anastasia, and tell him Mr Tob's sick. Tell him where to come.'

Without a word Anastasia left them.

It seemed a long time before he came. All the while Tob sat huddled and silent, Lizzie kneeling with her arms around him. He spoke once, licking his lips. 'I'm thirsty, Lizzie.' When at last his father did arrive he was surprisingly calm, almost, so Lizzie thought, as if he had expected the event. He had not been idle during the interval.

'Duffy's taken the girl and her mother home in the dogcart,' he explained. 'It seems this girl was dancing

141

with Tob when it happened. They don't live far away – only the other side of Bushy Park. So Duffy will soon be back, and then we can carry Tob upstairs to his own room. How are you Tob, poor old chap?' But as Tob made no reply he continued talking to Lizzie. 'I've sent a lad running for the doctor. He should be here shortly.'

Anastasia had guessed Tob's needs, and now came in with a cup of tea for the invalid, who drank it greedily. Ashwolde took the opportunity to pull Lizzie out into the garden. He spoke in a low voice: 'We'll have to carry him up the back stairs. Perhaps, if the guests are still busy with supper, nobody will notice.'

'Hadn't you better inform Mrs Ashwolde?' asked Lizzie.

'On no account.' He was suddenly firm. 'I don't want Muriel worried. The party must go on. *Noblesse oblige*, you know . . . And . . .' His voice dropped almost to a whisper. 'This is a very important day for her and Maisie, you see. And if this got talked of – well, it might spoil Maisie's chances, don't you know. It's not the sort of thing a family likes to be blazoned about. As a matter of fact, in my opinion, it's a good deal worse than a bar sinister on one's escutcheon.'

Lizzie couldn't help thinking: That girl with blood on her dress, who lives only the other side of Bushy Park, she knows what happened, and so does her mother, and before another week is over, it will certainly be blazoned about.

Alex approached Tob again and, as if being friendly with an unknown dog, he patted his son's head. 'Are you altogether done up, poor old chap? What about a glass of brandy?' When Tob nodded, he scuttled away to fetch a glass, glad to be able to hide his feelings of shame and inadequacy in some useful action.

The boy sent running for the doctor came back with a message to say that Dr Harmer would be delayed about an hour as he was dealing with an obstetric case, but he'd sent a bottle of laudanum mixture to be administered to the patient. 'To stop the cough,' the boy explained, as he had been told to do. 'And make . . . the pain . . . easier.' He was quite breathless from running. Lizzie gave Tob the first dose.

As soon as Duffy returned, he helped Ashwolde to carry Tob across the lawn and round to the back of the house. Together they lifted him up the narrow servants' staircase, Ashwolde panting as he struggled to keep up with the younger and fitter man. Lizzie followed with Tob's coat and the towels. They laid him on his own bed in which Anastasia had already placed a stone hot-water bottle. At Lizzie's bidding, she fetched two more pillows, as his breathing was easier when he was propped up.

'The bleeding seems to have stopped now,' said Ashwolde. 'Did he lose much blood, do you suppose?'

Lizzie made no reply, but helped Duffy to take off Tob's bloodstained shirt and replace it with a clean nightshirt. The laudanum was gradually overcoming the pain in his chest, but he was growing drowsy.

'Well, I think I'd better be getting back to my guests,' said Ashwolde. 'You'll be staying with him, Miss Thorburn?' he asked, pausing at the door. The others followed him out; and Lizzie sat down beside the bed to watch.

In a little while Tob opened his eyes, and seeing her beside him he put a hand out over the sheet to grasp hers.

'Will you do something for me?'

'If I can Tob, dear, if I can . . .'

'Will you let your hair down over my face?'

She stood up and, taking the pins out of her bun, she leaned over him and let her hair fall like a curtain over his head.

'Now kiss me hardy girl,' he ordered, and when she did so he said softly: 'It's a sort of consummation.' But when he tasted her tears he exclaimed: 'Why, Lizzie, darling, you're crying!'

'I always was a crybaby,' she confessed.

'Angels' tears . . . wash away the evil in the world . . .' He sighed deeply. Very soon he was asleep.

She took the opportunity to slip out of the room in order to change her clothes. She could hear the music begin again below. Voices and laughter floated upstairs as guests left the dining-room and returned to the dancing. A faint aroma of tobacco hung in the air, so Lizzie guessed that her host had taken some of the men to the study to drink and smoke. She lit the candle by her bed and placing it on the dressing table she brushed and pinned up her hair once more. She took off Aurora's striped, taffeta skirt and laid it neatly across the bed; she unbuttoned the Honiton lace blouse and packed it carefully into her small valise together with her brush and comb and toothbrush wrapped inside her face flannel; she put on her daydress and changed her shoes for stout walking boots; she took her long cloak out of the wardrobe and hung it over the back of a chair. She was ready to travel. She was determined that if Tob was moved to hospital that night she would go with him.

It was Duffy who brought Dr Harmer up by way of the servants' entrance when he arrived at last. He was a kind man with menacing black eyebrows and a neatly pointed black beard. He used to joke with nervous patients saying he couldn't hurt a fly, that there was not an ounce of harm in him in spite of his name, and would the little boy (or girl) like to smack his hand? This often made children laugh, and the bolder ones did, occasionally, smack his hand, while anxious mothers, hearing his amiable joking, loosened a little their clasp on their darlings.

'Are you a relative, Miss Thorburn?' he asked. 'Duffy told me on the way up that you're a nurse.'

144

'I'm a friend of Aurora's. And I'm actually a medical student.'

'Really? Well now, that is interesting. You must be at the new London School of Medicine for Women then? You're the first I've met, so far, of the new breed.' He approached the bed. 'I'll need your help with examining poor Tob.'

'I'm not at hospital yet,' said Lizzie. 'And I know nothing about medicine; but I'll do my best.'

'That's all any of us can ever do, Miss Thorburn; and it's usually not enough.' He slipped a thermometer under Tob's tongue and took his pulse. 'Temperature 101, pulse 110,' he announced.

Tob was drowsy and obedient as Lizzie lifted his shirt and held him in a sitting position while the doctor percussed his back. 'Now listen carefully,' he said. He placed the third finger of his left hand just above Tob's shoulder blade and tapped smartly with the third finger of his right hand, half inch by half inch all the way down to the bottom of the rib cage. Lizzie heard the drum-note deepen where there was a cavity in the lung, and then suddenly become muffled by a collection of fluid, 'probably a bloodstained pleural effusion,' as he explained. He made her listen with his stethoscope at the point where Tob had felt pain when he breathed deeply, and she heard a scratching sound.

'It's what's called a pleural rub,' said the doctor.

On the other side of the chest, Lizzie could hear scattered tissue-paper crackles when Tob took a breath.

'Laennec invented the stethoscope,' said Dr Harner. 'Do you know how that came about? It's a good story. He was a Breton from Quimper, but he worked in a Paris hospital, where he had wards full of consumptives. TB was even more common at the beginning of the century than it is now. He didn't like putting his ear against their chests to hear what was going on inside, because they were mostly crawling with vermin in those days – and, indeed, some still are. He was also very keen on walking in the open air; and one day, while walking across a field, he saw some children playing with a long, hollow log. When one of them scratched one end with a twig his friends, listening at the other end, could hear the scratching loudly magnified, as Laennec did, too, much to his surprise, when he listened. So when he went back to his wards he rolled up a piece of card into a cylinder which he used as an ear trumpet. That was the first stethoscope. Later, he had one made in wood, and later still it became what we now use.' He took his stethoscope from Lizzie's hands and hung it round his neck. 'He was an observant man, and his mind was ready for what he saw. As the great Pasteur has said: "Chance favours the prepared mind." Shall we go outside, Miss Thorburn?'

Dr Harmer had never thought he'd live to see the day when he'd have to work with one of these new female medical students – strange creatures, neither man, woman, nor good fresh herring, as he imagined them to be. Yet this Miss Thorburn seemed a normal enough young person, as docile and disciplined as he could wish, and sensible what's more. He was surprised to find himself, if anything, exhilarated by the encounter. The fact was that Dr Harmer was a teacher manqué, and in Lizzie he found the perfect pupil, completely ignorant, but keen and intelligent enough to learn, and in any case a captive listener. In spite of his prejudices his professional pride pricked him into showing off his expertise a bit.

Lizzie covered Tob with a blanket and eased the pillows behind his head before following the doctor out of the room. They stood on the landing and spoke in subdued voices.

'Do his parents know how ill he is?' she asked.

'Oh, I think so. He's been ill for some years, you

know; but he seemed so much better after his stay in that sanatorium in the French Alps last year, that they all had hopes of his recovery. You're wondering that they don't seem much concerned tonight? Well, Mrs Ashwolde wouldn't want her daughters to nurse him for fear of the infection spreading to them. And in any case, they must carry on this evening as if nothing whatsoever is amiss.' He sighed. 'It's their sort of courage, you see. And of course, if the rumour got around of TB in the family, the girls' chances of marriage would be blighted.'

'What are Tob's chances of survival?' she asked impatiently.

'Not great, I'm afraid. If there was a cavity on only one side we could put gas into the chest to make that lung collapse, and so give it a rest from breathing. But that would make him use the other lung more, and as that too is diseased, the trouble would simply get worse. But I shall send him to the Brompton Chest Hospital in London. I can get a bed for him there. I know one of their specialist chest physicians. I was his house physician once – some time ago, you know. But my old governor's still there. And he's an expert in this new artificial pneumothorax.'

'What's that?' asked Lizzie.

'It's a very neat idea, but needs a skilled hand. A little inert gas (nitrogen is what they use) is inserted into the thorax to obliterate the cavity. This will probably stop the bleeding – unfortunately, in his case, not the disease. But he'll be well looked after – made comfortable at least.'

Lizzie hung her head, unable to speak.

'Oh come now, Miss Thorburn,' he protested. 'We must keep a stiff upper lip. Patients do die, you know.' She made no comment, so he continued. Knowledge, he thought, gives courage, although to Lizzie his instruction was adding only misery. 'I know it's hard to accept, especially when you've known the patient as a boy, as I have. Such a gifted child, he was! He could have been, he could have done, anything. But of course, with this blight on his young life what could his family do? That's why he was allowed to study art. It was useless to put him into business or the City. I believe he has a gift for drawing, though he's not as good as his sister, I'm told. Aurora's too good – too clever by half in my opinion. It's not good for a girl to be too good at anything. Gives them ideas . . .' He became aware that Lizzie might fall into this category of girls, and tried to make light of what he'd said. 'I suppose that's what you've got, Miss Thorburn? Ideas, eh? I can see you'll make a good medical student, though it goes against the grain to have to admit it. Women doctors! I never thought I'd live to see that day. Well, well . . .

'But back to the matter in hand. We were considering treatment. Complete rest is what our young patient must have. No walking. He must be carried.' He strode to the end of the corridor and back again to where she stood. 'I suppose tuberculosis is indiscriminate,' he mused, swinging his stethoscope like a clock pendulum, 'but it does seem to hit the brightest and best. When you think that Keats and Chopin, and the lovely Marguerite Gauthier who was the original heroine of Dumas's *La Dame aux Camellias* . . .'

'And the Brontë sisters,' Lizzie interrupted him.

'They too. And even the great Laennec himself. One can't help feeling bitter when one knows they all died young of TB. The first half of our century seems to have been most lethal. And when one considers that one in six of all young adults in our cities, even today, will die of it before they reach the age of thirty . . .' He folded his stethoscope abruptly and put it in his pocket. 'But the ravages of the disease, though still terrible, are less now than they were. Only forty years ago, as many as

148

a quarter of our urban population succumbed to it. So we are making headway, slowly. There's no known cure for it yet, but prevention is possible, if only all people of goodwill come together to prevent it.' He looked at her quickly, thinking she seemed turned to stone by what he'd told her. Had he perhaps been too dramatic, over emotive for a female student? It was how he would speak to a fellow doctor; and if these women wanted to be doctors, well then, they must take the blows inflicted by disease and accept our common human condition equally with their male counterparts. He paused for a further few seconds to remind himself that she was a friend of the patient's sister, and so must feel some personal involvement in the case. She did look rather down in the mouth, and he certainly didn't want her to fail him by growing hysterical when he needed her help, so he resumed his discourse on a more optimistic note.

'But of course there are things we can do in our struggle with the disease.' He could hear the melody of a well known Strauss waltz rising from the rooms below and was slightly annoyed that he couldn't put a name to it. 'TB is the great epidemic of our time,' he said. 'We must treat it as an infectious fever. That means isolation of infectious patients in sanatoria. Overcrowding among the poor must be reduced, and the nutrition of the lower classes improved, as well as hygiene, of course. Spitting should be prohibited in enclosed spaces.' He sighed. 'Perhaps, one day, some form of vaccination as for smallpox . . . It's a programme that might daunt the hardiest. We won't cure it in my lifetime; but perhaps in yours, Miss Thorburn . . . Who knows?' He was a little worried that the girl made no response whatever to his eloquent plea; but he reassured himself that, no doubt, she had learned something from him. 'I'm going to the station now, Miss Thorburn,' he said. 'I'm going to reserve a carriage for our patient on the mail train to

London. It leaves, I believe, soon after four a.m. I daresay Ashwolde will want to accompany his son.'

'I will go with them,' said Lizzie. She held out her hand. 'And thank you, Dr Harmer. You have been very kind.'

He was much relieved that she seemed to have come back to life. 'When he wakes,' he said, 'give him a double dose of laudanum. We don't want him having a massive haemorrhage while on the train, do we?' He returned to the sickroom to pick up his Gladstone bag, and then quickly left the house, going down by the servants' staircase as he had come.

Tob was more wide awake than she'd realised, for he said suddenly: 'They'll send me to the Brompton this time, Lizzie. I always thought I'd end up there.'

'I shall go with you, Tob,' she said calmly. 'So don't be afraid.' She poured another dose of laudanum into a spoon. 'It stops the coughing and bleeding.'

He nodded. 'I know. And gives me dreams too.' But he swallowed his medicine.

She turned down the wick of the lamp near his bed. 'Go to sleep now, my love,' she murmured.

She went to the window and stood looking at the garden below, bathed in moonlight, at the jasmine-scented archway leading to the weeping willow, the secret trysting place which would never be visited again. She couldn't see the stables and the coachyard which were on the other side of the house, but she could hear, coming from them, sounds of traps being moved, of carriage wheels and horses clattering over cobbles, shouts of drivers, laughter and gay voices crying out farewells. The birthday party was ending. It must have been well after midnight. She had another three hours to wait before leaving for the station. She knew she must keep her feelings, like horses, under a tight rein or they would gallop away out of control. She stared up at the moon, so cold, so solitary, and remembered Shelley's poem:

> Art thou pale for weariness
>   Of climbing heaven, and gazing on the earth,
> Wandering companionless
>   Among the stars that have a different birth?

Many of her questions about Tob, much of the mystery surrounding him were explained, once she understood the nature of his illness, the long struggle he had endured knowing he might never recover, never be strong enough to marry and support a wife and family, would probably die young . . .

Muriel Ashwolde entered the room so hastily that she didn't see Lizzie standing at the window. She went straight to her son, lying now without pain in his deep sleep. She bent down and kissed his forehead gently, then stifling a sob with her lace handkerchief she turned and was about to go when she saw Lizzie. Muriel drew herself up, dabbed her mouth with the handkerchief, and said: 'Oh, Miss Thorburn, I'm so glad you're looking after my son. You've been wonderful, I hear. And Alex tells me you'll be travelling with them to London later tonight. He's trying to get a little sleep now, but he'll call you in good time.'

'I will do everything I can to make Tob comfortable, Mrs Ashwolde,' Lizzie promised, coming forward with outstretched hand. 'I'm most awfully sorry all this happened at such a time. I do hope it hasn't quite spoiled Maisie's party.'

'Naturally, we are all sorry,' Muriel agreed majestically. 'These things are sent to try us, I suppose. But I am very grateful to you. We all are.' She lingered as if she wanted to say more.

'I shall always treasure happy memories of 'Green Arbour',' said Lizzie. 'I enjoyed playing croquet on the lawn.'

Muriel suddenly looked relieved. 'Ah, yes. The garden

is delightful in summer, Miss Thorburn. I'm so glad you enjoyed the croquet.' And, lifting her large nose and the hem of her skirt, she swept out. She stopped for a moment in the corridor to wipe her hands on her lace handkerchief. What a blessing it had been after all, that the girl had been in the house, and so had saved her and her daughters the responsibility of nursing Tob! There would have been blood and sputum and other unmentionable things, which no doubt the coarser fibres of her class of person would be more suited to cope with than herself.

Lizzie was surprised, as they stood in the yard, that the noise made by the dawn chorus of birds didn't wake everybody up. A riot of competing songsters claiming territorial feeding rights for their newly-hatched young filled the air as blackbirds, thrushes, chaffinches, robins, wrens, tits and even sparrows all voicing the triumph of procreation, let slip a deafening *Jubilate Deo* from a thousand tiny throats.

Tob was carried to the wagonette on whose back seat, long enough for six or even eight passengers, he was able to lie. Lizzie covered him with a thick, plaid rug, and placed a cushion under his head. As soon as they reached the station, Duffy located the carriage reserved by Dr Harmer on the waiting train, and with the help of a porter and his mailbag trolley they managed to wheel Tob to it. Duffy stood mournfully at the door till the train began to move. Tob lay still, sunk deep in opiate ponds of slumber all the way to Waterloo; he did not stir, even when the train jolted to a stop at intermediate stations to pick up mail. No passengers came aboard at such an early hour. Ashwolde sat without speaking in one corner opposite Tob, Lizzie in the other. Half-hypnotised by the rhythmic clicking of the train wheels, she felt her eyelids droop, felt herself being carried off into sleep when she heard Alex talking in quick, urgent tones.

'I suppose you were outraged by what happened this afternoon, Miss Thorburn?'

She shook herself awake, trying to remember her outrage, trying to think back to the afternoon, yesterday afternoon, only twelve hours, but it seemed decades of life ago.

'You feminists want equality with men, I believe, in all walks of life; but I wonder if you ever think how weak men are – if you have any idea of the power, the sexual power you have over men?'

She guessed, with a slight shock, that he was going to talk about that pinching of her bottom in the hall, and was angry with him, angry because he'd woken her, and more so for thinking the matter worth bringing up at a time when his son, lying opposite him, was at death's door.

'My God! What power over us you women have when we fall in love with you!' He gazed out of the window and spoke as if to himself: 'Love swipes the feet from under you with one stroke of a Samurai sword, and brings you to your knees. You stretch out your hand like a pauper begging for a pennyworth of hope. And then it pushes you into marriage!' he added bitterly.

'What's wrong with marriage?' she asked.

He turned towards her and, as if remembering her presence, checked his anger. 'It's all right for women, I suppose,' he said. 'It's what all girls want, isn't it? For them it's security, and social status, and having children, and being able to dress babies up in pretty frills. But what women forget is that nature makes men lustful.' Indignation raised his voice again. 'They have this wild animal, you know, imprisoned between their thighs, which leaps up with a terrible desire, crying out for deliverance. It's not their fault, it's how God made them.'

153

Lizzie glanced at Tob to reassure herself that he couldn't hear what his father was saying; she clasped and unclasped her hands in her lap. She felt terribly embarrassed, though she realised that Ashwolde had, in all probability, merely drunk too much whisky.

'Marriage is all right as long as your wife wants children, but when she's had enough of them and turns you out of her bed, what's a chap supposed to do then? Our Christian religion insists on monogamy, adultery causes scandal and misery, and in any case is too expensive even for the very rich, and brothels are dangerous to health. What sane fellow wants to risk picking up syphilis? And any little harmless patting of a buttock is regarded by decent girls like yourself as an insult and filthy lechery! Women are cold fish,' he added, turning away once more to gaze out at the dawn-grey landscape beyond the window.

His revelations of the secrets of his married life opened up a frightening abyss in Lizzie's imagination. Things were not, were never, what they appeared to be, and life, it seemed, was difficult even for the well-heeled. A gust of conflicting emotions seized her tired spirit. What could she say? What could anyone do? She felt rather sorry for Ashwolde, but she quite understood that if his haughty wife gave way to his sexual demands she would probably end up with a baker's dozen of thirteen instead of three children, and become like some of those poor women in the East End of London with a toddler always clinging to her skirts and a baby forever crying at her breasts; and the small fortune she had inherited would soon dwindle away into feeding many mouths, into grocers' and haberdashers' and doctors' bills. The problem seemed insoluble. Moreover, Lizzie was still angry that he could worry about his own difficulties when his only son lay dying before him, and she resented being burdened with his troubles when she herself already had more

154

to carry than she thought she could bear. She sighed. 'Mr Ashwolde,' she said. 'I have altogether forgotten the little harmless lechery.'

He turned again to look at her, and began to laugh. 'You really are an amazing girl,' he said. 'Quite out of the ordinary.'

At Waterloo, he found a porter and a bathchair. Tob coughed a little as they lifted him into it, but he did not bleed again. Outside the station they hired an old four-wheeled growler, whose springs were none too good, and Tob groaned when the cab jolted, for by now the effects of the laudanum were beginning to weaken; but at least there was enough space inside for him to travel in a semi-reclining position. As soon as they arrived at the hospital, two porters carried him in. He opened his eyes as they laid him on a trolley, and looked around. 'Papa?' he asked. But his father was disappearing into an office with a staff nurse who wanted to record some details about her new patient. He caught Lizzie's eye and tried to smile. She came to the trolley quickly. 'Write . . .' he said. 'You will write?'

'I'll come and visit you, dear Tob,' she said, as he was wheeled away to the bed prepared for him.

Outside in the street the sun was shining. The long night's vigil was over and a new bright day had begun. Ashwolde stood on the hospital steps blinking like an owl in unaccustomed daylight, till suddenly he cried out: 'Oh Tob! My son, my poor boy!' and tears rolled unchecked down his cheeks. Lizzie put her arm through his, and they stood, linked together, weeping.

After a moment, she released him, wiped her eyes and blew her nose, and said: 'What we both need is some breakfast.'

Ashwolde, returning slowly to his role of gentleman, then hailed a cab and ordered the driver to take them to Brown's Hotel in Dover Street, where they breakfasted in complete silence. She was hungry, which, when she remembered that she'd eaten nothing since lunch the day before, and drunk nothing since that cup of tea in the kitchen while Anastasia danced on the table, was not surprising. They parted company after breakfast, Ashwolde to return to Waterloo station, Lizzie to Doughty Street.

'May I drop you off at your rooms?' he asked politely, as he hailed a cab.

'Thank you, but no,' she said. 'I want to walk a bit in the fresh air.'

He paused, with one foot on the step, and turned as if he wanted to say more, and she, afraid of further private confessions in a public place, said hurriedly: 'I will write to Mrs Ashwolde to thank her for all her hospitality. And please tell Aurora to look me up when next she's in town. And goodbye, Mr Ashwolde.'

'Goodbye, my dear,' was all he said.

Sunday morning bells were ringing as Lizzie set off to walk to Doughty Street, deep, demanding bells nearby, summoning people to church, and a lighter, more frivolous peal, like girlish laughter announcing from somewhere more distant that a wedding was about to be celebrated. She needed a wash and brush-up; she needed sleep if she was to cope with a normal day's work tomorrow, and Dax, whom kind Mrs Plumm had been looking after for the weekend, would need a walk, but she couldn't face going back to her digs yet. Dax would hurl himself into her skirt, and Mrs Plumm would want to know why she had returned so early in the day. She would be bursting with all sorts of questions Lizzie didn't want to answer about the party, which Mrs Plumm insisted on elevating to the status of 'ball'. She would demand descriptions of the house, the food, the dancing and the girls' dresses, and what popular tunes did the band play? Lizzie dreaded all this gossip, which only twenty-four hours ago would have given her pleasure to indulge in.

What she desired now, more than anything else, was a pause in time, a little space in solitude and silence in which to arrange all the events and feelings which had crowded upon her, leaving her battered and confused. She thought: Twenty-four hours ago I was a different person. It was as if many years had passed since she'd travelled to 'Green Arbour' to celebrate a birthday. She had walked in the beautiful garden, played croquet on the lawn, floated in a trance-like state on the little river, and had then entered Tob's house of dreams under the willow tree where the magic of love's recognition had encircled them with promises of joy and shy, fluttering hopes for the future. It seemed unbearably unjust that this sweet daydream should, so soon, be twisted into nightmare by the sudden flowering of scarlet poppies on a white silk dress. There, in the midst of music and rejoicing, vitality had ebbed from the body of her beautiful young man.

She heard the voice of Dr Harmer's harsh realism, and saw, in her mind's eye, Tob's grave being dug before he was yet dead. She flinched at her own imagining of earth being thrown on his beloved face as he lay in it. Indeed, indeed, it was a dusty answer that poor Tob had got from life. And later, when she learned of the cracks and crevasses in which Alex Ashwolde's life, his disappointments, his hostilities and even rage were buried, she knew that a sick heart hid behind 'Green Arbour's' smiling mask.

She would have liked to enter an empty church, to sit down there and talk to God in silence; but the churches were all full and noisy with Sunday worshipping. So instead she walked into Coram's Fields, deserted at this hour, and sat down on a bench and gave thanks to kind Dr Coram who had built a hospital beside his fields to house abandoned babies. Had God, too, like a despairing

157

mother, abandoned His children to a game of chance? Was Tob a playing card that had been discarded? Or did God still tip the dice with a directing finger? If so, why did he choose to create Tob, young, loving and beautiful, only to destroy him so soon? Perhaps, after all, Tob was just one of millions of tiny creatures caught up and swept along in the great uncaring evolutionary drive towards survival of the fittest. But Tob was not unfit; he was unlucky. At some time during adolescence, when he was least aware of it, he had been unlucky enough to stand too near a stranger in the street, or a fellow passenger in an omnibus, who from cavities deep inside his lungs had coughed tubercle bacilli into Tob's face. Perhaps, during the life class at the Slade, he'd sat drawing for too long too near to a consumptive model. Or had he walked too close to infected spittle in a pub? Everywhere in London, people spat; and in many pubs, brass spittoons were set on the floor for customers; it was inevitable that some of these places would have been swarming with germs. She remembered that time he took her to the Prospect of Whitby, and she'd said it was like going home to Yorkshire. As she had climbed the rickety stair to the wooden platform overlooking the river she had glimpsed through the open door a floor covered with sawdust to receive the abundant spitting as well as the beer spilled by customers.

She remembered, too, the sweet sensation of under-standing exchanged between them, as she and Tob sat together, watching a trio of Thames barges, their earth-red sails partly furled as· they came up on the rising tide, purposeful and slow, so heavily laden with coal they were, and low in the water. She remembered the sweet taste of port and lemon on her tongue, and Tob's smiling eyes, his carefree laughter and his shyness when he touched her hand. She gasped then, as a sob rose in her throat, and she began to weep, understanding, at last, the reason for Tob's absences and his long silences, and imagining the things he might have said if he'd been able to offer her a healthy body as well as a loving heart.

These were cruel realities she had to face as she sat there in the June sunshine. She had to call on all her reserves of strength to accept and endure the prospect of Tob's loss to come, and the loss of her own hopes kindled by the briefly-snatched happiness she had enjoyed with him. She was coming to terms, in her own way and in her own existence, with the implacable fate her ancestors had faced in their struggle with the ferocity and the waywardness of the North Sea. Her tears fell freely; there was no one to see her cry. Dr Coram had left his foundlings and his London fields to walk in more Elysian pastures long, long ago, and she was alone.

EIGHT

Aurora threw her bicycle down on the ground and quoted Tennyson crossly: '"The old order changeth, yielding place to new." But how I do hate changes!' She sighed, casting her eyes up to the blue sky over Bushy Park as if imploring help from heaven. 'So many of them, I don't know where I am!'

She sat down on the grass in the shade of a great oak while Lizzie propped her bicycle against its trunk. The biggest change in her own life, Lizzie thought, was buying this bike, which gave her wonderful freedom and the opportunity to escape from the grime and noise of London, the anatomy dissection lab with all its reminders of death, and to reach, if not exactly fresh fields and pastures new, at least a bit of space and the sight of great trees and grass expanses. Her bicycle was a promise of the new world about to unfold with the twentieth century. She didn't at all mind change. It was about time for a new and better order, which would be brought in by British inventiveness, enterprise, and all the wealth that it created, to be dispersed throughout the nation. What a wonderful machine the bicycle was! People of all sorts were taking to it; six MPs had turned up one morning at the House of Commons on theirs, and Marie Lloyd, dressed in bloomers, was riding across the stage singing: 'I'm as cool as any icicle/Riding on my bicycle.' Somebody called it the Bicycle Boom.

Lizzie sat down on the grass beside Aurora.

'I just hope that will be my last visit to 'Green Arbour' for a very long time,' said Aurora. 'And I hope the new tenants won't be too much of a nuisance.'

'Where will your mother live when she comes back from abroad?' asked Lizzie.

'Don't ask me.' Aurora seemed impatient. 'I have no idea. But that won't be for at least a year. They'll do all the health spas of Europe first, and then winter in Mentone.' She paused to watch two little girls bowling hoops along a path. 'As a matter of fact, I don't think she'll ever go back there. I expect they'll sell it after this lease runs out.'

'She'll miss her garden,' said Lizzie.

'Yes. She'll miss her garden; but the other things – Tob, and all that wretchedness – she'll be glad to leave behind.'

It was more than a year now, since Tob's death, and Lizzie was just beginning to leave it behind too.

'Papa, of course, will be in his element,' said Aurora, 'drifting from baths to bars and then to bridge tables. And it will give Maisie another chance. She'll be able to meet new people, China hands and India hands, bachelors on leave from the East and on the lookout for wives, men who won't know anything about Tob. She'll be out of those shadows.'

Ah! the shadows . . . thought Lizzie. How they clung to you, even when you tried to shake them off. They changed your way of looking at things, altered the spectrum, subdued the colours; but yes, they did make you focus the light better on what was essential: celibacy and devotion to work. No more romantic dreams wasting your time and energy. Absolute devotion to the Cause was what was needed from her now. Romance was for the likes of Maisie as she combed Continental spas for a suitable husband who had never heard of Tob's untimely death.

'What are you going to do about Anastasia?' she asked.

'Do? It's not for me to do anything really, is it? Duffy married her, so it's his business now. They'll stay on in the flat above the coachhouse, since the tenants have taken on Duffy to work for them.'

'But she's ill, Aurora. Too ill to work.'

'She got much better during the last months of her pregnancy, but she did seem to go downhill after the baby was born. I've asked Dr Harmer to take a look at her.'

'Such a lovely baby boy!' sighed Lizzie. 'With his quick-darting eyes and all his attempts to make friendly noises.'

'Yes. He is charming, I know. Just like his mother, though. Not a bit like Tob.'

When the baby was born in March of the year following Tob's death, Aurora broke the news to her, told her the truth. It had scorched her imagination like a branding iron. All the time he was initiating Lizzie into his magic world, covering their heads with bridal veils of green willow, making courtly love to her with his talk of secret temples in sacred groves, he was busy tumbling Anastasia into her narrow truckle bed in the servants' attic, or pushing her down on the stone flags in the scullery, lifting her petticoats up to her neck and pulling down her drawers.

There was a time, after she knew these things, when Lizzie had been unable to sleep, unable to concentrate, didn't want to eat, didn't want to do anything at all. Anatomy was specially difficult. It seemed impossible to remember all those unconnected facts. Prosy, describing the relations of the facial nerve to the mastoid process met Lizzie's uncomprehending gaze across the dissecting table.

'You're not listening, Lizzie. You're not even here. Where are you these days?'

Lizzie made no reply, but two large tears slowly rolled down her cheeks. At that, Prosy made up her mind to do something.

'I'm going to take charge of you,' she said. 'And you've got to do what I tell you.'

She led Lizzie out of the lab and marched her back to No. 3 Doughty Street. 'She's not well, Mrs Plumm,' she told the landlady. 'She needs bedrest and mollycoddling.'

Mrs Plumm took Prosy at her word, and cosseted her lady medical student lodger with broths, with junkets sprinkled with nutmeg, and with eggnogs whipped with sugar and brandy; and Prosy took Dax for daily walks after teatime, and then spent the rest of the evening reading aloud to Lizzie.

'What shall I read to you?' she asked.

'I've been trying to get through *Little Dorrit*,' said Lizzie. 'You might go on with that.' The book had a special significance for her because Tob had once asked her if she'd read it. That was on the day he took her out to lunch at Rules, a lifetime ago, it seemed, though she could still feel his ardent gaze on her straw boater and her mannish silk shirt and tie.

When, one evening, Lizzie commented that Dorrit was so tiresomely good that she wanted to shake some rebellion into her, Prosy knew her patient was on the mend; and when she began to laugh at the interview between the hero and an old flame he'd been lucky enough to escape marrying, Prosy knew all would be well. Laughter, she thought, is the cure for broken hearts. But it surprised her, nevertheless, that she seemed to have cured her first patient with no more medicine than a little merriment and a few small kindnesses.

Her cure was complete when Lizzie bought a bicycle for twenty pounds, a wicked extravagance but a beautiful object of desire in its shiny black paint, with a squeaky horn to warn traffic of her coming, and an acetylene lamp on the handlebars to light her road home after dark. When she rode out of the city towards the country she thought of Tob lying under the grass – the blessed grass that was growing over him now. Time and the earth would obliterate, equally, his charm and his sins. I must forgive him as I must forgive God, if I'm to get on with living at all, Lizzie told herself. And had not Tob, after all, only attempted to do what other men did, squeezing into what he knew would be a very short span of life, the experiences they stretched over their biblically-allotted three score years and ten? At last came the day when she felt able to cycle down to 'Green Arbour' with Aurora, to see Anastasia and her baby, Tob's son, and afterwards to talk about it openly.

'They didn't christen the baby after Duffy, nor after Tob, did they?'

'No. They've chosen to call him after the great liberator from ancient penal laws, Daniel O'Connell. The child will inevitably be called Danny Boy. No doubt his mother is already crooning him to sleep with the song.'

'Do you feel any responsibility for him? He is your nephew really.'

Aurora considered the matter in silence for a moment. Anastasia was a silly impulsive girl who had squandered her youth and beauty; and Tob – poor Tob! – had been greedy and selfish. He hadn't thought much about Anastasia, had he? Well, they had both paid a high price for their midsummer madness.

'Tob has infected Anastasia, you know,' she said. 'That's what Dr Harmer thinks. Galloping consumption is his diagnosis.'

'Oh, no!' Lizzie protested. 'No, not that . . .' She knew,

of course, that protest in the fight against the disease was not enough.

'But no,' Aurora continued, 'he's not my responsibility. He's Duffy's boy now. Duffy knows all about it. And, as a matter of fact, he seems to love the baby as if it's his own.'

'Duffy's a good man.'

'I think it's because he loves Anastasia. Always has. So I suppose he forgives her. Love works wonders.'

Wonders – and despair and disappointments too, thought Lizzie, in her shadowed world. And Aurora, who had been chewing a stalk of grass reflectively, said: 'The lower classes do sometimes seem capable of unexpected nobility.'

Duffy's nobility was to be tested to the limit as the summer dwindled into autumn, and the child he had adopted as his own fell sick, and the poor man found himself supporting a fretful feverish baby as well as an ailing wife.

'Dr Harmer has managed to get Daniel a cot in Great Ormond Street Hospital,' said Aurora. 'He'll be under the care of Dr Still.'

'Dr Still?' echoed Lizzie. 'That's a bit of luck. Dr Still is famous. He's even got a disease called after him. A pioneer, really, in this new kind of medicine dealing with children. Paediatrics, they call it.'

It was in October, when Lizzie was studying the eye – its attachments to the orbit and the thick optic nerves crossing in the middle of the brain at a point near the pituitary gland, which the ancients believed was the seat of the soul – that she received Anastasia's letter. It was carefully written with hardly a smudge of ink or a crossing out.

Dear Lady Doctor Miss Lizzie
    I know Miss Rory has told you about our Daniel's

fever. I know he is very sick. Dr Harmer is very kind, I think he tells us the truth but a woman's eye sees more I do believe. I cannot visit my wee fella in that London hospital I am not too well myself and tis too far. It would be the greatest of all blessings if you could spare a few moments to see Daniel and to tell me what's going on up there among the big doctors and my baby. I know you have a kind heart Miss Doctor Lizzie and I bless and beg you.

Respectfully
Anastasia Duffy

On the next visiting day, which was a Saturday afternoon, Lizzie took Dax with her on a lead. She let him run loose as soon as they crossed the grass in Coram Fields. She was caressed by the afternoon's mellow sunshine, its long soft shadows, and Dax's delight as he ran about sniffing at familiar smells. She felt almost happy again, and smiled as she came face to face on the path with another lady Dachshund owner, and foot to paw with a little Dachshund bitch.

'Our dogs seem to be making friends,' said Lizzie, and after a few minutes, so were their owners. Almost before she knew it Lizzie had agreed to a mating of dogs, when the time was ripe, and had promised to become enrolled in the recently founded ladies' branch of the Kennel Club.

'Ladies are not allowed in the Kennel Club proper,' said her new friend. 'That is reserved exclusively for gentlemen and dogs. The Duchess of Newcastle is Chairman of the ladies' branch,' she added. 'She breeds Borzois.' She handed Lizzie her card which read: Lady Bescoby. She explained that she often found herself in this part of London because she had a philanthropic interest in the Children's Hospital, and sat on committees organising the collection of funds for it. Lizzie had no calling card, but gave her name and occupation.

'My word!' cried Lady Bescoby. 'I *am* pleased to make your acquaintance! Not only because of your Dax but because of your valour in breaking into the fortress *manned* by doctors!'

Lizzie laughed. 'I daresay, one day, we'll break into the Kennel Club too.'

'That'll be a great day,' said Lady Bescoby. 'The dogs will be happy then, but heaven help the gentlemen!'

Dax didn't get a very friendly reception from the ward sister at the hospital, who peered frostily at him over her bifocals. 'You'll have to carry that dog,' she said. She would have liked to forbid him entrance to her ward, but she didn't know how to cope with the creature without his mistress. 'We can't have his paws on the waxed floor, you know.'

'I'll carry him,' said Lizzie. 'He'll be very good, I promise.'

The ward sister conducted her to a side ward where Daniel Duffy lay. As they were about to enter, a young house physician caught sight of them and approached quickly. Sister was glad to be able to leave Lizzie with him as she had so many other visitors to attend to.

'I'm very glad you've come,' said the doctor. 'The poor child's had no visitors; and we don't know quite who to communicate with. You're not a relative?' He looked her up and down doubtfully, swinging his stethoscope.

'I know the child's mother. She's too ill to travel. I'm a medical student myself.'

'Well, that'll make things a lot easier for me,' he said, smiling. 'You must be at the LSM then? Perhaps you'll be able to explain things to the parents. I'm Still's HP. He'll write to their general practitioner, of course, when the time comes; but I feel some less formal approach should be made to the mother.'

167

'She's a young Irish girl,' said Lizzie.

'That fits, doesn't it? Those Irish country girls coming to the city from the fresh clean air of their green island have no resistance to TB. They seem to go down like ninepins. I suppose she's pretty ill, and that's why she's not been up here to see us?'

He led her into a small, darkened cell containing a single cot. She was beginning to think it cruel to keep a sick child alone in the dark when she saw him and understood at once the reason for his solitary confinement. Only a few months ago he had been a glowing, playful baby; he now looked shrivelled inside his skin. He lay on his side with rigidly-arched back and wide-open, staring eyes; the bright red curls so like his mother's were darkened by sweat where they stuck to his white forehead; and as Lizzie bent over the side of his cot a wave of tiny twitchings passed over his body.

The young doctor spoke softly: 'He doesn't like the light; and noises irritate him. But I'll turn him gently on his back so you can feel the neck stiffness.'

'He's terribly ill, isn't he?' Lizzie hesitated.

'Well yes, of course. It's tuberculous meningitis. There's no getting over that, you know. An infant has absolutely no resistance to it. One hundred per cent mortality.'

They stood, one on each side of the cot, and for a moment of truth looked straight into each other's eyes.

'My God!' whispered Lizzie.

'He watches the fall of a sparrow,' he said quietly.

'And of this child, too?' she asked.

As soon as Lizzie put her right hand behind his head and lifted it a little the baby uttered a peculiar, high-pitched scream so unnerving that Lizzie quickly withdrew her hand, and Dax under her other arm pricked up his ears and whimpered.

'It's one of the terminal signs,' said the HP. 'That piercing cry.'

When they left the side ward he tickled Dax's ears and smiled. 'You didn't like it, did you? Clever dog! You knew there was something wrong. But don't worry too much, old chap. The child's heavily sedated.' He glanced up at Lizzie. 'You will contact the mother – very soon?'

Lizzie thought about the young house physician as she walked back to her digs. His large, intelligent eyes were full of suffering. For those few seconds, when they had looked at each other across the abyss of the dying child's cot, they had seen each other's souls. The way he'd spoken of the falling sparrow made her believe he must be a true Christian. It was comforting to reflect that at least his religious faith would support him as he walked through the horrors of those children's wards. Here I am thinking of him as if I knew him, she thought, and I don't even know his name.

She walked on and saw ahead of her No. 48 Doughty Street, the house where Dickens had once lived, the house in which his sister-in-law, Mary Hogarth, had died. Lizzie glanced up at the windows, as yet uncurtained against the autumn evening, and wondered in which room it had happened. Dickens was able to use the event to metamorphose his sorrow into art, and by writing had, perhaps, purged the poison of it out of his system; but she, who was no novelist, would have to write to Anastasia to tell her the dreadful news without the aid of art, quickly, before her baby died, must somehow insert a crumb of comfort to nourish her, a little hook of hope for the poor girl to cling to before the waters of sorrow rose up to swirl her away into her own death. Galloping consumption was Dr Harmer's diagnosis. Ah! What a legacy of pain and poisoned lives Tob had left behind him . . .

In the mornings, fog rose from the ground of gardens in Henrietta Street, scattered in the lingering noonday sunshine of early November, but gathered again by evening thickly enough to veil the street lamps and blur their light. Tennis nets at the London School of Medicine for Women had been taken down and folded up; tennis rackets were stowed away in cupboards; girls in white skirts no longer flitted across the grass like moths. The windows opening onto the verandah had been firmly closed. Inside, there was a hiss of steam from a kettle, clinking of teacups and a hubbub of girls' voices in the common room when classes finished for the day and grey autumn afternoons darkened to dusk.

The charming, old-fashioned house was considered spacious enough when the school was founded in 1874. There were only seventeen students then, but by the late 1890s, although an extension was being built, it was full to overflowing. It was, at last, a successful enterprise that the Dean presided over. The students all revered Elizabeth Garrett Anderson. For twenty-five years, with patience, persistence, good manners and a steely will, she had battled against what had seemed insurmountable obstacles. She had been, once, a lone crusader: no university would admit her, no medical examining board would allow her to sit their qualifying exams; but, in the end, her reasonable voice had prevailed against prejudice, vested interests and the unrestrained trumpeting of the *British Medical Journal*. In 1862, when she'd failed to gain entry to St Andrew's University to study medicine, the *BMJ* had commented: 'It is indeed high time that this preposterous attempt on the part of one or two highly strong-minded women to establish a race of feminine doctors should be exploded.' For some reason the French had been more liberal, more sympathetic to her cause. On the same occasion *Le Temps* (gratefully echoed by the *Englishwoman's Journal*) wrote: '*Votre cause est gagnée devant l'opinion publique . . . L'Europe vous regarde: la France vous applaudit.*' And, in time, public opinion had supported her in England. When at last she had qualified as a doctor in London, and obtained, through an examination which she'd taken in the French language, the degree of MD from the Sorbonne in Paris, she'd set about working for a school with access to a hospital for the training of other women doctors after her. In this she'd been supported by some of the great and the good, by a few eminent scientists and philanthropists, and by sixteen thousand ordinary women who had signed a petition to parliament praying for the admission of women to the medical profession. It was an irony of history that the opposition to female doctors, based partly on contemporary prudery and fear of sex – its argument being that it was dangerous to national morality for women to dissect the naked corpse in the anatomy lab and to treat the naked body in a hospital ward in the presence of men – rebounded like a boomerang on those who used it. The same prudery had fuelled the desire of many women patients to be treated by doctors of their own sex.

Prosy poured boiling water into one of the teapots in the common room. 'You've missed three weeks of work,' she said. 'You'll have to work extra hard to catch up on all this stuff about the middle ear.'

'I know, I know,' said Lizzie. 'There's no need to remind me.'

'We've only got six months before Second MB.'

'Don't bully me, Prosy. I'll do it in my own time.' Lizzie held out her cup for tea. After she'd added milk, she said thoughtfully: 'Fishes don't have ears, do they? They must be deaf.'

Prosy wasn't interested in fishes. She had left them behind her now and was working through the great mound of unmastered facts still ahead of her. Lizzie thought she had rather a one-track mind, but she was grateful for the biscuits Prosy provided at teatime. They were baked by her mother and sent up to London from

171

the country vicarage by parcel post. Lizzie took one out of their tin box before finding a seat. She picked up the current issue of the *LSM Students' Magazine* from the table beside her and flicked over the pages.

'What sort of a doctor do you think you'll be eventually, Prosy?' she asked.

'There's not much choice, is there?' Prosy sat down beside her. 'Only the best student of our year can hope to get the one and only house job at the Royal Free. I'm not good enough for that.'

'There's the job of MO to women post-office workers that Henry Fawcett has kindly made for us,' suggested Lizzie. 'It's advertised here. Or you could be medical superintendent of a lunatic asylum in Ireland – Mullingar, it says.'

Prosy made a face. 'No. I shall be a missionary doctor in India. That would please my father.'

'Biscuits are good, Prosy dear. Too good for Indian missions. Do mission doctors marry?' Before Prosy had time to answer she raced on: 'Do you think that the Eustachian tube, which joins the middle ear to the throat, was a gill slit when we were fishes?'

'How your mind does jump about, Lizzie! I don't know about the gill slit and the what's-his-name tube, but yes, I suppose so, sometimes – marry, I mean – if they're men. But women doctors must be celibate. How would they be doctors if they had hordes of children hanging on to their skirts?'

'They could get rid of skirts I suppose,' said Lizzie. 'But not so easily the hordes.' Prosy was like a mole, dig, dig, digging, for months and even years to get through her dark mound of facts. She was, of course, the salt of the earth, but still a mole.

'A mole is blind, isn't it? Adapted to darkness . . .' Lizzie mused, thinking: Better adapted than we are for this sort of blind burrowing through a heap of facts.

'We're doing anatomy now, Lizzie, not evolutionary biology,' said Prosy, tartly.

Lizzie nodded amiably. But she was finding that her own zoological fancies did somehow act as pegs on which to spread the anatomical nets she was trying to construct. They helped to organise the thousands of incomprehensible facts into patterns. They were attempts to seize chaos and fix it into some sort of order. With a sudden flash of memory she thought of Maisie walking round her mother's garden, describing it as 'orderly disorder'. That garden was a form of art. And might there not be an art even in anatomy?

'I'd like to look after sick children when the time comes,' she confided to Prosy.

'There's that new job for women at the Children's Hospital in Shadwell,' said Prosy. Lizzie nodded thoughtfully.

'You're wonderfully dedicated, Prosy,' she commented over her second cup of tea. 'And, of course, you're right.'

Prosy regarded her sternly. She suspected her of faltering in her loyalty to the Cause. She thought this weakness was probably the aftermath of her recent illness. 'I believe I am, Lizzie,' she said. 'And so will you be – dedicated I mean – once you're quite yourself again.'

Lizzie glanced around her at the other students and decided that that was the common bond between them all: dedication to the Cause. Although much lampooned and laughed at for being either tall, thin and bespectacled with their noses forever in their books, or else short, stout and cigar-smoking in their attempts to 'ape the man', she didn't consider them eccentric; they were, in her opinion, the salt of the earth. They all came from ordinary middle-class families, rather wealthier than her own. The father of one was a colonel, of another a naval chaplain. A bishop had fathered one, the owner of a brickworks another. None of them smoked cigarettes, let alone cigars, and most of them wanted to be medical missionaries, in which ambition the Queen herself (God bless her!) supported them. The rest, though not fired by the same religious zeal, were acutely aware of being a minority group, a small band of women determined to wrest from a still largely unwilling society and a hide-bound profession the privilege of learning and working on ground hitherto worked only by men.

The word most commonly used to describe them was 'strong-minded'. It was a derogatory term. For a woman to have opinions, or even ideas of her own, at variance with the majority was to push her into the 'lunatic fringe'. That they were strong in their determination to study medicine, Lizzie accepted. She preferred to think of their minds as being rational and so more resistant to fashionable follies. There were Miss Morris and Miss Cleaver, both full of kindness and common sense, and Flora Murray, who had been able to get rid of the aprons they all wore over their dresses in the dissecting lab and operating theatre, by substituting a short white drill coat with useful pockets for stethoscope and notebook.

They were, she supposed, an earnest lot. They were not interested in the more usual pursuits of young ladies of their day: fashion and flirtation and the minutiae of gossip concerning these; they had more important things to do than waste their time on trivia. There was one among them though, who was less purified salt. Whenever any male lecturer, or the occasional young doctor from the Royal Free came to tea and tennis at the school, he inevitably gravitated towards this girl. The others confided to each other in subdued and solemn tones that she was a *femme fatale*. Lizzie often wondered in what lay her fatality. She was not particularly beautiful, nor especially charming, but was said to 'carry herself well'. She decided that her mysterious power could be simply explained if one thought of her as like a good ship: well built fore and aft.

It was Lizzie's brother George who was to blame for the next distraction from the requisite dedication. He turned up at No. 3 Doughty Street, having docked in the Port of London and booked into a hotel near Covent Garden, and immediately put Mrs Plumm in a flutter with his manly stride, his blue eyes and ready laugh.

'You absolutely must come, Lizzie!' he declared, in between mouthfuls of homebaked scones served with homemade apple jelly in Mrs Plumm's dining-room. 'It's the event of the century, this Emancipation Run of all the motor cars. They're going to drive all the way from London to Brighton. And can you bring another girl?'

He had somehow got hold of four tickets for the Motor Car Club breakfast at the Metropole Hotel. It was being held to celebrate the passing of the Light Locomotives on Highways Act, which permitted horseless carriages to proceed on roads at a speed not exceeding twelve miles an hour, unaccompanied – as was necessary before – by a pedestrian waving a red flag. Lizzie judged Prosy to be too dedicated for this jaunt and, perhaps, too nun-like to relish the gargantuan breakfast that was promised in order to fortify competitors and guests for the race. Her ticket announced that a full English breakfast of bacon, eggs, sausages and kidneys with croutons was to be served, together with a choice of wines, beer, tea or coffee. She invited Aurora instead.

After it was all over she realised she must have been a pawn in the hand of fate. George and Aurora took one look at each other as they shook hands and knew immediately that it was the Real Thing, the once-in-a-lifetime, the forever kind of falling in love.

'It's something about the way he walks,' Aurora confessed later. 'I shall have to draw him. That sort of swaying stride, a swagger really, as if he owned the earth he walks on . . . It gives such an impression of masculine power it does make me swoon a bit,' she admitted.

'That's only because he's just come off a ship!' Lizzie scoffed. 'He hasn't lost his sea legs yet, that's all.' But Aurora didn't listen.

'And his wonderful fiery hair! And the way his eyes spark!' she bubbled on. 'It's as if he were charged with electricity!'

'Perhaps he is,' allowed Lizzie with sisterly realism. 'Like a conger eel.' But there was no damping Aurora's enthusiasm.

On the damp, drizzling morning of Saturday, 14 November, however, when they settled down to their pre-race breakfast, Aurora was unusually silent. Perhaps his electric charge had given her a shock? Lizzie, too, was not exactly shocked, but certainly surprised to see across the white expanse of the hotel breakfast table, the sad serious eyes that she had last looked into over a cot at the Great Ormond Street Children's Hospital. George had met Dr Still's HP, and made friends with him, in the offices of a shipping line whose cargo-cum-passenger vessels sailed between England and the West Indies. The young doctor was applying for a post as ship's doctor on one of these; Lizzie presumed his job at the hospital was coming to an end. George had forgotten to introduce them so she still didn't know his name. As she leaned across the table, trying to hear him give it, an outbreak of cheering prevented her from catching it. She heard him say: 'Impossible to talk in this noise. Perhaps afterwards . . . ?' But a further burst of cheering cut him off, as the Earl of Winchelsea rose to his feet and solemnly tore a red flag into shreds. No sooner was this done, than the President of the Motor Car Club, Mr H.J. Lawson, leaped to his feet, glass of claret in hand, to propose a toast to the motor car, prophesying that in the century so soon to come, horse traffic would be completely eliminated and its place taken by motor transport. Many people present thought him crazy. Crazy, too, they considered his costume, which he'd had tailored specially for the occasion.

George expressed his sartorial judgement: 'He might be a yachtsman, in a pantomime.'

'The leader of a Hungarian band, I think,' said Aurora, slyly glancing at him sideways. And they both laughed.

But Lizzie didn't object to his outlandish dress; she thought him far from crazy. Sometimes, the mad ideas of today turn into the accepted opinion of tomorrow. She responded to his enthusiasm; she was excited by the new cars, by the possibilities in them which she could imagine.

A hunting horn blared out, suddenly, to call the competitors to assemble, and everybody left the table to rush outside. Lizzie was separated from her party in the general scramble, which hustled her out of the hotel and on to the Embankment. She could see above the heads of the crowd a great gold and purple banner which Lawson was waving as he climbed into the pilot car. After him came a curious contraption which Lizzie, when she caught sight of it, thought looked like a double penny-farthing bicycle with a seat slung between and a folding hook over it.

'There's Gottlieb Daimler!' somebody cried. 'Did you see him?' Lizzie saw a foreign-looking man in a heavy wool coat and a peaked cap getting into his car.

A second hunting horn sounded for the start of the race. Lizzie ran alongside the procession as it began to move, but stopped to watch while one car had to be pulled by real live horsepower, in order to start its motor. There were fifty-eight cars in all, but only thirty-nine of them were able to start. They set off across Westminster Bridge to bursts of cheering mixed with some jeering from onlookers.

In her newspaper the next day, Lizzie read that only fourteen finally arrived to enjoy the triumphant dinner for the victors at the Brighton Metropole Hotel that evening. Most of the rest had 'conked out' by the wayside. A few had arrived very late having had to go into reverse gear whenever faced with a hill, and it was rumoured that one had been put on the train for Brighton after being driven along a country lane to give it an authentic mud splashing. The glorious fourteen were met by the Mayor and a great crowd, and directed into Dupont's Stables for the night. The word 'garage' had not yet entered our vocabulary.

George spent the remainder of his short leave tracking Aurora, doggedly. He turned up at the Rocket Street house and introduced himself to her grandmother; he turned up at the Slade where he sat on the stairs reading a newspaper, tearing off bits of it from time to time and scribbling messages on them which he persuaded the porter to pass in to Rory wherever she was – in lecture theatre or studio. Eventually, she found it easier to throw up her studies altogether and spend the last of his leave with him.

'I'm going to Jamaica with your brother,' she announced. She was radiant with joy, so radiant that all common sense had been burned out of her, was Lizzie's opinion. When Rory saw the expression on Lizzie's face she tried to explain: 'It's all been so sudden. Like fork lightning – shattering really – a *coup de foudre*. But don't worry. I shall make him marry me. And in the meantime, I'm going to paint all those beautiful black people and all that exotic foliage and flowers.'

George's radiance was more subdued when he told his sister that Rory had booked a cabin for herself on his next voyage to the West Indies. He seemed nervous, apologetic even. 'We haven't had time to get a special licence here;

178

but I daresay we can be married in Kingston. We shall eat yams and bananas for the wedding breakfast and drink coconut milk laced with rum.' He laughed, but he watched her face closely. 'Don't worry, Lizzie dear. I know we're flouting all the conventions; but it will come out right in the end.'

'I hope it will. I just hope you won't crush her with your male dominance.'

'Crush her?' George was shocked. 'How could I? She's uncrushable. That's why I admire her so much.'

'You've always been a bit of a *conquistador*,' she said, and thought: Desirable, and sexually attractive, but also to be feared . . .

'*Conquistador* or not, I'd rather you didn't tell Mother yet. Leave that to me. We'll be back in the New Year.' When she said nothing, he continued: 'Come to think of it, Rory's rather like Mother. Indomitable, don't you agree? With that queenly carriage . . .'

Lizzie's thoughts scuttled back to the *femme fatale* at the LSM and the way she carried herself. This was also something to do with evolutionary biology: the mysterious attraction between the sexes. Rory had fallen madly in love. Anyone could see that; but Lizzie noted a sense of desperation in her eagerness to run away from London, the Slade, and her family ties. It seemed to her that Rory had all too easily found a paid housekeeper to look after the old people in Rocket Street. 'I daresay Papa will breeze over the Channel now and again to visit his mater,' she had said. It was difficult for Lizzie to imagine that poor little bundle of cloth, which had been thrown out of a hansom cab into her arms, as anybody's mater, but of course she must have been his mother once. Underneath Rory's plans, Lizzie could detect a still raw mourning for her brother. He had been someone who had shared her childhood and could read her thoughts and moods. That intimacy had been mutual; she knew

179

her brother through and through. Was this knowledge something she wanted to bury with him? Rory had not expressed her grief openly. With that high, haughty nose and the assumption she must have held since infancy that she was born into an elite, came the acceptance of *noblesse oblige*: you did not show your pain publicly, you did not let the side down by succumbing to your grief. But Lizzie knew she suffered and was still suffering, that she was lonely and crying out for love.

When Lizzie stood on the quayside, surrounded by well wishers waving and smiling as the boat slid away on the Thames, she shouted up at Rory standing on the deck above: 'Good luck! Good luck!' Rory was sailing away from 'Green Arbour' and all its clinging nightmares; she was rushing into a new life strange enough to obliterate the past; in a way she was abandoning her own sinking ship.

Pushing her way through the crowd in an attempt to keep up with the steamer's momentum, Lizzie waved and cried out: 'And happiness! Happiness!'

NINE

On Monday morning, Lizzie stood, notebook in hand, pencil at the ready, and looked across the end of the bed at the man sitting up in it. If he blushed, it didn't show. In an era when most labouring men drank heavily and he drank more heavily than most, his face, already suffused by a beery glow couldn't possibly reveal a blush. He stared at her truculently. She had asked him a straight question and he would give her as straight an answer. Everybody peed didn't they? Even this lady doctor student must pee under her skirts. So what of it? But before he had time to reply she shot another question at him – a series of questions. 'Was it painful to pass water? Was the stream poor? Was it difficult to start? Did it ever stop in midstream?' Anyone would think she was a Yankee with a repeating Gatling gun the way she fired questions at him! He glared at her balefully. He was complaining of all those things. Well, he'd better tell her the story from the beginning; but as he didn't want the whole ward to hear, he beckoned her to come closer. So Lizzie dragged the bedside chair towards his pillow and sat down to listen.

'When I were a young lad I were foolish like most young lads. I went with a dirty woman who gave me the clap.'

Lizzie wrote without looking up. What on earth was the clap? Whatever it was, it made it very sore for him to pee. Later, this became more and more difficult, so he knew things must be getting blocked. Then one evening, after a few pints, when he badly needed to empty his bladder and found he couldn't, he had pushed up the end of his clay pipe to clear the blockage.

'And did it work?' asked Lizzie. It was a novel sort of catheter.

'It did and all,' he replied, and was relieved and rather surprised to find he'd made his lady student laugh. 'For a while,' he said. But he had bad luck, for one day, maybe he was a bit rough, or the blockage was worse, the pipe stem broke inside him and he couldn't get the broken end out. 'That were the start of real trouble,' he confided. 'After that it were dribble and stop all the time.'

Lizzie asked him to lie flat in the bed. She turned back the bedclothes and examined his abdomen; she felt the top of his enlarged and thickened bladder, gently because it was tender to pressure; she percussed it and could hear the dull note over the enormously distended sac of fluid. After writing all this down she listened to his lungs, took his blood pressure and examined his heart, and asked him how much he drank.

'No spirits,' he said, virtuously; but he admitted to swallowing six pints of beer a day. She made a mental note that it was probably more.

'You'll not get that in here,' she said.

'Not bloody likely,' was his rejoinder.

The surgical ward round was held next morning, by which time she had to present her notes in the clear grammatical précis that was required of her. It was a daunting task to have to read aloud what she'd written, before her chief and his entire entourage of house surgeon, starched sister in blue, and subservient nurse in pink cotton dresses, and his posse of white-jacketed students on this, her very first patient; but she did so firmly and clearly.

Mr Barrow looked at her quizzically when she finished. He couldn't help but admire the calm, straightforward way she'd tackled what might, in some students' presentations, have been an embarrassing case. And her notes were correct and precise. Why! She might have been a man!

'So, you think there's a piece of clay pipe in his bladder, Miss Thorburn?' No X-rays were as yet available to prove or disprove it, and he had his doubts, although the HS had told him that, on passing a catheter into the man's bladder to relieve his retention of urine, he had struck some obstacle. Possibly a stone? Mr Barrow placed a hand on the patient's abdomen; and Lizzie noticed the light, delicate and sensitive touch – the traditional 'lady's hand' of the good surgeon. 'What makes you believe his story?' he asked.

'I think he's a reliable witness,' she replied. Mentally, he commented that she was surprisingly confident for a girl: an independent, self-reliant sort of person.

'Heart and lungs all right? What was his blood pressure?' he asked.

'Systolic 160, diastolic 90,' she replied.

'Well, we shall see what the trouble is when we operate tomorrow,' he said. Had she been a male student he would have made a sporting bet with her. When his small procession left the ward, his eyes twinkled as he remarked to sister: 'She's a bit of a card, that Miss Thorburn!'

Lizzie visited her patient again later that day. He was worried at the thought of being an 'operation case'. Surgery was always a risky business, and Lizzie was too truthful to pretend otherwise; but she reassured him as best she could. Mr Barrow was an excellent surgeon with a very good reputation for success in operations.

Moreover if nothing was done, she explained to her patient, if he refused to have his obstruction removed (whatever it might be), his kidneys would be fatally damaged and eventually he would suffer a good deal more than his present discomforts.

'You do talk straight. That's one thing in your favour, Doctor,' he said. She noted with satisfaction that he had moved her upwards in his evaluation of respect due.

In spite of her optimism, she, too, was anxious. Only last Monday, she and Prosy had come across Miss Twill crying in the cloakroom. Miss Twill (who would one day chain herself to railings, smash windows and be carried off to Holloway jail screeching: 'Votes for Women!') was weeping uncontrollably because her surgical case had died over the weekend while she was playing tennis with her cousins in the country.

Prosy had patted her shoulder and spoken softly: 'Don't cry. The Lord has taken her into one of His many mansions. She is at peace with God.' And Lizzie had said shortly: 'People do die. It's a fact of life. But it's not your fault. You did your best.'

There was always a risk attached to surgery, so it was not undertaken lightly. The chief cause of fatality, apart from loss of blood, which it was usually possible to control, was infection. Albert Boyce Barrow belonged to the younger generation of surgeons, who had rejected Lister's antisepsis with its carbolic spray mist to kill germs in the operating theatre, for the new concept of asepsis, or prevention of infection by scrupulous cleanliness. Mortality from post-operative infection was steadily declining, although asepsis was far from perfect. Mr Barrow used to leave his coat in the dressing-room outside the operating theatre. He put on a heavy rubber apron the colour of terracotta garden pots, over his waistcoat and trousers, and rolled back his shirtsleeves to the elbow before 'scrubbing up'; but he wore no rubber gloves. These were still hidden in the next century.

On Wednesday morning, when Lizzie was expected to help the surgeon with her first operation, she assiduously soaped and scrubbed her hands, her forearms and especially her nails, under running water; but she wore no mask, no cap over her hair, and her long dress was only partially covered by a clean apron. She stood opposite Mr Barrow with the anaesthetised patient between them, and handed him the instruments pushed into her hands by the theatre sister. She watched him catch bleeding points with Spencer Wells forceps and helped to lay them neatly away from the incision. When the bladder was opened and drained, the surgeon picked out the end of a clay pipe thickly encrusted with lime and phosphate deposits and looking like a piece of wreckage rough and shaggy with barnacles and seaweed from being long submerged under the sea.

'There's your clay pipe, Miss Thorburn!' he cried, giving it to her and making her blush with embarrassment at the general laughter so caused. 'And for that I'll give you a very good testimonial when the time comes!' which promise made her blush even more deeply. As a more immediate reward she was allowed to insert two of the ten skin sutures when he closed the abdominal wound.

When, ten days later, she removed all his stitches in the ward under sister's eagle eye, she presented her patient with the remains of his pipe stem. He was delighted with his trophy, wrapping it up tenderly in layers of newspaper and unwrapping it every time he had visitors to admire it. Their heads bent to his while he told them about his wonderful lady doctor-to-be. Several pairs of eyes from his bedside followed her as she moved about the ward, and she felt, for the first time, a patient's admiring gratitude – one of the rewards a doctor may reap. It was like incense in the nostrils, a wonderfully fragrant homage, a pleasant, but potentially dangerous, stimulant to self-esteem.

It also took Lizzie by surprise; all she had done in this affair was to listen and record her patient's story as he told it. She learned by it one of the paradoxes of medical practice: a doctor often receives praise for saving a patient's life when he has done very little to merit it. He also often receives scant thanks when he has spent many anxious hours and made great efforts on his patient's behalf. Her hospital training was beginning to teach her all sorts of things not included in the printed curriculum, things impossible to learn from books, which would, in time, change her attitudes and her personality itself, slowly and subtly without her being aware of what was happening.

On the day when Lizzie and Prosy had passed their second medical exam, they had gone for a walk in the Strand, arm in arm and in very high spirits, and finally entered an ABC teashop to celebrate their triumph over tea and cakes, and to talk, already with nostalgia, of what they were about to leave behind them. The old London School of Medicine for Women was being extended and rebuilt, and the pretty verandah and the garden it overlooked would be incorporated into a new laboratory. Elizabeth Garrett Anderson was about to relinquish her post as Lecturer in Medicine, although she would remain Dean of the school for a few more years, yet. The girls agreed the place would soon be unrecognisable. And now that they themselves were moving on, they wanted to offer some sort of valedictory over the teacups to their chief, their pioneer, the first woman to qualify in medicine in England.

'Nobody like her,' said Lizzie. 'With her genius for common sense.'

'And tact,' said Prosy. 'That's what she always showed when dealing with opponents. The soft answer that turneth away wrath. And, do you know,' she said judiciously, 'I do believe she wouldn't have done it if she hadn't always dressed so well.'

Lizzie glanced at her friend with amusement. That was unexpected, coming from Prosy, who always looked as if she'd been pulled through a hedge backwards, with collar crumpled, shoe-laces undone and shirt buttons sometimes missing; but she did agree there was some truth in what Prosy said. Elizabeth had gauged, with sound psychological insight, the effect of her image on the public, and had always taken pains to dress appropriately. Her most prudish enemies could never accuse her of immodesty or of flaunting her femininity; her pro-femininity opponents could never truthfully declare that in appearance 'she aped the man', and all the conformists in society had to admit that she never appeared *outré*, Bohemian or in any way mad.

'But the real reason for her success,' Lizzie claimed, 'was that she knew she was right, she was always rational, and she persevered.' The girls drank their tea in thoughtful silence.

Without Elizabeth Garrett Anderson's lectures the dear old school would never be the same again. It had been a happy, protected environment for gaining new and often strange knowledge, for accepting the discipline of regular, arduous work and acquiring a certain scepticism, which they would all need later in life. Hospital would be very different, they told each other; and so it proved to be.

Hospital life was like no other they had ever known. Here they were thrown, unceremoniously, into the pit of all that was sad, bad and probably irredeemable in the human condition; here they were brought face to face, not as spectators, but as workers, in the often dirty and squalid struggle for survival of the sick poor. The

Royal Free Hospital in Gray's Inn Road was so named because its founder, William Marsden, a compassionate and far-seeing surgeon, wanted a hospital for the poor who had no powerful friends to write letters of recommendation for them, as was the usual method of gaining admission to a hospital bed. Poverty and sickness were the only qualifications necessary in his hospital, which became known as the Free, and later, when Queen Victoria blessed it with her patronage, the Royal Free. It was Elizabeth Garrett Anderson and her committee at the LSM who persuaded the Royal Free, which had no students attached, to grant access to its wards for clinical experience to her girls, in exchange for an annual rent, and so it became the first medical teaching hospital for women. But there were no women on the staff. The consultants and even its junior staff were all male. There were two or three qualified women doctors acting as registrars who were permitted to keep medical records, but as yet, they were not given responsibility for the care and treatment of patients. They did, however, teach the students.

The new students, when loosed onto the wards, were known as clinical clerks. They were allotted individual patients from whom they had to obtain details, in each case, of the history of the disease and the symptoms suffered, as well as cope with each patient's personality and distress. They had to learn to observe accurately and to interpret as impartially as they could. Although, in their own lives, these girls held strictly to the Victorian moral values they had been brought up with, they found that in the wards these values no longer had quite the same worth. There was no place there for old-fashioned notions about the deserving and undeserving poor. To cure disease if possible, to alleviate pain always, were what was demanded of them, quite irrespective of whether the recipients of these graces were deserving or not. The morals of patients were irrelevant, what mattered was their need.

Lizzie quickly discovered that dealing with the sick could not be learned from books. It was a skill she must acquire in other ways than through her lifelong addiction to reading. Her textbook of pathology could tell her that the classical signs of inflammation were *calor*, *rubor*, *tumor* and *dolor*; her teachers could suggest possible causes of it and the frequency with which these occurred; but she had to see and touch the swelling, wring out the steaming hot poultice to wrap round and, hopefully, to relieve the patient's pains, and observe his reactions before she could really appreciate what was going on. One student, one perhaps more thoughtful than most, had stuck up on the notice board of the common room a Chinese proverb: 'I hear and I forget. I see and I remember. I do and I understand.' Lizzie thought it a very apt description of the process of becoming a clinical clerk.

You had to 'clerk' on the surgical wards for six months, on the medical wards for another six, and then there was midwifery. As the Royal Free had no maternity beds, the students had to go elsewhere for this part of their training. Some went to Dublin where the teaching of obstetrics at the Rotunda Hospital was said to be the best in the British Isles. The tenement slums of Dublin swarmed with children on every landing, the fertility of the Irish poor was legendary, and babies were born there at every hour of the day and night, so any student who delivered the large numbers of babies available 'on the district' could acquire wonderful experience. Prosy, who had some distant relative married to a minor cleric at St Patrick's Cathedral in Dublin, was offered accommodation in their house while she delivered her cases in the city; but Lizzie, knowing nobody Irish, chose to go instead to Queen Charlotte's Hospital in London, where she was the only female student at the time, and where the atmosphere of hostility towards her was almost palpable. Those among the staff and students who were not openly rude to her, simply ignored her. She was a foreigner among them; she began to feel like some poor irrelevant 'kaffir' from Timbuctoo. It was a painful experience.

She was lodged in the nurses' home; she was fed and slept there in between attending deliveries in the labour ward; but she was regarded as something strange and perhaps dangerous. None of the nurses greeted her or even bothered to pass the time of day with her. Perhaps they had no spare time to pass; but Lizzie, privately, was of the opinion that they resented her presence. They preferred male students who were, after all, good matrimonial quarry.

A few days after her arrival at Queen Charlotte's she watched a Caesarian section on a young woman with *placenta praevia*. The placenta in this case was attached so low down on the inside of the womb that it would inevitably get torn during natural labour, causing massive haemorrhage with probable loss of the baby and, perhaps, of the mother as well. Caesarian section was therefore less risky than normal delivery. When Lizzie, standing at the back of the operating theatre, unable, because of the crowd surrounding the operating table, to see any more of what was going on than the back of the surgeon's head and the sister's unusually careworn face, and feeling uncomfortably hot, bored and disgruntled, suddenly heard the small plaintive cry of the newborn infant lifted out of its mother's womb and held in the air while its umbilical cord was tied, she came to life. A lump swelled in her throat and her eyes filled with tears – shameful, weak tears, she thought. She was glad, then, that she stood in the background unobserved.

Later that day, the surgical registrar who had been helping with the Caesarian, spoke to Lizzie during a prolonged delivery in the labour room.

'I'm going to put on forceps,' he said, 'to speed things up a bit. You'd better watch.'

So she stood behind him as he sat on a high stool facing the baby's head, covered with a black down, which was just beginning to show between the mother's bent legs. A young HS stood at the other end of the high bed dropping chloroform carefully, drop by drop, onto a mask that he held over the mother's face. Lizzie saw the registrar slip the steel forceps, first one then the other on each side of the baby's head while the uterus was quiescent. The midwife, whose hand was on the woman's belly, signalled when the uterus hardened in contraction, and then the operator pulled gently on his instruments. Quickly, and miraculously, it seemed to Lizzie, the head slid out, to be followed, at the next contraction, by the shoulders. Then the child lay there on the red rubber sheet till the cord was tied. Lizzie picked up the tiny body, slippery with skin grease, and handed it to a nurse who stood ready with a towel. 'It's a boy, my dear!' the midwife announced; and the mother gasped: 'Oh, thank God! Thank God!' Within two minutes, the little creature cried out his response to the cold world he had been pushed into; and again, Lizzie was assailed by a flood of feelings of shock, joy, and what she supposed must be a form of simple, maternal love.

Afterwards, when she stood at the sink washing her hands beside the doctors, she commented: 'What a mercy we have anaesthesia now!'

The registrar answered, quite genially to her surprise: 'And what a mercy the Queen approved of it!'

Lizzie thought: Approved (God bless her!), in the face of all those good Christian men who regarded the pains of childbirth as the right and proper punishment of all women for the original sin of Eve; but she didn't express her thought aloud. As he was drying his hands, he added:

'Did you know that the first child Simpson delivered under chloroform was a girl, who was christened Anaesthesia after his invention?'

'Oh, no!' she exclaimed, laughing. 'How awful for the poor child!'

'I daresay she was proud of her name,' he said. 'She should have been.'

'Think how she would have been teased by her friends,' said Lizzie. 'But I expect she called herself Anna, didn't she?'

'I never heard the end of that story; but I know some others about Professor Simpson. My father was a student at Edinburgh, you see, and studied under him.'

'What was he like – Simpson?'

'A small man with a very big head, my father used to say. Short and stout but very speedy, and always so busy that if you wanted to talk to him you had to walk along with him. And he walked so fast that all the pompous professors had to run to keep up.' He laughed. 'You're a Yorkshire lass, aren't you?'

'From Scarborough,' she said.

'I'm from Yorkshire too. Pickering's my home town. My name's Selby. Horatio Selby.' He looked at her steadily, expecting her to laugh again, but she didn't. Instead, she told him she was born in a house called Trafalgar.

'Well, I hope you're not going to be the death of me,' he said, and smiled. 'You may call me Ratty if you like. That was my nickname at school. I suppose you have a name?'

'Lizzie,' she said. 'Thorburn.'

'Lizzie,' he repeated. 'But I think we'd better be more formal on the wards.'

She got back to the nurses' home late that night, and went into the dining-room to help herself to a bedtime snack of cocoa and a slice of bread and butter. The place was empty; but a young night nurse came in to swallow her half-time titbit. Lizzie must have been smiling, for the nurse smiled too, and sat down opposite her at the long table.

'Had a good day then?' she asked.

'Wonderful!' beamed Lizzie over her cocoa.

Here, too, she could feel the ice breaking.

During the weeks that followed, Dr Selby, besides helping her to put on forceps, deliver breech presentations, turn breech into occipital presentations, and to stitch torn perineums, also initiated her into some of the hospital gossip and jargon of the time. The surgeon who had performed the Caesarian was, he informed her, Mr Bank, known as Dogger; and the theatre sister whose face was crisscrossed with interconnecting lines was known as Clapham Junction. Dogger Bank, in spite of his nickname, was not a student wrecker when it came to finals, but Professor Partager, the bad-tempered sarcastic head of the department, who was known as Professor Porcupine, or Porky for short, was a real pig in the practical exams.

'You want to keep out of his way if you can,' Ratty Selby warned her.

After a fortnight, she was sent out 'on the district' to deliver what were expected to be normal easy deliveries in the dwellings of the poor. She had to make her way into overcrowded rooms where whole families slept together in one bed, where water to wash the mother before childbirth had to be heated in saucepans in the basements of tenement buildings and carried up narrow unswept stairs to the woman in labour, who was often drunk and lay moaning on a bed of newspapers for want of any cloth, where the husband was usually drunk and the only assistant available was some kindly but dirty woman whose skirts were laden with dust from streets strewn with horse dung and whose willing hands had black, untrimmed nails.

'How are you getting on out there in our British jungle?' asked Dr Selby when they met one Sunday morning, he on his way to breakfast, she with her hat crammed anyhow on her uncombed hair, and bleary-eyed from lack of sleep.

She answered him with another question: 'Why on earth do they all drink so much? It only makes our job more difficult.'

'They say gin is the quickest way out of Manchester,' he said. 'I expect it's the shortest route out of London too. You must have been unlucky last night. Saturday's always the worst for drink, you know.' He was smiling at her hat and the picture of disarray she presented. 'More babies die on Saturday nights than on any other,' he said. 'From overlaying. It's not infanticide. The mother hauls the crying infant into her warm bed to stop it crying and smothers it in a drunken stupor.'

Lizzie opened her mouth to speak. She wanted to cry out that she'd already had so many burdens and difficulties to deal with during the night, that she was so dreadfully in need of sleep, she could really bear no more. But she closed her mouth and said nothing. She simply turned and fled from him. For a few seconds, he watched her disappearing back. Perhaps learning is harder for women, he thought. He couldn't help laughing a little at her disarray.

'My eyes were opened to a lot of horrors,' she confided to Prosy when they met again. 'But I did manage to deliver fifty-three babies. Prosy had tucked an even larger number of cases under her professional belt in Dublin. During that virtually sleepless month the two girls had acquired what every doctor must have: experience. It was pleasant, when it was all over, for them to be able to talk about it in the students' common room at the Royal Free.

194

Miss Twill informed Lizzie, on her way out of the room, that there was a letter for her on the notice board. 'It's been there for ages,' she said. 'And by the look of it it's been halfway round the world before getting here!'

The letter was addressed to 'Miss Thorburn. Medical Student'. It was written in an unknown hand, franked and franked again by the postal service. The stamp showed that it came, originally, from America. It had first been sent to 30 Doughty Street and returned to the post office with 'NOT KNOWN HERE' scrawled across it. It was then sent to the London School of Medicine for Women, from where it had been forwarded to the Royal Free, while she was at Queen Charlotte's. Lizzie opened the envelope, unfolded the letter and looked quickly at the signature written in a careful, but not by any means cramped hand: William Westerleigh. Who was he? She sat down and read the letter slowly.

Dear Miss Thorburn
    Your brother George and his wife asked me to bring you news of them on my return to England. Unfortunately, I was unable to do this at once because almost at the outset of my voyage home I was taken ill with typhoid fever and was put ashore in the Barbados, where I was shovelled into a cottage hospital of sorts. I must say I was very kindly cared for by black nurses, but was unlucky enough to suffer several unpleasant complications of the disease which still further delayed my homecoming. By the time you receive this letter you will no doubt have heard that George and Rory were married in Kingston, Jamaica, myself acting as one of the witnesses the law requires. Rory has decided to travel with her husband wherever he goes, so you may not see her for some time. They were, when I last saw them, both well and very happy.

I am now acting as ship's surgeon on a yacht bound for Chesapeake Bay and Baltimore. Everybody on board is perfectly fit, but the owner, who is a very rich man, is followed by his own peculiar Albatross. He is obsessed by the fear of acute appendicitis while at sea, and wants a surgeon at hand to remove his appendix if need be. I only hope I don't have to do it. So there is very little work for me as you may imagine; but I tell my conscience it is a way of convalescing, and also, I hope, of seeing something of the United States of America when we get there. Meanwhile, may a good wind fill your sails – or at least a bunkerful of good coal stoke your engines! Fortune follows the brave.

With kind regards, and hopes that (who knows?) we may meet again some day.

Yours sincerely

William Westerleigh

Lizzie showed Prosy the letter. 'You can have the stamp,' she said.

Prosy was a keen stamp collector. She examined the envelope closely. 'I haven't got this one. It's a Great Lakes Steamer under the words United States.' Then she read the letter.

'He seems to think I'm going on a journey,' said Lizzie.

'So you are Lizzie. We all are.'

It was more by chance than design that Lizzie travelled home to Yorkshire for that Christmas with Dr Selby. She was standing at the entrance to King's Cross station, admiring the new advertisement for Pears Soap pasted on a wall – Millais's curly-headed boy in a green velvet suit staring up at the lovely soap bubbles he had blown out of his clay pipe – when Dr Selby suddenly spoke: 'Are you by any chance travelling to York today? What a bit of luck – for me, I mean, if I may accompany you.' She allowed him to carry her portmanteau as well as his own, while she held Dax in her arms. It was a thrilling journey for Lizzie, chiefly because he treated her to luncheon in the dining-car, a thing she'd never enjoyed before. She was greatly impressed by the excellent meal that was produced from a hidden galley at the end of the carriage, and much amused by the waiter, very spick and span in his LNER uniform, who, in spite of the lurching of the car, danced gracefully towards her, flourishing and flicking his white napkin with more elegance than purpose as he served her mutton chop.

Dr Selby insisted on her trying a glass of claret.

'Even a lady doctor can relax and enjoy a glass at Christmas,' he said. Lizzie could see that he was enjoying his. His rosy plump face beamed at her across the narrow table. The space between them underneath it was so small that, occasionally, their knees touched, accidentally, Lizzie felt sure. He was the sort of man, she guessed, who enjoyed his creature comforts but was not selfish about them. He would, she believed, want others to be as happy and comfortable as himself. By the time they reached the coffee she regarded him as an old friend.

'What I can't quite see,' he said, raising his glass and looking at her through the dark red liquid, 'is why you lady medicos sacrifice your youth and vigour to doing all the hard work you do, when you are unable to use your qualification afterwards.'

'More and more jobs are opening up to us,' she said. 'Most of the girls at the Royal Free go into the Indian mission hospitals at present.'

'I wasn't thinking so much of fields of work,' he said, twisting the stem of his glass from side to side. 'I was thinking of that effort and dedication all gone to waste when you girls marry and have babies.'

Lizzie was annoyed to find herself blushing, and blamed the claret. 'I think most of us will remain celibate,' she said. 'We embrace celibacy for the Cause.'

'Oh, but that's terrible!' He was indignant. 'Such a waste of potential – all these might-be-good wives and mothers going into virtual nunneries!'

She glared at him accusingly: 'You're regarding us simply as breeding material, aren't you, Dr Selby?'

'It's how Darwin regards us all, Lizzie. And I wish you'd call me Ratty.' He was twisting the stem of his wine glass quite vigorously now, precariously, Lizzie thought, fearing that the train might swerve suddenly over a bend in the track and the wine spill on the clean, white cloth.

'I'll call you Ratty because that's how you make me feel today,' she said, crossly. 'And Darwin will just have to eat his hat!'

He was rather pleased that he'd annoyed her. He smiled benevolently across the table and murmured: 'Poor Darwin!'

At York, they parted company, he to go to Pickering, she to Scarborough; but on New Year's Eve he came to call at Newborough End. Matilda took to him at once. There was no need for Lizzie to explain what a kind and helpful teacher he'd been to her at Queen Charlotte's; the fact that he came from Pickering was sufficient claim to Mother's esteem. His youth and friendliness won her affection too. And as it happened that Dr Beverley had also been invited for the evening, the two doctors immediately joined each other to talk shop, and Lizzie's conversation was not required.

In the dining-room a festive high tea was laid out. George and Rory were not present because they were somewhere in the West Indies; but Katy had brought her fiancé, whom she'd met while governessing her girls on a summer holiday in Ostend. Mother placed M. Van de

Putte on her right. He was a Belgian businessman, at least a decade older than Katy. Mother was accepting him with as good a grace as she could muster. To her way of thinking it was a pity he was a foreigner; mercifully, he was not a Roman Catholic but an English-speaking Protestant from the coal-rich region of his country. Lizzie thought him rather dull, but very attentive, if not obsequious to Katy. It was already plain who would be the boss in that marriage. Edward, his moustache somewhat curbed by time and common sense, sat on the left of Dr Beverley, who took the end of the table opposite Mother, with Cissie on his right. Ratty, who was enjoying himself, ate his way enthusiastically through thin slices of succulent Yorkshire ham with pickled onions, through some of the best Wensleydale cheese he'd ever tasted with Bessie's homebaked oatcakes, and through several of her mince pies.

After tea they adjourned to the lilac sitting-room. Lizzie noticed that the wallpaper had faded opposite the window, and in one corner there was a suspiciously darkened, probably damp, patch; the chintz covers of the chairs were worn and the carpet near the doorway was frayed; but Ratty saw nothing amiss. He seemed altogether enchanted by the calm domestic scene: Cissie leaning tensely over the piano, and Matilda, her face smoothed under the soft lamplight, singing simply, without any concert platform tricks, a sentimental song he loved. She must have been in a romantic mood to choose 'Jeannie with the Light Brown hair'; and as soon as he heard the opening bars, Ratty leaned his head on the high back of his chair and abandoned himself to blissful listening.

Matilda pressed him to stay overnight; but he explained he must go home to Pickering that evening, as his mother would expect him to accompany her to church the next day.

As he was about to leave, Flo bustled into the hall with

her two children, and Lizzie's attention was immediately distracted by them. He was amazed by the way she took them in her arms. She seemed overwhelmed, her face transfigured with joy. It was how he imagined girls looked when they were in love, but not when they were handling other people's children, and these the offspring of her mother's former housemaid! He thought it very odd, and because he felt bewildered and at a loss, he held Lizzie's hand for longer than he intended as he said goodbye because he was searching her face with unspoken questions. She let her hand rest in his, but she was not thinking about him at all; her expression was simply full of a vague, absent-minded happiness. She was standing under the hall gaslight, around which a bunch of mistletoe was tied, throwing an intricate lacing of light and shadows over her face and shoulders, and for a moment he was tempted to kiss her under cover of the licence permitted in this silly season of the year; but he hesitated, fearing to rouse her angry resistance, and turned away. As he did so, he saw Katy in the dining-room doorway watching him with gleeful malice. Half a dozen voices called out happy New Year greetings as he left the house. He tried to distinguish Lizzie's voice among them but could not, amid the confusion of echoes in the street.

That night, Katy went into her mother's bedroom for a bedtime gossip. She sat down on the edge of the bed; but before she could begin to analyse Dr Selby or to tear apart Lizzie's feelings and intentions, Matilda put a hand on hers and said firmly: 'Please say nothing, Katy. There is nothing to say. Nothing has grown yet. With your sharp tongue you might nip it in the bud.'

Katy smiled. 'All those nothings must add up to something. But I'll not say a word to Lizzie.'

TEN

Eighteen hundred and ninety-nine. Faces lengthened at the sound of those numbers. There was a sadness in it, and a menace, too, like a bell tolling through the mind's ear. The great century was dying and the new one just around the corner was still hidden and, perhaps, to be feared. The dumpy little Queen, decorous and dowdy and undeniably good, who had presided for so long over the epoch to which she gave her name, was old and frail and could not be expected to live much longer. It had been a period of undreamed-of industrial growth with increasing wealth fuelled by British inventiveness, and of unimagined changes in the way people lived and worked and travelled about; it was a time when the Empire had scattered large, pink stains far and wide over the map of the world.

Britannia was now so great it was beginning to be feared that she had reached her apogee and there was nowhere for her to go, other than into decline. A few uncertainties, like rats around a cornstack, were nibbling at the edges of the self-confidence, the faith in progress, the philosophy of the work ethos of her people. The belief that the Anglo-Saxons were peculiarly fitted by God, or by natural selection, to colonise and rule the world,

201

spreading their superior civilisation with their advance – a task that soldiers as well as missionaries were eager to do – was no longer everywhere held sacrosanct.

Occasionally, disquieting reports came home from overseas that some of these Indian Babus seemed to be more civilised than their rulers, and quite a lot of the rest didn't want to undergo being civilised anyway. Moreover, it was continually reported in the newspapers that foreign navies were growing bigger than Britain's, and that her armies, spread out so widely in the world, might be unable to hold that thin red line in a crisis. Added to these anxieties, was an uncomfortable feeling that in spite of Browning's assertion that God was in His heaven and all was right with the world, it was obvious that labourers locked into factories, as well as the urban homeless, couldn't hear the larks nor see the dew-pearled hillside which so reassured the poet, and that in spite of all the Queen's efforts to be good, and of her people to follow her example, things were somehow going wrong.

Hard-working, middle-aged and well-enough-off persons might, with justification, look back on their century and be content to rest on their laurels when they considered all the great reforms: abolition of slavery, reduction in the hours of child labour, universal free education, and suffrage for most adult men; but sometimes they stirred uneasily in their armchairs when they read in the newspapers of some nameless old woman who had eaten nothing for a week and was found frozen to death in a doorway in Spitalfields, or when they heard the gossip in the clubs about the unsuccessful attempts made by Gladstone, the Grand and Good Old Man and former Prime Minister (now gone to his well-earned resting place), to persuade prostitutes into a better way of life. They had listened, it seemed, to his eloquent pleas, but very few were willing to abandon their trade.

There were other things happening, too, which made

the respectable classes frown, things illustrated by all the new words creeping into the language: plutocracy, *nouveau riche*, and conspicuous consumption. It was disturbing, to a generation brought up on Samuel Smiles's *Self-Help* to practice frugality and condemn the wickedness of waste, to read that a ten-course dinner could be purchased at the Army and Navy stores and delivered to your door. It was rather shocking, too, to half-believe the rumour that someone was putting pips of wood into red fruit pulp and selling it as raspberry jam. A whole new concept was entering business with the advertising industry: that of printing and selling lies for profit.

Aurora didn't much care about the nineties being a *fin de siècle*, somehow contaminated by sinister moral decay. She loved the free-flowing sinuous curves of Art Nouveau even if they did suggest a loosening of sexual inhibitions; she didn't regard Aubrey Beardsley's drawings as shockingly amoral as some critics did, but thought of his hand as using a pen like a sword, keen, clean, cruel and elegant enough to slice through the piled up rubbish of the bourgeois mind; but she didn't go back to the Slade when she'd had enough of wandering over the seas with George, and returned to London. Old Mr Ashwolde had died during her travels, and his little, birdlike wife did not linger long in Rocket Street after his departure. They had left the house to Aurora and it was now a land base for George as well, whenever he came home from sea. Instead, she threw herself into the Arts and Crafts Movement, attended meetings and lectures on Fabian Socialism, hoped for Women's Suffrage and read William Morris's works avidly. She looked back now to the Middle Ages as a time of innocence and contentment. 'Individual craftsmen are being replaced by machines,' she said. 'Art and imagination are getting lost. Even our English eccentricity is being crushed into conformity by mass production.'

Lizzie heard her complaints, but thought of the Middle Ages with less romanticism. She remembered the Black Death, and medieval law courts where torture was the right and proper method of extracting the truth about an arguable matter, and shuddered at the thought of burning witches and heretics as a punishment for clinging to strange beliefs. Not much sweet innocence there. She would have liked to follow Rory towards Votes for Women; but she just didn't have the time. She was now concentrating on her last studies before finals, so was more concerned with her own than with public affairs. In the eye department she was learning her own new vocabulary: strabismus, diplopia, exophthalmos and acute glaucoma. In the ear, nose and throat department she learned to differentiate tonsillar exudates and, under the heading of 'Infectious Fevers', to discriminate between the rashes of measles and scarlet fever. She still had skins and orthopaedics to deal with, but in the meantime was having coaching with Prosy on two evenings a week from Ratty Selby, who, since he was himself studying for the FRCS exams in order to be a surgeon, was temporarily out of work and grateful for the fees they gave him for tuition.

They met in Mrs Plumm's dining-room, after supper had been cleared away. They sat with textbooks open on the red plush tablecloth and discussed their difficulties and incomprehensions. He was a good tutor, clear-headed and not long-winded, who could tell an anecdote to illustrate a point, or make a joke on which to hang a fact. So, for most of that momentous year they were all three in a sense cocooned by their studies and quite unprepared for the shock, when it came on Wednesday, 11 October, of the declaration of war against the Boers.

On the following Sunday they decided to cycle to Hyde Park, to try to gauge public opinion as well as enjoy some amusement by listening to the orators at Speaker's Corner. On the way, they ran into a wildly cheering mob. In the middle of it all sat the old Queen in a high, open carriage. She was not waving, nor smiling; she sat with bent head while tears poured down her wrinkled cheeks.

'Let's hope the war will prise her out of her Balmorality and back into the real world,' said Ratty.

Lizzie, pitying her, was silent. Later, she asked: 'What's this war about anyway?' Some said the Boers were denying Britons the right to vote in areas where they laboured; other suggested they were really fighting for control of goldmines. Whatever the causes, the war undammed an enormous wave of patriotism. Thousands volunteered to fight, although the newspapers warned them they'd have to fight over harsh terrain, hot and full of hostile 'kaffirs'. War fever was whipped up by the papers; and Lord Harmsworth, proprietor of the new *Daily Mail*, who described his readers as loving a good hate, set about encouraging them to hate the Boers, whom they'd never met and hardly heard of before the war. Other, less reputable dailies, printed heady headline draughts of jingoism to brace Tommy Atkins's muscles and shrivel his thinking power. The British didn't entirely lose their sense of humour, however. Lizzie saw a cartoon in *Punch* of two urchins discussing the war. One was telling the other: 'The Boers will cop it now. Farver's gone to South Africa and tooken 'is strap!' It made her shiver, not least because it made her wonder how many little English boys were rather glad to see 'Farver' go overseas taking his strap.

Within a few weeks, surprising facts began to filter through to public awareness. Over half the enthusiastic volunteers from urban areas were found, at medical examination, to be unfit to hold a rifle, let alone carry a heavy pack and march for miles across hostile country.

They were puny, their growth stunted by childhood malnutrition, with muscles undeveloped and legs sometimes deformed by rickets. This was especially prevalent in men from northern industrial towns where sunlight, in the long winter months, could not easily penetrate the smoky pall from millions of coal-burning home and factory fires. It came as a shock to the comfortable middle classes to realise that a great many Britons were actually half-starved. And how, if our fighting men were too weak to fight for us, could the Empire be defended? Statistics suddenly became popular, and medical officers of health found themselves unexpectedly in demand to answer all the questions that were being asked.

Life expectancy, it was discovered, was far higher and infant mortality far lower among the rich, and among the clergy (why the clergy?) than among the poor. More than half the children at present living in the East End of London would not live to see their fifth birthdays. An infant born to rich parents, it seemed, had four times the chance of survival of his poor neighbour. The worst outlook of all was reserved for the babies of young women who were unwed. They were still being abandoned in places where Dr Coram's successors could pick them up, or being dumped in filthy homes under the care of ignorant, paid foster mothers. All Britons were free men, proud of their liberty and their laws, before which it was said they stood equal. And now they all had equal votes; but in the matter of wealth and living space, and now, it seemed, in health, they were markedly unequal.

With growing indignation, Lizzie read a letter from a *Times* correspondent, a doctor working in a Lancashire cotton-mill town who wrote: 'Where I work, the death rate is fifty per thousand; in the rich and royal borough of Kensington it is eleven.'

Large numbers of more-or-less fit volunteers were

loaded into steamers after the unfit had been weeded out, and set sail for South Africa, many never to return. At first, it looked as if the might of Britain was going to be defeated; but by May 1900, with the relief of the long seige of Mafeking, fortune was beginning to favour the home country. Lizzie and Prosy did not take part in the manic jubilations in the streets after the good news of Mafeking because they were about to sit their finals and were too busy studying. Nor did some of the other girl students, who had lost brothers in the war. 'Do you know what the word Mafeking means?' asked Flora Murray. 'It means a place of stones.'

The day of the finals was a bright Monday morning towards the end of May. Lizzie woke early, dressed carefully and swallowed some breakfast with more sense of duty than enjoyment. She met Prosy at the examination hall along with other girls from the Royal Free, all rather quiet like Milton's pensive nun, 'sober, steadfast and demure' by comparison with the boisterous male medical students from other hospitals. The written papers were not too menacing, she told Prosy, if you kept your head, answered only what was asked, and alotted each answer only its proper share of the time available. It was the orals and practicals that were universally dreaded.

'You won't have any acute cases,' said Ratty, trying to bolster his pupils' confidence. 'They'd be too ill to travel to the examination. What you'll see are long-standing chronic cases with pretty obvious physical signs, and some of them will know quite a lot about their own diseases.'

And so it proved for Lizzie, who discovered in her medical practical that her 'case' had an enlarged liver and a hard swollen spleen. He was a Westcountryman with the Bristol habit of adding an *L* to all terminal vowels. When Lizzie asked him, had he ever been abroad he replied: 'Oh, arr . . . ! It was in Egypt I got diarrhoeal something chronic; but it wasn't till Indial and Burmal that I got malarial.' She did wonder if he'd said too much, but couldn't refuse such bountiful information: it was manna from heaven.

In her surgery exam she was presented with a woman who had an ulcerating cancer of the breast, and later, a man with a lump above the collar bone which gave her the opportunity to discuss with the examiner goitres, lymph glands and cysts of the neck. This particular lump was a pulsating swelling which Lizzie diagnosed as an aneurysm of the carotid artery.

'You won't want to cut into that,' said the examiner with ghoulish humour, which made the patient cover the lump defensively with his hand.

She felt she was sailing through it all with great good luck, till she came to the day of the midwifery orals. She and Prosy entered the hall together and were directed to separate tables. To her horror, Lizzie found herself facing Professor Partager. I must be calm, she told herself; I must keep my head. I must not let the side down; I must do battle for the Cause. She sat down, took a deep breath and folded her hands on her lap. He is only a man, after all. He doesn't look too fierce. No bristling porcupine quills beneath his cuffs. I must not dither, nor be a fool.

He asked her what she knew about *placenta praevia*, and she replied that it was attached low down inside the uterus in a position inconvenient to the baby, the mother, and the obstetrician. He looked at her quickly over the tops of his glasses; but he didn't smile. 'Can you elaborate on what you mean by "inconvenient"?' he asked. He leaned his elbows on the table between them, pressed the tips of his fingers together and regarded her so severely that her heart began to sink; but at least he didn't interrupt her during her attempts at elaboration. He then asked her a few more questions, and at the end of her ten minutes he gave her the faintest of smiles.

'I am not too familiar with the female student,' he said, 'but I think I can say that you have acquitted yourself commendably – yes, quite commendably.'

He rose, she rose; he proffered his hand which she rather shakily shook, and added unexpectedly: 'And I wish you the best of luck!'

She left the hall, stupefied by her feelings of relief and elation. Ratty and Prosy were waiting for her in the corridor outside with excited questions: How was it? Did she stumble? Did she make mistakes? Was he a perfect beast? Prosy had been examined by Dogger Bank, but had sailed easily over him on the subject of twins in a primip and had not, she thought, been wrecked.

'When I told him I'd done my mids at the Rotunda we talked about Dublin, where he'd done his, too. And that took up a lot of the time.'

'And old Porky, Lizzie, was he nasty to you?' asked Ratty.

'Not at all,' she replied. 'Surprisingly. He said I'd done quite commendably.' And then the girls laughed, and seizing each other round the waist, they ran down the corridor crying out: 'Quite commendably!' till the invigilator emerged, agitatedly, from inside the hall and told them to keep quiet.

Two weeks later, Ratty went with the girls to see the exam results pinned up on a board in the same corridor. When they caught sight of their numbers in the columns of the successful, the girls uttered shrieks of delight and, turning away from the wall, began to embrace total strangers in the crowd. They were all so bemused by the emotions of the day that they accepted without question this embracing, all except Ratty who, when Lizzie threw her arms round him, pushed her away angrily, thinking: I am no more than a stranger to her. With that great heart of hers she loves all humanity, not me alone. Lizzie was too excited to notice his glowering, but Prosy, always more careful and thoughtful, put her hand in his and said gently: 'We wouldn't have done it without your help, Ratty. We owe you a great debt of gratitude.'

It was only later in the day that Lizzie remembered Ratty's angry face. She knew they would not be seeing much of him now that exams were over, so she decided to write him a little note of thanks.

Dear Ratty

I want to thank you very much for your help in turning this female into a doctor. I don't think I would have scaled the heights without the help of your knowledge and expertise, for which I shall be eternally grateful.

I hope we shall meet again soon. My sister, Katy, is to be married next month, and my mother is planning a party in London to celebrate her wedding, along with my qualification. I hope you'll join us on that day. No doubt you'll be hearing from Mother soon.

Meanwhile my very kind regards.

Lizzie

Poor Selby was not as lucky as his pupils were in their exams. He failed his first attempt at FRCS and realised he'd have to get a job – not a hospital house job which was virtually unpaid, though you did get board and lodging for working yourself to the bone, but an assistantship in general practice where he could earn enough in six months to keep himself going for another six months of unpaid study. However, he hoped he'd still be in London on the day of Mrs Thorburn's party.

The new Russell Hotel, which Lizzie had passed by many times during the years of its building, opened on Saturday, 2 June with a great fanfare of publicity and its picture in the *Illustrated London News*. From the leafy gardens of Russell Square opposite, you could stand and admire, or gaze at it in stunned silence according to your artistic tastes. To Lizzie, it seemed an exhibition of Victorian floribundance pressed down and running over. Its architect, Fitz-Roy Doll, who claimed some remote under-the-blanket ancestral link with royalty, had designed a building that might have echoed the splendours of French Renaissance chateaux built by Kings had it been built of white stone. But its skin rejected the aristocratic pallor of a French façade in favour of the ruddy complexion of an English beef-fed plutocrat and shone in the summer sunlight with the coarse vivacity of common earth in bright red brick. Elaborate decorations flaunted themselves on each of its eight storeys, and there were five tiers of balconies under a roof of burnished copper, which, in the coming century, would slowly turn green with verdigris. Outside the ground-floor windows, chubby terracotta cherubs twining garlands of flowers, danced from pillar to pillar on feet of clay. There was noble marble inside: marble floors, and a splendidly-carved rose marble staircase, and in the restaurant, marble pillars topped by white statues clutching at scanty draperies which seemed to be slipping off.

Nothing less opulent would do for the grand dinner Matilda was planning to celebrate all the triumphs of that momentous year. She knew it was daring, even, perhaps, wicked for her to abandon her lifelong habits of frugality in a frenzy of squandering; but such triumphs, she argued, came only once in a lifetime, in two lifetimes, if you counted her own with her children's: the marriage of a daughter to a rich man (although, unfortunately, a foreigner), the academic crown of another daughter, and the return of George from sea. It would be the first time for a decade that he'd be based on land for the whole summer in order to repair, modernise and refurbish the Rocket Street house. And the year 1900 alone demanded to be marked – didn't it? – with some suitably grand gesture.

So she booked a round table for nine in the gaudy restaurant, booked a room where the young couple, newly-wed in a short civil ceremony, could spend the night before she joined them to cross the Channel on their way to Belgium. There they would be married all over again in church, followed by a whole day of feasting, as was the custom, so she'd been told, with guests leaving the table between courses to relieve themselves or take a walk in order to work up a flagging appetite for still more food. Well, she wasn't going to be outshone by this Belgian son-in-law. She would show him what English hospitality could be like. The day was fixed, her special guests invited, their places at her table arranged with the head waiter: the bridegroom on her right, George and Rory on her left, Lizzie beside Katy, with Ratty on *her* right sitting between her and her friend Prosy, and to complete the circle, George's ship's doctor friend, who'd been invited to fill the place of the extra man needed. Edward did not come to London for the event because he had to mind the shop; and Cissie stayed behind to look after him.

That morning, in the registrar's office, Katy had not worn white. Her white bridal clothes were packed with tissue paper in her trunk ready for the big church wedding in Belgium. She had worn a suit of deep blue and a small hat, covered all over its crown with pink roses. She'd been nervous when it came to the promises required of her and at the signing of her married name. Her husband hovered over her as she inscribed it: Katy Van de Putte. The registrar smiled indulgently as he blotted it with unblemished pink blotting paper. 'When I first took on this job forty years ago, half the brides couldn't sign their own names,' he said.

'Whatever did you do then?' asked Lizzie, craning over her sister's shoulder to see the book.

'They used to sign in the right place with a cross.'

And Matilda, standing in the background with Katy's bouquet of pink roses in her hands, spoke up in a firm voice and with a strong Yorkshire accent: 'We do seem to 'ave coom on summat, then.'

Katy changed for the evening into a pale blue gown with a lacy frill at the neckline, which revealed her thin shoulders. It embarrassed Lizzie, though it seemed to amuse the others, to see how difficult it was for her bridegroom to keep his hands off her. Lizzie, who had been ordered by her mother to buy a new outfit for her sister's wedding, wore it for the evening too. It was a skirt and jacket of heavy tussore silk of a colour called *café-au-lait*, and with it she wore the Honiton lace blouse which had been hidden away in a drawer since the night (could it be as long ago as five years?) of Maisie's birthday ball.

She felt elated and carefree, and her happiness showed in her face and in the way she moved. She had passed her finals and now had no more examination crags to scale; the burden of the last six years had dropped from her, and she was basking in the sun of her own success without any thought of tomorrow. Moreover, she was enjoying, with unconcealed gusto, the cornucopia for all the senses which the Russell Hotel provided: a spectacle of brightly-clad ladies flanked by well-groomed gentlemen in sombre elegance of black coats and starched white linen, their oiled hair gleaming under the brilliant new electrically-lit chandeliers. She felt she could be proud of her own party among all the swells. Prosy, it was true, wore a rose-coloured dress handed down to her by several elder sisters, but she did display her mother's garnet necklace which winked cheekily under the lights. Rory was resplendent in amber silk with great amber

213

drops falling from her ear lobes and a chain of amber beads about her throat. Lizzie, watching her, thought: She is glowing like her amber, glowing with happiness. A string orchestra was charming the diners with 'Little Dolly Daydream', smoothing the careworn brows of businessmen with romantic fantasies, and bringing a flush of hope to the cheeks of young, unmarried girls. It was a pleasure to feel the crisp, white table napkin, and to catch the scents of good cooking which drifted to her nostrils.

Lizzie glanced across the table at Matilda and smiled, thinking of how much they all owed to her, and how right it was that she should sit there in her gown of black velvet with absolutely no jewellery to adorn her, and only her beautiful white hair to crown her as she should be crowned, a queen, which was what George had called her as he led her to the table: Queen of this night. Ah! her adored and adoring George! When he said things like that Matilda could even forgive him for marrying (secretly, too, in the brain-softening heat of a tropical island port) that haughty Miss with her sharp eyes and her expensive clothes.

Last of Lizzie's senses to be pandered to was her taste for oysters, which came sprinkled with lemon juice. She swallowed them one by one, relishing their flavour of the sea and the soft texture they relinquished in her throat. Glancing up after swallowing the last she caught William Westerleigh's large, serious eyes studying her, and suddenly blushed. Was he criticising her for being greedy? Perhaps she'd spilled some oyster juice on her new silk jacket? But no. When she looked down, she could detect no shaming stain.

William, although a shy and not a talkative man, was an acute observer of the social scene. From an early age, perhaps because he was the youngest of a large family, he had tried to read the human psyche by its

214

outward masks, and possessed what his mother called 'a second sight into the soul'. He had not missed the glances between Lizzie and her mother, had noted the still beautiful widow's confident, happy bearing, and judged that she was probably a benevolent if powerful matriarch. That she exerted a certain control over each of her guests was plain to see. It amused him to think of her as like one of these new telephone exchanges with invisible wires connecting her to each seat at the table. Selby was obviously under her influence. William guessed by their affectionate glances that she had already ear-marked him as her second son-in-law. Comparing her to her daughters, he wondered if they, in time, would grow to be like her. No. Not the bride. Time would not be so gracious to Katy who he foresaw might become waspish with age. But Lizzie . . . Ah, there was a difference to her sister! Lizzie was capable of great love. There was a sureness of generosity in the way she walked, and a great warmth in her voice and in her gestures. She was clever, too, but in spite of her cleverness she was still innocent, holding, he believed, to the great simple ideals of the Hippocratic oath she had so recently taken, and even, perhaps, of his own interpretation of *Ars longa. Vita brevis*: to be eager for knowledge but humble in the face of the unknown, to put your patient's interests first, to be compassionate in healing. She was one of a small band of women who were going to push the infant century into a new and better epoch of history. He saw it all with Tennyson's vision. There would, of course be 'prudes for proctors, dowagers for deans', but it was the 'sweet girl graduates in their golden hair' on whom they fixed their hopes. He had never forgotten his first meeting with Lizzie in Great Ormond Street Children's Hospital, how they had stood on either side of the dying child's cot. The memory of it had haunted him for months. He remembered saying:

215

'He watches the fall of a sparrow', and her reply: 'And of this child too? . . .' He remembered the deep wells of grief in her eyes. Above all, she was truthful. That was what excited him now, as she met his eyes over the tops of their wine glasses: the absolute honesty in hers.

'I must congratulate you on your success, Miss Thorburn,' he said, reaching out his glass of Chablis towards hers, but unable to touch it because the distance between them was too great, and then turning to Prosy beside him: 'And you too, Miss Watkins. You have both done so well.' He couldn't help envying that lucky fellow Selby as he sat, beaming with self-satisfaction between the girls whom he'd coached for months. During that time he must have got to know them both quite well.

They all began to talk about the exams, laughing at the poor student who, when shown a specimen in a glass jar, had mistaken a cancer of the skin for a pickled ear, and pitying Miss Twill who had diagnosed a loud systolic murmur of the heart as a pleural rub.

'And then there's the tale of W.G., the cricketing Grace, probably apocryphal,' Selby began, his voice a little louder and his smile a little broader from the wine he'd drunk and the attention he was getting, 'who was presented with a skull in his anatomy oral.' The examiner, pointing to the *Foramen Magnum*, through which the spinal cord, with its blood supply, rises to join the brain, had asked him what it was. And Grace, who already, at that date, sported a magnificent beard, had laughed a great jolly laugh and said: 'There's many a pint I've tossed down that hole!'

William joined in the laughter, but it nettled him to think that this young doctor could tell such good stories when he, who had travelled the globe, couldn't think of one that might amuse the company. He was, he told himself, as so often in life, an outsider, a spectator of the happy throng. He wondered how he could gain Lizzie's

216

attention. He determined that when the dinner ended, he would insist on calling a cab for her and taking her back to her digs. In that way there would be the possibility of some conversation with her. Unfortunately, things did not go the way he'd intended. First, there was the necessity to bid the bridal pair a last goodnight before they disappeared upstairs in one of the hotel lifts, then, as they all moved towards the hall to wait for the commissionaire to call the cabs, Matilda spoke to him. 'I believe we are all staying in Rocket Street tonight, Mr Westerleigh, so I think we can all travel together to George's house.' She must have known, in some recess of her mind, that the house belonged to Rory; but she always referred to it as George's house, or even George's town house. It was a small snobbery, but it irritated William.

Then Prosy turned to him. 'And what have you been doing all this time?' she asked. 'The last we saw of you was a postage stamp from Baltimore.'

'I stayed there for several months,' he said, 'sitting at the feet of Osler at the John Hopkins Hospital.'

'Ah! Osler . . . How wonderful!' she sighed. 'They say he's the greatest physician alive today. I believe his lectures are quite spell-binding, such are his eloquence and his great knowledge. You must tell us of your adventures in the New World some day, Dr Westerleigh.'

Miss Watkins was, undoubtedly, a well-meaning person, but she would keep him talking, holding him a prisoner of politeness while out of the corner of his eye he could see Selby helping Lizzie with her cloak, preparing to depart with her, not giving him the chance even to say goodbye. And at last it made him angry to have to watch Selby shepherding both the girls in that proprietorial manner out into the street through the pseudo-rococo, cupid-sprinkled porticos of that hideous hotel and into his beastly cab. Selby was a lucky dog.

Ratty got out of the cab first and, giving Lizzie his hand as she stepped down to the pavement, he said: 'I say, Lizzie. Do you think you could help a chap out of a hole?'

'Well, of course Ratty – if I can. What is it?'

'I've signed up for an assistantship in general practice in the wilds of Gloucestershire, starting August the first. But now I've been invited to join a sailing trip in the Hebrides. It's the holiday of a lifetime, Lizzie. I shall never get such a chance again.'

'Well?'

'Well, I wondered if you'd do the first fortnight as a locum for me?'

'Me? A woman doctor, Ratty? In the wilds of Gloucestershire? They've probably never heard of women doctors there. What about your Westcountry practitioner? What will he say?'

'Oh, I think I can fix it – if you're game. It would be a great opportunity for you, you know.'

It would, indeed, Lizzie thought. The opportunity of a lifetime for me. And a great piece of luck. She suddenly remembered William Westerleigh's letter: Fortune follows the brave. Well, she must be brave now.

A fortnight later, she received a telegram from Oban: STUBBS EXPECTING YOU STROUD SUNDAY 3 P.M. GOOD LUCK. RATTY.

PART THREE

Dr Lizzie

ELEVEN

Rain fell remorselessly that Sunday afternoon. It thrummed on the metal roof of the platform as the nippy young porter ran to extract Lizzie's bicycle from the luggage van. Then, balancing her portmanteau on the carrier over the back wheel, he led her towards the station yard. Departing passengers were hurrying to meet friends with carts, or, pursued by gusts of rain, were climbing into cabs as quickly as they could, but Lizzie could see nobody she imagined might resemble Dr Stubbs. When, at last, the train moved off on its way to Gloucester, the only remaining pony trap she could see sheltering in a corner under some trees was an open wagonette. Her porter whistled to attract the driver's attention, and he emerged unwillingly into the rain.

'Are you Dr Stubbs's man?' asked Lizzie.

'I am.' He lifted his head moodily.

'I expect you've come to meet me.'

'I come to meet a young doctor; but I ain't seen 'im yet.'

'It's me you've come to meet. I'm Dr Thorburn.'

He stared at her in disbelief as the rain dripped steadily off the peak of his cap and streamed off the head and flanks of the patient horse.

221

'I never 'eered nothing of no lady doctor, see,' he said at last. 'Dr Stubbs never said nothing about a young lady doctor. Never 'eered of such a thing. Are you sure you're Dr Thorburn?'

'Quite sure.' Lizzie opened her Gladstone bag and pulled out her stethoscope in an attempt to prove her professional status. It seemed to convince him. He nodded, muttering: 'Who'd a thought it?'

'I rather thought Dr Stubbs would meet me,' she said.

'Oo, 'e can't do that. He's injured, see,' the man explained. 'Fell off 'is 'orse and broke 'is arm.'

'Oh,' said Lizzie. 'Well, you'd better help me get this bike up into the cart.'

He slid off his box and, with the porter's help, heaved the cycle up. She tipped the porter before seating herself, and then, thanking her lucky stars for her good waterproof cape, she opened her umbrella.

'Does it always rain like this down here?' she asked as they began to move.

'Pretty well,' was his reply. ''Tis good for the cabbages.'

'Well, I'm not a cabbage,' said Lizzie.

'No,' he agreed. 'But there's 'uman cabbages as I know of.'

'I daresay,' said Lizzie. After that, conversation lapsed as they trotted through muddy lanes lined by dripping trees and hedges. She caught an occasional glimpse of fields and hills beyond and guessed it might be a pretty enough landscape in better weather, but it certainly did not lift her spirits on that afternoon. She wished she could have brought Dax with her. He would have been some company for her in this unfamiliar, rain-soaked scene, but Dax was sick. He had been pining and listless for several weeks. She couldn't bring a sick dog to a new job for an unknown employer in what was, to her, a foreign country, so she'd left him in London in the good care of Mrs Plumm for the two weeks of her locum.

222

All in all it was a bad Sunday. Even the name of the village they were making for sounded bleak: Stonington Malreward. Perhaps, she thought it was on some Saxon piece of land given to a Norman conqueror at the muster of survivors after the Battle of Hastings, and had proved to be unproductive ground.

The village was surprisingly attractive, even in the rain. Old cottages and a few grander, eighteenth-century houses clustered round a central green. The doctor's house, a small Georgian gentleman's residence, was reassuringly geometrical in shape, its respectability enhanced by a pair of pillars upholding a lintel over a handsome fanlight and a door on which was a splendid brass knocker and a brass plate emblazoned with the doctor's name and qualifications. Lizzie could smell wood smoke as she dismounted, and sniffed appreciatively.

'Will you stable my bicycle with the horse?' she asked, tipping the driver sixpence.

'Oh, Arr . . .' He seemed wonderfully mollified, even going so far as to touch the peak of his cap. 'Thank you, Miss.' He watched her as she marched with her portmanteau in one hand and her Gladstone bag in the other towards Dr Stubbs's front door.

A maid with wild hair and a dab of coal dust on her chin opened it and led Lizzie to the doctor's study where she stood in the doorway, her folded umbrella dripping onto the carpet. He rose from his winged armchair when he saw her. His right arm, which was tied up in splints, rested in a sling beneath his coat, and his fingers emerged between buttons and drummed on the surface of the cloth.

'Excuse me,' he said. 'I can't shake hands, as you see.' He gestured towards the splint. 'You must be Dr Thorburn's wife?' A look of irritation passed over his round rosy face. 'Dr Selby never said anything about a wife. Is the doctor coming in out of the rain?'

'I am Dr Thorburn,' said Lizzie.

A look of disbelief, followed by horror and then rage, took possession of his mobile features.

'Good God!' he cried. 'What's this? A woman doctor? Why – I shall be ruined! All my patients will desert me for my rival Dr Byrnes in Brookthorpe.' He sank back in his chair. 'How on earth did this happen?'

'Didn't Dr Selby tell you I was a woman doctor?' asked Lizzie. She was terribly shaken by her reception, but angered, too, by the rudeness of it.

'No. He did not. All he said was that his mother needed him in Yorkshire to deal with family matters arising out of his grandmother's sudden death, and that you could replace him for a fortnight.'

'Oh.' Lizzie's heart sank as she understood the depths of Ratty's perfidy; but she managed to stammer: 'I'm sorry about your mistake. I thought you were aware of my unfortunate sex.'

'Mistake?' he bellowed. 'Mistake? It's not *my* mistake. It's deception. It's that young fellow's criminal fraud. And how do I know you weren't accessory to it?'

'I certainly was not!' she cried angrily.

'Well, whoever is most to blame, we're in a horrible mess. Here I am, unable to get about on a horse or in a pony trap, with nothing but a female to do the visits. You'll have to go back to wherever you came from, young lady.' His voice trailed off in lamentation. 'You're no good to me.'

At that moment, his wife pushed past Lizzie into the room. She was a little woman with quick movements and a quick, clear voice.

'Now just calm down, Stubbie, will you? Poor Miss Thorburn is wet through, and if we don't take those soaking garments off her we'll have a patient with pneumonia on our hands.' Ignoring her husband's glare, she took Lizzie's hand. 'Now come with me, Miss Thorburn.

We've got a fire burning still in the kitchen range, though this is supposed to be summertime, and Molly will dry your cape, and your boots, too, while I give you a cup of tea. And Molly –' she called down the corridor towards the kitchen as she led Lizzie away, '– the doctor will have his tea on a tray in the study today.'

'Thank you, Mrs Stubbs,' said Lizzie, when they sat before a big open log fire in the sitting-room. 'You're very kind. But I shall have to go back to London at once.'

'My name's Penelope,' said the doctor's wife, smiling. 'And you can't go back to London today as there's no train now till tomorrow morning. You'll have to stay the night. And, indeed, your room upstairs is quite ready for you.' She paused, and then added: 'I think you'll find Stubbie quite amenable in the morning.'

'I shall not be amenable!' declared Lizzie aggressively. She was dreadfully disappointed at the way things had turned out, but too angry to cry. 'I should never dream of working for such a bad-tempered, prejudiced old man!'

His wife tutted gently. 'I'm afraid you've seen him at his worst. He was naturally upset just now. He's finding it difficult to be good, stuck as he is inside his splint. He's fractured his humerus, you know. He can do the morning surgery but he can't write prescriptions. He has to dictate these to the dispenser. And he can't ride, or drive a trap, and cycling is out of the question, so he can't do the sick visiting. And then you were rather a shock. But he's a very kind man, really. Inside that harsh exterior he hides a heart as gold and soft as butter.'

Tarnished brass and rancid butter was what Lizzie suspected he was hiding, but didn't say so. 'No doubt you see him through rose-coloured spectacles,' she said. 'I suppose that's how most wives see their husbands. To me he looks most unfriendly – a grisly bear, and dangerous when roused.'

His wife laughed as she poured the tea. 'Stubbie, a grisly

bear? Oh, no!' She handed Lizzie a cucumber sandwich. 'Men have to be managed, my dear. And bears have to be trained to dance, you know, when they're kept on a chain – as, of course, all men should be.'

In spite of herself, Lizzie found her anger and disappointment melting under the influence of this woman's pleasant voice and her very welcome tea, but she was determined to sit on her high horse a little longer.

'It's not my job to manage men, or grisly bears either,' she said. 'It's my job to heal the sick.'

Penelope Stubbs felt like laughing at the girl's prim expression, but being something of a diplomat she checked her laughter and said nothing. She knew she'd need all her skills to work on her husband later that night, reminding him of his desperate situation, persuading him that a female doctor would be better than none, that the girl seemed agreeable and sensible too. She was pleasantly surprised when Lizzie remarked: 'I do love a log fire. I could smell the wood smoke as we came up the High Street, so I knew there must be a log fire somewhere.'

Breakfast on Monday morning proceeded in complete silence. Lizzie found she was very hungry and ate her bacon and egg and crisp toast with relish.

'Young Pete Posser came in with a message about half an hour ago,' said Mrs Stubbs, refilling the doctor's cup.

'Oh?' he looked across the table at her. 'What did he say?'

'It's his sister,' replied Mrs Stubbs. '"Baby's head is stuck", is what he said. "Can't get out. Nothing doing."'

Lizzie put down her cup, suddenly. There was a short silence. 'Is his sister in labour?' she asked.

'Primip,' said Dr Stubbs. 'You've done your mids, I suppose?'

226

'Queen Charlotte's,' said Lizzie shortly. 'I had fifty-three deliveries.'

'You'll have seen some difficult cases then.'

Lizzie wiped her lips on her table napkin and rose from the table. 'Someone's got to see to her,' she said.

'Take my mids bag,' said the doctor. 'You'll find my forceps inside. And there's a bottle of chloroform. Goats Marshes. It's a couple of miles along the Berkeley Road. Show her the map, Penny.'

Mrs Stubbs took Lizzie into the surgery at the back of the house. There, a large scale Ordnance Survey map was pinned up on the wall behind the doctor's high desk. Mrs Stubbs pointed to Stonington Malreward and then drew her finger along to Goats Marshes. 'It's a miserable sort of place,' she said. 'And the Possers live in a hovel. But at least it's not raining.'

Lizzie strapped Dr Stubbs's midwifery bag to her own Gladstone on the carrier above the rear mudguard, and set off cycling as fast as she could, her heart beating more quickly and her imagination awhirl with hopes and fears of what she was about to meet.

Goats Marshes was nothing but a low-lying field, rank with rushes. There was only one dwelling to be seen, a wretched cottage whose thatched roof was falling apart. No well-tended garden surrounded it, but what looked like a rubbish tip leaned against one wall. A few purple loosestrife still flowering added a little colour to the scene, and as she wheeled her bicycle along the muddy path a flock of lapwings rose into the air and veered away uttering their cries of lamentation. She could see smoke rising from a chimney so she knew the place was inhabited, and was glad because if there was a fire there'd be some hot water, too. A boy of about twelve came to the door. 'Has the doctor sent you then?' he asked. As she entered the low-ceilinged kitchen a bedraggled woman emerged from an inner room and greeted her: 'You must

227

be the midwife. Thank God you've come.' A cry of 'Mam! Mam!' called her back to the bedroom.

There was no sign of any husband, of any male at all except the boy, Pete. Lizzie told him to find a bucket and, if possible, a basin too. 'I'll need all that hot water,' she said, glancing at a kettle steaming on a trivet by the open fire. In the inner and only other room, was a double bed covered with bloodstained newspapers on which lay a young girl of no more than sixteen or seventeen. She was too exhausted by her long labour to cry out lustily, but she kept up a continuous moan of 'Mam! Mam!' to which her mother responded by wiping her forehead with a damp and dirty rag. The girl was naked except for a pair of old and torn, black woollen stockings rolled down to her knees. There was no furniture in the room apart from the bed; in the kitchen there was a central table but only two upturned wooden crates for chairs. Lizzie saw that there was no possibility of sterilising her instruments. She would just have to trust to luck that Dr Stubbs's forceps, carefully boiled before being wrapped in a clean white linen cloth, had not been contaminated by any fingers since.

With Mam's help, she turned the girl round so that she was lying across the width of the bed, then she ordered Mam to hold her daughter's bent legs apart so that she could see what was going on. It wasn't easy. The room was dark, even in summer, the only light coming from a tiny cobwebbed window in the kitchen and the low flickering red glow from the fire.

'Bring me one of those crates to sit on, Pete,' she ordered. 'And put that saucepan down on the floor here beside me. And have you got a mug?' Into the saucepan which he'd brought instead of a basin, she poured some of the hot water and washed her hands in it. Into the mug, which was clean enough although chipped, she poured more water and added a teaspoon of carbolic. She placed the bucket on the ground beneath the girl's legs and, taking some cotton wool, dipped it in the carbolic wash and cleansed, as well as she could, her patient's swollen labiae, through which a tuft of the baby's black hair was just peeping. Lizzie didn't think she could trust Mam to drip chloroform onto her daughter's face, so she had to lean across the unresisting girl and do it herself. Then she inserted the forceps and waited. As soon as she felt a flicker of contraction in the uterus she pulled gently. The head came out with surprising ease, followed quickly by the shoulders.

She tied the cord, cut it, and then lifted the baby, limp and slippery, a helpless scrap of humanity about to take its first breath of air, and was suddenly caught by a passionate longing to have and to hold the child, to possess it, to protect it from all dangers, a desire to call this little creature hers. And then, as suddenly, she was numbed by the knowledge that in all this she would forever play a secondary role. For her there would always be the lesser joy of holding a stranger's baby in her arms, but never the all-engulfing happiness of mothering her own. Well . . . she reminded herself, it was a sacrifice she had already made; she had placed her unborn, unconceived infant on the altar of the Cause. There was no sense in quibbling with the gods now.

'It's a girl,' she said. She looked up at Mam, whom she realised was a lot younger than she seemed, for although she had several teeth missing and two deep furrows of despair ran down from nose to chin on either side of her mouth, she still had a lot of thick, black hair. The woman quickly left her daughter's head to inspect the newcomer. She took the infant in her arms and carried it into the kitchen where, on the table she had made ready a box fitted with a scrap of blanket. 'My little pearl,' she crooned, when the infant uttered a cry. 'My baby girl.' Tears poured down her ruined face.

Lizzie was occupied with cleaning up her patient, dropping the afterbirth into the bucket along with blood and newspapers. The young mother had begun to call again for her Mam, who went to her, carrying the baby wrapped in its inadequate blanket.

'And no paps nor pobs now, only the breast for Baby,' Lizzie warned. She was afraid they'd cram all sorts of filthy dummies made of lumps of gruel in twists of cotton rag into the child's defenceless mouth and kill her with infantile diarrhoea before she reached the age of one month. 'And have you a blanket for your daughter? She's shivering.' Mam fetched an ex-army greatcoat from a pile of old clothes in one corner of the room and spread it over the girl, tucking it round her as she lay, happily bewildered with her baby cradled under one arm.

'What she needs now is a good cup of tea,' said Lizzie, washing her hands in the remains of the hot water and wiping them on Dr Stubbs's linen cloth. And luck, she thought. A good deal of luck. 'I'll call again tomorrow.'

As soon as she was outside in the fresh air, she drew in a deep breath of it. Good God! What a place! What a life – no, not a life at all, only an existence, of sorts . . . And what had that new baby, that little Pearl to look forward to in this new century of ours? Lizzie could see that at least she would be loved. If she survived her first month she would be loved; and that was something.

'We can't charge the Posser family anything,' said Dr Stubbs. 'People like that have hardly enough money to buy bread.' They were sitting round the empty grate in the study after supper.

'How on earth do they manage?' asked Lizzie.

Dr Stubbs, who was smoking a pipe, puffed before replying: 'They give a hand with the haymaking, help with the cider apples when they're ready for gathering . . . occasional casual labour. And they collect firewood from hedges and copses. They live no better than gipsies really. Shanghai Lil is what folks round here call Mrs Posser.'

'What does that mean?' asked Lizzie innocently.

Mrs Stubbs explained: 'It was a bunch of sailors docking at Sharpness who first gave her that name, and it stuck. She waylays the timber waggons on their way from Bury Woods to the saw mills in Stonehouse, and lifts her skirt at the drivers. Or so people say.'

Lizzie's hand flew to her mouth as she imagined it: Did they lie in the open marshy field? Or did Mam drag her men into her hovel to the only bed shared by her daughter, her son, and the new baby – all witnesses to the scene – and do her work on a layer of newspapers? Mrs Stubbs blinked when she saw the effect her words had on Lizzie, but her fingers didn't stop working. She was knitting a sock on four steel needles. 'I'll give you a shawl for the baby,' she said. 'Made by our Mothers' Knitting Circle. You'd better take some butter and a few eggs when you visit them tomorrow. And a bar of soap as well.'

Nothing more was said about Lizzie's return train to London. By the end of the week, as Lizzie went about the cottages and outlying farms, attending to the humdrum sicknesses of daily life (tonsillitis, which needed hot drinks and a dose of Dover's powder at night, trouble-some coughs to be soothed by Gee's linctus, and a measles rash for which she prescribed nothing more than boracic eye lotion to prevent conjunctivitis), it became obvious to her that there was a large number of patients who couldn't be charged anything. She began to wonder how Dr Stubbs himself survived above the poverty line.

'He gets it out of rich patients,' his wife explained. 'A two shilling fee from a farmer becomes two guineas at the manor. And for the rest we use a debt collector.'

Lizzie caught sight of the debt collector one morning

as he reported at the surgery entrance, which was at the side of the house. He was a bespectacled little man wearing a shiny black suit and bowler hat. He carried a notebook in which he wrote down all the sixpences, and even tuppences being paid off weekly by the patients, and over one shoulder was slung a canvas bag, in which all the cash was kept.

On Friday, there were two letters in the post for Lizzie. One was from Mrs Plumm with the sad news of Dax's demise. When Lizzie spoke of it that evening in the study after supper, Mrs Stubbs did put down her knitting, and leaning across to Lizzie, who sat on an upright chair between them, she patted her hand.

'He was a veteran in canine years, I suppose,' said Lizzie. 'I half expected it really.'

'Dogs, like men and women, all have to go to ground,' remarked Dr Stubbs gloomily.

'I shall have to concentrate now,' said his wife picking up her knitting once more. 'It's always tricky turning the heel.'

Her second letter Lizzie took to bed with her and read over again. It was from William Westerleigh who was about to depart for the far East – Japan, he wrote, saying it would be his last voyage before he settled down to serious work. And would she, out of the kindness of her heart to a traveller far from his native land, albeit a self-exiled one, would she write to him now and again telling him what she was doing so that he could imagine her at work?

He had been admiring the new Liberty wallpapers Rory and George were pasting up inside their Rocket Street home, swarming all over with Morris designs of honeysuckle and convolvulus, while Lizzie herself must be cycling between hedges of the real stuff. He didn't think she needed Liberty images when there were wildflowers all around her. 'To tell the truth,' he wrote,

'I find the new wallpapers altogether too vociferous. Personally, I prefer a sedate wall.' And would she drop him a line c/o SS *Miranda* at the shipping offices in Colombo or Port Said, where he could pick up mail on his way back to England?

He is a Romantic, Lizzie thought, with his wildflowers all round me. She remembered the purple loosestrife growing near the Posser hovel on Goats Marshes. Then she placed the letter between the pages of Frederick Treves's *Surgical Applied Anatomy*, which she kept on the bedside table with her candlestick. She couldn't read tonight. She had too much to think about. She fell asleep thinking of Dax trotting faithfully behind her on all those explorations of London they'd made together when she was a student.

During Lizzie's second week, several requests for visits from the new young lady doctor were received. Mrs Stubbs, who wrote down names, addresses and complaints under appropriate day and date columns in the big Visiting Book, nodded with satisfaction. The girl was being accepted after all, and Stubbie would have to eat his words. She, herself, had always believed that women patients, if given the chance, would often prefer a woman doctor.

Before Lizzie set out on her rounds, Mrs Stubbs gave her directions and sometimes a few tips with occasional thumbnail sketches of the people to be visited.

'Miss Mailer,' she said, 'is a very respectable, middle-aged lady, and quite well off. You can charge her five shillings. She's got what she calls an intractable sore throat.'

Miss Mailer lived between the post office and the village grocer's shop, in an unpretentious but substantial house overlooking the green where once, twenty years ago, she'd watched her father bowl against the famously-bearded cricketing doctor, W.G. Grace. Her father had been a haberdasher in Dursley, and a widower, whom his daughter gave her marriageable years to care for; and for this he repaid her well after his death. She left the town for the village she'd fallen in love with on that sunny cricketing afternoon of her youth, bought a house there, and became a village philanthropist, teaching in the Sunday School, helping the slower children with their reading as well as with their bible studies, and giving good, nourishing teas afterwards to some of the needier attenders. This lady lived, as Lizzie realised, at the other end of the spectrum of Gloucestershire country life from the likes of Shanghai Lil.

When Lizzie was admitted to Miss Mailer's front parlour she noticed on the central table an open book, and glanced at the title. It was *Uncle Tom's Cabin*, which had reached this English backwater nearly half a century after it had helped to ignite a civil war in America and in far-off Russia had made Tolstoy weep for the black slaves. Lizzie could see Miss Mailer was not well, though she hadn't taken to her bed and was fully dressed in a wine-coloured gown with a modestly high neck. She was a handsome woman in her fifties, with thick, brown hair only faintly tinged with grey above the ears, and steady, intelligent blue eyes. Lizzie found her slightly feverish when she took her temperature.

'You're the first woman doctor I've met,' she said. 'I envy you. I envy you your work and your freedom.' Lizzie, who was counting her pulse said nothing. She had noticed on the palms of her patient's hands a curious rash of dry papules like small, pink, paper medallions. 'Perhaps we could be friends,' said Miss Mailer. 'I should so like us to be friends.' There were enlarged glands in her neck and also, Lizzie found, when the wine-coloured dress was unbuttoned, under her armpits.

'Come to the window where I can get a better light on your throat,' said Lizzie. What she saw then was a long, glistening, ulcered streak over each tonsil. 'It's not at all like an ordinary tonsillitis,' she said. 'I think you ought to see Dr Stubbs to get another opinion.' She prescribed a soothing throat paint, and made an appointment for Miss Mailer to attend Dr Stubbs, privately, that afternoon in his study. 'Will you be able to come out?'

'I shall drive myself in the governess cart,' replied Miss Mailer.

'Wrap yourself up well, then. You're running a slight fever.'

Lizzie told Dr Stubbs about his appointment over lunch. 'It's the snail track ulcer of syphilis,' she told him. 'I've never seen one before, but it's just as it's described in all the books.'

'But that's impossible!' he declared. 'A syphilitic ulcer? Miss Mailer? Why, she's over fifty! And absolutely respectable, too!'

His disbelief was shaken when he saw her throat and the rash on the palms of her hands. Like Lizzie, he felt himself in a bit of a quandary. He could not suggest to this virtuous lady that she was harbouring secondary syphilis until he was absolutely certain of it, but, if she was, it was imperative that she should be treated quickly in order to prevent the catastrophic tertiary stage of the disease from taking possession of her. Wassermann, whose blood test was to make the diagnosis so much easier for later physicians, had not yet publicised his discovery. There was only one course of action. He must wire for a specialist, a venereologist, to come out from Bristol to examine Miss Mailer.

What happened in that interview, Lizzie never knew. She kept tactfully out of the way as soon as she saw the great man drive up to the front door in his well-sprung, comfortable, closed carriage pulled by a pair of well-groomed bays with glossy, well-fed rumps. She helped Mrs Stubbs prepare a splendid tea in the sitting-room to refresh the consultant after he'd made his examination.

'And is this the young lady who first saw the patient?' He turned and beamed benignly on Lizzie as she stood, deferentially, at the door when he was leaving. 'Well! Well! Remember it. You'll never see a more typical case. Beginner's luck, eh Stubbs?' The two men exchanged smiles, excluding her. The consultant took his top hat from Mrs Stubbs's humble hands and put it on his head, and the country doctor, in spite of his sling and his splint, hurried out with him to the garden gate, his every gesture expressing delighted subservience to his chief. It was all part of the professional hierarchical game in which the men knew the rules learned at school, in team games and in later training, and in which Lizzie could take no part. She felt, a little sadly, that she would always be an outsider here.

It was only after the great man had gone, that Stubbs confided to her: 'You were absolutely right, Dr Thorburn.'

Two months ago, Miss Mailer had allowed into her house an acquaintance of her father's later years, a Danish sea captain who, having sailed his ship through the Sharpness Canal to Gloucester, took the opportunity to visit his old friend's daughter in that English village with the quaint name, and stayed there for several days while his cargo was being unloaded and the ship's stores replenished.

'She will have to go into hospital in Bristol to receive an unpleasant course of mercury medication,' said Stubbs.

'Poor Miss Mailer!' said Lizzie. 'What about the man? He needs medication too.'

'He's gone on his way by now. That sort of fellow spreads his favours far and wide.'

The case of Miss Mailer's sore throat raised Lizzie's status in the Stubbs household to such a degree that

Dr Stubbs began to talk to her over the glass of whisky toddy he took every evening to help him sleep.

'I met Elizabeth Garrett, you know,' he confessed. 'More than once. It was when she came to the Middlesex in the sixties. I was a student there at the time. She couldn't get any medical school to admit her legally; but she was doing a sort of self-training on the wards under the patronage of our surgical chief. He was helping her all right; but we students, we didn't like that at all. We all felt a woman wasn't the real thing, don't you know, would break up the camaraderie, stop our jokes, clean up our bad language if you like. We didn't want her joining the club. So we signed a petition to push her out of the medical school. It put her back for a while.' He paused. 'I suppose she was a nice lady really. Can't even remember what she looked like.' Shamefacedly, he glanced up at Lizzie from his corner by the fireplace. 'We were backwoodsmen, all, weren't we?' It was the nearest he ever came to an apology.

Lizzie was silent. That was it, she thought. Elizabeth Garrett couldn't join the club. She had to get all her training on her own. And were other women also unclubbable? Lizzie thought they probably were; and they, too, would all have to go their ways alone.

But on Saturday evening, when she went upstairs to her room to pack her valise in readiness for her departure to London, Penelope Stubbs followed her. She presented Lizzie with an envelope containing her fortnight's wages, which Lizzie took with a sudden feeling of triumph.

'They're my first wages!' she exclaimed. 'Isn't that wonderful?'

Mrs Stubbs nodded and began to speak rapidly, punctuating her phrases with nods, like a sparrow pecking crumbs: 'And we're grateful – very grateful to you, Lizzie – for helping us out. We're both grateful.'

237

'Oh, Mrs Stubbs – Penelope – I've been so happy working here.'

'I suppose you wouldn't care to stay on with us for six months?' Penelope asked suddenly.

Lizzie turned in amazement from her packing. 'But – do you mean –? What about poor Ratty?'

'I'm not too worried about that young man,' said the doctor's wife. 'And as I guessed you'd be willing, I sent this this morning.' She showed Lizzie a copy of a telegram Molly had taken to the post office for her: SELBY NO LONGER NEEDED. THORBURN WILL DO.

TWELVE

Don't you think five inches a bit *too* radical?' asked Lizzie, scissors poised in the air. Penelope was helping her to shorten her skirts, which were becoming excessively mud-splattered on wet days. Her trunk, so kindly and carefully packed full of her clothes and books by Mrs Plumm, had at last arrived at the station to be picked up by Dr Stubbs's man.

'Not at all,' replied Penelope. 'Everybody round here already regards you as so extraordinary, that another inch or two less of skirt won't make any difference to your reputation.'

'Extraordinary?'

'Unfamiliar, then. And therefore freakish.'

'Is that what they call me – a freak?'

In fact, she was called Dr Lizzie. It was during her first week in Stonington that Penelope told her at supper how she and her husband had made bets on what her name might be in the days when they thought she was a man. They knew it began with *A*. Dr Stubbs bet sixpence it was Arthur; Penelope put her money on Algernon, and was looking forward to calling the new locum Algy.

'As a matter of fact, it's Alice,' said Lizzie. 'But I'm always called Lizzie.'

At that moment, Molly came into the dining-room carrying the cold, sliced meat, and having heard what was said, immediately set about spreading the news in the village.

Whatever her reputation, she was soon in demand, especially when children were ill, perhaps because she kept in her pocket a paper bag filled with dolly mixture. Every child who opened his mouth to have his tongue and tonsils looked at, was given a sweetie and, if he made no fuss, two.

Both the postman, who delivered a weekly letter with interesting foreign stamps addressed to Dr Thorburn, and Molly, who put the letter beside Lizzie's plate at the breakfast table, passed on the news that she had a sweetheart. The current theory among the women of the village, was that he was a sailor. Since the stamp was never the same, he must be moving about the world. A little distant romance added to Lizzie's value because it gave them something to talk about and, since the facts known were scanty, something to speculate on as well. The post office clerk was soon able to inform those who were curious, that Dr Lizzie was writing weekly to a certain Dr Westerleigh. Not a father, nor a brother, he must, of course, be a fiancé. Lizzie, herself, looked upon him rather as a reader of a journal she was writing to order her own thoughts as much as to entertain him.

She mentioned her most interesting cases, described the countryside and the villages she visited, and she told him about her two new friends: Miriam Mailer, with whom she spent most Wednesday afternoons (Lizzie's half day), and the lady of the manor who gave her tea, occasionally, on Sundays (her day off). Miriam Mailer she described as a good woman full of unselfish ideals who spent her life trying to help the less fortunate. She had even offered to do some nursing for any of Lizzie's patients who might need it. 'I can do so little,'

240

she said. 'But I can do something. If I could just light a candle in the imagination of some child, to throw a little wider circle of illumination, or strike a spark of curiosity towards an unexplored corner of his knowledge, then I'd be satisfied.'

The name of her disease had never been spoken by either of them, though each silently felt its presence between them. Miriam was still being treated by her specialist, and there was every hope that he would be able to check its advance. Sometimes, when Lizzie watched her friend, busy about the house or talking about her children in the Sunday School, she wondered about that Danish sea captain. She saw him in her mind's eye as tall and slim, handsome, though of course no longer young, with crisp, grizzled curls and bright, mocking eyes and a laugh and manner which swept away all fusty, small hypocrisies, a man used to dealing with the elements and basic human needs. And yet he did this evil to Miriam . . . Did he harbour any guilt along with that infection in his bloodstream? And did he ever fear the nasty way of dying which, if he had no treatment, awaited him?

She wondered, too, about Miriam. Did she secretly mourn her lost lover? Or did she, when she stood at her bedroom window looking out on the quiet village green, tremble with delicious fear to think how near she'd come to scandal and tragedy? Perhaps she smiled a little ironic smile when she reflected how little all the pious people attending church services on Sunday knew about her hidden life.

Lady Bescoby of Stonington, too, had her ideals. What an extraordinary coincidence that was! Lizzie had been called to see a housemaid who had slipped on stone steps as she carried some empty wine bottles to the cellar, and had fallen and cut her arm on the broken glass: a nasty gash which needed stitching. It was a mild September morning when Lizzie arrived at the manor, and the heavy, hobnailed front door of the Tudor house was wide open. She pulled the bell rope and heard the bell clanging through empty rooms. As she waited, she could see stone floors and low-beamed ceilings and a brightly sunlit corridor opening to a garden beyond.

A prim parlourmaid dressed in black with starched white cap and apron reprimanded her. 'You should have gone round to the back to visit Violet. But now you're here I'll take you through.'

She led Lizzie into the housekeeper's room where Violet was brought to her. The girl's forearm was bound up with strips of bandage torn from discarded linen sheets through which blood was seeping. Lizzie unwound the bandages gently.

'I can't very well offer you dolly mixture for being so brave,' said Lizzie when she had finished stitching. 'That's what I usually give the children who don't cry.'

'Will it leave a bad scar, Miss?' asked Violet.

'Not too bad I hope,' said Lizzie. 'And in time it should go white.'

The housekeeper, leaning over her shoulder to inspect it, commented: 'That's one thing a woman can do better than a man I suppose, and that's to sew a fine seam.'

She led Lizzie to a drawing-room walled with oak linen-fold panelling, where the lady of the manor sat at a mahogany desk inlaid with marquetry. When she turned round to face Lizzie she looked bewildered for a second before saying: 'Coram's Fields, wasn't it?'

'Why! Lady Bescoby!' cried Lizzie. 'I had no idea you lived here!'

'And how's your little dog?'

'Gone the way of all flesh, I fear. And rather recently, too.'

'Oh! I am sorry. I remember the little fellow well.'

After that, Lizzie was invited to stay to lunch, and then to coffee, which they drank on the terrace overlooking the garden while a family of dachshunds played around their feet, and after that to inspect the garden.

'It's really what I live for,' Mary Bescoby confessed. 'Chiefly my roses. They're past their best now, but you must see them in June – if you're still with us. Bliss it is, then.' She paused by a bush of red roses with a delicate scent. 'It's "General Jack". He's simply smothered with blossom in June.' She stooped to smell a flower. 'Dark red, the colour of blood.' She laughed, turning to Lizzie. 'I daresay you see too much of that.' They walked on to the next bush in the rosebed. '"Mabel Morrison",' she said. 'A white sport of "Baroness Rothschild". Very naughty. And she does turn a bit pink when the weather's hot. But you can't see that now. She's finished flowering. How's Dr Stubbs? Poor old Stubbie's going to miss his hunting with the Berkeley this winter.' When they reached the end of the path and stood looking back at the old house, and the dachshunds began to scamper home, she added: 'I suppose someone like you must think I lead a life of idle riches.'

Lizzie, watching the antics of the little dogs, was smiling. 'I remember you were busy with philanthropic schemes when we met in Coram's Fields,' she said.

'I try to do my bit. But down here in the country I give my heart to my garden. It's a small thing, of course, but I take the view that if I can create an oasis of peace and beauty for those who walk in it I won't have entirely wasted my life.'

All this, Lizzie recorded for William Westerleigh's amusement.

In his reply, which was posted in Aden and reached her three weeks later, he described her and her two new friends as the 'Three Graces of Stonington', who deserved a better reward than that endowed by the Ordnance map. 'You can guess which one I give my apple to!' he wrote.

Because he was so far away and she couldn't watch his face as he read her letters, she was able to write freely and truthfully what was in her mind; and he wrote to her in the same way, recording what he saw and what he was thinking. They were certainly not love letters; but there was in each, something that smouldered in her imagination, making her think about him afterwards. Sometimes, she was aghast at what he'd written about her. But he doesn't know me! she would inwardly remonstrate. He has built an image of me that isn't me. And she feared that when they met again, which was what he persistently hoped for, he would be disappointed in the reality.

Dr Stubbs planned to open a new surgery in Framthorne, in an outlying area of his practice, and he wanted Lizzie to 'man' it on Wednesday mornings. It was to be held in the front parlour of Mrs Holder's house, which stood beside the Frome not far from where the little river opened out to gush into the Severn. In Stonington, Dr Stubbs employed Nellie Birt to dispense his drugs, who was not a trained pharmacist but the retired village school mistress. Scrupulously, she weighed powders and folded them into neat packets, and meticulously, she measured lotions and potions into bottles before labelling them. There was no drug dispenser in Framthorne, so Lizzie was instructed to give her prescriptions to the patients, who would hand them, each with a threepenny bit, to Gubbins, the carter from Saul, who, keeping one penny for each transaction for himself, would then hand them to Nellie Birt and the next day deliver the medicines to Mrs Holder for distribution to their claimants.

There were not many patients at Lizzie's first Wednesday surgery, and only two or three prescriptions for Gubbins to carry to Stonington, but she was aware, as she mounted her bicycle and rode away, of being an object of interest. Bedroom curtains twitched, and old men standing on a corner turned to stare as she rode by. I suppose they're gawping at me because I'm like a bearded woman at the circus, she thought, lowering her head over her handlebars and peddling as fast as she could. Someone to be laughed at, that's what I am. But it was a beautiful October noonday, and she was free to do what she liked. So she decided to explore the Arlingham peninsula which jutted, a firm rectangle, into the waters of the Severn, forcing the great river to turn a horseshoe bend around it.

She cycled happily down lanes hedged with scarlet-berried hawthorn, with purple-berried elder, and golden leaves hiding sloes, all draped with old man's beard in thick folds of green and grey, as leafy and fluff-seeded a knitting together of stems, as densely patterned, as any of the new curtains sold by Liberty's. She bent her head and smiled, remembering William's letter. He didn't like vociferous wallpaper. He preferred a sedate wall. Well, she wasn't sure about walls but she did like a vociferous hedge in autumn; she rejoiced in its abundance as the triumph of a year's growth.

At Arlingham, she found herself in the middle of orchards, the source of the famous local perry cider. The little golden pears still clung to their branches but were outshone by the brilliant colours – yellow, orange and crimson – of their slowly withering leaves. Lizzie stopped to look at them. As soon as the pears began to fall men, women and children from nearby villages would come together to collect them into baskets which would be emptied into circular stone troughs in farmhouses, where heavy stone wheels would be pulled by horses round and round over the fruit, pounding and crushing it into a pulp, squeezing out the juice to be fermented in wooden vats. After that it would be stored in oak barrels till the following summer, perhaps longer, till it was ready to drink at tastings and auctions, which Penelope Stubbs described as 'wild junketings'.

Lizzie rode on towards the river and, leaving her cycle propped up against a hedge, she walked down to the edge of the Severn to stare with a shock of wonder at the apparition on the opposite shore. She was looking at St Peter's church in Newnham, rising in red sandstone walls and turrets above rocks known as Newnham's Ladder, which displayed such a richness of different reds and yellows it seemed like an old Turkey carpet spread below the entrance to an oriental palace. 'It's an unlucky church,' Dr Stubbs had told her. 'And fairly modern – the fifth erected on those rocks.' All the four previous churches on that site had foundered in floods, collapsing subsoil, or fire; but to Lizzie it was a fairy-tale castle fit for a modern Sinbad.

She walked along the riverside path and, turning a corner saw that the tide was very low and there on wide sands, cattle stood, some grazing desultorily. She wondered what they could be eating. There was no one about, and she feared for them in a rising tide. The second highest tide in the world rolled up the Severn, she'd been told, often in sudden, dangerous rushes, and at its highest, when it was called the Bore, it hurled itself upstream, pushing the river back, rippling in white-topped crests that overturned boats and threw into its treacherous turbulence any fisherman foolish enough to be still afloat.

She caught sight of the ferryman's cottage and his boat tied up on the bank, with a stand of salmon-catching putcheons laid up for the winter. The salmon fishing season was over now till next April, and all along this stretch of the river were fishermen's shacks and groups of these long conical baskets. Peering down into them Lizzie could see just how a salmon might swim in but be unable to turn round and swim out.

The ferryman emerged from his house to get a better look at her.

'I'm worried about the cattle,' she said. 'Won't they get caught when the tide comes up?'

'Don't 'ee fret,' said the man, grinning. 'There be plenty of time yet to call 'em in.' The words of an old song flashed through her memory: '*O Mary go and call the cattle home/Across the sands of Dee . . .*' But in that song poor Mary was drowned.

'What do they find to eat out there?' she asked.

'Not much on Pimlico Sand. Chewing the cud is what they do there. Maybe a bit of samphire on the far side. That's salty. They do like the salt.' He watched her, slyly measuring her reactions to his talk. 'And it be very good to eat, too, cooked with a bit of buttermilk sauce.'

'Sounds good,' said Lizzie, feeling suddenly hungry.

'You be the new lady doctor then?'

She nodded. 'It's my first day here.'

He jerked his head sideways, indicating the south Arlingham shore. 'There be a man downstream as is sick. He might pick some samphire for you if you can cure him.' With a cackling laugh he turned back into his doorway.

Lizzie had received no request to visit this man, but she decided to call. 'What's his name?' she shouted after the ferryman.

'Bert Weston. Been here a long time.' And he cackled again.

She retrieved her bicycle from the hedge and rode off to find him. At first she couldn't see any house, but after a quarter of a mile or so, she caught sight of two plumes of smoke coming from a dwelling which proved to be a pair of railway carriages propped up on pillars of brick. They were in need of a coat of paint, and the roof was held down by boulders. Beyond, lay an upturned boat beside a neglected vegetable plot where haulms withered on ridges above potatoes not yet dug up. On one side stood a group of apple trees, dreadfully deformed by the Atlantic gales blowing upriver but still somehow managing to survive and fruit, for around their roots lay unharvested heaps of little apples.

Sitting on the steps at the entrance to the first railway compartment, a woman wrapped in a black shawl was smoking a pipe.

'Good morning!' Lizzie greeted her. 'Does Bert Weston live here?'

The woman made no reply but removed her pipe and, grinning, pointed next door. Though her cheeks were raddled and half her teeth missing, her hair was coal black. She had a long, fierce nose and dark, glinting eyes. Lizzie thought that if she sat on a broomstick instead of those steps, and had a black cat perched on her shoulder the picture would be complete.

She knocked on the wall of the second compartment and shouted: 'Mr Weston! It's the new doctor! I'm coming up!' There was no response to her call, but she clambered up and pushed open a creaking door.

A very thin old man sat miserable and motionless in a sagging basket chair beside a stove. A pile of driftwood lay on the floor beside him, and a mug half-full of black tea. He said nothing when she repeated that she was the doctor, but when she asked him if he was ill he stared at her, and then whispered as if in fear of being heard: 'Poisoned.'

He refused to say any more, but agreed to take off his coat and lie on the bunk bed attached to the wall so that she could examine him. She sounded his lungs, listened to his heart and felt for lumps all over his abdomen, but found nothing abnormal. As she turned away from him, swinging her stethoscope and wondering what to do next, she saw on the wall facing her a fishing net shaped like a child's shrimping net but bigger than a man.

'Is that a fishing net?' she asked. 'I've never seen one like that before, shaped like a letter Y.'

For the first time, he showed signs of life. He sat up and swung his legs off the edge of the bed. 'Oh, arr . . .' he said. ''Tis me lave-net.'

'For salmon, is it?'

''Tis for hunting salmon. Made it meself. Dad taught me how to do it – make it and use it. And his Dad afore him did the same. 'Tis a secret craft. But I'll tell you.' He winked at her and tapped his nose with an assumed cunning. 'The landstaff is of ash, see. But 'tis a special branch of ash. And the rimes (them's the wide arms) is of new young withy. Got to be springy, see.'

'It must be heavy to carry,'

'Oh, arr. Heavy. And a man in the prime of life to carry it. You run through the shallow water, see, to where you spy the mark of the salmon jumpin' upstream. 'Tis what you call the loom of him. And then you scoop him up. 'Tis like shovelling coal. You never see him, mind, not till he's in the net and you throw him up in the air.' A look of pleasure passed over his withered face. 'Arr, 'tis like a Y for Yesterday. And 'twas like yesterday that I were usin' it. But all those yesterdays won't never come again.'

'I can't find much wrong with you,' said Lizzie. 'I think you just need feeding up to get your strength back.'

He shook his head and stood up. He put on his coat and shuffled back to the stove, which he opened in order to add more driftwood.

'What did you mean by saying you'd been poisoned?' demanded Lizzie. He lifted his head and nodded towards his neighbour.

'You mean she gave you something to eat which has upset you, and now you imagine she's poisoned you?'

There was a long silence. Lizzie sat down on the edge of the bunk and waited.

'Not that sort of poison,' he said at last. ''Tis in the air.

She's put a spell on me. Tells me I'll be dead before the year is out.'

'But that's ridiculous. How can words poison you?'

'She 'as powers, that one – powers you don't know nothing of.'

'And anyway, why does she want you dead?'

'She covets my 'ome, see. Wants it for 'er daughter.'

Slowly, he told Lizzie the story. Ever since his wife died, over a year ago now, the old witch next door had been telling him to go into the workhouse where he'd be fed and looked after. He'd soon be too feeble to do it for himself anyway, she kept saying. The place would be better with her daughter in it, who was only sixty. And when, at last, he told her to go to hell with her covetousness, because he'd never go into the workhouse but would stay here by the river where he'd lived all his life till he died, she raised her right hand and cursed him solemnly. And from that day forwards he had pined and sickened. Called herself a herbalist she did, and had many cures to her credit, so it was said. But how many people had she done to death? She knew about secret medicines, and poisons, and black magic, too, and some of the old river magic, he did believe.

'There's no such thing as black magic,' said Lizzie firmly. 'Nor river magic either. Now just you listen to me. I'll have a word with that witch of yours. And I'll send down a tonic for you. And you must cook yourself porridge for breakfast. And take some milk with that tea.'

He shook his head, but he did clasp her hand before she left.

His neighbour was still sitting outside her door when Lizzie came out. She surveyed Lizzie sardonically as she watched her mount her bicycle. 'He'll be dead before the year's out,' she said.

'Just you leave him alone!' said Lizzie angrily. 'He's my patient now, not yours.'

The old woman said no more but spat noisily to one side of her wooden steps.

A mist was rising from the river as Lizzie rode back. It was stealing gradually inland, cooling the afternoon. She shivered, telling herself it was certainly a strange place here, along the Severn, mysterious and full of memories of a way of life, ancient even before the Romans came. River magic, indeed! And the old fisherman really did believe her nonsense, too.

She stopped at the ferryman's cottage to tell him that Gubbins, the carter from Saul, would bring a bottle of tonic medicine to the Framthorne surgery, and someone would get it down to him. Could he possibly take it up to Bert Weston? The ferryman agreed, but shook his head so morosely that Lizzie wondered if he, too, could be under that black herbalist's spell.

'Oh yes, I know Ma Tinker,' said Dr Stubbs that evening, when Lizzie reported to him her visit to the railway carriages. He was clumsily trying to light his pipe with his left hand, so she struck a match and held it for him. 'She knows a thing or two about herbals,' he said, when the pipe was lit. 'And I'm not hostile to her medications. If they keep grumblers and chronic incurables away from my door, I'm grateful to her. After all, it was an old woman like her who showed Withering the properties of digitalis – that she could cure the dropsy with foxglove tea – though of course, she had no notion of how it worked on the heart. But it needed Withering's scientific training to establish the safe dose.'

'What herbs does Ma Tinker use, I wonder?'

'Valerian from rock walls to calm excited nerves, mosses to cover septic wounds. And she does make a medicine that cures rheumatics, so I've heard. I believe it's a stew of willow bark, so it's really just the same as my salicylate mixture.' He puffed and paused before adding: 'These people can be poisoners, too, you know.'

'Ma Tinker's poison seems to be a curse rather than a potion,' said Lizzie.

Dr Stubbs stared moodily into the fire as he smoked. 'These river people are strange folk,' he said at last. 'A very ancient race. Still some remnants of the British tribe, Silures, along Severnside, you know. They had their own gods: Nodens was Lord of the Severn, his power controlled the Bore. The Romans, when they first saw the Bore, were panic-stricken, thinking the river was erupting like Vesuvius; but the priests of Nodens could foretell the tides and warn of the coming of the Bore, which must have seemed miraculous to the ignorant in those days. He's a lave-net man, Bert Weston, isn't he?'

'He was,' said Lizzie. 'I doubt if he could lift one now, let alone run through the water with it.'

She despatched a bottle of *Mist, ferri, cum strych.* via Gubbins, and hoped Bert Weston's appetite would have improved by the following Wednesday.

The next day a letter arrived from Colombo. Molly dropped it on Lizzie's place at the breakfast table, and ran into the kitchen to inform cook.

'He's reached Ceylon,' she announced. 'That's what it says on the stamp. Where's Ceylon?'

'Dunno,' said cook. 'Foreign parts, likely.' She gave Molly a conspiratorial wink as they shared a little thrill of imagined romance. They would have been disappointed had they read the letter.

'Colombo still hot and humid,' William wrote, 'I suppose it doesn't really cool off here till January.' And then, disjointedly, he continued: 'Have you ever thought about the different kinds of lies? The old joke about there being three sorts – lies, white lies, and statistics – is really not fair to statistics, which, if gathered carefully by people without axes to grind, and reported honestly and impartially, can reveal surprising facts.'

He had been reading William Farr, the founder of the

252

science of vital statistics, and declared that his 'Report to the Registrar General' was gripping stuff, as easy to read as a novel, and quoted one of his purple prose passages: 'The children of the idolatrous tribe who passed through the fire to Moloch scarcely incurred more danger than is incurred by the children born in several of our large cities.' And did Lizzie know that more lives had been lost in England through infant deaths than in all the wars of the last century? The adult death rate had been reduced by vaccination to prevent smallpox, by sewer drainage which had abolished cholera and was reducing typhoid deaths, and even tuberculosis was being gradually vanquished by better living conditions; but infant mortality remained the same in 1900 as it was a hundred years ago. 'What do the babies die of?' William asked her, and immediately replied: 'Some, inevitably, of congenital defects, of pneumonia and other fevers; more die of starvation, life being cheap and food dear; but most die of summer diarrhoea.' Not so long ago, ten thousand babies died of it in one summer, in London alone. The annual epidemic was so well known and taken for granted that undertakers always made a supply of tiny coffins ready for the summer months.

'Children are our national asset, our future hope,' William wrote. 'Their price is above rubies; they are more valuable than the Gold Standard, and yet we allow them to be destroyed like this. It used to be thought of as demonstrating Malthusian principles – that populations die when they exceed their food supply. And later, as all part of Darwin's survival of the fittest. But' – and Lizzie could hear his indignation bursting through the lines of his letter – 'Dr Ballard of Leicester's recent paper has exploded that myth. He has shown that death from infantile diarrhoea does not follow starvation or sickness, since in over half the cases it kills previously healthy babies. Moreover, it is a preventable disease. So why is it not prevented? This is a most abominable state of affairs. It demands the attention of doctors. We must attend to it. But how? That is what I must think about next, when I sit idly on deck in the shade of an awning while the ship skims over the surface of the Bay of Bengal.' He signed himself 'Affectionately', and added a postscript: 'We shall have to work on the mothers of these infants. Today's parents are the first generation to have been compulsorily educated in the three Rs. Of health education they have received none whatsoever.'

Lizzie folded up this long letter. In using 'we' was he assuming royal privilege, did he mean there was a general public duty we all had, or was he speaking, more personally, to himself and herself? That raised quite a lot of questions in her mind.

Lizzie could hear a certain amount of hilarity coming from behind the surgery door as she worked on the following Wednesday morning, and thought she could detect a clinking of mugs when the door opened to admit a patient. This week, Mrs Holder's kitchen was full of patients waiting to see her. Some, no doubt, had come simply to look at her as much as to have their ailments treated. She wondered if Mrs Holder, besides collecting the coins for attendance, might not be selling cider to the attenders, but made no criticism when she accepted a cup of tea and a sandwich at the end of her session. As soon as she'd said thank you and brushed the crumbs from her bodice she rode off to Arlingham.

Her tonic mixture had certainly done nothing for Bert Weston. He was obviously worse. He'd taken to his bunk bed, where he lay, motionless, with his face to the wall. There was a stuffy, uncared-for smell in the room; ashes, dead and grey, lay in a heap on a tin beneath the unlit stove, and a chamber pot full of urine stood beside the bed. She could see she hadn't cured him,

254

but at least she would empty that chamber pot before she left.

'Did you take your medicine?' she asked.

''Orrible stuff,' he said. 'And I'm no better for it.' When he sat up, Lizzie could see his withered neck and bony upper chest in the open neck of his shirt.

'Have you been eating anything?'

'What's the use?' he sighed. 'I'm on the way out. Slipping downstream. Can't 'old steady against the tide.' He lay down again and shut his eyes, and Lizzie knew he'd lost the will to live. He needed a stronger magic than her bottle of tonic could provide.

Ma Tinker was waiting for her as she came out with the chamber pot. Lizzie heard her laughing as she emptied it over Bert's vegetable garden. The sound was suddenly overwhelmed by a blood-curdling lament, which filled the air. For a moment of horror, Lizzie stood still, but looking upwards she saw, flying in arrow formations overhead, skeins of wild geese. They had come from northern, ice-fast tundras to find their winter feeding fields on the salt marshes of the Severn. Those piercing calls were not of sorrow but of joy on recognising the New Grounds below Arlingham and the end of their long journey.

It was as she cycled past Arlingham church on her way home that she saw the Vicar busily raking leaves which had blown into the graveyard and across the path from the orchard beyond. He was a big, burly man, six foot at least, with a massive black beard. He stood upright to rest his back for a moment and, in his long black cassock with the rake in his hand, he looked like Neptune with his trident. Nodens, she thought, Lord of the Severn. An idea was taking shape in her imagination. She dismounted and pushed her bicycle through the lychgate. He greeted her, and when he propped his rake against the wall of the porch and went inside, she followed him into the church.

*   *   *

255

The boy ran on ahead, skipping about on the sea wall. He obviously found this more fun than his usual activities as altar boy. The Vicar and Lizzie strode side by side after him, each carrying a Gladstone bag. The cold, northerly wind blew up their skirts before them, pushing them on and hastening their speed.

'I've never done an exorcism before, you know,' he said. 'I had to get special permission from the Bishop to do it.'

'You'll have to don your vestments in the open air,' she said. 'There's nowhere else for you to change.'

As soon as they arrived, he put his bag down on the ground by Bert's door and pulled out his white surplice and violet stole. As he dressed, he had to wrestle with the wind, which was snatching at the hems of the surplice and fluttering the stole's silk ends. He shouted at the boy to dress too, and then he took out the silver censor. It was difficult to light as the wind kept blowing out the matches. Lizzie, after seeing with satisfaction that Ma Tinker was staring through her window at them, went inside to tell Bert about the impending exorcism.

He was lying on his bunk with his eyes closed.

'Bert,' she said. 'I've brought the Vicar to see you. He's going to purge the evil out of you and make you well again.'

He opened his eyes and struggled to sit up, clutching his grimy blanket to his chest. She fetched an old cushion from his chair to help support him, before summoning the priest.

'I ought to cleanse the air round the place first,' he said. 'But as it's so cold I think we'll dispense with the air outside. Go ahead, boy!'

The child climbed the steps holding the censor, and as soon as he was inside he swung it with gleeful vigour producing great plumes of scented smoke as he marched backwards and forward across the room.

'God Who by death overcame the power of death,' chanted the Vicar, following in the child's steps as closely as he could in the confined space, 'beat down Satan quickly! Deliver this place from all evil spirits, all vain imaginations and phantasms. Bid them harm no one but depart to the place appointed them, there to remain forever. God, Incarnate God, Who came to give peace, bring peace. Amen.'

By this time Bert was trembling, and his eyes stared in fright at the Vicar's right hand, raised above his bed.

'Almighty God, Who art the giver of all health and healing, of all strength, and of peace, we commend this Thy servant, Bert Weston, to Thy loving care, beseeching Thee to work Thy holy will in him to Thy great glory. Through Jesus Christ Our Lord. Amen.'

There was a short silence while the Vicar dipped his right thumb into a little pot of oil.

'Bert Weston,' he intoned, 'in faith in the power and will of our Lord Jesus Christ to heal and make you whole, I anoint you with this holy oil.' He then made the sign of the cross, in oil, on Bert's forehead, with the words: 'In the name of the Father, the Son, and the Holy Ghost.'

It was all too much for Bert, who fell back on his pillow sobbing, while the Vicar raised his hand in blessing over him.

When it was all over Lizzie looked around for Ma Tinker. She wanted to triumph over her, to relish the Vicar's greater power over hers; but Ma Tinker was nowhere to be seen. Vanquished, Lizzie thought complacently, she has retreated to her den to hide her humiliation.

They walked back along the river path, Lizzie striding ahead of the Vicar, the boy trailing behind to pick up a feather or throw stones into the rising tide. The rough winds seized the Vicar's cassock, buffeting it about to reveal sturdy boots and hairy shins beneath. It blew mercilessly, making his eyes water and his nose drip. Although he didn't look so much like Nodens now, Lizzie confided: 'I thought you looked so like Nodens, Lord of the Severn, you know. Quite apart from the exorcism, I thought you would impress Bert Weston with your superior magic, and so dispel Ma Tinker's miserable little curse.'

He laughed. 'Well, as a matter of fact I thought you looked like the nymph drowned in Severn waters. Let's hope we've done the trick between us.'

A week later, Bert Weston had risen from his bed and had walked along the river shore collecting driftwood for his stove. Two weeks later there was a good pile of it drying nicely under the floor of his house, and the potatoes had been dug and stored in sacks between the brick pillars which supported it. He was in his garden ignoring the damp wind which blew steadily upriver when Lizzie called. He was bending over his carrots, shaking them free of earth and examining them for carrot fly when he saw her. He greeted her cheerily, told her the Reverend had called on him and given him some calf's-foot jelly made by his wife. He referred to Ma Tinker as 'that old bitch', accompanying the description of his neighbour with a hearty spit to leeward. Lizzie was amazed at the change in him. How had it happened? How had that exorcism brought about this cure? Faith did move mountains, religious people declared. Could this be a miracle then? Or was it due to mesmerism? Perhaps the man she thought of as the Reverend Nodens had exerted a force of will strong enough to heal him. Whatever it was that had been done, Bert Weston was undoubtedly better.

She didn't see the Reverend Nodens again till the first Wednesday of the New Year. She was sitting at her desk in Mrs Holder's front parlour in Framthorne, had just dipped her pen in the inkwell in order to write the date, 3 January, in her big casebook with the marbled paper covers, when she was aware that the noise in the kitchen waiting room seemed to be louder than usual. They *must* be drinking cider in there, she thought, though Mrs Holder had hotly denied it when challenged. Lizzie paused, pen in air, remembering that the season was still within the twelve days of Christmas, so a certain amount of hilarity was to be expected, when a sudden hush fell, and the Vicar burst abruptly into the surgery. He seemed agitated. He stood before her desk and stared as if hunted at the walls around them before he spoke. 'I'm afraid I have some bad news for you.' His voice boomed like a sermon in the small room. Lizzie could hear the continuing silence in the kitchen, could imagine the expectant faces of those straining to listen to him.

'You must keep your voice low,' she warned him. 'The walls here are thin, and every word you say might be heard next door.'

He dropped his voice and leaned over her desk; somehow his bent position and his new conspiratorial whisper diminished his prestige and dignity. 'I'm afraid you'll be upset. I'm sorry,' he said.

'What's happened?'

'It's Bert Weston. He's hanged himself on one of his apple trees. You wouldn't think they'd take the weight of a man, would you – those stunted trees.'

'Oh, no . . .'

'Only a foot from the ground too, – his feet were when I saw him – the body, I mean. But there's no doubt he did it.'

'What a terrible thing!'

'I was called out on New Year's Day by Bloor. That's the ferryman down there. He'd found him. Swinging in the wind, he said, when he went to the camp with a bottle of beer, or drink of some sort, to share with him – to celebrate . . .'

'How dreadfully sad. And I thought we'd cured him, between us.'

'We did, Lizzie. We did. We gave him a short reprieve from misery for six weeks, nearly two months really . . . I wonder what went wrong.'

'It's that wicked woman. Willing him to die. She was too strong for all of us.'

'You did your best, Lizzie,' he said with sudden warmth. 'More than that. You were marvellous. Such an imaginative move – by a doctor, I mean – to think of such a thing, even if it didn't work out in the end.' In his confusion, he took her left hand and pressed it, playing absent-mindedly with her fingers. 'You're a marvellous girl,' he said.

'It was your miracle, not mine,' said Lizzie, taking her fingers from his grasp.

He stood up abruptly and, without another word, went out through the kitchen leaving Lizzie rather stunned. It was his wife who'd made that calf's-foot jelly for Bert Weston, wasn't it? What a mercy he was married! Imagining the possibility of having to cope with a proposal from the Vicar, even though he was splendid enough to figure as Nodens, Lord of the Severn, filled her with alarm. Poor Bert! He was lonely after he lost his wife; he knew he was losing his salmon-catcher's vigour; he fell ill with marsh-mist melancholy, and he died of despair. He did grasp at a few weeks of hope, but then, as the year ended, he had remembered Ma Tinker's prophecy: '*Before the year runs out* . . .' She had defeated them all in this battle for Bert's soul. And, no doubt, her daughter was already clearing out his cabin prior to taking possession of his property. She wondered what they would do with the lave-net. Poor old man!

Lizzie tinkled the bell on her desk to summon the first patient. He lurched into the room and sat down opposite.

'Good morning, Doctor,' he said, and a blast of alcohol wafted across the space between them.

'What's the trouble?' asked Lizzie, thinking: And it's not yet 10 a.m.! She would definitely have to speak to Mrs Holder again about the cider.

THIRTEEN

'You have no idea how much the Japanese appreciate the beauty of nature,' William wrote. 'Can you imagine the British spending a public holiday admiring trees? That's what they do here: go out in hordes to the country and walk about, feasting their eyes and marvelling at the colours of their maples before the leaves fall. And I have seen such paintings here! They have a special style of landscape painting quite different from ours. I just wish Rory could see them. I know she'd love them. I saw one of the sea, of a great wave rising up, its white crest curling and breaking, that was pure genius.'

His letter didn't reach Lizzie till Christmas. He wrote it on his way to Australia and posted it in Sydney. She could imagine him walking up and down the deck of SS *Miranda* in his white ducks, his hair thick and very black, as she remembered it, and his deep blue, eager and intelligent eyes not missing a thing. She thought of his sailing into the antipodean summer as snow fell softly and silently on Stonington.

Everybody was busy making preparations for Christmas. There was the life-size crib to construct in the lady chapel of the church; there was extra training for the choirboys who were expected to tour the village and all the great houses of the neighbourhood, to stand around front doors and porches swinging their tin cans containing lighted candles and singing lustily and more or less in tune about an old Slav king called Wenceslaus who delivered winter fuel to the poor, and whose feet got so hot they melted the snow he walked in; and there was Miss Mailer's Christmas party for her Sunday School children. Lady Bescoby's cook made dozens of little sponge cakes topped with sugar icing for their tea, Penelope Stubbs buttered and sliced quantities of bread to be eaten before the cakes, and Lizzie put handfuls of dolly mixture into twists of paper which she tied with coloured ribbons bought in the haberdashery section of the general store, so that each little guest could have a packet of sweets.

The party was held in the schoolroom. Desks were pushed along the walls, a long trestle table was put up and covered with Miss Mailer's tablecloth, and the food laid on it. After tea, the schoolmistress played the piano for the singing of 'Daddy Wouldn't Buy Me a Bow-Wow', which the schoolmaster conducted, fielding, good-naturedly, all interruptions in the form of barks and growls from the boys and giggles from the girls.

Dr Stubbs was beginning to write prescriptions again. His injury had taken longer to heal than a simple fracture because the shoulder joint was involved, and there was fear that he might be disabled by arthritis after the bone had knitted. So, when his splints were removed by the surgeon at Berkeley cottage hospital, he was ordered a course of massage and Swedish drill once a week at the hospital, and Penelope had to oil and rub his shoulder joint daily, at home. He took on more work in the practice, but he was not yet able to ride or drive a horse.

'Do you think you could stay on with us till the summer, Lizzie?' he asked her. 'There's a young man at Bart's who may be able to help me then; but I'll need you, meanwhile.'

So Lizzie was still in Stonington when the Queen died on 22 January and all the bells in all the village churches of Severnside tolled their message of woe into the cold air. The great Queen was dead. Many wept openly when they spoke of her. She had lived so long and had grown to be such a familiar background to their lives that it seemed a personal loss.

The SS *Miranda* was coaling in Malta, and William was on his way home, when the news of the Queen's death arrived by telegraph. Her going stimulated him to write to Lizzie about our good English queens, about the influence of women rulers, and how many more would be needed at all levels of government in the new century. 'Women don't cry havoc and let loose the dogs of war, do they? They are more concerned for the health and safety of their children. They don't have much desire to gallop about in hordes to achieve power or conquest over weaker enemies.' Lizzie wasn't so sure, remembering childish history books with pictures of the British queen Boadicea riding her chariot into battle and slicing Romans up right and left; but she continued reading the letter. 'Although all those many qualities of physical strength and courage, of aggression and ruthlessness, are, no doubt, still useful in outposts of Empire, and, of course, were very useful in the days when we lived in tribes as hunting nomads, they are rather an encumbrance to living in modern cities. We no longer need good fighters so much as people who are able to get along together in peace and consensus. Women are better at this sort of thing than men. What I hope is that when women have a bigger say in the running of governments there will be no more wars. Of course, I'm aware of the growing German threat. In Germany, women are confined to the three Ks, *Kirche*, *Kinde* and *Kuche*, and can have no say on the affairs of the state. The new influences must come from England. It may be that now, when we are more dependant on machines than on big biceps, women, who have, for centuries, been regarded as the weaker vessel, may prove to be the stronger. They are biologically shaped to care for their offspring, thence for others – perhaps, with time and training, for society as a whole. They are less egotistic than men, so might develop altruism enough to work for a new world whose aim would not be self-aggrandisement, nor the amassing of money for self but for the benefit of all. Is this an impossible dream?'

Lizzie didn't answer that. She knew William would be back in England as soon as his letter, which she folded and placed with his others in the drawer where she kept her gloves and scarves. He was, she thought, something between a preacher and philosopher. She did sometimes wonder what he would do next.

The coming of that spring as it crept over fields, valleys, rivulets and copses seemed a miracle to Lizzie. Everywhere, birds were singing, and the dawn chorus of maters and nesters in the doctor's garden in Stonington was so loud that she woke up startled in the early hours, long before breakfast time. The little wood she had to cycle through on the way to Framthorne was carpeted with white flowers of wood anemone so thickly that it made you think there'd been a fall of snow. The yellow iris began to appear on banks of drains and freshets where the kingfisher shot like a blue arrow in search of food.

'The elvers will be swarming soon,' said Mrs Holder. They were enjoying a cup of tea together after the morning surgery. 'Never a year went by but I used to go down to the elvering. But I'm too old for it now.'

'Elvering?'

'For baby eels,' said Mrs Holder. 'They come up on the highest tides, mid-March, at the full moon.'

'Where do they come from?'

'Nobody knows. But 'tis very far. Thousands of miles they do say. How they find their way up here, 'tis a proper puzzle.'

Dr Stubbs was more informative. They came, he told her, from the Sargasso Sea, whose warm water was their cradle, and whose rich nutrients fattened them before they were swept off in the Gulf Stream towards freshwater rivers. They came like invading armies every spring, year after year, had done so from time immemorial, rushing up with the tides into rivers where they spent who knows how many years before returning as adult eels to their spawning grounds far away in the Atlantic. It was a bit of a mystery why they travelled such enormous distances. Probably something to do with the water temperatures necessary for spawning. Perhaps coastlines had slipped and floated away from each other millions of years ago, carrying eels with them while the creatures still persisted in seeking out their old familiar haunts. It was so much of a mystery that Lizzie decided to observe the spectacle for herself.

So, on the Wednesday evening just before the Vernal Equinox, as darkness fell and the not-quite-full moon was rising, with the highest tide of the year expected, she stood on the riverbank below Framthorne, armed with a box-like muslin net lent to her by Mrs Holder and an old, lidless kettle belonging to Mrs Stubbs.

There was quite a crowd on the bank, but it was not noisy. People were talking, if at all, in subdued voices, all intent on what they were doing. Most of them were men and boys, but there were a few women, notably old Mrs Girder, whose family had, for centuries, held a royal licence to fish for elvers, some of which had to be sent to Gloucester in the old days to provide for a bishop's breakfast, and some to Berkeley Castle as a delicacy for the Earl's table. Old Mrs Girder was dressed in men's clothing and wore waders up to her thighs; but Lizzie, still in her long skirt, was, she realised, most unsuitably outfitted for this dipping. She remembered that time when, as a child in Robin Hood's Bay, she had paddled out to the collier brig to get her buckets filled with coal. Aunt Clara had simply lifted up her petticoats and tied them round her waist with string. Nobody had thought anything of it. Emboldened by this memory, Lizzie sat down on the grass and peeled off her stockings, which she dropped, together with her skirt and belt, beside a clump of reeds. She glanced anxiously up and down the bank before she stood up. She needn't have worried; all the elverfishers were too busy with their nets and buckets to notice her indecency.

At first, when she stood with her ankles sinking in mud, she couldn't see anything unusual in the water. She was simply aware that it was terribly cold as it swirled past her knees. The moon, which had been partly hidden by scudding cloud, now emerged very clear and bright; there was a murmur from the crowd, and Lizzie saw suddenly, beneath the surface of the water, another surface gleaming and translucent but rolling like waves. It was not a second thickness of water but a host of elvers on the move, madly wriggling as they swam, nosing always out of the salty water towards the fresh water of the river Frome. Each one was three or four inches long and quite transparent. They would have been difficult to see by day, the eye being deceived into mistaking them for ripples in the current through which other objects could be observed, but in the dark their skins caught and threw back beams of light. Two men standing near her held lanterns over the water the better to catch reflections from the glassy fish. In the light from their lamps the whole river seemed to be filled with elvers, a great shoal like a multifaceted mirror turning under the waves.

Lizzie stood there making what must have been a ridiculous figure in her white drawers, had anyone bothered to glance in her direction, while she witnessed her miracle. She was possessed by a profound feeling of awe. This mysterious annual pilgrimage of elvers had been happening for so long, it was impossible to imagine the span of time. They had come surging out of the Atlantic, pushing their determined way into obscure rivulets all along the coast, before history, before kings and their conquests were ever heard of; they belonged to a story more ancient even than the Egyptian dynasties recorded on the walls of tombs. She imagined the priests of Nodens catching and eating them in that magical, far-off time, holding a festival to celebrate this abundance of food at the coming of spring, rejoicing as she was doing now.

Lizzie leaned down, dipping her net into the flood, saw a thin boy's legs beside her own and, looking up into his face, exclaimed: 'It's Pete Posser, isn't it? How's Baby Pearl?'

''Ullo Miss Doctor! She's fine and fat,' he replied.

So she had survived. 'And the rest of the family?'

He nodded. ''Tis for them as I'm catching these. Lovely fried.' He grinned, and then bent to the serious task of filling his two buckets.

'How will you get them home?' she asked. 'They'll be heavy, those buckets.'

'Oh, I'll take me time,' he laughed. 'Plenty of time.'

She nodded. Time, she supposed, was the only thing he did have plenty of, apart from this sudden gift from heaven of spring elvers. She soon filled her own kettle of fish. Then she dressed quickly, lit her acetylene lamp and, hanging the kettle over the handlebars of her bike, she began the ride back. On the way, she passed an open farm cart. Someone shouted a greeting at her and, glancing up, she saw Pete Posser. She was glad he'd managed to get a lift for at least some of his way home.

William's next letter to Lizzie announced his arrival in England. He was staying in his mother's house in Bristol, and suggested a meeting on Easter Sunday to explore the countryside round Berkeley. 'I would very much like to pay my respects to any mementoes that remain of the great Dr Jenner of Berkeley, who lived a quiet, unpretentious life one hundred years ago, caring for the sick, enjoying an evening of good talk and music with a few congenial friends, and observing what went on about him. By his introduction of the smallpox vaccination he has probably saved more lives than any other doctor before or since. Do you know how it came about? He overheard a milkmaid say she would never get smallpox because she'd picked up cowpox on her fingers from a cow's udders. Smallpox then was a terrible scourge, killing a third of those who fell ill with it, and ruining the faces of the survivors. Cowpox could be regarded as a minor ailment, but it must, if what the milkmaid said was true, be in some way nearly enough related to smallpox to convey protection from the worse disease. Of course, at that time, he knew nothing about germs. He used a little of the liquid from a cowpox vesicle to inoculate a boy, who, when later exposed to infection, did not contract the disease. He then repeated the experiment on others with the same result. And who knows what vaccinations against other ills may, in future, be in use, as a result of this experiment?'

So, on Easter Sunday afternoon, they met at Berkeley Road railway station and cycled down towards the little town built around the massive Norman castle.

They were both rather shy at first, glancing at each other warily, grateful for being able to share a tourist's interest as a motive for their meeting. It was a cool but fine, dry afternoon, the hedges a delicate green fretwork, primroses peeping out of banks at the roadside, and birds everywhere, singing in manic mood. Lizzie examined him surreptitiously as they rode. He was well dressed, almost to the point of being a dandy in his good, tweed jacket and knickerbockers and knee-length, green wool stockings. He didn't wear any cap, and his marvellous black hair blew about his forehead and ears as he cycled. There was something ascetic about his lean features, she thought, and then wondered if it was possible to be ascetic and a dandy at the same time.

He raced down a hill faster than she did and waited for her at the bottom. 'You're just as I imagined you'd be!' he called out as she caught up with him. She felt a lift of happy relief that he was not disappointed, and mocked him. 'Did you imagine I'd grown old and grey within a year?'

They stopped on a bridge over the little Berkeley Pill and gazed at the stream which once had carried ships from Bordeaux with cargoes of wine for the castle cellars, and tub-like row boats of Severn fishermen with their tolls of salmon, eels and lampreys for the castle table.

'Lampreys?' echoed William. 'Didn't some king die of eating a surfeit of lampreys?'

'Ugh!' exclaimed Lizzie. 'Have you ever seen one? Disgusting creatures – black and wriggling and all sucking mouth! How anyone could swallow one I can't imagine.'

'What a pity!' said William. 'I'd been planning to order lampreys on toast for tea. Perhaps, on second thoughts, I'd better not.'

In the church of St Mary the Virgin, they found Jenner's grave in the floor of the chancel. The plain, stone slab was simply engraved with his name and dates, and those of his parents, his wife and son, all buried with him. It pleased

William that, in death, Jenner was as unpretentious as he'd been in life. As they turned to leave the church, they saw the fourteenth-century tomb of Thomas, Lord Berkeley, and his wife Lady Katharine, their effigies lying stiffly side by side, he helmeted, in armour and with sword, she in alabaster draperies with a girdle round her hips, their faces smudged by time's corrosion but their hands still piously pressed together in prayer. Lord Thomas washed his hands of the regicide by claiming that he was not in residence at the castle when rebellious Mortimer, with the support of the Queen, his mistress, who for years had raged against a husband who loved pretty boys, caught and imprisoned Edward II there. Nobody knows who did the deed, but the weapon was a red hot poker, rammed up the King's arse.

Lady Katherine, who outlived her lord, performed many good deeds, perhaps in expiation of the guilt of murder committed under her roof, not least among them, her founding of the still flourishing Katherine Lady Berkeley Grammar School.

After they had enjoyed a leisurely meal of soft boiled eggs and bread and butter, in a cottage advertising 'Teas', William and Lizzie cycled back to the station.

'I think this was the nicest Easter Day I've ever spent,' he said, as they stood waiting for his train. To her intense annoyance a deep blush spread over her face and neck. It made him smile, and his look softened. 'I hope we can meet again like this?'

'That would be nice.'

'I only get every other Sunday off.'

'I won't be staying with Stubbs much longer, you know.'

He was alarmed, wondering where she would go.

'I shall go back to my old digs with Mrs Plumm in Doughty Street. You can always write to me there.'

They could hear the rumble of the approaching train.

He wanted to touch her glorious, golden hair, to stroke her cheeks and kiss her lips, but was afraid that if he did any of these things the dam of his reserve would break, releasing such a flood of love that she would flee from him for fear of drowning. He knew he must proceed cautiously, allowing her time to adjust to him; but there would be no time at all now, because here she was about to disappear again in London.

He made up his mind, suddenly. 'I've got a week's leave at the beginning of May, Lizzie. I could put up at the Berkeley Arms. I daresay I could hire a dogcart. And then I could drive you about when you do your visiting – be your cabby. And we could talk – about the cases you see – and, oh, lots of things. And when I'm not with you I could study in my room for my membership exam. What d'you say?'

The train was beginning to slow down at the platform.

'No need to stay at the Berkeley Arms,' she said briskly. 'It's too far away. Why not put up at the Bullfinch on Stonington Green? They say it's comfortable, and not too dear. And the Stubbses would like your company, too, in the evenings.'

'What a wonderful idea! Yes, I'll do that. Goodbye till then, Lizzie!'

Her eyes were shining, and she was laughing as she watched him chasing up the platform to find the guard's van for his bicycle. He managed to get a seat by a window and, leaning out as the train moved away from the station, he stood waving till he could no longer see her.

Lizzie was left full of uncertainties but absurdly happy. William was clearly eager to be with her and excited by her presence, and yet he hadn't touched her once that afternoon, not even her hand. What did that mean? She stopped on her way back to Stonington and picked a field daisy from the side of the road. She was tempted, like any village girl, to pull its petals off one by one: he loves me, he loves me not. Her count ended on 'he loves me not', but as she threw away the plucked flower head she laughed because she didn't believe it. Good heavens! What a fool she was, thinking about him in this way! She had a job to do, and falling in love was not part of it. All the same, she found her spirits soaring, and her imagination racing as she thought of his coming visit to the Bullfinch on the Green. They were going to drive about the countryside together in May – the best month of the whole year. Lifting her eyes from her handlebars and seeing some April rain clouds on the horizon she prayed: 'Please God, don't give us too much rain!' And then laughed aloud. 'Cabby,' he'd said. He was going to be her cabby!

'I'm afraid Nurse Barnes is going to need your help at Hope Farm,' said Dr Stubbs.

Lizzie was not delighted to hear this news because it was already growing dark and Hope Farm was beyond Arlingham; but at least it was dry that April evening.

She was grateful for her strong headlamp when a weasel tried to cross the road in a hurry, making her swerve to avoid it. As she did so, the beam of her light fell on a badger turning away into the hedge. Farmers round here didn't like badgers because they kept on burrowing, throwing up mounds of earth which blocked the drainage rhines, damming up water and flooding fields. But what a handsome animal that badger was!

It was very dark when she entered the wood and so quiet that she could hear, above the swish of her hard tyres on the muddy track, the trickling of a stream as it ran half-hidden by hart's tongue ferns over its stony bed. She was glad to be in open country again when she left the wood, and grateful for the moon rising.

In the brightly-lit kitchen at Hope Farm, a girl of

twelve was calmly distributing to six younger brothers and sisters, bowls of bread and milk, sprinkling sugar over them with thoughtful concentration. Her orderly, practised movements revealed that she knew what she was doing, had done it all before, whereas a wild-eyed skivvy not much older, who was drawing warm water from an urn beside the range, was trembling with fear of what was going on upstairs. The midwife took the jug of water from her and then led Lizzie up to the bedroom where a woman, still in her thirties, lay white and clammy on the sagging mattress of a big brass bed. A single oil lamp burned on the mantelpiece.

'It's an occipital presentation, but the head's still high,' said Nurse Barnes. 'And she's very, very tired.' Then raising her voice: 'Aren't you, Mrs Drew, my dear?' And then to Lizzie in a whisper: 'She's been at it for twelve hours, Doctor, and it's her eighth,' after which her voice rose cheerfully: 'But don't you worry, Mrs Drew, my dear. The lady doctor's here now, and she'll help you out of this.'

Lizzie went to the bed and took the patient's hand. Mrs Drew turned her head and managed a smile. Complications were common in grand multips, Lizzie remembered. The woman's pulse was rather rapid and thready. After examining her, Lizzie knew this would have to be a high forceps delivery, which would be difficult to accomplish in the dim light and sagging bed.

'Let's get all these children off to bed,' she suggested. 'Then we could carry her downstairs and put her on the kitchen table. Could your husband help carry you downstairs, Mrs Drew?'

The patient shook her head wearily. 'Don't want him around,' she murmured. 'Don't want to have to worry about him at a time like this.' Nurse Barnes explained that they'd sent him off to look at a cow, which happened to be calving in a field at the same time as his wife was in labour.

As soon as the children were putting each other to bed under the efficient command of the eldest, Lizzie and Nurse Barnes carried the mother down and placed her gently on pillows on top of the deal table. The midwife administered chloroform while Lizzie kept a hand on the uterus. As soon as there was a contraction, Lizzie was able to pull on the forceps, and then the baby's head emerged, followed quickly by the rest of him. He was a large boy.

The mother opened her eyes and a few tears spilled from them when she heard she had another son. 'Bertie,' she murmured. 'After the new King.'

The uterus was ominously flabby; the afterbirth had not yet been expelled.

'You'll be able to have a lovely cup of tea soon,' said Lizzie, encouragingly, as she waited.

Nurse Barnes went to the range and pushed the kettle on to the hottest plate. By the time she returned to their patient, blood was oozing out and beginning to drip onto the stone flags. She exchanged glances with Lizzie. They both knew that haemorrhage from a retained placenta would kill Mrs Drew unless it was stopped.

The neck of the womb was still wide open, so Lizzie was able to insert her right hand quite easily. Very gently, she felt for the edge of the placenta and, finding a loose flap, she began to peel it away with her forefinger, gradually and steadily, even as blood gushed and dripped down the legs of the table and onto the stone floor, until she could feel the whole thing under the palm of her hand. It fell with a plop into the waiting bucket. Meanwhile, Nurse Barnes had loaded a syringe with a solution of ergot, which she injected quickly to stimulate the exhausted muscle to contract, so closing the myriad bleeding points. Lizzie gave a sigh of relief when she felt the uterus harden.

'Nice and hard, like a cricket ball,' she said. 'Now you can have that cup of tea. I expect you're thirsty.'

'Parched. Right parched,' sighed Mrs Drew.

'Keep your head down for a while, my dear,' warned Lizzie. 'You've lost a lot of blood, so you might faint if you sit up suddenly.'

It was her husband who nearly fainted when he came in, still in his dirty boots, and saw his wife, white as a ghost lying on the kitchen table in a pool of blood, while the midwife fed her sips of sweetened tea from the spout of a feeding cup. There was blood all over the floor, and the young lady doctor was trying to mop up the mess.

'Bessie!' he cried out. 'Bessie, love!' He fell on his knees and, grabbing her limp hand, burst into loud sobbing.

'She's all right now, Mr Drew,' said Nurse Barnes loudly, as if talking to the deaf. 'She's going to be all right now. Just you go out the back and take off those boots. And we could do with some more water.'

He stamped out, shouting for the skivvy to give him a hand. Lizzie could hear the creaking of rusty iron as he pumped water, and the bumping of buckets on the cobbles in the yard.

Later, after he'd carried his wife upstairs, and Nurse Barnes was tucking her into bed, and the skivvy was on her knees washing the kitchen floor, he was allowed to hold his new son in his arms.

'Thank you, Doctor,' he said. 'And as my new calf is a heifer, I shall call her Lizzie, after you, if I may be so bold.'

'You may,' Lizzie laughed. 'But seriously, your wife won't be back to her old strength for some time. She's lost a lot of blood, so will be anaemic for a while. You'll have to feed her up with good red meat, liver and beef, as she needs iron.'

'I will, I will,' he agreed eagerly. 'I can't understand it. 'She's always had them so easy before.'

'He's a big baby. And her eighth in twelve or thirteen

years. The womb's just worn out. She's had a hard time, you know. It was touch and go really.'

'Oh I know that, Doctor. I know that.' He swallowed convulsively. 'And she's a good wife. None better. I'll take care of her now, Doctor. Don't 'ee fret.'

Lizzie was sure he'd take care of her. He loved her; she could see that; but the best thing for her would be to have no more children. And how was that possible?

'She'll be feeding baby Bertie herself, no doubt,' she said. 'That'll stop her getting pregnant for a while. And I think it would be best if she didn't have another baby too soon.'

'I won't touch her, Doctor!' he promised impulsively. 'I swear to God, I won't touch her!'

Lizzie guessed he was promising the impossible. How could he, young, strong and ardent as he obviously was, remain celibate though forced to lie with her in that farmhouse double bed? And how could she, still only thirty-five and obviously fertile, not get pregnant again soon? It was a fact accepted by common wisdom that if a wife refused her husband too often, she would lose him to another more willing bedfellow, and that would be a pity for them all. If only there were some way . . . Lizzie thought. 'I'll prescribe an iron tonic for her,' she said. 'Send one of your boys to fetch it from Mrs Holder in Framthorne.'

And what a pity it was, too, she reflected, as she mounted her bike, that there was no way of giving blood direct into veins. That would certainly get iron into them quickly.

She was happily relaxed and satisfied with her night's work as she rode home. Wispy clouds wiped the face of the moon fitfully, revealing and then shadowing the massive stone tower of St Mary's church at the end of the lane. Then, as she approached, moonlight suddenly blazed over the orchard behind the tower making two hundred blossoming pear trees glitter like an army of crusaders in white battle array. The sight was so unexpected and so beautiful it made her gasp. She halted and, wheeling her bicycle through the silent churchyard, she stood staring, while images from the recent hours slipped across the screen of her memory.

It had been a difficult and dangerous delivery, but the mother was alive and the baby was a fine, healthy boy. A glow of relief, of elation filled her. She could say to herself, without false pride, that she had succeeded. Yes, she possessed a skill, and she had been able to use it when it was most needed. She had been at the right place at the right moment; all the faculties inherited from her ancestors, everything she was and, with learning, had become, had joined together to help her deal with the crisis she'd just faced and had mastered. A sudden sensation of joy, of being seized and lifted by a wave, exploded within her, drenching her with happiness. She was gazing at a huge pear tree of great age. It was the leader of that angelic host. Its mantle of white blossom shifted and shimmered in the moonlight, like feathers being ruffled by a mysterious wind, like wings; and suddenly she laughed aloud. It's my Archangel, she thought, remembering her childish vision of the ice angel brooding over the White Sea port in Great-uncle Mills's story. It had been the goal of his long sea voyage once, and tonight it was the summit of her own journeying. This bright night of fulfilment would burn forever in her memory. Had she, Lizzie Thorburn, an unimportant and still rather ignorant female assistant to an obscure country doctor, not been at Hope Farm, Mrs Drew would certainly have bled to death.

'Oh my Archangel! My manifestation of whatever God there is – I am thankful.' She supposed, as she took to the road again, that she must have had some sort of vision, or even hallucination. She rode as fast as she could through the dark wood, too dark now outside the narrow beam from her lamp. She didn't want to see any other, less pleasant, ghosts among the trees.

There was a light in the hall of the doctor's house to welcome her return, and by her bed was a glass of milk and a piece of shortbread, put there by Penelope's thoughtfulness; and a stone hot-water bottle was waiting to warm her feet when she climbed into bed.

FOURTEEN

May was even more lovely than April in the Vale, as grass sprang into its greenest, lushest growth, hawthorn smothered hedges everywhere with cream, and clusters of cider-apple trees behind every farmhouse flushed pink as the flowers opened.

'It's a sort of English garden of Eden,' said William flicking the horse with his whip, 'in the wonder-lovely month of May . . .'

They were on their way to Chill Woods up on the Edges. Dr Stubbs had grumbled when the call came, saying it was really too far beyond the radius of his practice, but the girl, Grace, who came to fetch Lizzie, and now sat, anxious and scowling in the back of the dogcart, had persuaded him. She had walked a long way to get help for her sister. 'It's the Miss lady doctor we need,' she said, urgently pleading. 'Special like. Ellen is bad, real bad, bleeding like she had no cork in her.' But in spite of these ominous words, Lizzie's mood was cheerful and confident as she sat beside William and watched with pleasure his strong fine hands controlling the reins.

'I feel like Samuel Johnson,' he said, 'when he wanted nothing better than to spend his life driving briskly in a post chaise with a pretty woman.'

Lizzie blushed with surprise and pleasure. 'It's not exactly a post chaise,' she said.

He laughed. 'You're so matter of fact, Lizzie. You should allow me a little flight of fancy sometimes.'

Lizzie blushed more deeply, this time with shame.

'You're so forthright and truthful. You speak out what you think. I envy you that. It's one of the things I admire about you. I find it difficult to say what I feel. My upbringing trained me to stoicism and to suppress unnecessary chatter. Sadly, I find my upper lip is often so stiff I can't speak when I should.'

'You're speaking now,' said Lizzie, encouragingly. 'You put it very well too.'

It took over an hour to reach the charcoal burners' settlement. The last half mile was uphill, which slowed them down, and the last few hundred yards so steep they had to dismount and walk beside the horse along a dirt track to the clearing, where a smell of woodsmoke hovered. There were signs of woodcutting, stumps of felled trees and stacks of logs around the camp, in the centre of which stood strange beehive-shaped constructions which Lizzie guessed were the charcoal furnaces, each built of columns of faggots into an upturned funnel which was covered with a thick layer of turf to damp down the fire inside. Two smoke-blackened figures nodded without smiling as Grace and Lizzie approached.

William led the horse towards a semicircle of trees. 'Don't worry about me,' he said. 'I shall be quite all right with my book.' He patted a bulging pocket of his jacket. Glancing back, Lizzie saw him stooping over a clump of foxgloves. She noticed how he bent his head and touched the purple spires most tenderly with those beautiful, strong hands of his, as if their tubular blooms were children's heads. He looked up and met her eyes and, smiling happily, waved his novel, *Emma*, before retiring into Jane Austen's quiet, rational world.

At the end of the glade was a group of wooden shacks, roughly roofed with branches and thatched with straw. Into one of these, Grace led Lizzie. It was no more than a bothy with an earth floor on which stood an old iron stove with a cracked and rusty flue pipe, which must have smoked abominably when the fire was lit. The only other furniture in the room was a rickety table and two upturned wooden crates acting as chairs. A ladder led to a room above.

'You can go up, Ma'am,' said Grace, as Lizzie hesitated. 'Ellen's there.'

A girl of sixteen or seventeen lay on a mattress on the floorboards. Instead of sheets, there were thick layers of old newspapers; there was no pillow on which to rest her head with its great tangle of black hair. Her cheeks bloomed with a bright flush, and her eyes burned with unnatural vitality. She was surprisingly attractive, and it startled Lizzie to see such beauty in these surroundings. She was reading a novel of the sort Matilda would have described as 'penny dreadful', which she now placed, print downwards on the floor beside her. Its title, Lizzie noted, was *Her Wildest Dreams*.

'You be the lady doctor then?' she asked. Her tongue moved over dry lips, and a look of fear flicked across her great dark eyes.

Lizzie tried to smile reassuringly. She took her patient's temperature and found it high, felt her pulse, which was rapid, and noted the pool of blood between her legs, which were naked, for she wore no skirt.

'I'm that parched,' said Ellen, 'I couldn't have believed you could work up such a thirst.'

From the top of the ladder Lizzie called down to Grace to demand a mug of water for her sister. The girl drank it greedily while Grace stood and watched her.

'Gentleman he was – or so we thought,' said Grace, ''till Ellen missed her monthlies. And then he said there

282

was to be no wedding bells 'cos he was wed already. Well, Pa would bloody kill her if he knew, so what she do?' She took the empty mug from Ellen's hands. 'What can you do when gin and the hot bath I give her up the hotel don't work?'

Grace was employed as a chambermaid in a hotel in Stroud, and Ellen worked there in a casual capacity when the place was busy, scrubbing floors, fetching and carrying hot water, helping Grace make the beds. Grace had her own attic bedroom, and sometimes Ellen slept there with her, no questions asked.

'Ellen is feverish,' said Lizzie 'She needs lots of fluids. So could you make her some tea, Grace? One of the neighbours, I daresay, has a kettle of boiling water.' And when Grace departed down the ladder Lizzie knelt on the boards beside her patient and asked: 'What happened?'

The girl's eyes filled with tears. 'I loved him,' she said. 'I really loved Alec. Smart Alec, Grace calls him. Well, he was smart. And I thought if I married him I'd get away from here, from Pa and his drinking fits, and all the dirt. All me brothers and sisters have left one by one, since Mum died, except Grace. Only the two of us left now.'

'How many periods did you miss?' asked Lizzie.

'Only three. I never showed nothing. But when I knew he wouldn't marry me I was scared. He dropped me like hot coals when he knew I was gone, like. He did pay the 'bortionist hisself. He knew I couldn't.'

Lizzie was rather scared, too. She knew she was getting into deep and dirty water. 'Where was it done?' she asked. 'And who did it?'

'Nasty little rat of a man – friend of his, he said. Did it together, they did, with me lying with me knees up on a kitchen table in the basement. I screamed when I saw his black finger nails, and wouldn't let him touch me, till Alec made him wash his hands in the sink.' Lizzie shuddered. 'And then he held me down while his friend did it. Stroud it was. Not far from the hotel.'

'What did they use?' Lizzie was curious.

'It was an umbrella rib,' said Ellen. Lizzie winced. 'Hurt something horrible. But I didn't bleed much, not then, not till I began to walk home.'

'You walked all the way from Stroud?' Lizzie was shocked into indignation at last. 'Why, it must be four miles at least!'

The girl nodded. 'Walking didn't bother me,' she said. 'It was the pains that come on on the way.'

'When was it done?'

'Last week. Six days gone. But I'm not right. I keep shivering, and yet I'm that hot. How long'll it take to get right again?'

Lizzie didn't answer. Instead, she took her syringe out of her Gladstone bag and filled it with a dose of ergot, which she plunged into the girl's buttock, 'It's to stop the bleeding,' she explained. 'And may make you squeeze out a few more bits of fleshy stuff as well.' She put away her syringe and stood up. 'Do you think you could sit in a basin of warm salted water every day to wash away the blood? And drink plenty of tea, water, anything,' she added.

'Pa wants to give me stout,' said Ellen. 'He don't know nothing, of course. He thinks maybe it's scarlet fever coming on.'

'A little stout won't harm you,' said Lizzie. She snapped her Gladstone bag shut and, clutching its handle in one hand, she climbed down the ladder.

A burly, bearded man was waiting for her below.

'What you bin doing to my Ellen then?' he demanded truculently. He swayed a little as he spoke, and Lizzie could smell the beer on his breath across the room.

On his return to the camp, Grace had intercepted her father to warn him of the lady doctor's visit. 'Ellen's

284

bleeding something terrible,' she'd said. Of course, he was suspicious and angry, although to Grace's way of thinking he should have been glad he didn't have to bear the shame of his neighbours' eyes on Ellen's swelling belly. He was always like a tormented bull when he'd been drinking anyway. And William, noticing his anger and his drunkenness, followed Grace to his door.

'She's very ill,' said Lizzie, cautiously playing for time.

'Kept the truth from me, she and her sister. Thought they could fool me, did they? Fell for that smart Alec, that gentlemen from Gloucester then? Silly bitch!' He undid the buckle of his belt. 'What she needs is a bit of my medicine, Miss Doctor, or whatever you calls yourself.'

Lizzie stood her ground at the bottom of the ladder.

'Don't you dare!' She spoke quietly, but with such intensity that he blinked. 'And what good would it do anyway?'

Surprise at Lizzie's defence of his daughter made him take a step backwards. He swayed widely and, to save himself, grabbed at the table, and then sat down suddenly on one of the wooden crates.

'It 'ud teach her a lesson,' he muttered.

Lizzie glanced up over his head to see Grace standing in the doorway with William behind her. He didn't speak, but raised his horse whip to reassure her.

'You've been teaching her that lesson for years,' Lizzie went on. 'What good has it done? It's not the sort of medicine that cures anything – only drives people away from you.'

He stared down at the floor and shuffled his feet. He was beginning to feel sorry for himself. 'Leaving me alone in me old age . . . only come back when they're sick . . . That's the way of it . . .'

'They run away from you because of all the *B*s,' said Lizzie, pursuing her advantage mercilessly.

'Where be the bees, then?' he demanded, mystified.

285

'Beer, bad temper, bullying, the belt and bruises,' she replied, censoriously. There was a long silence, during which he wiped his forehead with his hand, and sighed. 'Oh, arr . . .' he agreed. He felt uncomfortable. He was not used to admitting his faults; and this strange young woman's accusing stare increased his discomfort to such a degree that two large tears spilled unexpectedly from his eyes and rolled down his leathery cheeks. 'All alone in me old age . . .' he muttered.

'Well, Ellen mustn't be left alone,' said Lizzie briskly, 'She's very ill, and she needs nursing. Grace will tell you what to do.'

She passed him with her head in the air, but she was very glad to get out of the place and, once outside, found she was trembling. William felt it, too, as he gave her his hand to steady her when she climbed to her seat on the cart.

'Pure genius,' William murmured. 'The way you handled that bully.' He fastened the chocks to the wheels to slow them down on the hill.

As they emerged from Chill Woods and descended the steep track towards the Vale, a sparrowhawk, which must have had a nest full of young somewhere in the woods above, swooped suddenly in front of them, startling the horse. It was William who uttered an exclamation as he pulled on the reins. He had seen loosened feathers and a limp brown head hanging from the hawk's claws. Lizzie, her mind full of the painful scenes she'd just witnessed, hardly noticed it. She was stunned by the spectacle of nature's profusion all around them, confused by the continuous Magnificat of birdsong that accompanied them. On this heavenly May morning, when the whole earth was clamorous with glad renewal, the contrast between her inner and outer worlds was so great, so irreconcilable, that she felt disorientated. She felt as if she was living in a glass aquarium full of murky water in which she swam with other spectral fishes round and round, forever gazing outwards towards the bright air which they could never reach, and she asked herself: Which is the real world?

For a time, they drove in silence. Once or twice, William glanced sideways at her, respecting her solitary mood, but at last he asked: 'What was all the trouble there, Lizzie?'

She began to tell him slowly, trying to place into a coherent, medical case history, all that she'd seen and felt: the horror and injustice of it, the girl too young and beautiful to have to struggle so with all her demons at once – poverty and filth, the loss of love, the fear of disgrace, a criminal abortion done by the man with dirty finger nails who had almost certainly given her a puerperal infection – all these horrors telescoped into a few days of that poor girl's life, all lived through over again in remorse and nightmare as she tossed, feverishly sweating on that miserable bed.

'She ought to be in hospital,' said William. 'She probably has septicaemia. You'll have to get her moved.'

They came to a level stretch of road, at a place known as High Cliff, from where they could see spread out below them the great green plain, and on its rim the silver Severn gliding to the sea. William's heart leaped at the sight; and he remembered *Comus*. He pulled the horse to a standstill so that Lizzie could admire the view, thinking: What a pity it was that women have to wear hats to hide their crowning glory, but promising himself that one day he would tell her how like Milton's goddess of the river she was. One day he would overcome his shyness and speak to her eloquently:

Sabrina fair
   Listen where thou art sitting
Under the glassy, cool, translucent wave,

In twisted braids of lilies knitting
The loose train of thy amber-dropping hair.

But Lizzie's thoughts were far removed from twisted braids of lilies. 'There's no treatment for blood-poisoning, is there?' she asked.

'There's anti-streptococcic serum,' he said. 'But it's scarce, expensive, and would take time to get hold of out here in the back of beyond.' He put his left arm round her and gave her a little hug. 'But she'd get decent nursing care in the cottage hospital.'

To their dismay, when they arrived back in Stonington and had talked things over with Dr Stubbs, they discovered that the nursing care so much needed would not be easily obtained.

'An unmarried pregnant girl who's had a criminal abortion and is now suffering from puerperal fever!' cried Dr Stubbs. 'Of course she'll not be allowed inside the cottage hospital! Quite apart from the moral outrage, she's dangerously infectious to other patients.'

'What do you suggest then?' asked William.

'We might get her moved to the workhouse infirmary,' said Stubbs. 'I'll send a note to Dr Waller. He's in charge there.'

They were sitting round the lunch table, sipping coffee.

'Do you think I ought to inform the police?' asked Lizzie suddenly. 'After all, a crime has been committed. And if the girl's got septicaemia she's going to die as a result of it.'

'It would be manslaughter at least, if not murder,' said William.

There was a short silence.

'You're a doctor, Lizzie, not a policeman,' said Stubbs. 'It's your job to look after and, if possible, ease the sufferings of the sick. The law is none of your business.'

And he certainly didn't want his assistant getting mixed up in a nasty case of this sort.

Looking across the table at her, William could see the misery stamped on her face. 'This has been a rough experience for you, Lizzie,' he said. He knew it was something she was going to have to ponder over, analyse and, finally, store in her memory, learning what she could from its bitter aftertaste. When he left the house he turned in the porch and took her hands in his. 'I wish I could help you, Lizzie,' he said.

'You do William,' she murmured, looking at him and trying to smile. 'You do.'

He turned her hands over, then, and kissed the palms one after the other. 'Such competent compassionate hands,' he said.

For the rest of that day, Lizzie felt his kisses tingling on the palms of her hands. Several times she turned them up to examine them, sure that the skin must be inflamed, and surprised to find it looked perfectly normal, no redness, no blistering, just the remembered imprint of his lips. When she closed her eyes for sleep that night she saw again his bent head and the tender curve of his cheek. She wished then, that she'd stroked it gently, coolly, gratefully for his kindness. His name floated through her half-dreaming mind as scents from Penelope's garden drifted into the room on the night air. It was not the scent of sweet williams; it was too early in the year for their flowering. It was the scent of lilies of the valley, planted below her open window. 'Sweet williams . . .' she murmured, as she fell asleep. 'Sweet williams . . .'

The usual weekly letter for Dr Lizzie did not arrive at the Stonington post office that week. Instead, here was this slim and rather elegant young man driving her about in a hired dogcart. It didn't need great reasoning power to deduce that he must be the letter-writer. More than one lace curtain was tweaked aside in a front parlour window to permit a peeping of curious eyes whenever the pair drove away from the village green, and more than the ordinary number of regulars came into the Bullfinch each evening for an odd pint or two in the hope of catching a glimpse of the stranger from foreign parts.

'Fetching,' was the adjective bestowed on William by the younger section of female opinion, 'and a bit of all right. That's what.' The older women were more moderate with praise. 'Oh, arr . . .' they said. 'Might do for 'er then.' The men made no comment at all; but at least they didn't spit after he'd passed by, which was an indication that this foreigner from beyond Gloucestershire might even be accepted as one of them, when he'd lived in the village for twenty years or so.

Lady Bescoby and Miss Mailer both issued invitations for Lizzie's half-day off. So William enjoyed a pleasant lunch in the panelled dining-room at the manor, and a delightful tea in Miriam Mailer's cosy parlour. A great deal of admiring attention was mixed in with the hospitality. It amused Lizzie to see how his shyness melted under this warmth. He was soon telling them about Japan and the colours of the maple trees; and he excited them greatly by describing how he'd taken part in a tea ceremony with dainty little ladies who were Geisha girls.

'There's no impropriety, you understand. It's all a ritual of good manners and fine talk.' And then he added: 'It's really a civilised grooming process. It's what you see apes doing in zoos, you know – grooming translated into high art.'

There was no doubt he was popular with the ladies, which made Lizzie happy and proud of him.

Events moved quickly in the remaining days of Ellen's

short life. Dr Waller took her into the workhouse infirmary, into a small cell in the fever block, which was
isolated from the rest of the hospital – a bare room with
whitewashed walls and no curtain at the window, so that
the place could be easily fumigated after her departure.
And she was provided with her own particular nurse, a
girl of twelve who had been born in the maternity ward
and whose mother worked in the nursery as a cleaner.

Dr Waller's face grew grave when he spoke to Ellen's
father and her sister Grace. They knew his solemn tone
of voice was meant to banish hope.

'She's going to die, Pa,' said Grace as they walked home
to Chill Woods. 'And it's all that smart Alec's doing.' She
began to blub, and very soon she blurted out the whole
truth, declaring: 'He ought to be punished for what he
done! He ought to pay for his wickedness, same as our
poor Ellen, not get off scot-free.'

Pa agreed with her. He wanted revenge, bloody quick,
not only for the damage to his daughter, but for the insult
to himself as her father. He was a little afraid, too, that in
some way he might be blamed if rumours of the felony
reached the ears of the law. So he decided to play the
injured father. It was on that long walk home that he
and Grace agreed to go together to the police station in
Stroud, to spill the beans and demand justice. So Smart
Alec was arrested and, to save his own skin he turned
King's Evidence, informing on his friend in exchange for
the promise of a lighter sentence for himself. Penelope,
who had her ear to the ground in matters of local affairs,
relayed all this to Lizzie.

Lizzie was anxious to see Ellen once more, but the
Frenester workhouse, known as the Spike, was a long
way from Stonington. It would take the best part of
Sunday to get there and back.

'Let's go,' said William. 'It'll be my last day here with
you. Let's take a picnic.'

Penelope packed lunch and lemonade for them in a wicker basket, adding a small jar of honey and some jam tarts she'd baked, as a present for Ellen. William was in good spirits and sang as he drove south through winding lanes. It was not long before they caught glimpses of the Spike, so called because the spire of the workhouse chapel tower was visible for miles across the Vale, and, indeed, acted as a landmark for all tramps making their way towards it.

The workhouse was a large complex of red stone buildings with outer and inner courtyards and many linking corridors. In the front garden, some old men sat on benches in the sun. They nodded and grinned as Lizzie and William passed by on their way through a stone archway to an inner yard, where several little girls were skipping with a long communal rope. 'If it was Monday, they'd be inside the schoolroom chanting multiplication tables,' said William. 'And I'm sorry to say, getting caned rather too frequently. Workhouse education inclines more towards the rod than to the stimulation of a child's mind. It's not of the most enlightened kind.'

'They seem happy enough today,' remarked Lizzie.

They reached matron's office through another archway. She was a plump, harassed woman who panted a little as she hurried them along grim, brown-painted corridors and out across a worn grass patch to the fever block.

'She's sinking, of course,' she explained, speaking of Ellen over her shoulder as she walked. 'But she's taking her time. These young, strong girls do struggle. They don't go easily.'

The child-nurse sitting by Ellen's bed rose as they entered. To Lizzie and William she looked like an illustration from a Kate Greenaway nursery rhyme book in her blue-and-white-striped cotton dress, with her starched white apron and frilled mob cap, and her little black, highly polished boots.

'Is your patient eating anything?' asked Lizzie.

'A bit of porridge for breakfast like,' came the reply. 'And a dear little bit of taters mashed in milk for her dinner.'

'She might like some of these,' said Lizzie, handing the honey and jam tarts to the child, whose face suddenly shone at the sight of them, with such pleasure, that Lizzie couldn't help smiling. 'I daresay Ellen will let you have a taste of them, too,' she added, 'if you behave yourself.'

'Oh thank you, Ma'am,' said the child. She placed the treasures on Ellen's bedside table, and then made a quick bobbing curtsy before leaving the room.

Ellen was propped up on pillows, dozing, but she opened her eyes when she heard Lizzie's chair scrape the floor. Her clammy forehead told Lizzie of fluctuating fever, her pallor, of how great had been her loss of blood. Above her hollow cheeks, her eyes seemed larger and brighter than ever as she stared at Lizzie for a moment in silence.

'It's me lady doctor,' she said at last. 'So you've made me better then?' She glanced at William who had pulled up a second chair on the other side of her bed. She must have thought him a member of the staff because she greeted him politely: 'Good morning, Sir. Thankful I am, Sir – to be here.' He thought she was probably under the influence of opium, and smiled encouragingly, but she shut her eyes and took a long sighing breath as if even this effort of speech had been too much for her.

It would be useless, Lizzie realised, to try to read to her. She had brought with her a copy of Conan Doyle's short stories, intending to read one aloud to Ellen; but it was obvious that the girl's mind was wandering too much to appreciate Sherlock Holmes.

Lizzie asked: 'Is there anything you need, Ellen?'

She opened her eyes again and stared round the room as if she wasn't sure where she was. Her hands, already thinner, patted the folded edge of coarse calico sheet, smoothed it and pressed it, smoothed it and pressed it with repetitive gestures.

'There were a spring-water well,' she said dreamily. 'In the woods. Fetching water like, when I were a child. And sometimes I paddled down the stream. Lovely it was, so clear, the cold water gurgling, lovely between me toes . . .' She stopped and sighed again, a long, slow sigh. 'Like that poem we was learned at school . . .'

William leaned towards her and began to recite in a sing-song voice:

> I come from haunts of coot and hern
> I make a sudden sally,
> And sparkle out among the fern,
> To bicker down a valley.
>
> I chatter, chatter as I flow
> To join the brimming river,
> For men must come and men must go,
> But I go on forever.

'Forever,' murmured Ellen. 'That's it. Forever . . .' Her face beamed with happiness.

Lizzie was afraid she might burst into tears, but she managed to say: 'Can I bring you anything, Ellen? What about some lemonade?'

Without looking at her, but still smiling, Ellen replied: 'It's all right, Ma'am. So clean . . . It's all right now. Forever . . .' And she took another long, shuddering sigh.

As they walked back along the grim corridors William said: 'That sighing breathing – it's uraemic. She's going to die of kidney failure.'

Silently, they climbed into the dogcart for the journey back to Stonington; they didn't speak till they'd left Frenester behind them. Then William broke the silence.

'I always thought that thing of Tennyson's rather bad poetry, you know,' he said.

'It made Ellen happy.'

'Quite remarkable, wasn't it? The way she glowed.' He glanced at Lizzie and was startled to see tears running down her cheeks. 'Why, Lizzie, darling! Darling Lizzie!' he said. He pulled the horse to the side of the road and dropped the reins and, putting his arms round her, he held her as she wept.

'It's such a waste of life!' she sobbed. 'So cruel! So unjust!' Nature is wasteful, he thought, evolution cruel, and the world unjust. It was a doctor's job to mop up spilt blood, mend broken bones and, when possible, ease the pain of a patient's passage here on earth, while the priest exhorted the sufferer to endure for the sake of paradise after death. But it was not the time to state the obvious, so he simply held her, murmuring: 'Don't cry, Lizzie, don't cry!' till her distress had subsided, and then he wiped away her tears with his own handkerchief.

'I'm sorry,' she said, 'to be so unprofessional.'

He tried to reassure her, telling her she'd be all the better as a doctor for being able to feel her patient's plight. 'It's a razor's edge, you know, we doctors have to tread between being able to understand – and that does mean to feel – a patient's troubles, and to retain the faculty for clear judgement in a case.' As she made no comment, he continued: 'It's not easy to be so near a sick person and yet have to separate oneself. There must be this distance between,' he added gently, 'or we'd all crack up and end our days in asylums for the insane.'

Ibsen, in his great play *The Doll's House*, which William had seen performed three times on the London stage, had allowed his heroine to escape her cosy domesticity in order to grow up to be an adult, free woman, but how she would cope with the harsh realities in the world outside her little home he did not relate. Watching Lizzie,

William thought he could have told the playwright a thing or two about the trials and tribulations the New Woman had to face. When they moved off once more, he added, softly: 'But in the intervals between horrors there are consolations, you know. The amazing beauty of the natural world. And then there's friendship, exchange of ideas, and infinite jest.' And possibly love, he thought, but didn't voice that hope.

Lizzie didn't sleep well that night. She had dreams of water. She was paddling out to sea in Robin Hood's Bay where a boat was drifting, rudderless. Great-uncle Mills was leaning over the side; he wanted to catch her hand; she was trying to reach him but the waves kept pushing her back. Then, as she nearly grasped him, it was not Great-uncle Mills any more, it was William being carried away from her by the tide. She was in a wood then, paddling upstream towards a waterfall which spouted out of rocks between green banks where ferns and wild arum lilies grew. She was wearing a bouncy lilac skirt like in Uncle Mills's flat-back, and the boy on the other side of the stream was holding out his hand to help her across. She knew it was forbidden to cross the water, but she wanted to pluck a lily at his feet. As she stretched out her hand its lovely purple flowering head turned into a giant arum, *Dracunculus Vulgaris*, the big, black stinkhorn she'd seen in a botanical book; and that variety, she knew, was poisonous to touch. Later, there would be scarlet berries. She woke with a pounding heart and a feeling of relief that she'd escaped some nameless danger.

On Monday morning, after breakfast, Stubbs's wagonette was to take William to the station. Lizzie saw him to the porch. 'I've enjoyed your visit,' she said.

'So have I, Lizzie. Of course. So much . . .' He held her hand and looked into her face searchingly; but she dropped her eyes and released her hand. 'You'll write?' he asked.

She nodded. There was no time to say more; William had a train to catch, she had a surgery full of patients waiting to see her; but later in the day she felt a little sadness creeping over her. Next morning when she woke, she didn't look forward to the day as she had when William was near at hand, and later in the week she realised her appetite for life seemed to have lost its keen edge. There was no excitement to it. And when, during her work, she sometimes said to herself: I must tell William that, and knew she couldn't, his absence checked her eagerness. She was missing him. She was about to leave her friends in Stonington too, and the thought of living in London, with all her former student chums scattered, Prosy in India already, made her heart sink. There would be George, of course, from time to time, and Rory in her newly-decorated Rocket Street house, who was expecting her first baby.

She spent her last Sunday in the Vale saying fare-wells. To Miriam Mailer she gave her copy of *Trilby*, a novel she'd read more than once. It was a bestseller, was also dramatised by its author, George du Maurier. Lizzie and Prosy had queued for hours for gallery seats, to see Trilby, the Parisian artists' model, pose 'in the altogether'. Unfortunately, the censor would not permit this indecency, so they were disappointed that no more than her bare arms were visible behind a screen; but they did enjoy the thrill of watching Beerbohm Tree as the wicked Svengali, mesmerising Trilby into singing like an operatic star, till he fell ill and died, when poor Trilby collapsed ignominiously on stage. The play was all the rage in London for a time; and the hat Trilby wore – a soft black felt with an indentation in the crown – became so popular an item of men's wear that no young man in the swim of things would appear on the streets without one. Lizzie wrote on the book's title page: 'To my friend, Miriam Mailer, with affection.' And Miriam, clasping *Trilby* to her bosom, declared she would never forget Lizzie as long as she lived.

They walked together to the garden gate where they shook hands solemnly, and then Miriam suddenly asked: 'So you've said goodbye to William? I do hope it's not for long.' When Lizzie said nothing, Miriam spoke urgently: 'He loves you truly, Lizzie. You only have to look into those beautiful, sad eyes to see that.'

Lizzie was surprised to hear Miriam speak so, and slightly nettled, too, when she thought of anyone else but herself looking deeply into William's eyes.

'Such a love as he has for you,' Miriam pursued her pleading. 'It's a once-in-a-lifetime thing, you know. It's rare, Lizzie. You mustn't cast it aside.'

Lizzie laughed as lightly as she could. 'My dear Miriam, such a Romantic you are! But romance is not for me. I have work to do.'

Lady Bescoby came straight to the point. 'Are you going to marry that delightful doctor of yours?' she demanded.

'He's not mine!' declared Lizzie indignantly.

'More's the pity. Such a handsome man! And if you don't, I do believe you'll break his heart.'

Breaking William's heart seemed suddenly cruel, and rather painful for Lizzie as well. 'I want to be a doctor,' she objected, 'not a doctor's wife.'

'Ah, well!' sighed Mary Bescoby. 'I expect you'll get married in the end like the rest of us. But you won't desert us altogether, will you? I hope you'll come back in June to smell "General Jack" and see my "Mabel Morrison" blush as the temperature rises.'

They walked out onto the terrace where, immediately, a crowd of dachshund puppies hurled themselves around their feet. Mary picked one up and, stroking its head, she examined its face closely. 'I'd like to give you one to keep you company in London.'

'Oh, I say!' cried Lizzie as she took the little bitch from her friend's arms. 'What a wonderful present! You couldn't have thought of anything that would please me more!' She tickled the dog's ears and murmured: 'Daxie. I shall call you Daxie.'

Penelope was practical with her farewells, tucking a paper bag full of homemade scones into a spare corner of Lizzie's trunk. 'No good giving you butter,' she said. 'That would only melt in the heat of the train. And jam might ooze out from under the lid. But here's some Arlingham perry for you to drink with friends.' As she wrapped the bottle carefully inside a flannel petticoat, she added: 'Stubbie thinks you and William would make a good team, you know – professionally. To me, you seem so suited. And what a nice man he is!'

Lizzie stood fiddling awkwardly with the buckle of her belt.

'Well, you'd better make your mind up, Lizzie,' said Penelope. 'If you don't snap him up soon, someone else will.'

The thought of someone else snapping him up annoyed and rather alarmed her, too. Was it possible she was just a little jealous of this non-existent someone?

Dr Stubbs stood at the gate while her trunk, travelling valise and Gladstone bag were loaded on to the wagonette, and the new puppy, tied to her new leather leash, was tucked under Lizzie's arm. Penelope kissed her. 'I shall miss you,' she said. 'I've enjoyed your company, and our evening talks.' Dr Stubbs was wordless with farewell; but he shook Lizzie's hand with such a powerful pumping action that she couldn't help remarking that his shoulder muscles had certainly regained their former strength. He grinned rather mournfully, and stood waving till she was out of sight.

When they had travelled at least ten minutes in silence, and Daxie was comfortably asleep in her lap, Lizzie tried a little conversation with her driver.

'How are your cabbages this year?'

'Bad. Slugs got at 'em.'

'I'm sorry to hear that. Can't you do anything about it?'

'Oh, arr . . . I kill 'em off with beer. I puts out a saucer of beer and they crawl into it and die of drink.'

'I suppose it's quite a nice way for them to die.'

'Better 'n they deserve. Buggers they are for beer. Slugs is buggers anyway, and that's the truth. There's no denying it.' After that, exhausted by speech, he said no more.

FIFTEEN

London seemed surprisingly dull and uneventful after the busy Stonington days. Her idle hours made Lizzie feel uneasy, especially when she thought about her future. In the mornings she walked with Daxie in Coram's Fields. Dickens must have walked here, she thought, so near to his Doughty Street house; and, indeed, he had put a female foundling from Dr Coram's hospital into his novel, *Little Dorrit*, giving her the uncomfortable name of Tattycoram: a wild, unruly girl, as Lizzie supposed children without proper families to prune their wilfulness tended to be – as she herself might have been, had she been motherless.

She borrowed *Edwin Drood* from the public library and read it with eagerness, wondering how Dickens had meant to finish the story had he lived long enough. How imaginatively he set the scene! 'Not only is the day waning, but the year. The low sun is fiery and yet cold behind the monastery ruin, and the Virginia creeper on the cathedral wall has showered half its deep red leaves down on the pavement. There has been rain this afternoon, and a wintry shudder goes among the little pools on the cracked, uneven flagstones, and through the giant elm trees as they shed a gust of tears.' In the quiet, orderly cathedral city all is not well: a hint of evil creeps into the reader's mind, and the menace of murder burns in the red sky. But who would do the deed?

Trying to plot the missing end of *Edwin Drood*, and walking with Daxie in Coram's Fields, could not entirely keep at bay her anxieties. She had some money in the bank, accumulated during her work as assistant to Dr Stubbs, but it would not last for ever, and she had no job now, nor much hope of getting one. She scanned the advertisements in the medical papers. The position of Medical Superintendent to the Asylum for the Insane in Mullingar was still vacant, either never filled, or left in a hurry by the previous incumbent. A lady doctor was needed in the Port of Suez to examine women and children returning from India and the Far East for quarantine purposes before they were permitted to travel on through the canal, homeward bound. It would, she thought, be the perfect job for any woman doctor seeking a husband. There would be plenty of bachelor Indian army officers and Indian civil servants returning to England on leave and on the lookout for a suitable wife; but Lizzie wasn't on the lookout for a husband. Severely, she reminded herself that husband and children, all the warmth of fireside family life, were not for her. Sometimes she argued against herself: Didn't Elizabeth Garrett marry and have children? Well, yes . . . But only in her late thirties when she was well established, professionally, and had won her battles. Lizzie's battles were only beginning. So marriage with William was unthinkable – and yet she thought about him every day, and with increasing misery as time went by and no letter from him arrived through the post.

She was missing his letters, and she was missing him. What had happened to him? She knew he was studying for that difficult higher exam for membership of the Royal College of Physicians. Was he so absorbed in study that he had forgotten her? Or had he decided that, after all, they were ill matched? Perhaps getting to know her better during that week he had spent in Stonington had opened his eyes to her faults? She combed through her recollections of their hours together, of their conversations, trying to find any hints of reasons why he didn't write. She wondered if her breaking down in tears during that drive back from the Spike had disgusted, or disappointed him, had made him think she was too weak a woman to be a doctor; but she couldn't forget how tenderly he'd held her, calling her 'Lizzie, darling Lizzie'. That hardly denoted disgust and disappointment. She remembered how once he'd said: 'We're very different, Lizzie. I am an observer of life, not a partaker in it as you are. I stand on the edge of the river and watch the swimmers in the water while you plunge in and strike across the stream.' Perhaps he had come to the conclusion that they were too different; but she remembered, too, that he'd said: 'Our very difference is the reason why we could make the two halves of one whole.'

All the time she was out walking with Daxie, her mood was swung from hope of hearing from William tomorrow to fear of never seeing him again, and back through uncertainty to hope once more, until at last, one morning, she sat down on a bench in Coram's Fields, picked up the dog and, tickling the little bitch's ears, said softly: 'The fact is, Daxie, the dreadful truth is that I must be in love.'

She hadn't felt like this over Tob, she reflected. That affair was different. She hadn't really known what was happening then. Love had caught her unawares like a force of nature, like a hurricane slowly gathering speed and sweeping her off her feet, before throwing her down in its calamitous rush. After Tob's death, her heart had closed up, had shut out love. She was older now, her intelligence more focused. She was clearly aware that to pursue her chosen career she must remain celibate; she was aware, too, that in spite of her reason, her heart was making a fool of her, so she lectured herself: Falling in love is like walking into a form of slavery. All that she'd struggled for, the freedom and independence that she'd fought so hard to achieve and had so triumphantly won, were being imperilled. But her heart told her that William was kind and understanding about the Women's Struggle. And he did have such deep, sad eyes. The strongest pull he had on her, in fact, was that he needed her. Although he had been ready to stand up for her against Ellen's great, bullying father with that ludicrous little whip, she sometimes wondered if it wasn't he who needed her protection. William was cleverer than she was, and older; but there were times when he seemed so young and vulnerable that she thought of him as a child. She remembered the evening when he prophesied that some day women would be sitting in the House of Commons.

'God forbid!' Dr Stubbs protested. 'We don't want the hand that rocks the cradle rocking the parliamentary boat!'

'Oh Stubbie, don't be such a stick-in-the mud!' said his wife.

'And if women are to invade our man's world who will do women's work in the home?' pursued Stubbs.

'Machines will be developed to do most of it,' William explained. 'Machines will do the work of servants in time to come.'

Stubbs waved his pipe in the air. 'You are a hopeless dreamer, William,' he said.

William was hurt and angry to be so dismissed, and Lizzie, reading his feelings on his face longed to protect him. She knew his idealism would inevitably be bruised by the rough world, and that made her feel older and wiser than William.

By the end of a fortnight in London, she believed it was all her fault. It was she, herself, who had pushed him away by her coldness. The hardness of heart she had assumed in order to strengthen her singleness of purpose had convinced him that she would never love him; her lack of response had discouraged him so deeply that he'd given up trying to win her. Remembering Mary Bescoby's prophesy, she began to worry that perhaps she had, indeed, broken William's heart. So sensitive a man would be easily cast down.

And it was she who had wounded him. Was he now sitting, hopeless and desperate and unable to concentrate on his studies, in his mother's house in Bristol? She thought of Miriam Mailer's words: 'It's a once-in-a-lifetime thing. Such love is rare.' Regret flooded her for what she had roughly refused and deservedly lost.

And then his letter arrived.

He had been appointed Registrar at the Bristol Royal Infirmary, had been thrown head first into the deep end, as he put it, with several wards full of patients to get to know, and all their records to read and keep in proper order, as well as all the new medical cases sent in by the chief; but Sunday was to be his first day off. And would she travel down to Bristol on Brunel's Great Western Railway to the station at Temple Meads where he would meet her? 'Telephone from the Great Western Hotel at Paddington,' he wrote. 'There's a telephone there. Ask them to connect you with the hospital and let me know the time of your arrival.'

Though she had admired, from afar, the telephones installed at the Royal Free Hospital, Lizzie had never used one before. She found the manoeuvre terribly exciting. She heard a bell ringing at the other end and a woman's voice answering, then waited while strange sounds, clicks, buzzes and, perhaps, footsteps sounded in her ear, and then suddenly she heard William's voice.

'Is that really you, William?' she asked. 'How wonderful to be able to talk like this! It's a miracle really, isn't it? You sound quite near, too, though you are a bit squeaky. I'm so excited, I can't believe it!'

When William replaced the receiver he was, for a few seconds, dazed with joy at her enthusiasm, till it dawned on him that her delight was probably not so much for hearing his voice, as for the telephone itself. He remembered her excitement at the Motor Car Club lunch, and recognised that she must be someone who was entranced by new inventions. All the same he couldn't help laughing a little as he hung up his white coat in the staff cloakroom and handed over his weekend responsibilities to the other registrar.

Lizzie opened the carriage window as the train arrived, and leaned out, trying to identify William in the crowd on the platform. He was scanning the windows of the incoming train when she saw him, saw his well-cut suit of grey worsted on his lean body, saw the black felt trilby on his head and thought: Really, he is quite the dandy! As soon as he caught sight of her he snatched the hat off his head and, waving it high in the air, began to run up the platform ahead of her carriage. She used to say in later years, that it was then, at the moment when she saw his face, eager as a child's before a Christmas party, that she decided to marry him. When the train came to a halt, he was standing just below her carriage door. He pulled it open, and she, in her eagerness to get out, tripped on the step and fell straight into his arms, which her mother would have considered an improper action, since they were not engaged, no proposal of marriage had been uttered, and no declaration of love had ever, as yet, been spoken by either of them. There was no need for any of these formalities. Any passerby on that Sunday afternoon in June, would have seen, with one glance at the radiance in their faces, what was happening to them.

He didn't take her straight home to his mother's house. He wanted to show her something of his native city of Bristol on the way, so he hired a fly from the rank in the station yard and ordered the driver to Clifton to look at the fine eighteenth-century houses there, and then to the great open space of the Downs, which he described as the city's green lung, and lastly to Brunel's suspension bridge over the Avon Gorge. Here they dismounted, asking the driver to wait, and walked across, admiring the view up and down the river, the steep cliffs on either side and the great drop down to the water below.

'It's awfully far down,' said Lizzie, peering over the railing.

'Somebody or other tries to jump off it nearly every year,' he said cheerfully. 'Not so long after it was opened, when a young lady tried to jump to her death, her crinoline filled like a balloon and held her up till she landed gently in the mud.'

'What a mercy!' Lizzie exclaimed. But she was thinking more about the first transatlantic liner Brunel built, which must have chugged its way under the spot where they stood, out of the Avon and into the Bristol Channel and then across mountainous seas to the New World.

William's mother's house on Ashley Down was large and rambling, surrounded by informal gardens planted with some uncommon trees. At the gate were shrubberies of rhododendron encroaching on the drive, but at the back of the house, where he led her, was a sunny lawn, and there on a white-painted, metal chair sat a plump, smiling widow dressed in black with an old-fashioned, starched white cap on her head, and a fine gold watch suspended by a chain round her neck. It was with the help of this timepiece that she ordered her hours quietly into their proper routine: attendance at meetings to organise good works, chiefly, but not exclusively, to do with the running of the hospital; corresponding with all her four daughters who were in India working in a school for Indian girls, and overseeing the thrifty but not frugal management of her house with its four servants. She was a calm, comfortable person, perfectly adapted to her function and her times.

'Come and sit down, my dear,' she said, as Lizzie stood hesitating. 'Phyllis will bring out the tea in a few minutes. I've heard such a lot about you from William, but, of course, I'd rather see you for myself. William's very good at diagnosing diseases, but it takes a woman's eye to size up a character.'

Rather nervous about being sized up, Lizzie sat down gingerly on another small ironwork chair, while William wandered off to watch a pair of house martins. They were nesting under the eaves above a yellow rose that clambered all the way up the back of the house to its roof. His mother, following her gaze, remarked: 'They come back year after year to the same spot, as you can see by the number of nests and the mess they make. But I wouldn't disturb them for the world. And their guano is good for the Banksia rose.'

'Is that its name? It's lovely.'

'Scented, too,' said Mrs Westerleigh. 'Called after Joseph Banks. You know about him, I expect, since he sailed with Captain Cook to collect all those strange new plants. Captain Cook sailed from Whitby. I believe you come from that part of the world?'

'Well, my ancestors did.'

Phyllis emerged from the house with a tray of tea, thin slices of brown bread and butter, and a pot of honey.

'Thank you, Phyllis,' said her employer and, when she'd left them, added: 'Phyllis was brought up at Muller's orphanage, just down the road. She's a very quiet girl. I once asked her what it was like there, and she told me they were given everything they needed except love.' She looked up and, noting Lizzie's steady sympathetic attention, she thought: She's all right, this Dr Lizzie. She has a loving heart. She'll look after William nicely when I'm gone. 'William wants to be a paediatrician, you know,' she continued as he rejoined them. 'I expect you know what that is?'

'Oh, mother! Of course she does! She's a fully-qualified, practising doctor!'

'Well, paediatrics is a very new sort of medicine, William. You told me so yourself – that there are no paediatricians in the provinces yet, and only Dr Still in London. It was when he was under Dr Still at Great Ormond Street that William fell in love with paediatrics. Wasn't it, William?'

'Well, it is said in London that the only thing doctors know about paediatrics is Dr Still's telephone number.' He bit into a piece of bread and butter and smiled across it at Lizzie.

'William's going to be the provincial Dr Still. And, of course,' his mother rattled on, 'we do need these new children's doctors if we are to do something about the terrible loss of child life in our cities. William tells me that in the East End of London, and in the poorer districts of all our northern industrial cities, half of all children born don't reach their fifth birthdays.' She paused, and watched Lizzie's face to see how this news was taken.

'You were going to think out what to do about it, William,' said Lizzie. 'Did you find any solution?'

'Hmm . . . Yes, perhaps,' he admitted. 'As a matter of fact the French are doing it already.' He then explained how, a decade ago, the French government had become alarmed at the fall in their birthrate. ('Not a worry for us over here!' said William.) Germany had a steady birthrate, so it was feared that a time would come when France had too few fighting men to put into battle against her old enemy. Their public health records revealed that a great many infant lives were lost, especially among babies whose mothers, for one reason or another, could not breast-feed their young. So somebody came up with the plan to open milk stations, or *gouttes de lait*, a form of clinic where mothers could obtain milk free and, at the same time, a little instruction in hygiene and baby care.

'What a good idea!' said Lizzie. 'Schools for mothers . . . And are they working?'

It seemed they were. It was William's idea to open one in England, preferably in an industrial city where the need was greatest. All the babies brought to the clinic would be weighed and examined, and any sick, or failing to thrive, would be referred to a paediatrician.

'But, of course, I won't be able to do all this alone. I'll need expert help.'

'And I suggest you use this dried powdered milk that's now available. It's less bulky than the fresh, and less likely to go sour.'

'Good idea,' he nodded.

'You'll probably have to get the town hall to back you.'

He nodded again. 'That's what happened in France.'

After tea, he took Lizzie to view what he called the 'arboretum'.

'Is your mother a Quaker?' asked Lizzie.

'Yes. Most of my forbears were.'

'And you, William, are you a Quaker, too?'

'Not entirely,' was his brief but smiling answer.

He showed her an ancient, evergreen tree she'd never seen before. 'It's a strawberry tree, *Arbutus Unedo*,' he said, touching the bark. 'This was my fortress when I was a boy. I used to climb into it to escape from my sisters when they were too overpowering. Would you like to try the strawberry fruit?' He reached up to pull down a branch and plucked a small hard fruit that did look rather like an unripe strawberry. 'Try it.'

She bit into it and immediately spat out the bitter taste,

which made him laugh. She thought of telling him about her pear tree which grew into an archangel, but decided to wait till she knew him a little better.

'I was lucky in having a happy childhood,' he said. 'It's my belief that unhappy children make unhappy and, perhaps, even bad adults.' He stopped beside a maple. 'It's not as good as the ones I saw in Japan,' he said. 'But it's coming on, slowly.' He picked a finely-dissected, pale green leaf, and gave it to her. 'There's such a lot we could do for children, Lizzie, you and I . . .' They had reached the end of the garden, which overlooked a wide valley studded with grazing sheep. On the far side of it, a field of ripening wheat sloped upwards to the horizon. 'We could work together, Lizzie, go into practice together. What do you think?'

'Oh dear!' she cried. 'Oh dear!' She was besieged by all sorts of contradictory feelings. Was he offering her professional work or a proposal of marriage? 'I really don't know . . .' She felt dreadfully confused.

They walked back to the house by way of a path which led to a little wooden summerhouse with a thatched roof where they could sit and look out over the valley.

'You're afraid of losing the freedom you've won. Is that it?' he asked.

'Freedom for me means freedom to work,' she said, at last. 'Celibacy protects that freedom.'

Slowly and deliberately he removed the pins from her hair and let it fall about her shoulders. 'When the wheat is ripening over there,' he said, 'there'll be poppies growing in it. And then I shall pick some, and crown you with red flowers. You'll be more than ever like Demeter the corn goddess then.'

He was taken aback by the sudden look of pain that passed over her face. It was not till several years later that she told him about the splashing of scarlet poppies over a white silk dress at Maisie's birthday party.

'I don't think much of celibacy,' he said. 'Just think what you and I could teach each other, could learn from each other. The celibate knows very little about the other half of humanity. I do believe he tends to become egocentric in time. Celibacy cauterises and blunts the common touch – that's a gift you have so much of, and I so little. I need you, Lizzie, not only for my work but for myself.'

'I'll have to think about it,' she said.

With a sudden inspiration he pressed his advantage saying: 'And if you come into practice with me I shall buy one of the new motor cars.'

She touched his hair. It was such thick, black hair with a dark blue sheen, so beautiful that she couldn't resist leaning forward and kissing him boldly on the lips.

'Oh, my dearest girl!' he cried. 'I only hope that one day I'll make you as happy as you're making me!' He knew then that she would come to him trailing clouds of glory, and he would sink himself in her and be forever safely wrapped in her radiant goodness of heart.

He used to say, when he was old and, perhaps, was forgetting the facts, that he was never sure if Lizzie married him for himself, for the partnership in general practice he offered her, or for his brand new, three-wheeler, two-seater Tri-Car. 'It was rather like a bath-chair,' he told his grandson. 'But it did have a petrol engine.' He smiled, remembering its habit of sputtering to a stop, and how often he'd had to borrow one of Lizzie's hatpins to clear the blocked jets. But in spite of it all, they'd got the car to go. What fun they'd had! And once, on a straight, downhill road, they'd even managed to reach a speed of 30 m.p.h.